THE SWEETEST OBSESSION

A SMALL TOWN GRUMPY SUNSHINE ROMANCE

NICOLE SNOW

ABOUT THE BOOK

My brother's best friend owned my heart until the day he drenched it in kerosene and burned it down.

Grant flipping Faircross is so *not* the reason I'm coming home.

I don't care if he's gotten bigger, meaner, and grumpy enough to flash freeze the sun.

So what if he's up in my business the second I arrive?

I'm smarter now.

I'm only back in Redhaven for my sick mother and to talk some sense into my sister before she marries a toad.

Grant ran me off once and I'm not running back.

I can handle the drama, the messy secrets, and an unexpected stalker just fine.

...or maybe not so fine.

When Prince Anti-Charming charges in to protect me, it's kinda hard to say no.

When I find out he's a single dad with a heart bigger than a prune, it gets harder.

And when his lips storm mine with a growl that says *"stay,"* oh God.

Are we really doing this again?

Especially when an old tragedy resurfaces with hard truths, stinging tears, and one brutal question.

Will our sweetest obsession finally deliver us or destroy us forever?

I: ONE LIFE (GRANT)

*W*ell, damn.

That's definitely a dead body.

I tilt my head back, looking up at the pair of heeled loafers twisting slowly over the grand ballroom of the Arrendell mansion.

We're standing on the upper walkway looking down over the massive checkered floor. I'm so far away that the dead woman still looks tiny, dangling from the central chandelier.

Her own weight makes the whole thing sway gently with a morbid chiming of glimmering ornaments.

I cock my head to the left and right, frowning up at the body.

Next to me, Junior Sergeant Micah Ainsley huffs, cocking his head to the right, his pale-blue eyes pensive.

"Don't know how else to call it, Captain Faircross," he says. "It's a textbook suicide. Pretty clear-cut."

I grunt in numb agreement.

Not much way it can be anything else, of course, but I can't help scrutinizing the scene anyway, considering where we are.

Call it a cop's overdeveloped instincts for detail, but I need to be sure, dammit.

Because right now, looking at this woman dangling some fifty feet off the ground, hanging there by a trailing velvet red curtain drawn into a noose, I'm not fucking feeling it.

Oh, I am feeling lots of other things.

I don't know.

Maybe it's because it happened in *this house*, but even if it hadn't, I'd still get a damned funny feeling about this whole mess.

The woman looks like she was in her late forties or early fifties, her dark-brown hair just starting to grey. She's short, a little thick. Her body hangs slack inside the severe plain blue-and-white pinstriped uniform dress that's typical for the mansion staff.

The women gathered below, nearly breaking their necks as they stare up at the scene, are wearing the same thing.

Same apron. Same thick beige stockings. Same low-heeled leather loafers.

Even the same hairstyle with their hair pulled back into tight, no-nonsense buns.

The deceased has a round, square-set face with deep laugh lines despite the puffiness already starting to set in.

There's a terrible purple bruise around her neck, just visible past the twist of garishly red velvet.

Despite the plainness of her outfit, her nails are painted a vivid scarlet.

I scan the room again.

The walls all around the grand ballroom are draped with floor-to-ceiling velvet tapestry that sheet past the walkway where I'm standing, evenly spaced at broad intervals. They pour down like runners of blood to the ballroom floor below.

There's one conspicuously absent on a diagonal from

where Micah and I stand, just around the corner of the square walkway.

It's easy to see what happened.

She stood at the railing of the walkway and pulled the drape loose from its overhead fixtures, then dragged the full length of it up. Must've done it in the dead of night—considering it's about six in the morning right now, and her appearance tells me she's been dead for three to five hours.

She could've tied one end of the drape around the upper walkway railing, then knotted the other end to weight it.

I don't want to think how many tries it took her to toss the end until it caught just right on the chandelier and let the rest swing back to her.

From that point on, it would've been easy.

Undo the knot.

Tie the end into a noose.

Jump.

Leaving her life behind with a damning question.

Why?

According to the Lord and Lady of the house, one of the younger girls on the live-in housekeeping staff woke up early to get started on her chores. She came into the ballroom, saw the woman hanging, and screamed—sending the entire house scrambling to call into town.

To the Redhaven PD, namely.

To me.

"Oh, my, this is dreadful," Lucia Arrendell hisses at my other side, wringing her thin hands.

Her aristocratic face twists, a caricature of dramatic distress. Even this early in the morning, she's in a deep wine silk robe with perfect makeup, her white-streaked icy-blonde bob so stiff it barely moves with all her fluttering.

I just stare at her as she sniffs loudly.

"To think, the poor dear was so unhappy that she'd turn

to *this.* God. But we always include mental health coverage as part of our employee insurance policy. I don't understand, I just wish—"

"Quiet," I mutter. "I'm trying to think."

The air goes cold.

Well, colder.

I wouldn't be surprised if Lucia Arrendell never heard those words in her pampered life. Definitely not from the offended gasp she gives back, but before she can do more than open her red-painted mouth, her husband—standing at her back in a burgundy velvet smoking jacket and black silk pajama pants—silences her with a hand against the small of her back.

"Now, now, dear," Montero Arrendell drawls in his exaggerated Clark Gable accent. "I know you're distressed, but do let the detectives focus on their work, yes?"

He meets my eyes over the top of his wife's head like he's doing me a big fucking favor.

No matter how conciliatory and smooth he sounds, I see what's behind those impenetrable green eyes.

They're empty.

Stone-cold.

Measuring me.

Probably asking about my price, assessing whether or not I can be bought to keep this out of the press. The Arrendells have a little bit of a reputation problem to deal with right now.

It's been a few months since their son turned out to be a prolific serial killer and my lieutenant's new wife almost ended up as his latest victim. Ulysses and his accomplice, Culver Jacobin, died in police custody in an apparent suicide.

But the whispers are alive and well.

Two suicides connected to the same rich family in just a few months?

4

People start to wonder.

Including me.

"Tell me her name again," I clip, watching below as Lieutenant Lucas Graves and Officer Henri Fontenot move through the assembled staff. Their voices sound distant, turned into hollow echoes by the far reaches of the ceiling as they take statements from the house personnel. "How long has she been working here?"

Lucia makes an irritated sound, but then seems to get over herself.

"Cora, I believe," she says quietly. "Yes, her name was Cora, I... oh dear, what was her last name again? She made the most delightful coq au vin, and she always remembered to pick up this wonderful orange blossom hair mask for me. Oh, I'm so *terrible* with names..."

Right.

You can remember her damn cooking and shopping trips, but not her name?

"Lafayette," Montero fills in, smoothing a finger over his thin black mustache. He's still watching me, unblinking, like we're playing a game of chicken. I'm not interested. "And I believe we hired her ages ago? It was April, I recall. A delightful spring day. The hawks were out."

I don't give two shits about the hawks or all these diverting details.

I just file everything away into a deep, dark file in my head.

I've long since learned that taking the direct approach with an Arrendell is useless. The best thing to do is watch. Listen. Read between the lines.

Then wait for the right moment when something slips.

If I'm being honest, there's not much waiting to be done today.

Whatever pushed this woman to the edge, there's little

doubt that it's suicide, and after studying Cora Lafayette a little while longer, I sigh and jerk my head to Micah.

"Go with Henri and cut her down. We'll get the county coroner in, confirm ID, notify the next of kin. Standard procedure."

Micah frowns. "You want to wait until the autopsy? Knowing the cause of death might give them a little closure, at least."

"I... yeah." I clench my jaw, watching that slow depressing sway of the dead woman's feet.

Closure.

That word stings like hell.

Too much death in this damn haunted house.

Earlier this year, one of those deaths was confirmed to be Lucas' sister, too.

The first victim.

After years of having to accept that Celeste Graves was just *missing*, that she'd run off and left him, Lucas finally got the closure he needed on his poor sister.

But Celeste wasn't the only person who went missing that night.

Rumor had it that Ethan Sanderson—a man I grew up with, a man I loved like a brother, a man who was desperately in love with Celeste—had either run away with her, or else killed her himself and fled.

I knew better, though.

Ethan, he'd have never run off without telling me or leaving his sisters in the dark. I knew him well enough to know he'd never murder the woman he loved. So with Celeste dead and her case shut, that leaves the question.

Where is he?

What happened to Ethan?

Where's my fucking closure?

What the hell happened to my best friend?

And what about his family; what about—

Fuck.

I can't bring myself to think her name.

Even after all these years, the ache of missing her stings. Just as fresh as if she only left yesterday.

No.

Like I only drove her away yesterday.

I never got a chance to apologize. Maybe I never will.

I don't know if she's ever coming back.

There's a part of me that wants to break my silence. To demand that Lucia and Montero cough up that information, spill everything they know about my very personal lingering mystery.

For all their big fluffy speeches as First and Second Selectman of Redhaven, North Carolina, waffling on with *We can't express enough how sorry we are for our son's actions* and *Our apologies to this beautiful town for the horrors its citizens have faced,* I think they know.

Yeah, bull.

They know more about what their son was really up to than they let on.

"Captain?" Micah presses.

"Yeah," I finally confirm, tossing my head at him. "Get going. Call it in."

He nods sharply and walks off, slipping his fingers between his lips and whistling toward the ballroom to get Henri's attention. I watch Henri glance up, then peel his tall frame away from the crowd and walk toward the red-carpeted stairs.

I beam a long look at Montero first, then Lucia. "Mr. and Mrs. Arrendell, where are your sons right now?"

For just a moment, the look in Lucia's steely-grey eyes turns almost black with hatred.

Just the tiniest slip of her mask—because we both know where *one* of her sons is.

In the dirt. Forever.

The murderer a murder victim himself.

And his untimely demise happened with the Raleigh PD and not locally, but our badges aren't that different. It's not hard to tell what she thinks of us.

Lucia Arrendell blames me.

She holds the entire Redhaven police crew responsible for her son.

Still, she pins her mask back in place, her smile cooling, once more the grand duchess talking to the plebeians whose names she never bothers to remember.

"You know, Sheriff—"

"Captain," I correct. "Redhaven PD isn't affiliated with the county sheriff."

Her lips twitch sourly before that frozen smile returns. "*Captain.* Xavier's off in Dubai, closing a new real estate deal, you know. And Vaughn—oh, you know, he's always too busy to call home to his mother. Who knows."

Yeah, I've wondered about that for a while.

"Aleksander, though, he should be around here some-where. I thought I passed him in the hall just a minute ago?" Lucia makes a great show of looking around, then raises her voice. "Aleksander! Darling, are you around?"

I just watch her skeptically.

Montero looks almost bored, hovering as silent and watchful as a crow. There's something especially odd in his eyes today as he glances at the body of Cora Lafayette. The dead woman swings as Henri and Micah work carefully at the knotted drape tied to the banister.

Lucia clucks her tongue, staring down the hall.

"*Aleksander?* Come on out. I know you're both there."

Both?

I get my answer when a girlish giggle answers.

A few seconds later, he comes shambling around the corner of the hallway branching off from the upper walkway.

He's not alone.

Aleksander Arrendell is the impeccable portrait of a man who's graced nearly every fashion magazine cover in the world. His tailored linen shirt hangs off him over the latest designer jeans, his longish platinum-blond hair swept artfully to one side. His face is slim and fox-like. The same otherworldly green eyes that run in the family complete the eerie look.

I've never interacted much with Aleksander, but I know him on sight the same way I know the rest of this little town.

The woman on his arm, that's another story.

I know her so well my fucking heart plummets to my knees.

Rosalind Sanderson.

Little sister to my missing friend Ethan—and to *her.*

The woman whose name I won't let my mind even whisper.

And it hurts like hell to see Rosalind this way, her skimpy silver dress half-falling off her bony frame, her honey-blonde hair a disarrayed mess, her lipstick a smear.

She's damn near falling over in her strappy heels, barely held up by Aleksander's firm arm perched around her shoulders. Her dark-green eyes look dilated and unfocused.

Mostly, it's the nails, though.

Her nails are painted screaming red, loud and blinding.

The same glossy shade as the dead woman's, weirdly enough.

That doesn't sit right with me.

They're both staggering, too, clearly either drunk or high.

High, I'd guess, considering they both glance at the

dangling body like two teenagers sneaking a naughty peek at some X-rated film they aren't supposed to see.

It's a struggle not to wince when they both burst into a laughing fit, nuzzling at each other like catnip-drunk felines.

Fuck.

Part of me wants to rip Ros away from him and send her right home.

Only, I haven't seen her in a while.

Not since the last time my little girl Nell got mad at me and "ran away" to sulk with Ros until she felt like speaking to me again.

I've been too busy with my promotion to captain and—if I'm being honest with myself—avoiding painful memories associated with her sister.

Hell, for the longest time growing up, I thought of Ros as *my* baby sister.

When a man does that, he doesn't much like the idea of his baby sister dating Aleksander fucking Arrendell of all people.

She really couldn't pick one of the nice, boring boys her own age?

I also don't like the change that's come over her one bit.

That's not Ros.

The Ros I knew wouldn't be able to look at a dead body without breaking down in tears.

Not hysterics.

She used to be the shyest thing, full of air and sun, innocent and withdrawn. The girl in front of me looks more like a stranger wearing Ros' skin.

Her ma's not gonna like this either—if Angela even knows.

Goddammit, does Ros know Angela's back in the hospital?

I must be wearing some kind of sour look I can't hide. Because Ros stumbles to a halt as she catches sight of me.

All the color drains from her face and her eyes widen as she stares up at me.

"O-ohhh," she falters. "Hi, Grant!"

"Ros," I grind out, reminding myself she's not my little sister.

Not my kin, meaning I have no right to say anything, much less condemn her dating life.

Lucia thins her lips. "Do you think you two could compose yourselves well enough to speak with the police captain? Or are you late for another party?"

Aleksander smirks devilishly.

"Oh, come now, Mummy." He fakes this cringe posh British accent that only makes me angrier. Rosalind giggles and looks away from me guiltily. "You should be nicer to your future daughter-in-law."

Daughter-in-what-the-fuck?

I stiffen and stare.

"Daughter-in-law?" I echo before I can stop myself.

"Well now," Montero tells his son, clearing his throat. "I suppose we can excuse a little young mischief as long as we keep it in the family."

Rosalind bites her lip, smearing her lipstick more, and leans into Aleksander, holding up her left hand.

In the low sickly orange light, a large diamond embedded in gold flashes like a drawn dagger.

"He asked me last night," she says with the same sheepish smile I used to see when she was a little girl, always begging the big kids for their approval and affection. "Of course, I said yes! Um, please don't tell Ophie yet, Grant. She doesn't know... and she might be kinda pissed."

As she damn well should be.

Ophelia's baby sister, getting tangled up with *this* family?

I growl "fine" almost on auto-pilot before I realize what she just said.

"Wait. Hold up. Ophelia... Ophelia's back in town?" I hold my breath, bracing for the gut punch.

Then it hits me dead-on.

That old familiar pain.

That wrenching loss, stronger than ever.

That sense of *longing*, stretched across a decade without her like a man straining on a torture rack.

Ros licks her lips, still watching me like a little girl who's afraid of being punished.

"Yeah. Just today," she says quietly. Behind her, Micah and Henri lower Cora Lafayette's body down slowly into Lucas' waiting arms. "She's driving in from Raleigh-Durham right now."

Oh, I think, as the past rushes up to meet my face like a brass knuckle uppercut.

Oh, shit.

II: ONE BAD MEMORY (OPHELIA)

I swear, I have the world's worst luck with rental cars.

The last time I had a car give out on me, I was driving through the Pacific Northwest on a scenic road trip during a short sabbatical.

I'd rented this nice Lexus convertible so I could enjoy the show with the top down, but all I'd gotten was a face full of smoke when the radiator blew right outside of a cozy little place called Heart's Edge, Montana.

At the time, I felt lucky to hitch a ride into town with a friendly ranch girl named Libby, who dropped me off at the mechanic's with a little teasing about how it happens so much they're starting to think it's aliens.

This time, though, I don't think aliens have anything to do with it.

It's just good old-fashioned Redhaven bad luck.

And my luck is definitely running out as the Corolla I rented sputters and gasps just as I'm cresting the final hill before the familiar drop down into the valley cupping the town.

It's strange coming home this way.

I haven't seen this town in ages—and if it wasn't for life happening, I'd be happy to never see it again.

But fate keeps driving me back here one nasty blow at a time.

First, the job loss. The recession slammed Florida pretty hard and the Miami hospice center where I worked 'regretfully' served me a pink slip when budget cuts knifed through the staff.

My sister Rosalind was acting weird as hell on the phone, too.

Spacey, out of it, distant, evasive.

In our last video call, her eyes were bloodshot and sunken in like she'd been crying hard. But when I asked, she just giggled, avoided looking at me, and swore up and down she was fine.

No, I don't think she's fine.

And after losing our brother, Ethan, seeing Ros struggle is too much.

It scares me to the bone.

Old memories of Ethan keep surfacing, too, dredged up by the national news coverage of the Emma Santos murder case, plus the Arrendell tie to the deaths of so many girls, including hometown cold case Celeste Graves.

Then there's my mother.

Even as I fight the car to the shoulder and slam the brakes on before gravity takes hold and pulls me into an uncontrolled skid downhill, my eyes sting.

My mother is dying.

Again.

And I don't know if I can survive it a second time.

For her sake, I have to.

I jam the parking brake on and scramble out, shivering in the early October chill.

Yeah, I've been a Florida girl for too long. The autumn cold creeping over North Carolina leaves me feeling as naked in my thin sweater as the leafless branches of the dense poplar and pine trees around Redhaven.

I pop the hood and look inside.

I'm no mechanic—not even TikTok car-savvy—but at least I can tell nothing popped loose this time. There's nothing obvious, nothing smoking, sparking, or broken.

Crud.

Well, at least this time I know it's not the radiator hose.

Frowning, I brace my hands on my hips and look down the hill into town.

Redhaven looks as picturesque as ever in its silence.

It's the kind of perfect Stepford village in every horror movie where eventually you find out that underneath the gorgeous colonial homes and peaceful forests and pristine glassy lake, there's a horrible secret waiting to swallow up the unsuspecting.

A witch buried under a massive tree with blood-red roots.

Townsfolk who turn into cannibals by night.

Cults and rituals and evil sacrifices in the woods.

Or maybe it's just one weird family with a million rumors and their fingers in everything and too much money for their own good.

I eye the majestic dark house up on the peak of the opposite hill, then swing my attention down to the town square with its majestic statue of the town's founder.

Another Arrendell, go figure.

It should only be a quarter-mile hike downhill into town, and at this time of morning Mort's Garage should be open and empty except for old Mort himself. I can already see him falling asleep over his corncob pipe, about to tip his chair back with his bad habit of rocking it in his sleep.

But as I pop the trunk to see if I can dig up something warmer to keep my teeth from chattering on the walk, I'm caught by flashing lights from below.

A white van with red and blue lights darts away from Redhaven's narrow cobbled streets and bolts onto the highway up the hill, followed by two cop cars. As the van zips closer, I can just make out the logo on the side.

Raleigh County Coroner.

Oh, no.

Here we go again.

My soul compresses into a lump of black dread.

I clutch a fist against my chest and breathe roughly.

No, no, please don't let me be too late.

Please don't let the cancer eat my mother while I was on that flight from Miami to Raleigh, *please*—

The van whizzes past, followed by the cop cars.

My heart knots with a different feeling as I catch a glimpse of the man in the driver's seat of the second car.

Holy hell.

I haven't seen him in so long, I can't be a hundred percent sure. But I think it was him.

I think that was Grant Faircross.

Just a glimpse of a broad frame, dark hair, a starkly defined brow that always made him a perma-grump, set in a brooding scowl.

No—I must be imagining things.

All these memories reaching up and making me see people I'd rather forget.

That couldn't have been Grant.

My heart can't take seeing him right now.

"That's not your mother in that van," I tell myself.

No way. It's not logical.

I'd have gotten the call no one ever wants long before anyone loaded her up and took her away.

So as the cop cars pass, I try to refocus on practical things.

Like rummaging around in my suitcase until I come up with a long-sleeved Henley I normally use as a nightshirt and pull it on over my clothes. It's not much, but at least it cuts the wind while my skin prickles with goose bumps.

As I zip the suitcase and slam the trunk shut, I notice the sound of an engine coming up behind me. Maybe it'll be somebody I know and I can hitch a warm ride into town. I turn toward the growl of the approaching vehicle.

Just in time for one of the cop cars that just passed me to pull up to the curb behind me, easing to a halt and parking.

I blink.

...they turned back for me?

Well, I guess that's their job, anyway. I'm just so used to big-city cops that I forgot about that small-town personal touch.

What I could never forget is the familiar body language of a man built like a human tank and carrying himself with the weight of a mountain.

I could never forget the way he makes my heart stop cold.

Grant flipping Faircross steps out from behind the wheel of his patrol car, unfolding himself with that slow-moving grace I never thought I'd see again.

The car bounces up by at least an inch as he stands with his weight no longer pressing down.

God.

When we were younger, Grant was an absolute wall of a boy, always taking up too much space and drawing the eye without trying.

Now he's grown into a fortress of a man, so broad and muscled that his deep navy-blue uniform shirt looks like it had to be custom made to fit the breadth of his chest. Same goes for the black Redhaven Police Department jacket draped over his mile-wide shoulders.

There's just one difference.

That iron-cut, arrogant jaw I remember is obscured by a wild scruff of dark-brown beard, framing the stern line of his mouth. His deep hazel eyes look like the last rays of a brassy sunset, watching me mysteriously, framed in heavy, weathered lines.

All the new edges to a familiar face that reminds me just how much time has passed.

Just how much distance stands between us now.

Somehow, my heart doesn't care.

Just seeing him again makes me feel like the spindly, knob-kneed girl I used to be. I almost forget how easily he can be a sledgehammer to the heart.

There I was, trailing after my older brother and his best friend like a lost kitten.

Completely hypnotized by Grant's stone-cold silence, his gruffness, his mystery.

Like half the girls in Redhaven, I thought I was going to be the magic one who could get through to him when all he saw was a skinny pipsqueak who wouldn't go away.

I want to hate him for *that*, too.

But I'm not that girl anymore.

I'm a grown woman with a life and problems of my own.

I don't need Grant Faircross to notice me.

Except as he stands there, looking at me with his thick, coarse hands resting on his hips and the wind whipping at his chocolate hair with just a hint of silver, I'm frozen.

Absolutely tongue-tied since I won't admit to being awed.

I can't handle this right now.

It's too much, too soon, when everything else piling up has me feeling as fragile as blown glass. So ready to shatter in an instant if he utters one harsh word.

But he doesn't say anything at all.

He just reaches inside the patrol car, retrieves a battered brown cowboy hat from the dash, and settles it on his head.

My breath stalls.

Ethan's hat.

My brother used to wear that freaking thing everywhere, ever since he was a kid, never caring that it was too big for him. Then one day he just chucked it onto Grant's head and said, *If you won't say we're best friends, you big asshole, at least wear this dumb hat. That way I know we're cool.*

Grant didn't say a word.

He never did.

The man could never string a single sentence together in emotional-speak.

Oh, but he'd worn that dumb hat, all right.

And seeing it settled on his head now, the broad brim shadowing his eyes and the leather band still dotted with those turquoise beads I carved ages ago into the shapes of crude, tiny butterflies...

I'm gone.

I feel myself falling down, ready to cry.

I'm actually *glad* when Grant doesn't say one word.

He just strides past me, his steps long and lazy with a terrible hint of swagger.

So, he still carries himself with the aura of a man who knows just how much space he takes up and how much strength he packs in the slightest movement.

There's a breathless moment when he brushes past me.

When my lungs remember how to work, I can even smell him.

Something like woodsmoke and fresh, clean, earthy masculinity.

His scent slaps me back to that unspeakable night so long ago.

A time when I thought nothing of being buried against Grant's chest, secretly burning and hiding against him while he held me, comforted me, kept my crumbling world from falling down.

He let me inhale him then until I couldn't smell the salt of my own tears pouring down my cheeks.

Then he's gone, and I'm back in the dreary present.

Wrapping my arms around myself, I fight a chill that runs deeper than any cold.

Turning, I watch as Grant prowls to the front of the car and its open hood. Even with the raised metal in the way, he's so broad that when he bends over the Corolla's innards, I can still see his shoulder protruding past it.

Beautiful.

Not even a *Welcome home, Ophelia.*

But maybe he's never forgiven me for leaving.

You're gonna run, Philia? That's your answer? Fucking running away from Ethan?

Then don't come back.

It still stings like it did the first time he killed me with those words.

I haven't seen him since that day.

Until now.

And what a sight for sore eyes I must be, back in Redhaven with my tail tucked between my legs, as miserable and small as if I never left at all.

If he's the least bit torn up, he doesn't show it.

Grant fiddles with something inside the car—and his rough, sandpapery voice emerges from behind the hood. "Radiator hose popped."

"It did not. I *checked.*" I instantly scowl.

"Should've checked harder," he growls. "Damn thing can look like it's still together, but once the seal breaks you're not going anywhere, Butterfly."

Ugh, that nickname.

The big idiot can still cut me open with a single word.

It really is like I was just here yesterday.

To him, I'm still the starry-eyed little sister who doesn't know what she's doing, who has to be watched like the unwanted tagalong.

If Ethan were here, he'd smack Grant on the back of the head and tell him to be nicer to the butterfly nerd.

But Ethan's not here.

Just his ghost, making the silence between us so tense it's suffocating.

While I'm fighting the bitterness on my tongue, Grant fiddles with something inside the Corolla. Then he straightens and slams the hood shut with a deafening *boom!*

The car bounces on its wheels.

"That'll do you for a few." He lifts his head, fixing those unreadable mocha-dark hazel eyes on me. "Long enough to get you over to Mort's. Wouldn't drive it any farther."

Thanks, Dad, I start to snap.

All these years without so much as a note by pigeon, and he *still* thinks he's the boss of me.

But I remind myself again that I'm a grown woman now.

Not that little girl.

Definitely not *Butterfly*.

And I need to leave that bratty ego in the past, along with everything else. At least he's just helping this time instead of doing a controlled demolition on my heart.

"Thank you, Grant." I force a smile.

There's something so strange about the way he's looking at me.

I guess some things never change.

I never could tell what he's really thinking, what he's about to say, if he bothers to say anything at all.

When I was younger and hadn't had the hopeless

romantic knocked out of me yet, his silence always seemed so mysterious, this cryptic harshness begging for a gentle touch.

Now, it's just frustrating.

Not knowing what to say while he stays silent.

But my heart climbs up my throat as he steps closer.

The space between us vanishes.

It's like there's an invisible red thread stretching from me to him, and instead of growing more slack as he draws near, it just pulls tighter, winding me up in knots.

He stops in front of me, looking down at me with shadows for eyes glowing beneath the brim of his hat.

Right before he shrugs his powerful shoulders, slides out of his jacket, and—thrusts it at me?

What?

I blink at the jacket dumbly.

What's happening doesn't register until it does.

Oh.

Oh, crap.

He... he noticed I was shivering and underdressed.

That, too, is totally Grant.

The mute giant who won't say a word when he's not snarling at someone, but when something needs doing, he notices, all right.

Like jerry-rigging my car.

Like keeping me warm.

I take the jacket hesitantly with my heart coming undone.

For a frenzied second, my fingers brush his.

It's a bitter sort of wonderful, the sizzle of his skin against mine. I wish he wasn't wired into my blood like he's a missing part of me, awakening dormant feelings I thought I'd stamped out forever.

Of course, there's no reaction from him.

None.

But now I'm shivering with more than the cold as I slide his jacket around my shoulders and slip my arms into the oversized sleeves. I draw it close until I'm enveloped in his lingering body heat and that dizzying woodsmoke scent.

This jacket is so large I could nearly wrap it around me twice, the sleeves falling far past my hands and the hem dropping almost to my knees.

It's like being wrapped up in him.

But it's also not the same.

You don't want that anymore, remember?

Do I?

Those are old memories trying to live in the now.

A broken, girlish crush that doesn't belong to me anymore. But his scent lingers from the collar of the jacket.

My chest goes tight.

So tight.

And it's nothing like the explosion of hurt that hits me as Grant says, with absolutely no warning, "I still miss him, too, Ophelia."

Holy shit, holy shit.

I can't breathe.

Just like that, he knocks the air out of me.

This harsh reminder that while he lost a friend, all those years ago, I lost a brother, and we'll never get Ethan back.

It's my turn to lose my voice. My lips part, but nothing comes out.

I stare at Grant, frozen to the spot.

His expression never changes, but I'm—dammit, I won't cry.

Not in front of him when it hasn't been five minutes.

I cried my tears dry years ago and put everything to rest, so I still have a smidge of pride.

Pride he lets me keep.

Because as soon as he moves around, I no longer have to

look into those hazel eyes and wonder if that giant rock feels anything at all.

Those words, however heartfelt, don't match that closed-off expression.

I just want to see it once.

I want to see *some* feeling on his face, to show me that Ethan ever meant anything to him at all.

No, that *I* ever meant anything.

But he's already walking past and I can't see anything at all.

He's leaving, so I don't expect the warm, heavy hand that falls on my shoulder, burning me even through the dense layers of his jacket. This calming weight settles all the awful, squirming things zinging around inside me, pressing them down, down, *down* until they stop making me shake.

"Stopped in on your ma this morning," Grant says. "She's looking good. Can't wait to see you again."

"You went to see her?" I swallow, somehow finding my voice past the stunned shock.

"Just being neighborly."

That gentle hand falls away.

I turn too quickly, heart in my throat, and watch as he walks back to his patrol car. His broad shoulders sway with the rhythm of his steps.

It's so strange to think that after all these years, Grant's been here with my mother.

Not me.

But I'm the one who ran away, aren't I?

Yet, I'm so close to breaking into wretched sobs right now —this time with relief because I know for sure that coroner's van wasn't taking Mom away.

"Then who?" I ask faintly. "The coroner's van, I mean."

Grant stops at his patrol car, one big hand on the driver's side door, the other on the roof, glancing back at me.

"Maid up at the big house." He looks past me to the looming sharp outline of the Arrendell house. "Suicide."

"Oh, that's terrible! I'm so sorry for her family."

Again, Grant says nothing.

He just looks at me for a fraught moment—then ducks into his car.

The engine starts and the patrol car backs up before U-turning onto the road.

Just like that, he's gone, following the van with the poor dead woman out of town.

Leaving me alone on the side of the road with bad phantom memories and a heart he shouldn't be able to break again.

I turn to stare at the elegant house on the hill, hating its mystery, while the cold seeps in and numbs my bones.

III: ONE DAY AT A TIME (GRANT)

uck, I should've told her.

    I slouch at my desk at the dilapidated little Redhaven PD precinct office, staring at the paperwork on the Cora Lafayette case. My pen taps restlessly against the half-filled report.

I just need to wrap up my notes. Once we get the coroner's report, we can file this away. Should only take five minutes or so.

Instead, I can't stop thinking about it.

I should've *told* her.

I should've told Ophelia that her younger sister is engaged to Aleksander goddamned Arrendell.

I just couldn't bring myself to do it.

I could hardly get a fucking word out at all, not after seeing her for the first time in—damn, how many years has it been?

Too many after she went tearing out of Redhaven the second she was college ready, heading to nursing school out of state and never looking back.

Ten years.

I remember a girl—slim and lithe and headstrong—with a dancer's delicate build and a bulldog's determination.

Butterfly.

That's who she was back then, barely old enough to drink and an adorable pain in the ass with an attitude bigger than her frame.

The Ophelia who came back is a stranger and all woman.

And that woman doesn't need me dumping more trouble on her doorstep than she's ready to handle, especially with her ma's cancer relapsing. That's probably why Ros didn't want to fess up and tell her yet.

I should just trust her to know her sister.

She'll know the right place and time.

What matters is that it's not *my* place.

Doubt I could've spilled the truth without doing more damage, anyway. Hell, I almost didn't recognize Ophelia when I saw her, changed by time and the sorcery of growing up.

Somehow, those girlish features got refined into sophisticated elegance, but the glacial perfection of her face just can't be cold when her mouth is crooked and red and sweet.

Yeah, fuck me for staring at her *mouth.*

She's got this way of quirking her head to one side and biting her cheek like she's always about to laugh. The cold October breeze turned her honey-blonde hair from a tumble into a cloud, flaring around her in streaming wisps. They glowed like gold where the sun caught them, the entire mass caught up inside the collar of my coat.

Then there are those wide green eyes, gone angled and soft and wiser with age, yet still so innocent.

Still so familiar it kicks me in the face when I know the sharp mind behind that pointed gaze.

She's so much more than a distant memory when she's here again.

And I can't believe she's still got my heart tied up with nothing more than a glance.

Hell, if Ethan were around, he'd sock me in the mouth and tell me to keep my eyes *and* my dirty paws off his little sister.

He'd probably be right.

I'm pretty sure she hates me anyway.

She has every right.

After the way we parted, I'd hate my miserable, bitter, antisocial ass, too.

* * *

Ten Years Ago

"THERE'S something you're not telling me."

For such a skinny string bean of a girl, Ophelia's always been as perceptive as a mirror.

Sometimes I want to ask her how she always knows.

Only, I think she'd smack me clean across the face if I did.

We're sitting out back on her ma's porch. It's gotten to be a habit in the time since Ethan disappeared without a trace.

Almost ten damn years now.

I couldn't do much, not back when he first vanished.

I was only twenty then, still in college and working to get on the Redhaven PD. After that, I was just a rookie. As I've worked my way up to a proper badge, I've kept up the same habit, year after year.

I have to look in on the Sandersons.

On Angela, on little Ros, on Ophelia, just to see how they're coping.

I have to make sure they're okay.

Ethan would've wanted it that way.

I think he'd like me watching over them, even if he would've given me endless shit over it and laughed his dumb head off.

He also would've known I'd never stop looking for him, no matter how many years slip by without answers.

I just don't know how to tell Ophelia we finally have a clue and a new mess of questions, so I sink down in my patio chair and pop my beer tab.

She eyes me, sighs, and picks up her iced tea.

"You're just going to sit there and grump all evening, aren't you?"

My eyebrows go up. "Just drinking my beer, Butterfly. Shut it."

She laughs.

"You throw that on for the bug or because you actually like the songs?" I nod at her chest and the shirt she's wearing.

"The new album rocks! The symbol's just a fun bonus," she says.

Goddamn, does that outfit suit her. She's wearing an oversized t-shirt tonight with a print of Milah Holly's latest album cover on it. It's a purple butterfly smeared across a black background like a soul taking flight—if it wasn't just crushed and smeared by some clumsy asshole's hand.

Me, I don't get Holly's music, but almost every girl under thirty does when the singer belts out ballads about broken hearts and pure love and good girls pushed into being bad by some uniquely awful fuckboy.

"You're being all secretive again. Come on, what is it this time?" She huffs impatiently, sips more tea, and thunks the glass down on the little table between us. In the evening shadows, her eyes are green fireflies, as bright as the little glowing bugs dancing across the grass and trees of her blue-shaded backyard. "Did you find something new? With Ethan, I mean?"

Fuck, what's that saying about good deeds going unpunished?

I wonder if this girl's psychic as I shrug.

Truth be told, I'm a little embarrassed.

How could I not be, trying like hell to figure out where Ethan went for three damn years now and turning up with a big fat nothing?

If he ran off with Celeste Graves, if he got into a fight with her and—no.

I can't think that shit.

That's what half the town believes these days.

That he had something going on or he was so obsessed he lost his shit and disappeared them both.

Nah, I knew Ethan. He couldn't have pulled a hair on her head when he was mooning over her half his life and he just wasn't that type of guy.

A murderer? Even in some fit of fucked up passion or jealousy?

Not on my life.

For me, there are only two options.

One, he fessed up his feelings and she echoed them right back. They took off somewhere together to be happy without telling another living soul.

Or they didn't make it anywhere alive—and if we ever find Ethan, it won't be a happy ending at all.

It's just gonna be whatever's left of him. Hell, maybe Celeste Graves too.

Still, it shouldn't have taken this long to find the note.

I'm not sure I want to tell Ophelia about it. Not till I understand why he hid it where he did, almost like he didn't want it to be found.

"Hey." Ophelia swings her legs. Her feet don't even touch the ground. She's always been a short thing and I guess that's not changing. "I'll tell you a secret if you tell me yours."

"Seriously?" I side-eye her hard. "We're a little old for 'I'll show you mine if you show me yours.'"

"Don't be gross, Grant." She flushes hotly.

"Mm-hmm." I take a sip of my beer. "What've you got to tell me?"

"Nope. You first."

I shake my head slowly, looking away from her across the yard. Past the porch overhang, the sky is clear and deep blue, the stars just freckles in the night. "Your news good news or shitty?"

"Yep. Good."

"Then you go first. Let's hear something good for a change."

I'm already waiting for it when it comes—a slender fist thumping me in the arm. "You're just trying to avoid telling me. Promise if I tell you, you'll tell me."

I sigh heavily. "You are a goddamned brat."

"Asshole."

"Punk."

"Dick."

"You kiss your ma with that mouth?" I growl.

As I say it, I can't help glancing at her.

Yeah.

I'm thinking she's gonna be glaring at me like usual, but no.

She's got the weirdest look on her face tonight. Her skin's all soft and pink again, like the summer heat crawled up inside her when it disappeared with the sunset.

That mouth I know she kisses her ma with is plump and red, her lips parted, and when she catches me staring she looks away stiffly.

Hell, I do too when I know how messed up that is.

She's Ethan's kid sister. The ultimate forbidden fruit.

I damned sure shouldn't be eyeing her mouth or any part of her at all when I'm pushing thirty and I'm only here 'cause her missing brother was—*still is*—my best friend.

"I kiss my mom and anyone else I want," she says haughtily. "Jeez. I hope there are nicer guys than you down in Florida."

"Florida?" I frown. "What the hell's there?"

"University of Miami," she says triumphantly, flashing me a look. "I got a full-ride scholarship for my nursing degree. The letter came a few days ago."

My chest goes cold.

I stare at her in disbelief.

It's like my brain shrinks inside my skull as my world gets smaller and darker.

"Philia, you're—you're leaving Redhaven?"

"Um, yeah." Thinning her lips, Ophelia glares at me. "You could try being happy for me, you know."

"Congratulations," I bite off. "Why the fuck you leaving? NC State ain't good enough for you?"

"Why does it matter?" she flings back. "Christ, Grant, can't you just... like, be nice about something for once?"

"You know damn well what I'm saying, Butterfly," I snarl. "You and me, we're the only ones still looking for him. Even your ma gave up and had that fancy headstone put up. And now you're leaving? Fuck, you're up and quitting just like that?"

I almost regret my words as she winces.

Almost.

Because that twisting dagger lodged in my chest can't soften my words.

"I can't live my whole life around Ethan!" she flares. She lights up when she's mad, glowing like lightning, just vibrating from the inside out. "Do you think he'd want that,

Grant? Do you think he'd really want me to put my whole life on hold to keep chasing him?"

"Somebody's gotta. If it ain't us, then fucking *who?*"

Dammit, I can't stop how my voice rises.

My hand crushes the beer can till it dents inward with a loud screech and I drop it on the patio table. "Look, just 'cause he said not to look for him doesn't fucking mean we shouldn't."

Ophelia starts to snap at me—then stops cold, drawing up short, staring with her eyes big and shining like marbles.

The color drains from her face until she's as white as a sheet against the golden halo of her hair. "...what do you mean he said not to look for him?"

Fuck.

Me and my big mouth.

Sighing, I sink back into the chair like I'm trying to bury myself in it. The furniture creaks under me, and I close my eyes, steeling myself before I reach into my uniform blazer's pocket and fish out a folded slip of tattered paper to pass over.

She takes it with shaking fingers.

Confusion knits her brow as she unfolds it and stares down at the handwriting scrawled across the paper, slowly reading it out loud.

"I knew you'd find me here. Don't look for me, Grant. If you've found this, I'm already gone. There's something I need to do, consequences be damned." Her breath sucks in sharply and she presses her knuckles to her mouth. "This... this is Ethan's handwriting, where did you...?"

"Stuffed inside that old copy of *Where the Wild Things Are.* Same one I used to read to y'all when we were kids," I admit reluctantly. "He must've left it there 'cause he knew I'd take a while to look, and by then he'd be long gone if something went bad. I dug the book out since I was gonna give it to my aunt and uncle since they're trying to have a baby and all. Figured they could read it to their kid—and that shit just fell right out."

She works her lips, swallowing loudly. Her eyes glisten.

"So he... he really did leave us?"

"I don't know. Don't think so. That's Ethan's handwriting, all right, but—" I shake my head slowly. "Something feels off about this, Philia. I can't believe he would've done that, ghosting us without a word. You know it, too. You fucking know. If he was fixing to run off with the girl of his dreams, he'd have let us know where to find him."

"Wh-what are you saying?"

"There's some kind of message there, I don't—fuck, I don't fucking know, okay? I know I sound batshit insane."

"You sound like an asshole—as usual—but not crazy. Not at all." Her voice is so weak, her head bowed. In the dark I can't make out her face, but her thick voice tells me that she's struggling not to cry. "Why'd you even show me this? Why'd you show me if you don't know what it means?"

That dagger in my chest sinks deeper.

"I don't know."

"You don't know fucking anything!" she throws back, and when she lifts her head, it's not that she's trying not to cry— it's that she was hiding the tears coursing down her cheeks.

"Ophelia," I try, but the words won't come.

She glares at me for a breathless second—then chucks the letter right at me.

The air catches the cursed paper and sends it fluttering down on the table between us, this damning thing. "So you just... you're going to throw that at me and bring up all these old memories for what? So I won't leave? So I'll keep chasing Ethan's ghost instead of having a life?"

I almost rock back.

A shotgun burst to the heart wouldn't have the same punch.

"No, damn you!" I shoot back, and dammit, I'm trying not to yell but she just pulls it out of me. "Don't. Just don't fucking give up on him, okay? That's what I'm asking, all I ever asked."

"If you think just because I want to go to college, I'm giving up on my brother..." Ophelia stands. Her slender frame thrums with energy, with anger, shivering so hard that loose shirt shakes against her body, her eyes lit furious. "You don't know me at all, Grant. I'm going. I'm going, and you can't stop me."

"Never tried," I snarl, rising to my feet. "Go on. Fucking go to Florida. Leave your family." *Leave me,* I don't say, still tasting those bitter words. "You're gonna run, Ophelia? That's your answer? You're gonna run away from Ethan?" I grind my teeth. "Then get out. Get the fuck out of here and don't come back."

I don't mean it.

I don't fucking mean it at all, but there's this sudden scalding panic in my chest at the idea of never seeing Ophelia Sanderson again.

I don't know if it's because I'm having this crazy déjà vu over the thought of her disappearing just like her brother or if I'm actually wanting her to—

No.

I can't think about that shit.

I already planted my foot in my mouth so far it's blown out my ass.

Ophelia's eyes widen.

There's an instant hurt, where I know those tears aren't just for Ethan, but because I just stabbed her so brutally.

Then it closes over behind anger, her mouth setting with stubborn determination.

"Fine," she bites off, cutting and cold. "I will. If I don't come back, I won't have to deal with angry pricks like you. Get lost, Grant. I don't want to see you again."

Just like that.

Believe me, I know it's what I deserve.

Her ripping my beating heart out with a few savage words, sentencing me to the same fate that has me so piss scared.

But before I can say anything, she whirls around and she's gone, slamming through the back door of her house into the golden glow of her kitchen.

Just a last whipping slash of her baggy butterfly shirt before I can't see her anymore and I'm alone.

I stand there like the colossal idiot I am for the longest time.

The night hums with crickets and frogs, a whole world indifferent to my suffering and my stupidity.

I know I need to leave.

This isn't my house anymore, even if it's been a second home since I was a kid.

Even if those memories I cherish double as a torture chamber now.

Late nights watching movies in the Sandersons' living room, me and Ethan sitting cross-legged on the floor with our faces nearly pressed to the TV. We were glued to some bad monster movie or clutching our controllers tight as we tried to shoot every zombie.

Ophelia would sneak down way past her bedtime and curl up on the sofa, hugging her blanket with the red butterflies to her chest, glued to us like a little burr.

Tumbling around the backyard. Chasing each other through the woods bordering the property, telling ghost stories, daring each other to do stupid kid shit.

Back then, the three of us were inseparable.

The world made sense.

When Ethan disappeared, the glue holding us together came apart along with reality, leaving this chaos that has my dumb ass spinning in circles.

The screen door squeals behind me and I turn. "Ophelia—"

But it's not her.

Angela Sanderson steps out on the back porch, her movements slow and graceful.

She's the spitting image of an older Ophelia, grace and beauty refined into something more reserved and dignified and weathered.

Instead of Ophelia's shining green eyes, her mother's eyes are a soft, compassionate brown. She still wears a scarf over her tumbles of blonde hair, even after all these years. Used to be, she'd wear it to cover how her hair was falling out from the chemo while she fought off cancer, but now it's like it's part of Angela's whole look, a trademark modest thing.

Just as familiar as her gentle smile as she looks up at me, sighing. "Fighting again, are you? You two are like oil and water lately, sad to say."

"Guess so, ma'am." I grumble, trailing into a groan.

Smile lingering, Angela stops at my side, folding her slender hands in front of her and looking out into the night. The faint moonlight glows against her pale skin while those night sounds drone on.

"Do you know what your problem is? Both of you."

"We're both too mouthy for our own good, ma'am?"

"Sometimes," she admits with a touch of humor. She glances at me sidelong, knowing. "The real problem is neither of you ever say what you really mean to each other."

"I..." I cough.

Oh, shit. Am I that transparent?

Clearing my throat, I look away too quickly, staring up at the night sky.

37

"Yeah. I guess that's an issue. Too late now, though. She's made up her mind and she's goin' away."

"Away is never really *away,* boy. She'll come back. Spring break, Christmas, my girl wouldn't let me miss her that much." Angela pats my arm. "You'll get your chance to mend fences. But Grant?"

"Yeah?"

"Thank you," Angela says warmly, her eyes glimmering. "For never giving up on my son."

It catches me so off guard I don't know what to say, so I nod respectfully as my throat closes off. "Of course, ma'am. Ethan wouldn't give up on me."

Angela only smiles, squeezing my arm before she turns to go inside, leaving me alone.

I don't stay much longer.

This isn't my house—and it hasn't been a place where I truly belonged for a long damn time.

So I turn to walk around the side of the house and let myself into my patrol car.

As I pull away, there's a light on the top floor window.

For just a second, I see her.

A slender figure against the curtain that catches me and holds my heart captive.

I drink her in for the longest ten seconds of my life before I force myself to look away, back my car out of the drive, and head home with my vision red and blurred.

* * *

Present

THAT NIGHT WAS the last time I saw her.

Until today.

The worst part is, Angela was wrong. Ophelia avoided Redhaven like a root canal ever since the day she left.

Instead, she'd flown her mother and Ros down to Florida for vacations and holidays together. Ophelia's always been contrary like that, but I never thought she'd take my words so damn literally.

Then again, maybe I'm just overthinking it too hard today.

She's got a hundred heart-wrenching reasons to stay the fuck away from this town without the way I ran my mouth doing more damage.

Too many bad memories.

Too much spiritual rot in this town, really.

Some folks can taste it in the air. They wisen up and realize they don't want to stay and wait around for Redhaven to swallow them whole.

"Hey, Cap?"

Henri's voice yanks me from my thoughts. I blink, focusing on the letters that went fuzzy in front of me as I lift my head up from the report. "What?"

"No need to bite my head off, *mon capitan*," he snaps off mockingly in his French Creole drawl, grinning, completely unbothered by my snarling. He sweeps his mess of shaggy brown hair away from his eyes. "Just wondering why you're still here, that's all. Ain't you supposed to be picking Nell up from school?"

"*Fuck*. I completely spaced." I bolt to my feet, grab my jacket off the back of the chair, and realize I don't have it—I gave it to Ophelia. "Yeah. Gotta run. Thanks, Frenchie."

I angle past him, heading for the door. His voice drifts after me. "Y'all take care too, Captain Grump."

I don't bother answering that.

Don't know why the whole crew likes rubbing it in.

Hell, I'm not that *grumpy*.

I just don't waste time mincing words when point-blank says it a whole lot better.

I drop into my patrol car and roll through the winding cobblestoned streets of Redhaven at a grueling school's-out-twenty-miles-per-hour pace.

On the way, I pass Lucas Graves on crossing guard duty. I probably earned the dirty look he gives me as I pass. Everyone hates being the one to pull that shift, but somebody's gotta do it.

Considering he's got a pregnant wife whose classes are currently letting out right now, though, he'd probably rather be anywhere else. Not stuck directing traffic so hordes of munchkins can walk home.

By the time I pull up to the red-roofed, C-shaped building that houses all of Redhaven's small K-12 classes, most of the evening traffic rush has trickled out.

I'm expecting to see Nell standing on the front walk waiting for me. Probably hankering to talk my ear off about which teacher got stuck watching her with me being late—but instead I barely catch a glimpse of her disappearing into the back of a maroon Subaru SUV.

Oh, goddammit.

Am I really so fucking out of it I just forgot?

My parents are picking her up today.

That's why my internal Nell alarm didn't go off.

Sure enough, my ma pulls the driver's side door open for the little girl, my father already in the passenger seat—and before I can even pull my car over, Nell's head pops over the rear passenger side window.

"*Uncle Grant!*" she shrieks loudly enough to crack glass.

She comes flying out of the car before anyone can stop her.

Oops.

I hit the brakes and scramble out just in time to catch the almost-ten-year-old cannonball that slams into me.

Girl's got some legs on her and she's not even half-grown, clearing a two-foot leap to hurtle herself right into my arms.

I let out an *oof* as her full weight pounds my chest.

I recover quickly, though, wrapping my arms around her, supporting her while she buries her face in my neck.

Her familiar tumble of dark-brown ringlets tickle my skin.

"Hey, Nelly-girl." I squeeze her tight. "Sorry, I forgot Ma and Pa had you today."

Nell pushes her hands against my chest and draws herself back to look at me with her little brown eyes glinting with excitement.

"Ice cream! We're going for *ice cream*," she proclaims. "You're coming with us, right?"

I groan inwardly.

Nelly-girl knows what she's doing when she says it like that. Like it's already a foregone conclusion, and I need a Harvard law degree to convince her otherwise.

"Baby girl, you know there's a reason I asked Ma and Pa to take you today," I say. "I'm up to my chin in paperwork. Gotta go catch up."

My mother leans against the bumper of the Subaru, tall and curvy, her iron-grey hair pulled into a bun.

"You had time to drive out here," she points out, wagging a finger.

"No ganging up on me."

"Yes ganging up on you!" Nell chirps with a pout. "You work too much, Uncle Grant. And you don't eat enough ice cream. If you just ate more you'd smile."

"Is that so? Didn't know I had to maintain a minimum ice cream level to look pleasant." I arch a skeptical brow.

My father leans his arm out the passenger window,

offering me an easy grin past his thick silver beard. "You've already lost the argument, Son. Only question is if you're riding with us or taking your patrol car."

I heave out a heavy sigh, but he's right.

When it comes to Nell, I rarely win unless it's something deadly serious.

She's just too damn good at getting her way.

Guess that's what happens when you're not just the big cousin.

Can't put an easy label on what I am some days. More like the older brother she never had when I'm not busy being full-time dad.

"Fine, I'll take my car," I grind out. "That way y'all won't have to drive me back and eat up more of my time."

"I wanna go with Uncle Grant!" Nell proclaims, laying her head against my shoulder.

That's that, I guess.

We split up, and soon I get the full rundown of Nell's day as I tail my parents' Subaru for the ten-minute drive to the little ice cream parlor near the town square.

I'm used to it by now.

Thankfully, Nell doesn't need me to talk much, just as long as she's sure I'm listening and paying attention. She tells me how she wants to be a professional flower girl.

Probably because she got so much gushing attention looking cute as a daisy in Lucas' wedding. Big change from last week when she wanted to be a rocket engineer. I'm sure next week she'll want to be an architect or a postmodern painter selling NFTs.

What can I say, the girl's bright as hell for her age.

She yammers on about Miss Delilah and how she's gonna be sad to move on from her class and into Miss Nora's soon. But apparently, Miss Delilah promised she can come over and play, and when she's old enough, maybe she can even babysit the Graves' baby.

When she goes off about how huge Miss Delilah is now that she's almost ready to pop, I groan and remind myself to ask Lucas if Nell actually *said that* to his wife's face and to apologize if she did.

How the hell is someone related to me so talkative?

She sure as hell inherited the Faircross gene for no filter, though.

Girl never knows when to keep certain things to herself.

She hasn't stopped talking even when we get to the ice cream parlor. She waves impatiently, leading me inside, chattering away as we meet my folks and we all put in our orders and find a table.

My parents end up with modest scoops of mint chip and rocky road. I just snag a cone with the darkest chocolate I can find.

Of course, little Nell orders herself a towering sundae so complicated the poor girl behind the counter looks frazzled trying to keep up with all the fixings.

I balance my cone in one hand as I pull out Nell's chair so she doesn't drop that ridiculous sundae.

"Uncle Grant." She frowns at my cone. "That's *all* you're going to get? You're so *vanilla*, Uncle Grant."

What the hell?

She better not know what that means.

And it's dirt-black chocolate laced with almonds, thank you.

I choke on my next breath anyway while my dad chuckles. My mother hides a titter behind her hand.

"This look like vanilla to you? Don't you ever say that again," I growl, brandishing my cone at her. I slump down in one of those tiny damn chairs that feels like it's ready to turn into a pile of splinters under me. "That doesn't mean what you think it means."

"Huh?" Nell blinks at me innocently. "What does it mean then?"

"Maybe when you're older," I grumble.

Like hell.

I may be here raising her since her old man ain't, but I'm sure as hell not explaining *that* to her. There's enough dread with having The Talk at all when she gets older if my folks won't pick up the slack.

Knowing Nell, she'll be just as irreverent as ever and enjoy watching me squirm while I try to explain basic biology and safe sex and all that other crap that comes with growing up. I'm sure she'll already know more than I do from all the books she crams into her head.

Whatever.

I should know there's something up when she actually accepts my answer.

Nell normally never lets anything go without a little arguing, a little cajoling, a little pouting when nothing else helps get her way.

For now she just chirps "Okay" and buries her face in her sundae.

It's almost gone before I find out the reason.

"So," she says, licking a little whipped cream off her spoon, "I need a tent for the field trip."

I narrow my eyes.

My ice cream's long gone and I'm just idling, taking bites out of the waffle cone.

"What field trip?" I ask.

Nell blinks at me innocently. "The one Masie Jenkins has planned? The camping trip?"

"First I'm hearing of it." I know what she's doing. Acting

like she's just reminding me when she never brought it up at all.

That's the problem with being a cop raising a kid. Half the time you just teach them how to be better mini-criminals.

I clear my throat and say, "If it's a field trip, the school must've sent you home with a permission slip, huh?"

"Welll..." Nell twirls her spoon in the melted pool at the bottom of her bowl. "Um, Nana and Pop-pop said it should be okay."

My mother holds her hands up. "Don't look at me. I said to ask you, but you probably wouldn't mind."

"Uh-huh." I eye Nell. "What are you not telling me, Nelly-girl?"

"Um, well..." She bites her lip with a tight smile. "It's not a school field trip. Not exactly. But my whole grade is going! Camping next weekend. We'll be right there on Still Lake, not even deep in the woods..."

"Mm," I grunt skeptically. "And that means Masie's parents are going to be there, right? And at least two more adults for that many kids."

"Um..."

Oh, shit.

Here we go.

The reason she's dancing around.

"Out with it, Nell," I say.

She winces and lowers her eyes. "Masie's older sister is coming. But... but she's a really good chaperone! I promise."

"Junie? Like hell," I snarl. "Nelly-girl, she's only seventeen. Not even old enough to chaperone herself."

"Language, Grant! Not in front of little ears," Ma chides me gently.

"Oh, he says that all the time," Nell pipes up. "I'm used to it."

"Don't you switch this around on me. You're not getting me in trouble with my parents when you're in trouble with *me*." I frown. "Nell, you are not going on a field trip with—how many rug rats are in your grade? Eleven?"

"Ten." She juts her lower lip out.

"Right. Ten munchkins and one seventeen-year-old in the woods alone at night. You knew damn well I'd say no when it's a recipe for disaster, so you tried to be sneaky. Not nice." I shake my head. "It's not happening, and I'm gonna have to talk to the Jenkins about that plan, too."

"Uncle Grant!" Her face crumples into pure horror. "You can't. Everyone else is going!"

"And you're not everyone else, last I checked. Go ahead and hate me now, but someday you'll be glad I spared you the trouble. That trip's just asking for trouble. Missing kids, someone drowning, breaking a leg..." Look, I hate having to upset her like an ingrown toenail, but I'm not budging. "You're not going and that's final, Nell. You wanna go camping, I'll take you myself."

"What? But I don't *want* to go with you!" she flares. "You're a buttface!"

"Nell," my father says softly. He's a big man—almost as big as me before age started shrinking him down—but soft-spoken and gentle as a bear cub. The man raised me with the same gentle sternness he wields now like a master. "You know you're not allowed to talk back that way to your uncle."

"But he *is!* Buttface!" She whirls on him, her sundae forgotten, tears welling in her eyes.

"Nell!" my mother admonishes. "Use your inside voice." But then she turns a pleading look on me. "Surely, it won't be so bad for just one weekend, darling? Can't you find an adult for them? As long as they promise to stay out of the water and Junie checks in."

Dammit all.

46

I love my folks and I'd be hopelessly screwed raising Nell without them. Although they're part of this whole situation, we're not exactly co-parenting here.

I don't need them undermining decisions this big in front of Nell.

Only, it's too late.

She's giving me a tense, hopeful look, glancing between me and my father like she's begging him to veto me on this.

Fortunately, Dad has the good sense to keep his mouth glued shut.

"The answer's still no," I say firmly. "Considering you tried to pull one over on me, you're lucky I don't ground you. Now finish your ice cream so we can go home. I want your homework done before dinner."

Nell's nose scrunches up and her mouth quivers.

For a second, I think she's about to burst into a proper tantrum—but then she catches herself.

She's been doing that a lot more lately. Too grown-up to cry, trying to be a big girl and act ladylike. So after a few trembling moments, she sniffs and lifts her chin.

"I'm not speaking to you," she announces.

"Fine," I answer, exchanging patient looks with my parents. "As long as you get your homework done, you don't have to."

Nell doesn't answer.

Guess she's serious about the silent treatment then.

What the fuck ever.

That leaves things a little quiet and strained, the adults talking about Redhaven's latest gossip while Nell makes a very loud, spoon-clanking show of finishing her ice cream.

There's really not much else to say.

My parents and I keep in regular contact, and it's a small town—everyone knows what's going on with everyone else, and when you're not the gossipy type, there's not much to add.

I see enough truth behind the rumors up close, the petty and ugly and explosive.

That doesn't stop Ma from making a pointed comment about hearing a certain someone's back in town.

My father gives me a knowing look.

Shit, I should've expected this.

I just grunt and ignore them, but I guess it's proof how mad Nell really is when that doesn't even get her to prick up her nosy little ears. The kid's a diabolical little gossip in the making, always up in everyone's business and connecting dots most grown-ups wish she couldn't string together.

Half the time, I'm proud of her when she's smart as a whip.

The other half, I wonder if she's too old to keep quiet with a pacifier.

Some of the stuff that comes out of her mouth would make the Pope blush.

When everyone's done, I kiss my mother's cheek, let my father clap a friendly hand to my shoulder, then usher a sulking Nell outside to the car.

As I tuck her into the passenger seat and watch her to make sure she fastens her seat belt, something hits me.

Don't know what to call it. An instinct, I guess, like somebody just touched the back of my neck with ice-cold fingertips.

It makes me look up just in time.

There's a man across the street who makes me frown.

I don't recognize him, and I know damn near everyone in town.

All part of my job as the highest-ranking officer below Chief Bowden. It's also just part of living in a town with a population in the low four digits.

This guy, he's older, maybe early sixties. Gaunt. Grey hair combed neatly, despite the wild-eyed look.

Sunken cheekbones, deeply hollowed eyes that lock on mine like he wants something.

Never seen him before in my life. Could be a tourist since we've got a lot of people staying up at Janelle Bowden's B&B, The Rookery, currently at full capacity with the autumn leaves turning.

That outfit looks familiar, though.

Waistcoat.

Tailcoat.

Slacks.

White gloves.

Who the hell wears gloves this time of year in broad day—

Oh.

Yeah, I'm pretty sure I saw a few of the household staff up at the big house decked out just like that guy. The Arrendells really take the whole old-world butler thing to an extreme, right down to the uniforms.

Considering I just came from checking out a suicide up there this morning, I've got some weird-ass feelings about one of their employees standing out here in the middle of the street in his work clothes, just staring like he's never seen an irritated cop before.

I know I'm probably overthinking it.

The Lord and Lady of the manor who signs his checks are probably real fuckin' jumpy after the whole thing with their psycho son.

I wouldn't put it past them to send a minion or two to keep tabs on me so I don't try to kick up any more shit that'll harm their precious reputation.

I narrow my eyes at the man, flashing him a challenging look, but he doesn't move.

His expression never changes, even when I cock my head questioningly.

All right then.

I make a mental note to do a little digging, see if I can ID him, but for now I've got a little girl I don't want anywhere near anyone connected to the Arrendells and their depressing bullshit.

I settle behind the wheel of my patrol car and delay pulling out until I'm sure my parents are safely ahead of us.

The weirdo across the street doesn't seem remotely interested in them.

When I pull out, though, and check the rearview mirror, his head cranes, following me down the street.

Nah, I don't like this.

One more problem I sure as hell don't need.

* * *

BY THE TIME we get home, little Nell still hasn't relented.

I get the scorned princess act all the way through homework, dinner, and cleaning up for bed.

I'm not going to push at her.

She'll get tired of ignoring me in a day or two. She's a needy little kitten, thrives on attention, and I'm her favorite source. Ignoring me just hurts her, so she'll make up her own mind when she's good and ready to forgive.

I'm glad she doesn't push me away when I tuck her in and smooth her wild hair back from her brow. The minimal fussing, that's not too bad of a sign.

We'll probably be cool by morning.

Once I'm sure she's asleep, I settle on the sofa to finish up my case reports.

Usually, there's not much to report on, but we're in the thick of the last tourist season with a dead body. Between the suicide and two pairs of hikers getting into fistfights over prime camping spots and six different cases of shoplifting, I've got my hands full.

It's after midnight by the time I make up my mind to turn in for the night.

Only, as I stand, stretching my back until my spine pops, a sharp sound clatters out front.

That icy weirdness of cold fingers scraping the back of my neck hits again.

I tense, instinctively taking a careful sidestep as I edge toward the door.

When I peer out the front window, there's—nothing.

Predictable as hell.

But what else?

The motion sensor lights on the front porch aren't on, either.

Just in case, I crack the door, always aware of my service pistol hanging in its holster from the coatrack. No bullets in there, certainly. I always take 'em out when I come home in case Nell ever gets curious. Still, I've got a clip in my pocket and I can have that gun locked and loaded in under five seconds.

Don't think I'm gonna need any action tonight, though.

There's nothing out there at all.

Not even a shadow twisting in the night.

Probably just raccoons or foxes, fucking with garbage cans on the curb for scraps.

They always get a little hyperactive when the tourists move in and there's more trash around, more junk food thrown out. Night scavengers love a good feast.

Sighing until I relax, I close the door—but just in case, I trudge upstairs to peek in on Nell.

When I ease her door open, her bed looks flat.

Those cold fingers choke me as I bolt into the room, flipping the light on in a panic.

Sure enough.

Sheets thrown back.

Her backpack's missing from the hook on the back of the door.

"Nell?" I call, racing out into the hall. Bathroom door's still open, only she's not in there, fuck fuck fuck. "Nelly-girl, where are you?"

No answer.

Nothing as my drumming heart becomes a block of black ice.

Fuck my life.

Nell's run away.

Again.

IV: SHE'S THE ONE (OPHELIA)

I'm amazed the house hasn't changed in all this time.

Yet everything feels so different and that's even more remarkable.

Sure, it's the same split-level ranch house where I spent the best and worst years of my childhood.

Same pale-grey siding and cheerful bright blue trim.

Same covered front porch and big back deck.

The familiar overgrown backyard my mother let go wild during her last battle with cancer, only to declare later that she liked it better that way. Mom grew back tough as a weed, so she wasn't going to cut down *her* weeds when they grew big and tough, too.

The last time I was here, the house was full of life and sound.

My mother, my little sister, Grant storming in and out whenever he pleased.

Up until that night he told me to run and never come back again.

Tonight, as I unpack and stuff my clothes away in my

childhood bedroom, now turned into a guest room dotted with so many of my old things tucked away lovingly in the closet, it hits me.

The house is too still.

And I have no flipping clue where my sister is.

Ros barely said hello before she was gone.

Not a word about our mom, her eyes too bright, her smile too wide, way more interested in whoever she was texting than in saying hello to the big sister who probably feels like a stranger to her, considering I left Redhaven before she was grown.

And Mom... she's at the medical center on the edge of town.

The only patient in their little three-bed cancer wing.

I haven't been to see her yet.

I *need* to brace myself to see her like that again.

So for now, it's just me.

Me and Ethan's ghost.

He's not dead.

He's not.

I've repeated that unlikely mantra for what feels like ten lifetimes.

But every time, it sounds more desperate, more draining to believe something I know isn't true.

I still remember the day I turned on the TV and Redhaven was plastered all over national news. It was even trending on Twitter and half a dozen true crime podcasts.

Rich, weirdo philanthropic family, bad seed, serial murders, the kind of thing that gets crime buffs panting with excitement. I wouldn't be surprised if half the fall tourists are here hoping to get a glimpse of the Arrendells or dig around the Jacobin farm for more evidence.

Good luck with that.

Sniffing around the Jacobins is a good way to end up limping out of town with your butt full of buckshot.

I doubt there's any evidence left, anyway.

According to the news, the FBI swept in and took everything over from Redhaven and Raleigh PD, and they're still in the process of analyzing the DNA evidence to see if they can match them to any missing girls in the last twenty years.

It won't be easy. All they have left are half-digested bone fragments thanks to the grisly way the victims disappeared.

But I can't help wondering...

What if some of that DNA evidence holds a clue?

What if it points to my brother?

God. Am I ready for that?

Real closure, however awful?

Celeste and Ethan disappeared the same night.

The rumors were the worst part.

People saying Ethan did something terrible. That he killed her, kidnapped her—salacious small-town gossip that left me cringing every time I heard a whisper, or felt wary eyes on me any time I went out in public.

The other kids shunned me, snickering under their breath.
Murder girl.

Like I was guilty by association when my brother wasn't guilty of anything at *all*.

I know he wasn't.

And now I have a little proof.

Ethan never killed Celeste Graves and we know who did.

Which makes me wonder if the Arrendells killed *him*.

I've always wondered from the little things Grant let slip after the whole thing happened. He'd never been willing to tell me much, always trying to protect me.

But he had told me that Lucas Graves thought Montero Arrendell killed his sister, that Celeste was involved with the rich patriarch somehow. I guess that was supposed to comfort me, back then.

All it did was make me more desperate than ever to escape this bottomless pit of a town.

I stare down inside my empty suitcase.

I packed light because—I don't even know.

Maybe I'm still treating this like a social visit. Not like my life in Miami is over.

No job, my lease on my apartment is almost up, and I can barely afford the rent anyway.

I have a bad feeling I'll only be going back to Florida to pack up my things and ship them to Redhaven.

Fine.

That's fine, I tell myself.

My mother needs me in her darkest hour and that's more important than anything else.

Sorry, Grant. Guess I broke my promise to stay away forever, you huge jerkwad.

When I pull myself up from dreary thoughts I can't believe how late it is.

I totally lost track of time unpacking, but my growling stomach reminds me it's past midnight and I haven't eaten since I grabbed a burrito from the taco truck next to Mort's while he looked over my car and told me he wasn't letting me spend a penny on repairs when it was the rental company's problem and he'd bill them.

A little hometown hospitality, I guess.

But all I could hear were the whispers any time someone passed by.

Hey, isn't that...?

Oh my God, it is. Hasn't she been gone for ten years?

After the—you know. Do you think that's why she's back?

Oh, didn't you hear? Her poor mother...

I grind my teeth as I head downstairs to raid the kitchen.

Yeah, yeah. My poor mother.

Who doesn't want your pity any more than I do.

I throw together a quick turkey and provolone sandwich from what I can scavenge from the fridge, then wander into the living room to see what's on the late-night channels. But as I settle in and reach for the remote—

Creak.

The noise is way too loud when it's just me in the house. The silence of an empty space cracking with the sound of the front porch boards straining.

I tense, swallow, and fight back goose bumps as I crane my head toward the door.

Creak. Creak. Creak.

Deliberate, measured footsteps on the porch. Almost stealthy.

Oh, God.

I hold my breath.

A long shadow stretches under the thin gap beneath the door, the one my mother has been promising to fix with weather stripping for over a decade but never has.

My heart pounds wildly.

Silently, I squirm around until I can reach my phone buried in a cushion, struggling not to make a sound.

The steps stop, but that shadow stays, dark and ominous.

With shaking fingers, I unlock the phone and tap in 9-1, then pause, my thumb perched over the last number.

Creak.

And the shadow retreats, the light sound of those foot-steps moving away.

What the actual hell? Did they see me somehow?

Was it a burglar who changed their mind?

I wait another minute, straining to listen for—well, anything.

Someone rattling at the windows, testing the back door locks, but there's nothing.

With my mouth cotton dry, I slide off the couch and creep to the door. Stretching up on my toes, I peer out the peephole with my phone clutched to my chest.

Still nothing.

No one there.

Not even when I open the door, letting in the moonlight and the chilly night scent.

I stand on the porch, staring across the front yard.

It's like no one was ever here.

There's just calm starlight falling over the gabled roofs of Redhaven, bathing the sleepy town in the illusion of peace.

I won't have any peace until I'm sure, though.

So I keep my phone close and shove my feet into my boots, clomping down into the yard.

A quick circle reveals more nothing.

No one's been in the backyard, either.

I'd be able to tell when you'd have to stamp down a path through the overgrowth to get anywhere but the worn trail between the back door and the storage shed.

Did I just imagine it? Or did I just have a narrow miss with an actual break-in?

Maybe I'm just being jumpy after all.

Call it stress, being back home, worrying about my mother, about my baby sister, seeing Grant again, unpacking all these frothing memories I'd hermetically sealed.

I'm so tired, and not just physically.

It's no surprise if my brain keeps conjuring demons coming home to my doorstep.

I turn to let myself back inside, climbing up the back porch steps and—

Another rattle, this time from the shed's direction.

I freeze, breath hitching, the air cold in my throat until

it's like I swallowed a fist of ice. Poised with one foot on the step above, I listen to the heavy silence.

This is silly.

...it's probably just raccoons, right?

Possums. Mice. Bats.

Something normal and furry and annoying that goes thump in the night.

But I won't feel okay until I *make sure.*

I'll just check the shed, scare the critters off, and go to bed safe and sound.

With my breath rushing loudly in my ears and sweat icing my temples, I turn slowly and step back into the yard.

Every step down the path feels like an eternity. My fingertips are numb as I switch my phone over to flashlight mode.

Just raccoons, just mice.

And if it's not, well...

I may be short, but I can kick a dude in the kneecaps—or a little higher, if I really need to.

The years spent lifting orthopedic patients early in my career would turn any girl into a beast.

Only, there's no sign of motion when I stop in front of the shed. But what's that?

Light?

Yeah. Just little flickers of light through the windows.

Someone's in there.

Well, crap.

Crap, crap, shit!

Moving carefully, I peer inside the little window next to the door.

I'm expecting—I don't know.

A teenage punk. Some creeper, or maybe one of the Jacobins doing whatever it is the Jacobins do when they stalk around the hills at night hunting and making moonshine and God only knows what else.

I'm definitely not expecting a little girl.

She's small—no more than ten—and she's rearranged all the old junk in the shed to make a little playhouse.

One that's probably been there for a long time, considering the books and toys tucked on a shelf, and the nest of blankets and pillows she's made for herself in there.

The light splashes from her bright-pink phone screen. It's one of those kiddie things parents give their little ones that can only use certain apps and contact preset numbers.

She's crying.

The light from the phone's screen reflects off the bright streaks on her cheeks and shines off her tousled brown curls and soft brown eyes.

I have no idea who she is.

But I can't ignore a crying little girl, especially not one hiding on my family's property. So I pull the door open slowly, careful not to spook her.

"Hello?"

Her head jerks up.

"M-Miss Ros?" she gasps—then flinches back, shrinking against the wall. "Oh. Y-you're not Ros or Miss Angela..."

"No, sweetheart." I exhale softly.

So she knows my sister. Probably why she felt so comfortable sneaking into the shed.

I slip inside and hunker down, making myself shorter and keeping my distance so she won't feel cornered.

"I'm Ros' big sister, Ophelia. I came home to take care of our mom." I hold my hand out. "What's your name, hon?"

"N-Nell," she stammers softly, then bursts into a wail so abrupt it makes me flinch, loud and keening as she flings herself at me.

I catch her with a gasp, rocking back with my arms full of little girl.

"Hey, hey," I say, patting her back and wrapping my arms around her. "Hey, c'mon, Nell, it's okay. Everything's gonna be fine. Why are you in our shed, sweetie? Did you run away from home?"

"I-I wanna go *hooome*," she howls, sobbing against my shoulder. "I-I want my Uncle Grant!"

What.

I freeze.

Her uncle... *who?*

No.

No flipping way.

* * *

GUESS WHAT?

Way.

It's almost comical how some things never change in Redhaven.

Like the elder Faircrosses still having the same phone number, despite the fact that they don't live there anymore. It wasn't hard to get the relay going when I called to find them already frantic and on the hunt for Nell, only to loop Grant in with a gruff promise he'd be by in a few minutes to pick her up.

I'm so lost.

No idea what's going on.

But by the time Grant's patrol car skids into my driveway, I have Nell calmed down at the dining table, sitting with a cup of warm milk and honey.

She's in her pajamas, her bare feet dirty. I'm just wiping them off with a wet towel when a heavy knock comes at the door.

"That's Grant, all right." Standing, I rest my hand on top of the little girl's head with a smile.

"Oh, no." She stares down into her milk miserably. "He's gonna be so mad at me."

"You think? I bet he's going to be crazy happy to know you're safe. Don't worry, Nell." I wink at her, tweaking one of her curls. "I've been wrangling that big old bear since we were kids. I won't let him yell at you."

"You knew Uncle Grant when he was little?"

"I did," I say. "We used to be best friends."

Well... that's fudging the truth a little.

But I do remember those days fondly before Ethan's disappearance tore our hearts out, back when we were the Three Musketeers.

I'd better let Grant in before he breaks down my door, though.

So I pull away from Nell and pad over to open it.

Grant looks more haggard than I've ever seen him.

He's in his pajama pants with a plain grey t-shirt stretched across his broad chest, his feet bare, his wild waves of dark-brown hair disheveled. Even his silver-shot beard is a mess.

The last time I saw a hint of emotion on that cranky face was when we realized Ethan was missing and not coming back.

That night I'd seen him go through the wringer.

Despair. Grief.

Tonight, it's too familiar, torn with darkness.

Fear. Worry. And finally, sweet relief.

I have enough sense to step out of the way so he can see Nell before he's past me and rushing over to the table.

"*Nelly-girl.*" His normally steady rumbling voice cracks ever so slightly as he drops to his knees next to the chair and pulls that tiny girl into his massive arms.

"Uncle Grant!" she sobs, only this time it's happier as she flings her arms around his neck and buries herself against him. "I'm sorry. I'm sorry I ran off. Ros wasn't here and I got scared..."

"Yeah. You have to stop doing that, Nelly-girl," he rasps out roughly. "When you're mad at me, you *talk* to me first. You can yell at me all you want, but you can't run off in the middle of the night. What if something happens to you before you get to Ros? What if someone steals you off the street?"

"So she does this a lot?" I ask softly, pushing the door shut and padding closer, folding my arms around myself as I watch them.

Grant starts like he just remembered I'm here, looking at me over the top of Nell's head.

"Yeah. Precocious little scamp. She and Ros have this weird friendship because she's obsessed with the way everything smells in your ma's shop. When Nell gets mad at me, she runs away to the shop. Ros usually gives her candy and brings her right home. Can't say she's ever run off this late at night before or come here. I just left your ma's shop when my pa called."

I smile faintly. "I don't know where Ros is tonight, so I guess Nell got stuck with me and warm milk. But I think she comes here more than you realize. There's an entire playroom set up in our storage shed."

"I don't know what I would've done if she hadn't. Thank you." Breathing roughly, Grant buries his face in Nell's hair, holding her tighter. "Tell Miss Ophelia thank you, Nell."

"Thank you, Miss Ophelia." Nell sniffles, muffled against Grant's shoulder.

I don't know what to say.

I'm at a total loss, seeing Grant like this with a little girl he obviously loves very much. Enough to rip so much raw emotion past his stoic wall.

It's a side of him I've never seen.

A strange new facet to this man I thought I knew so well from forever ago. It cuts into me in completely new ways, reminding me how he used to be able to pull me to pieces with a single glance.

But I can't.

Watching Grant with Nell is enough to tell me that I don't know him at all anymore.

And I certainly don't need my chest tightening and fluttering this way over a man who might as well be a complete stranger to me now.

He'd just break my heart again anyway, wouldn't he?

I can't leave myself open for that a second time.

Still, I can't help murmuring, "Uncle, huh? But you're an only child."

"It's a long story." Grant curls his hand against the back of Nell's head, cradling her against his shoulder and holding her against him as he stands, lifting her off the ground, tucked in his arms. He gives me a long look. "I need to take her home and put her to bed."

I nod quietly.

He stops, faltering a moment as he adds, "If you want to come along, I can explain once she's asleep."

I understand without being told.

It's a delicate story. Probably one best not retold in front of little ears.

It makes me wonder who she's lost.

And why loss seems to be a way of life around here, so prevalent that it's already hurting someone so very young.

Still, I hesitate.

I should mind my own business and let Grant get back to his life.

I'm happy I was able to help, and that should be enough for tonight.

I also need to turn in. I need all the rest I can get to brace for tomorrow's visit to the medical center.

Instead, I find myself nodding, taking a step back. "Let me find my sweater and shoes. I needed to give your jacket back to you anyway."

"Keep it," Grant says, looking at me in that strange insightful way he has. "Until you get yourself something warmer. Seems like you forgot what winter's like around here after all that time in the Miami sun."

There's an edge to his words.

I can't quite put my finger on it, but it stings.

Whatever.

I won't let it get under my skin. And I won't back out of going either, even though I'm already having second thoughts.

I just turn away and head upstairs to fish out the thickest cardigan I have and get dressed, grabbing his loaned jacket last.

I try not to ask myself why I'm getting pulled into Grant Faircross again.

* * *

"She's my cousin."

I sit at the kitchen table in Grant's comfortable colonial cottage, waiting on tenterhooks. I remember when this used to be his parents' house, but then they moved into the Garrisons' old place when the Garrisons moved and the Faircrosses retired, leaving the cottage to Grant.

It's the little things, I think.

Almost like Redhaven is its own pocket universe.

All the same planets and stars, but they're constantly

shifting, forming odd new constellations that change how their gravity pulls on your heart.

Grant's gravity tugs on me tonight as he sets a steaming mug of mint tea in front of me, then settles down with his own mug in the ladderback chair across from me.

In the low golden light of the kitchen, he's like a wood sculpture, weathered and aged into a work of pure rough mahogany with his lingering summer tan. I swear, the man looks like he was carved from solid oak, and even as he's grown into a man with deep thought lines around his eyes, there's also something about him that's just...

Eternal.

Unchanging.

It's oddly comforting, especially when being back in Redhaven has me so unsettled.

But I frown, curling my hands around the hot ceramic until it warms them. "Wait... your Uncle Nathan and Aunt Melissa? The kid they had?"

"Yeah," Grant grunts. Something troubled flickers in his deep hazel eyes, lending a solemn air to the handsome stony crags of his face. He starts to take a sip of tea, then stops, looking down into the mug. "Their house burned down. Nell was barely a year old."

Oh, God.

My heart plummets.

Oh, I hadn't realized—my mother never told me.

It's like there was this secret embargo on Grant talk between us over the years, and now my heart hurts as I realize what I've been missing.

Before I can stop myself, I reach across the table, resting my hand on Grant's wrist.

"You don't have to say it," I murmur. "I'm sorry, Grant. I didn't mean to bring up something painful."

He looks at me oddly, then down at my hand against the

thick, dark hair furring his arm. I suck in a breath and pull my hand back, but that only earns me another unreadable look as he sets the mug down and runs his fingers through his thick, brown beard.

"I ain't mad, having to talk about them," he rumbles. "Just haven't had to tell this story in a good long while. Mice in the walls, I guess. Got through the electrical wiring. Some of the walls in that house were a century old. Brittle as hell. Just damned tinder. All it took was one spark." He shakes his head gravely. "I was on call that night. Got there before the fire trucks could make it. I wasn't supposed to go, but when I realized it was my aunt and uncle's address..."

I almost don't recognize Grant right now as he trails off.

That taciturn young man I knew has grown into a colder, older man, yes, but there's also *more*.

Some deeper, wiser, fuller sense of self.

Something that pulls at me in ways both old and familiar —and new and unsettling, too.

"I don't remember going in the house," he continues. "Next thing I know, there's smoke and fire everywhere, rafters caving in. They'd gotten to Nell's nursery and covered her with a wet blanket before the smoke got to them." He pauses, swirling the tea in his mug. "I was too fucking late for them. But little Nell, she was screaming up a storm, scared out of her mind. She was okay 'cause that blanket filtered the smoke, saving her little lungs. I snatched her up and got the hell out of there right before the roof caved in."

"Oh my God." I shake my head, willing him to continue.

"Yeah. It's just me and my parents now. We stepped up as a family, taking her in and sharing the responsibility. Nell mostly stays with me, but my folks keep her if I'm at work and she's not in school. She calls me her uncle 'cause it makes more sense to her, I guess, seeing how I'm so much older."

Holy hell.

That's a lot to take in.

I just let it process for a minute, then murmur, "I'm so sorry. It seems like I've missed a lot of your life. But I'm really glad Nell has you."

"You've missed a lot of everyone's lives," he flares.

And just like that, I'm ready to grind my teeth down to nubs again.

Stupid lunk.

Why does he have to rub it in when he's the one who told me not to come back?

I try to keep my voice level as I say, "You're right. Including whatever's up with Ros. By the way, has she been acting kinda funny lately, or is that just how she is now? I don't even know where she went tonight."

For a second, the big man across from me sits up taller in his chair.

My eyes narrow.

There's one thing I've always known about Grant Faircross.

He can't lie worth a damn.

He can stay quiet about something—he's insanely good at keeping secrets—but he sure as hell can't lie about it.

And even if there are so many little things different now, things that throw me off until everything feels real but not real... I guess that hasn't changed.

Because there's a familiar stiffness to his shoulders, a little guilty jerk, a tell before he answers like nothing happened.

"Haven't noticed," he drawls, slurping his tea. "Don't see Ros much these days. Been dealing with the tourists for weeks. Not much time to stop and talk."

Right. Like he ever makes time for chitchat.

There's a flash of irrational jealousy.

I picture Rosalind here every day, Grant stopping by Mom's shop to find her waiting behind the counter with her sunny disposition and bright smile and crown of golden hair. She has the kind of personality that would charm anyone, even the most dour, stubborn, rude, brave—

Down, girl.

Calm your tits right now.

I do *not* have feelings for Grant Faircross anymore.

Especially when he's hiding something and I need to know what.

"What do you know about my sister?"

"I told you. Nothing." Grant scowls.

"Dammit, Grant. You're acting like I'm still a kid and you have to protect me from potholes on my bike. If something's going on with Ros, just tell—"

"Where the hell you getting this from?" he snarls. "I told you, I haven't noticed shit. You got a problem with your sister, take it up with her. Don't get mad at me about it, Butterfly."

For a second, I stop and stare.

He shrinks back—as much as a human mountain like him can—knowing he slipped up using that old name I don't dare acknowledge.

"That's not why I'm—" I cut myself off, slapping my hands lightly on the table as I stand, shrugging out of his borrowed jacket. I drape it over the back of the chair, leave my tea untouched, and offer a sweet smile. "You know what? Never mind. Say hi to your parents for me, Grant. I'll stop by one day to see them when I'm sure you're not there."

While he glares at me, I turn around and march into the living room, heading for the front door.

Only, there's company.

Nell, just coming down the foot of the stairs. She's dragging some kind of mangled blue floppy horse thing with rainbow yarn for a mane.

A unicorn, maybe?

It's hilariously filthy and stained, but she clutches it like it's the most cherished thing ever while she scrubs at one eye and blinks at me.

"Miss Ophelia? You're going home already?"

That little girl makes my scathing smile genuine.

"It's past my bedtime, hon. Pretty sure it's past yours, too. Why are you up again, sweetie?"

"...I didn't get to tell you good night."

And there goes my heart.

"Oh, honey." I step closer, offering my hand. "Want a goodnight hug?"

Nell nods drowsily.

So I sink down on one knee and pull her into my arms, painfully aware of Grant's huge shadow in the kitchen doorway, watching us in vibrating silence.

"Promise me you'll be good, all right? No more running away. If this big dumb jerk is mean to you, if you're good and stay at home, then I'll take you out for ice cream."

Nell's woebegone look is a little too calculated.

"He's mean all the time. That's a lot of ice cream..."

"You'll have earned it. Because *he is mean all the time*," I throw back over my shoulder before standing again and ruffling Nell's hair. "Good night, munchkin."

"Good night, Miss Philia."

"Good night, *Philia*," Grant rumbles, stressing his pronunciation in a way that tingles my heart.

Nope.

Not tonight.

I'm not giving in to that pull, that gravity, that one-way ticket to hurt.

Absolutely not.

I *will* resist.

With one last silent, mutinous look at Grant—knowing damned well I'm being every bit the brat he thinks I am—I turn and walk out the door without saying a single thing in response.

* * *

IN HINDSIGHT, rushing out of my house in nothing but his jacket, an oversized t-shirt, athletic shorts, a too-thin cardigan, and flip-flops was probably not the smartest move.

Dumber idea?

Walking home in the dark without the jacket *alone.*

In North Carolina in the middle of a biting October night.

I only have myself to blame.

But the teenage girl inside me almost wishes Grant would chase after me, just to make sure I get home safe.

I don't have any business praying for special favors, though.

Our last run-in should've been a good reminder why I can never ask this man for anything.

* * *

I SLEEP SO POORLY it's a major chore to drag myself awake.

It's not just because I'm on edge, waiting to hear strange footsteps on the porch again or listening for ghosts that haunt this little town with too many secrets.

It feels like long, anxious hours lying awake, staring out the bedroom window, watching the leafless branches of gnarled trees clawing at the glass like starving things trying to get in.

Or maybe they're trying to drag me outside with them and force me to face everything I don't know I can withstand.

Everything I can't avoid forever.

When I pry my eyes open and check the time, it's dawn. I need to be at the medical center first thing.

God, it's so morbid.

There's a problem with my mother's DNR paperwork, something they can't get ahold of Ros to sort out.

Well, neither can I. She's ignored my last two voicemails and left my texts on read.

Ugh, what gives?

It's so strange to come home and still feel like I'm alone when my mom is barely in this world anymore and my sister has just...

Checked out, I guess.

But has she, really?

There's an annoying lump in my throat as I force myself through a shower, throw down an English muffin with jam, and drag myself out the door with a cup of coffee in hand.

My rental car's still at Mort's, so I'm on foot as I make my way through sleepy Redhaven. Its meandering streets flow through rows of picturesque houses that belong in a painting on a hotel wall somewhere.

Redhaven's a place where everyone walks or bikes unless they don't have a choice, especially during tourist highs when parking gets crowded.

Everything you could ever want is neatly arranged around the town square in the branching spokes of a wheel, just a few blocks away from wherever you happen to be.

Only, those few blocks feel like a fifty-mile death march by the time I reach the medical center.

Miles of people staring at me as they pop in and out of their cars and shops and houses to start the day.

That annoying double take as they realize I'm not Ros— no, it's the *other* sister.

The older one who ran.

The one who never got over what happened to her big brother.

Sure, a few people smile and beam me greetings, or wave and call out, *"Welcome home!"* But every glance, every hello, every startled *welcome* carries a weight like an elephant.

The weight of skepticism, surprise, curiosity.

The weight of avid greed, strangers asking for more of the scandal that's so personal to me, no matter how I try to run from it.

The weight of pity.

Oh, that poor girl.

All these years thinking her brother was a murderer when he's just been dead all along with the Graves girl. Guess he really did love her after all.

They're wrong.

I never thought Ethan was a murderer. The very idea was so ridiculous it made me gag.

I've always known there was more to the story than anyone dared guess. But I can't think about that right now.

Not when I'm standing outside my mother's hospital room, looking in through the observation window at her and wondering when the woman who raised me became so small under the sheets.

So old.

It's not like I haven't seen her regularly.

I always fly her out for holidays, random visits, a few times a year just for brunches and long weekends before she headed back home. But the slow march of years crept up unnoticed until it's like she's aged thirty years since I last saw her.

The last time was in my Florida condo, sitting serenely in front of the big sunny windows and looking out over the ocean with a small smile. Her beautiful face was aging gracefully with wisdom and peace.

Just last week, she was on the phone with me, talking about how happy she is that I'm coming home, and her voice was so bright I could easily imagine her strong.

But I see the grim truth in front of me now.

I see the quiet battle Mom fought so hard, the ravages of a pain she hid weathered on her face.

She's a sunken husk.

Her face is greyer, paler, more spotted than I ever remember.

Her cheeks are nearly concave.

Her skin is so thin it's like desiccated silk.

Like she's already part cadaver, her bones trying to poke through her skin, her hair brittle and showing her scalp past bristles of wiry dull yellow that used to be a warm honey gold.

Frankly, it scares me.

I wouldn't even think she was breathing if not for the dim fog on her oxygen mask.

It hurts.

It hurts so fucking much it's destroying me, knowing I'm standing here watching my mother die by inches and seconds and hopeless breaths.

I've been through this once before, back when she beat it the first time.

Even then, I never thought we'd get lucky twice.

I remember the last time, the cancer diagnosis, me and Ethan and Grant standing together in this painful huddle, trying not to hurt, to be brave.

Just three awkward kids staring down their first brush with death and how flipping cruel life can be.

I'm not that wide-eyed child who can't find the right words anymore.

Oh, but what I wouldn't give to have my brother here with me right now.

And what I wouldn't give for those rare moments back when an impossibly grumpy, overgrown bear of a man could be comforting and kind.

Now, I'm an exile.

A stranger to Grant's oak branch arms and his big, broad body throwing up a wall, blocking out the world and its threats.

A stranger to everything I'm struggling so hard to keep sealed—and failing—deep in my bleeding heart.

V: ONE BIG MESS (GRANT)

*I*t's like I'm fucking cursed.

I swear I'm spending more time at my job thinking about Ophelia than I am actually working lately.

That woman frustrates me so goddamned much.

Mainly because she won't get the hell out of my head while I'm pretending to focus on writing up what must be the twentieth vandalism report of this tourist season.

Damn punk-ass kids.

If rich people are going to bring their brats around this town to act out and shoplift, we'd all be better off if they'd teach them some manners first.

Honestly, we've gotta do something about it, because it gets worse every passing year and half the town's income relies on the tourist bucks.

All we need is a bad reputation for petty crime. Then all the city birds who migrate here with the seasons will stop flocking to get their fix of artisan furniture and home-brew beers and hand-tapped maple syrup, too scared off by rumors to spend their time and money.

Too bad every time I try to work out a plan of action so I

can make things work with such a small crew, my brain won't cooperate.

It snaps right back to that look on Ophelia's face.

That narrowing of her eyes that says she could see right through my bullshit.

Fuck.

How does she always *know?* Even after all these years avoiding each other?

Annoying as hell.

And why's she always gotta go snooping around up inside my damn head?

Only, I owe her one for bringing Nelly-girl home safe, don't I?

I had no idea she'd been building herself a nest in the Sandersons' storage shed. Maybe I should build her a proper tree house when the weather warms up, give her a place of her own that lets her run away without actually leaving my property in the middle of the night.

I get that sometimes she needs to be alone.

I'm definitely not the best at playing Dad. So yeah, it's okay if she just wants to kick me in the teeth and have a little privacy sometimes.

I just need to know my little girl's safe—preferably without hating my guts.

I'm man enough to admit it.

My heart would bust like safety glass if something happened to her.

No, she ain't mine, not by birth.

But by life, by tragedy, by fate, she sure as hell is.

Behind all the bluster and iron-fisted rules I make her live by, I just want the best for her.

"Would you look at that," a voice drawls from behind me, ripping me from my thoughts. "Feels like I'm having a flash-back. Last time I saw that look on your face, you were sulking over a *girl.*" Lucas goddamned Graves smirks as I spin my chair around to face him. "In fact, I think you were sulking over the *same* girl, if memory serves."

"Fuck your memory, man." I scowl at him.

That doesn't wipe the smirk off his face or out of his cat-green eyes. He just folds his arms over his broad chest as if to say, *Sorry, Cap, you don't intimidate me.*

That's the problem with small towns.

Everyone knows everyone and they get way too used to all their shit.

"I'm not sulking, Lieutenant," I growl. "I'm working out whether to fire every last one of you. We've got forty percent more crime reports compared to last year, and eighteen percent fewer arrests. Tell me why?"

From his desk across the room, Micah Ainsley pipes up with a cunning smile. The man glows like a Renaissance sculpture, tall and muscular, his albino skin bone-white. "We have sixty percent more tourists than we did last year, too, Captain."

Henri Fontenot glances up from reading on his phone, leaning against the wall near Mallory's dispatch desk. "You mean it was quieter than this last year? Huh. How did y'all not fall asleep?"

"Shut it, city boy," Lucas throws back. "It's busy for *us.*"

"N'awlins ain't the city, *mon ami.* It's just the country grown wild."

"I don't even know what that's supposed to mean," I mutter. "Is the peanut gallery done with its bullshit and ready to give me some real answers or what?"

I get an immediate round of cheeky salutes.

Mallory the dispatcher even twirls around in her chair without stopping her rapid-fire typing and throws one at me, too, then blows me a kiss.

Insubordinate brats.

All of them.

I've barely been captain of the Redhaven PD long enough to win a crumb of respect and I'm already about to have a stress aneurysm because I'm surrounded by professional jokers.

But I grind my (in)subordinates into line and get down to brass tacks.

Everyone sobers up as we settle down and discuss patrol schedules, throwing around a few theories for what we can really do about the petty crime wave. We talk about pulling together rosters of shop owners, trusted folks we can talk to about setting up more CCTV cameras here and there to catch any funny business.

The cameras are cheap as hell these days and pretty sophisticated. I know a few good systems endorsed by Enguard, the premier West Coast security firm. Home Shepherd has also been making a lot of fancy military grade drones repurposed for civilian safety, but I'm not sure their tech is in our budget yet.

After listening to Micah nerd out over the drones for ten solid minutes, we're signing off and divvying up duties, with only Henri clocking out when he's scheduled to be on call overnight while the rest of us pull day shifts around town.

Lucas and I are the last guys out.

As he stops by his desk to snag a fresh ticket pad I lean over and stop him, lightly thumping my fingers against his arm.

"Hey. You got a minute?"

Lucas flutters his lashes. "Well, Cap, if you're about to ask me to the Pumpkin Formal? I can make time for you."

I eyeball him hard.

"I liked you better when you didn't talk so much, funny man."

"What can I say? New wife, new baby coming means I'm a

changed man." He grins and sits on the edge of his desk, running a hand through his thick crop of black hair. "Seriously, though, what's up?"

I clear my throat, struggling to get the words out.

Lucas looks so damn happy now. I don't begrudge him for it.

I know there are plenty of old pains that still hurt him, even if he doesn't show it much these days. Closure or not, he'll always carry a little guilt over not being able to save Celeste.

Too familiar.

Our demons are too much alike.

We both lost someone dear to us the same night. I'm happy as hell he got a few answers.

And it's like he knows even before I say, "I can't stop thinking about the Santos case and everything it turned up about—you know."

"Celeste." He sobers. His sister's name comes out like an old prayer he hasn't uttered in months. "Yeah. It's bringing up memories with Ethan, ain't it?"

I nod slowly. "I'm wondering if we've got grounds to legally rip the seal off that case, instead of just asking questions?"

"You mean you want to pursue an active investigation?"

"Don't know yet." I sigh. "Hell, it'll probably take years for Raleigh forensics and the Feds to finish sifting through the recovered remains and writing their reports. They might get a DNA match on Ethan eventually, or they might not... Guess I just feel like maybe we should be looking around on our end. We've still got a lot of unanswered questions, but what we learned after the Arrendell bust could shed some new light on it."

Lucas cocks his head from side to side thoughtfully. "You're the captain, Captain. It's your call and I've got your back. But I think you need to ask yourself something, Grant."

"Yeah?"

"Who are you really doing this for? Yourself—or her?"

I narrow my eyes.

Fuck, he's got me there.

* * *

THAT QUESTION'S still on my mind as Lucas and I part ways and I drop into my patrol car to start my route.

We tend to split the town three ways with one of us taking the inner shops and streets and another one taking the residential areas. Another officer—usually Micah—plays park ranger out in the wilderness, keeping an eye on the tourists and the hillfolk alike.

Micah likes the woods more than any New York City boy should. I think because it's a good chance to bring his old German Shepherd out with him.

The man's also got an uncanny knack for just disappearing and catching people off guard, which is always a little weird when he's as pale as a ghost and you'd think he'd stand out like a sore thumb against the dark trees.

We've all got our talents, I guess.

Mine's brooding until it hurts, and that's what I do while I park my car on the edge of the central town plaza with a good view of the shops.

Figure I'll watch the patterns going on tonight, see if I can pick up on anything hinting at trouble. Probably dumb kids doing all the shoplifting, and kids are never as good as they think at hiding when they're up to some shit.

I never was.

Neither was Ophelia.

Hell, when we were kids, she was usually the one who

accidentally ratted us out when the three of us got up to some shenanigans.

It wasn't that she was trying to snitch.

She just got flustered and spilled the beans when her ma or my parents gave us a good grilling. Usually, it was worse when it was my folks. Growing up without a dad, Ophelia never learned the resistance it took to face down not one, but *two* parents with a straight face, and—

Fuck, there I go thinking about her again.

She's living inside my damn head rent free.

Maybe she always has, I don't know.

I just know I don't have the answers I need.

Ethan's disappearance has haunted me my entire adult life.

Growing up an only child, it meant a hell of a lot to have someone my own age who felt like family; like the brother I never had. Then one day he was gone, leaving behind a soul-sucking void.

As much as I hated losing him, what hit me the hardest was how rough it was for Ophelia when he just up and vanished.

Also, how little I could do about it.

If I'm being honest, I was on the fence about staying a cop early on. Didn't seem like there was much to it in a Podunk town like this where the real heinous crimes go unsolved.

It's still a minor miracle we took down one Arrendell prick and got closure on a few cases.

Back then, I was only half sold on police work, still thinking about getting into metal fabrication, something like that—and then that night happened.

Celeste Graves and Ethan Sanderson *gone*.

I realized fast if I ever wanted answers, I'd have to stay a cop and keep looking into their disappearances, if only to find some closure.

Not just for me, but for that gorgeous bewitching woman with her wild green eyes that could turn so sad in an instant, like she's remembering everything she'll never have again.

Then she ran off.

Because my dumbass pushed her away.

Because I had to bark my hurt at her instead of learning to keep a leash on my anger like a grown-ass man.

Growling, I roll up my sleeve to scratch my arm, lingering on the black butterfly tangled in barbed wire that traces my bicep.

Go ahead and guess what inspired that.

Pain has a way of bringing fresh ink to a man's skin like misery loves company. Some secrets are so loud they just won't shut up every time he looks in a mirror.

Maybe because he doesn't want them to.

Maybe because he needs to hear them to remember who he is.

Truth be told, I stopped looking as hard for answers after she ghosted and the only butterfly I had left in my life was the one branded on my skin.

What the hell was the point if it wasn't for her?

I'm jolted out of my thoughts like I'm thunderstruck when I glimpse blonde hair moving down the street, familiar body language, and for a moment my heart kicks like a gunshot.

Ophelia.

But no, it's not her.

It's her little sister, strolling arm in arm with none other than Aleksander fuckface Arrendell.

If I hadn't known her since she was knee-high to a frog, I almost wouldn't recognize Ros right now.

She's always been a sweet, prim girl. A bit of a modern green flower child—cottagecore like the kids call it these days—with a certain innocence about her.

A little too sheltered, maybe. After surviving her first run with cancer, Angela Sanderson turned into a loving, good-natured helicopter mom and it showed with Ros as much as it helped her.

But right now, Rosalind's wearing a clinging white satin dress, skintight in all the wrong ways that make me uncomfortable.

I don't want to see Ophelia's baby sister's tits hanging out like that. Especially when she's hanging all over that phony fuck.

Aleksander keeps an arm around her shoulders while he leans in close, nuzzling her neck right there in public like he's some kind of vampire.

Christ, it's not even Halloween yet.

There's lipstick stains on the collar of his stylish grey suit, his mouth as red as hers. Her makeup is dark and sultry, her nails still a bright, glossy red.

I don't want to judge.

I don't.

Sometimes, small-town girls just find themselves and change overnight, realizing there was a big-city vixen inside them all along.

Yet it's barely ten in the goddamned morning and I think they're both drunk off their asses, swaying from side to side as they stumble into each other. Not a single care given for the more conservative folks steering around them with looks of baffled distaste, then *second* looks when it hits them who that is sloppy-drunk and probably high on Aleksander's arm.

Damn.

If Ros really wants me to keep her relationship with Aleksander a secret from Ophelia, she needs to be more discreet.

Sooner or later, this will blow right through the gossip mill and have everybody and their dog whispering about it.

I give it a day or two before it gets back to Ophelia, and

there's a knock-down drag-out fight between the Sanderson sisters that could level the whole town.

Nagging unease eats at me.

I should say something.

Tell Ophelia the truth, warn her, give her time to process this shit before Rosalind sails in and drops an atom bomb on her. I hate that Ophelia's got to deal with this shit sooner or later on top of her ma's medical situation.

I care about them both, even if Ros is more like a younger kid I never knew half as well as Philia.

And I'm torn between loyalties, wanting to honor Ros' privacy but also wanting to do what's right for everyone's own good.

For Ros' own good, too, I think.

I may need to keep an eye on her before her boyfriend— no, fuck, *fiancé*—drags her into something real ugly she's not ready for.

My brain hurts.

I need more time to think about what to say to Ophelia— if I say anything at all.

Maybe I just need to clear the air. It's funny how she reads my silences like a favorite book, plucking out crap I don't want her to see, but when we start talking we just lock horns and start doing damage.

I start doing it, mostly.

I always say everything wrong.

When we were young, sometimes it felt like all Ophelia ever asked for was that I speak. And I never could, not clearly, not the way she needs.

That's me.

That's my dumb ass to a tongue-tied tee around her.

Even when she was little and I wasn't that much bigger, before she turned into someone so beautiful she could twist my tongue in knots with a single glance from beneath her long lashes.

When we were kids I didn't know how to tell her how much she and Ethan meant to me.

How they eased that loneliness an only child knows when he's the quiet kid in a gossipy little town.

So I showed her by picking on her, pulling her pigtails, like any kind of attention was good attention—and that pattern just stuck, even as we grew up.

I pull her hair, and she sucker punches me and tells me how much of a colossal dick I am.

I'm not completely sure how long I've wanted to hear something else.

But what I hear now, as I watch Ros and Aleksander disappear into the Sanderson family shop, Nobody's Bees-Ness, is my dash radio coming to life with a gritty crackle.

I'm expecting Mallory to tell me there's been another silly incident, kids tagging the trees out in the logging areas or another punk caught shoplifting.

"Unit four-oh-two? Call came in from the Sanderson house, GPS shows you're closest—some kind of trouble with an intruder, possible assault. What's your ETA?"

My heart stalls.

Intruder?

Possible assault?

Ophelia.

Clammy sweat sweeps down my brow as I wrench the handset to my lips.

"Less than three minutes," I say, twisting the key violently in the ignition. "Tell her to sit tight, Mallory. I'm on my way."

VI: ONE MEAN GRIP (OPHELIA)

I shouldn't feel as guilty as I do for leaving the medical center.

I tell myself it's only because I'd get in the way.

Yes, I may be a trained nurse, but without being on staff at the Redhaven MC I'd just be a liability if someone needed to get in there to provide my mother with emergency care.

She's the *reason* I became a hospice nurse, but when it's your own mother...

Sometimes, there's not much you can do.

Thankfully, it only took a few minutes to sort out an incorrect date on her DNR. Several more minutes for me to process the fact that my mother *signed* a flipping DNR without telling me.

Then there was nothing else to do but sit back at her bedside with her thin hand in mine and silently beg her to wake up, to come back to life, to be the same vibrant woman I still see in my mind, clear as day.

She wouldn't want this for me.

Stuck here in limbo, pining for her health, waiting for death like it's my own life ending too.

Although Grant told me Mom was fighting and she promised me she was fine on the phone, the attending nurse said she sleeps a lot. She didn't bat an eye the whole time I was there with my fingers tangled in hers.

But it's fine.

...it's not fine.

Mom hasn't been *fine* for a long time, and I almost wanted to yell at her for hiding her deteriorating condition.

For making it hit that much harder when I finally got to see her for myself.

I didn't try to wake her, no, not even to hear her voice.

Not when rest is exactly what she needs to heal and fight on.

So I came back home and started tidying up the house on top of trying to call Ros again. It takes six texts and two voicemails, but she finally calls me back.

Holy hell.

It's like she doesn't hear me at all from whatever strange planet she's on when I try to tell her how Mom's doing.

That's not my sister on the line.

There's something *wrong*.

She's giggling too much, slurring her words.

Then there's a male voice in the background before she shushes him and ignores me when I ask who he is.

"Ros?" I ask, trying to force down my bubbling frustration—and fear. On top of Mom being gravely ill, I'm worried to death that there's something awful going on with my sister. "When are you coming home tonight?"

"Tonight? Oh, Ophie, I don't know. Still have to do inventory at the shop," she says matter-of-factly. It comes out forced like a blatant excuse. "You need something?"

"Um, yeah, to see my sister? Ros, I've been back here for two days and you haven't dropped in for more than five minutes. What's going on with you?"

"It's just... busy. Calm down," she says defensively—and I catch Background Guy muttering again, even if I can't make out his words. "You remember how tourist season gets, right? Everybody wants their beeswax candles and scented soaps, and when that's over we get the online rush for the holidays when their people back home find out where they bought it from. Just chill, Sis. I've been doing this on my own for a while now. If you really want to see me, you *could* come help clean up the back room for storage. Packing and postal runs and all that organizing takes time. I mean, you'd know if you'd been here all these years..."

Ouch.

Guilt rips through me.

"Okay, okay. Maybe I deserved that." I sigh. "I'll stop by the shop once I'm done here, okay? Let me know if you need help with the back orders."

"Sure," she says, but she already sounds distracted again. Like she's checking out, pulling the phone away. "Later, Ophie."

"Ros—"

Too late.

I stare down at my screen, the phone blanking with a disconnected call, then sigh and push my face into my palm.

"Dammit, Ros."

I curl up on the sofa and spend a few hours surfing job sites, looking for work. I think I'm just in denial right now because all the listings I apply for are in Miami.

Part of me thinks this is all a temporary hiccup, I guess.

Mom will miraculously get better.

I'll blow in and fix whatever's up with Ros.

Then I'll escape Redhaven's dreary orbit a second time before it swallows me up the same way it did Ethan and so many others.

Before I start thinking of this place as home again and get

way too attached to certain people when I should know better by now.

Especially big, gruff, emotionally stunted people.

By the time I'm done with a few halfhearted job apps, I hear the rumble of a garbage truck pulling away from the curb. Considering how stuffy the HOA is around here—especially since it's run by Lucia Arrendell—it's best to get the cans in from the curb ASAP. I wouldn't put it past some busybody to report it if they're out there for more than two hours.

The joys of small-town pettiness and boredom.

Just another reason to get out of here without looking back.

I unglue myself from the sofa and step outside, shivering in my jeans, t-shirt, and sandals as the chilly afternoon makes the sunny sky a lie.

Ugh, I really need to go shopping and buy a proper coat.

As soon as I get done lugging the garbage cans inside, I rake a few leaves.

I'm by the curb when I almost slam into a tall figure on a jog. He materializes out of nowhere, blocking my path.

My breaths stop cold as I peel back in shock.

I've never seen this man before in my life.

He's tall, gaunt, older, with a deeply seamed face and hollow eyes burning with a crazed intensity. His grey hair looks deranged, twisted like a bird's nest, and in his tailcoat he looks like an Addams Family extra, pale and shadow-eyed.

Gasping, I step back, bumping into the trash cans behind me.

"Who are y—"

"You're next," he hisses—and he lunges, grabbing at my arms.

"Hey—stop!"

Strange, bony fingers dig into me.

He's nearly shaking me, making my teeth rattle as he drags me closer, staring at me wildly.

"You have to stay away." His voice cracks. "You... you have to stay away or *you're next!*"

"Let me go!" I scream, shoving at him, but he won't relent. He just keeps pulling. "Hey—hey! Get your hands off me right now."

I summon my sternest nurse voice, the kind you only use when the rare disgruntled patient starts blaming you for everything wrong in their life, or the leering old men who think nothing of asking for a hand job.

But the creeper only holds on tighter, bruising pain grinding into my forearms, the meanest grip I've ever felt from another human being laying hands on me.

He jerks me in so close we're almost nose to nose, staring into me like he's trying to devour my soul.

One look at his eyes tells me he's not well.

A storm of mental distress, already on the verge of breaking, if he isn't broken already.

He might do anything.

And it's a lot harder to defuse a mental health crisis when they're grabbing and shaking you apart.

My heart snarls in fury and panic.

"Mister, please. Let go of me right now," I grind out before my courage fails.

"You'll die," he whispers. "Get any closer and you'll be the next to—"

Holy shit, enough!

"Let. *GO!*" I screech—and I reach for the rake behind me, grasping it and swinging it around with all my strength like a baseball bat.

The rake slams into his side with more of a punch than I figured this flimsy thing could pack.

His grip loosens as he stumbles away, banging himself

into the yard waste bin I pulled out for the leaves and tipping it over. As he windmills backward the big bin joins him.

The clatter and tumble and banging noise matches the chaotic beating of my heart.

Now's my chance.

I sprint for the door like there's a rabid coyote on my heels.

I still hear him behind me as he staggers up again.

Dress shoes slapping the driveway, panting breaths, but I have a head start.

I bolt up the front steps and fling myself through the front door.

Then I slam it shut in his face before frantically twisting the lock, pushing myself against it for support, trying to just breathe.

Breathe.

I'm bowed over with my hands braced on my thighs, gasping for air that rips at my throat and lungs.

There's a terrible second of silence.

I think he's gone.

Until he slaps his hands against the door so hard and abruptly I almost black out.

"Leave it! Don't go near them!" he roars. "You're next— you're next!"

"I don't know what the hell you're talking about!" I shout back. "Go away, you fucking creep! I'm calling the cops!"

Oh, God.

There's another slamming sound against the door, making it rattle in the frame. I need help right now.

I back away, staring at the frosted inset at the top of the door. Just past the half-moon of glass I can still make out his silhouette.

Phone in hand, I'm panic dialing 9-1-1 when the silhouette flicks away.

He reappears at the window once, his freakishly tall shape so murky past the curtains, but only for a second.

Soon, it's gone again.

I hold still, frozen by fear until I throw myself at the window and fling the curtains open.

I can't see anyone now.

Not even his weird, lanky frame running away.

He's just gone like he never existed.

What the hell? Was he dangerous or was this some kind of sick early Halloween prank by a demented tourist?

But he didn't look like a vacationer at all. Not dressed up like that. Not with the insanity swirling in his eyes.

And his words...

You're next, you're next.

You'll die.

That feels more like a threat.

Still shaking, I retreat from the window, never taking my eyes off the empty front walk and driveway. There's nothing out there but the green waste bin as I fumble with my phone.

The dispatcher picks up immediately, thank gawd—and it's so weird to recognize Mallory Cross' voice on the other end, this sweet lady who's worked there for years.

"9-1-1, what's your emergency?"

"Mal?" I choke out, my throat hurting from the adrenaline rush. "It's... it's Ophelia Sanderson. Listen, someone just attacked me at my mom's place and... and they made death threats against me. I've never seen him before, I just—"

"Oh, honey—honey, calm down, and let's take it slow. Start at the beginning."

So I do, trying to jam every little detail I can into a two-minute panic call.

"Got it," Mallory says, clucking her tongue. "Sit tight and make sure all the doors are locked. I'm sending a patrol car right over."

"Thank you," I whisper, hanging up the phone.

Then I wrap my arms around myself tight and curl up on the sofa to wait.

You know it's bad when I'm hoping for him.

I actually want them to send Grant Faircross.

How can I settle for anyone else than the only man who's ever made me feel safe?

VII: ONE STEP FORWARD (GRANT)

*Y*ou want to see the shittiest parking job in the world?

Tell a man the girl he's been fixated on since high school was just assaulted in her own fucking home, then watch him nearly plow his car across her front lawn trying to get to her.

I bolt out of the car and take the front steps of her house two at a time.

Butterfly, fuck.

Just hold on.

I barely refrain from punching a hole through her door.

Mallory said there was some weirdo doing just that, so I restrain myself and knock, raising my voice to call out.

"Ophelia? It's Grant. Open up! There's no one out here."

There's a long moment, a faint sound of footsteps shuffling from inside. Then the door cracks open.

She gives me a mutinous look, her green eyes crackling.

"Are you saying I imagined it? You—"

"Fuck *no.* God, woman, put your claws away for five minutes. I was telling you it's safe to open up."

That's when it registers.

The way she's so flustered, skin red like she's just been in a scrap.

The bruises on her arms.

Fresh, reddish-purple, and still forming in the shape of someone's grubby goddamned fingers. The points where those fingers dug in the darkest.

I've seen it plenty of times on domestic calls.

Instant rage storms through me and the world recedes into a humming white haze.

"Motherfucker," I clip, reaching for her. "Who did this? Who hurt you?"

Ophelia's eyes widen.

She stares at me, then glances away, twisting to look down at her upper arms.

"Oh, I hardly noticed. Honestly, it looks worse than it really is..."

Bull.

I don't know a damn thing yet except for the fact that the man who grabbed her is *dead.*

I'm not thinking when I drop down on one knee in front of her right there on the porch while she stands in the doorway.

"Grant? What are you *doing?*"

"Let me look. I need to see the damage," I growl, brushing my fingers lightly over the soft skin of her forearm. The light shines behind her head, turning her honey hair into a gold halo.

"S-sure," she relents, letting me do my thing.

As worked up and furious as I am, touching Ophelia is a special kind of torture.

I keep it careful, keep it light, gently grasping her forearm and turning it so I can get a good look at the bruises.

"He grabbed you pretty hard, but he didn't break the skin. He hurt you anywhere else?"

"My neck feels a little sore," she answers, rubbing the back of it. There's something odd in her voice. "He shook me pretty rough, too. Snapped my head around a bit."

Okay, shit.

Now, he's a dead man and dismembered.

"He'll be lucky I don't hang him from the town square statue by his ballsack when I find him," I growl, standing and giving her a gentle nudge. "Let's have a look around and you can tell me what happened."

She gives me another weird look and takes a hesitant step backward into the house.

I follow, taking a quick glance around.

All my police instincts fire, quick and assessing, searching for details she might've missed in the initial panic.

The old house hasn't changed much from what I remember, all lush oversized furniture that doesn't quite match, clearly chosen more for its marshmallow comfort than for showroom style.

"You guys still keep the first aid kit in the bathroom?" I ask.

"...y-yeah."

Fuck me, I've never seen her so shaken. I can't help touching her shoulder.

"Hey," I say. "You're gonna be fine, Ophelia. He's not hurting you again. It's okay now."

"Is it?" she echoes faintly, her pretty green eyes round marbles as she stares at me.

"The hell wouldn't it be?"

"Um, you're actually *talking,* for one. I think the world's about to end."

I blink.

That's when I realize she's teasing me.

Before I know what's happening, I grin. If she's still joking, she'll be one hundred percent fine.

"Brat," I spit, lightly flicking my fingers against the center of her forehead. "Sit down and I'll get you the kit."

She flashes me a smirk and drops herself onto the couch, giving me a glimpse of full hips and jeans that cup her ass like they're trying to make love to it.

I pull myself away and head down the hall to the first-floor bathroom, trying not to let that vision stick.

Sure enough, there's a box in the little cabinet above the toilet, an old steel fishing tackle box that belonged to Angela Sanderson's husband before he died not too long after Ethan was born.

This box came out every time we banged ourselves up as kids, running through the woods like heathens and falling out of trees at least twice a week.

We'd come tumbling in from our adventures, after we dared each other to do stupid shit that risked our necks. It's a minor miracle nobody got more than a broken ankle over the years.

You name it, we got ourselves scratched up doing it, only to come dragging back before dark so Mrs. Sanderson could patch us up like a good medic and send me home to my ma covered in Bactine and Band-Aids.

The memory makes me smile as I hold the box—and I sober as it hits me.

Time passes like one cruel son of a bitch.

It's been decades since the last time Angela Sanderson patched me up. And now she's on her deathbed, while I'm taking this kit out for her grown daughter with a hundred awkward feelings between us, all while her youngest is about to get hitched to a giant asshole and start an entirely new stage of her life.

Funny how everything changes and mutates yet still stays the same.

Tucking the box under my arm, I head into the living room and sink down on the sofa next to Ophelia.

She glances at the tackle box. For a moment, her expression softens as she brushes her fingers over the top.

I can tell what she's thinking.

Most of the time, I can read her too well.

She's one of the few people here who makes *sense* to me, until she doesn't when she gets all pissed off and I have no idea what the hell I did.

But right now, it's not hard to tell she's sinking into those same memories.

The same memories that mean even when it's just the two of us, we're never alone. Not when we're haunted by the same nagging ghosts.

"Remember the tree house?" she asks softly.

I look up.

"No 'GURLS' allowed," I mutter, stressing the way we butchered the spelling. I gently brush her hand aside to flip the first aid kit open. "Except you. We made a one-time exception for the gentleman's club."

She laughs—and why the hell do I love that sound so much?

"Lucky me. But you said I wasn't *really* a girl, right?" She pokes my arm just above my wrist. "Jackass."

"Woman, that was almost thirty years ago. You were barely a toddler then," I point out with a snort. "You were a baby. Not a girl."

"And you and Ethan couldn't spell 'girl' to save your stupid lives," she retorts.

I lift my head, eyeing her skeptically—only to find her watching me with this almost challenging smile that makes it impossible for me not to smile back.

For just a moment, I stop and drink her in.

So delicate, yet so grounded and down-to-earth.

She's completely goddamned beautiful, and while she looks like her ma, there's also something else there entirely.

Something I can't pin down except knowing she probably inherited it from the unknown man who fathered both her and Ros.

With her blonde hair loose and cascading down around her face, her cheeks flushed, she looks like some kind of angel who crossed over into mundane life.

Yeah, I know how fucked up that is to say.

This sweet thing who'd give me a sugar rush forever instead of the bratty little hellion who occupies my thoughts every waking moment since she showed up again.

I'm a little helpless as I linger on her mouth.

That pink, soft mouth that'd feel like pure candy wrapped around any man's dick.

I know.

I know I shouldn't go there.

That lucky bastard who found out? He damn sure isn't me.

Not after I trampled her heart and still can't spend more than an hour with her without something combusting to shit.

I swallow a growl and remind myself to cool it, jerking my gaze away so I can dig through the kit until I find a little tube of anti-inflammatory cream.

"You want to tell me what happened? Start at the beginning." I reach for her closest arm.

"Huh?" She blinks like she's just snapped awake, then clears her throat and looks away. "Okay. Right. Um. So, I was out bringing in the trash bins and raking a few leaves because last I remember, Mrs. Appleberry will call the HOA if they're out past sunset. I mean, if she's still alive—"

"She is," I snort, smoothing the cream on her bruises. I'll photograph them after I'm sure the numbing cream is doing its work. It won't have a visible effect at first to count as tampering with evidence. "Called the HOA on me last week because my grass was a quarter inch high, and she doesn't even *live* on my street."

"But she loves her evening walks, bless her heart," Ophelia says dryly. "But yeah, I was just bringing the bins in and then there was this *guy*. I don't know where he came from. Really tall, scary-looking. Older. Grey hair. Crazy part is, he was wearing a suit. Almost looked like some kind of butler, but he was also wild. Totally rocked the mad scientist vibe. He scared the crap out of me. Thought it was some weird Halloween thing when he came barreling in looking like Lurch—until it obviously wasn't."

"Lurch?"

"The butler from The Addams Family?"

"Oh."

That's mighty interesting.

My brain snaps back to the man who was standing on the street staring at me the other day with Nell.

If there's a connection, it's not much relief.

If I'm right and that guy works up at the big house, I like it even less.

"What the hell did he want?" I ask, keeping my focus on my hands as I turn her arm to make sure I didn't miss a spot before reaching to start on her other arm.

It leaves my forearm pressed against her stomach.

If it's innocent, why does this feel so compromising?

Damn.

She's so warm through the shirt.

This perfect heated softness making me far too aware of her closeness.

Her scent makes my nostrils flare, this muted sweet

beeswax smell that's clung to her since childhood. Probably a side effect of a life raised around her mama's handmade beeswax products, especially when she'd pitch in a hand sometimes like every good kid with parents running a small biz.

There's also something about that smell that's just Ophelia Sanderson.

It guts me how much I've missed it.

I'm damn near intoxicated as I breathe slowly, listening to her.

"He told me I was next," she whispers, looking around like she's afraid this freak might come flying through the door. "That if I get any closer to 'them,' whoever he means, I'll be the next to die. He really seemed upset, almost manic. I don't know. Was he threatening me or trying to warn me?"

"Sounds awfully threatening to me," I say coldly.

"I thought so too—at first. But after he left and I finally calmed down, now I'm not so sure."

"Philia, he *hurt* you," I snarl.

"Yeah, but I'm just not sure he meant to. He looked wild, almost scared. I don't think he was thinking right." Ophelia bows her head, touching her fingertips to the bruises on her arm. "I hate to say it, but I don't think he meant any harm. Even if he scared me out of my wits..."

"Ophelia." I barely hold myself back from snapping. "When a strange man shows up yelling death threats in your face and throwing you around, he doesn't get the charitable interpretation."

Her eyes fall.

"...yeah. I guess you're right." She presses her lips together. "But he just left, too. He banged on the door a little after I locked myself inside and I think he tried to look in the window. I thought he was about to break in but then he was just... gone."

Gone, but most definitely not fucking forgotten.

"And if he comes back? What then?" There's an edge in my voice.

I want to hear it from her mouth.

I want her to show me she's still got the same stubborn common sense after all these years.

"I'll be more careful," she says. "I'll check before I go outside. Every time."

"Doesn't mean you'll be safe here if we don't know what he wanted. He'll probably be more stealthy next time," I point out before snapping the tube of cream closed and tossing it back into the kit. "You know what, fuck this."

"Excuse me?" Her brows go up.

"Pack your shit. You're staying with me tonight."

Ophelia's head jerks up, her green eyes flashing like warning lights.

For a second, I think she's about to pass out, and it's got nothing to do with her run-in with Evil Jeeves.

"I'm doing *what*? Why would I do something so insane?"

"Because I don't like the thought of you here all alone if that guy shows up again. Who the fuck knows when Ros will actually come home? You seen her?" I pull my phone out of my uniform and flick to the camera app. "Now hold your arms out and sit still so I can get a few photos for the report."

A frustrated little noise spills past Ophelia's lips, but she complies, thrusting her arms out straight so the bruises are more visible.

"Look, Grant, I'm not staying with you. I don't need a babysitter. I think I just overreacted. For all I know, that guy's someone's grandpa with a bad case of dementia. Confused about where he is or something. I bet the people who love him are looking for him everywhere. Is there anybody around town missing?"

I shake my head firmly.

"No, and if that's the case, we'll find out and have him home in a day," I say, quickly snapping several photos. "Considering the shit going on here in the last year, though, I'm not taking that risk. You wait around for a happy ending and you might not have an ending at all."

"Huh? It's not that risky—"

"Ophelia." I cut her off with a growl, locking my gaze to stubborn green eyes. "Listen, the last time we had creepy assholes following the new girl around, she wound up with one girl dead in her living room and a psycho trying to feed her to the Jacobins' pigs. With that kind of shit going on, I can't risk it being harmless." I stop, my jaw clenching, then force myself to add, "Especially not when it's you."

When I shut my yap, I notice she'd started to open her mouth. Her brows are drawn together in a furious line.

She stops and gives me another strange look I can't interpret as she frowns.

Her lower lip thrusts out in a bratty little pout I'm not fucking staring at.

Honest to God.

"I didn't tell you Ros hasn't been coming home. What are you hiding, Grant? What's going *on* with her?"

Ah, fuck.

I shouldn't have let that slip.

"Later. I'll tell you at my house." I haul myself to my feet.

"Nope. In case you hadn't noticed, I still haven't agreed to anything."

I dart her the world's dirtiest look.

Sweet Jesus, this woman and her pride.

"Philia, listen." Sighing, I turn back to face her. "Look at it like you're doing me a favor. Nothing more. Between you and me, my folks haven't had a real vacation in years. I'd like to let them get out of town before Christmas and away from any sketchy shit around here, but they've gotta be here to look after Nell when I'm at work, and with school, I can't let her go with them. I know you. I bet you're going stir-crazy, fretting nonstop when you're not with your ma. We could use a little help around the house to give my parents a break, let 'em take some time off. So, if you're willing, I'd really appreciate it if you stayed with me, kept yourself out of trouble, and helped me out with the munchkin. It'd kill a whole flock of birds with one stone. You won't have to be alone, looking over your shoulder while I track down your intruder, and I won't have to worry about Nell while my parents are gone."

Maybe that will push past her pride and let her actually accept.

But Ophelia just blinks at me, her mouth hanging open.

"What?" I frown. "What did I say?"

"...I don't think you've ever said that many words with feeling in your entire *life*, for one."

I groan, smacking my palm against my face.

"I do know how to fucking talk, Butterfly."

She laughs. "Do you? You had me fooled for a good long while."

"All grown up and still a pain in the ass."

"Well, you helped spoil me growing up. So yeah, you should know." She tilts her face up, eyeing me intently. "You promise you'll clue me in on Ros if I come?"

Honestly, I'd clue her in even if she didn't.

It's not hard to see how worried she is, and dammit, I never should've swept it under the rug in the first place even if my intentions were to save her some grief.

"Yes," I bite off.

Ophelia sighs.

"Fiiine," she grumbles, pushing to her feet. "But you'll have to wait here while I pack."

"You want me to help?"

"No." Her face flushes bright pink as she twists past me in the narrow space between the sofa and the coffee table without another word.

That damnably Ophelia Sanderson scent flares my nostrils again as the warmth of her body touches mine and leaves me burning. She throws a look over her shoulder as she heads to the stairs with a little toss of her shimmering honey-gold hair.

"Stay here. No boys allowed," she says.

Then she's gone, flitting upstairs, as warm and bright as if she hasn't just been assaulted.

Goddamn.

How does she do it?

No matter what happens, Ophelia Sanderson picks herself up and forges on, shining on like the summer sun.

Then again, she wouldn't be the woman who thieved away a piece of my heart ages ago if she didn't.

Whatever happens next, that's one jagged piece I'm sure I'll never get back.

VIII: ONE BIG SLIP (OPHELIA)

There are times when I feel like Grant Faircross can sear me open with a single glance and see all my hidden secrets.

Which is why I can't believe how dense he is sometimes.

And how completely oblivious he can be to the way he just delivered an earthquake, left me reeling by rushing to my side the second he thought I was in danger.

That closed-off, rude, blunt boy has grown into a man with an iron heart.

But there's something different about him, too.

There are times when the walls crack for the briefest second and his emotions show freely.

It almost makes me think he cares.

That there's something more than just the unwavering obligation to protect me because I'm his best friend's little sister.

God.

Doesn't he realize how many feelings he's kicking up?

Like the fact that I've always hated how it felt like Grant

just saw me as extended family, like his own little sister, a complete nonentity, not really a girl—or now, a woman.

But the way those dark-mocha eyes ran over me as he looked at my bruises, the way he *touched* me...

That was not the caring, distant caress of a big brother.

In that moment, Grant freaking Faircross made me feel every inch a woman and then some.

Also, it only took half an hour to pack my things, considering I'd just unpacked them and I hadn't brought much with me to Redhaven.

Grant waited patiently downstairs, though I heard him thumping around a bit in the bathroom to put the first aid kit away. The déjà vu hit like a freight train.

It's just *weird.*

Almost like years haven't been lost in time, tossing us back to those easier days when we'd spent our evenings together.

And if it wasn't for the gaping chasm left by Ethan missing, I'd smile.

The drive to Grant's cottage is short enough. I mean, technically every drive through Redhaven is pretty short.

I curl up silently in the passenger seat, basking in the warmth coming from the heating vents. Grant stays silent and brooding.

I try not to let him catch those little glances I throw him from the corner of my eye, desperate to read his mind.

What's he thinking now?

Does he sense the same tension in the air?

He's certainly turning over something in that big head of his. His brows always stitch together a stark line when he's deep in thought like gathering thunderheads.

And now that he's sporting this full, thick beard, it just adds another layer when his beard twitches, grinding his jaw like he can chew on those ideas until he gets to the truth.

I'm sneaky as I glance at him, but I get the feeling he knows I'm watching.

Do you know how long I've been watching you, though?

Do you know how much I wanted to know you before everything turned so crappy?

Sigh.

I'm not supposed to do this again.

I know I'm not.

I'm not supposed to be having warm, fuzzy feelings for Grant like I'm a kid with a crush all over again. Especially not after he's knocked around my heart like a tiger with a ping-pong ball.

But he's always been the compass, hasn't he?

The lodestone that draws me back.

No matter how much older and wiser and more immune to impulsive emotions I'd like to think I am, I'm still helpless to resist his magnetism.

When I was young and stupid, I used to think we were made for each other.

That I was the only one who could understand him because I was the only one besides Ethan who ever really tried.

Then I grew up and found out that broody men like Grant don't want to be understood.

They're content to be these enigmas put on the Earth to drive women like me insane.

Honestly, they're a little like self-absorbed children who don't quite realize relationships are a two-way street—even friendships—and it's not all about finding people who are just sidekicks along for the ride with a moody, intense, mute main character.

Yeah.

In case it wasn't obvious, my post-Redhaven love life

hasn't been stellar. When I think about the men I've dated ever since I left, my stomach twists with a truth I hate.

I've always been trying to find another Grant.

Someone who's snarly and blunt and kind of a dick.

But actions speak louder than words.

Grant's actions have always hinted that under his grouchy surface there's a kind, thoughtful man who puts others first.

Not a completely selfish asshole with a hard-on for his own dark, tormented image.

Why else would he be dragging me off to his house and asking me to help with Nell when he's made it clear he just wants to look after *me?*

Poor guy.

He thought I couldn't say no to helping with the kiddo and he's totally right.

Even if it wounds my pride a bit to be lured in so obviously, I can't deny it.

I think this could be good for me, though.

I've been looking for a happy distraction from Mom, from Ros, from Redhaven and its sinister crap.

Plus, little Nell is a perfectly adorable diversion to help keep me from fixating on a thousand heart-wrenching worries over Mom.

She's also waiting for us when Grant pulls into the driveway of his cottage. His parents are there, too, their car parked by the curb while they take turns pushing Nell in the wood-and-rope swing hanging from the large oak tree that casts its shade over Grant's neatly tended front yard.

The grass looks like it's a quarter inch longer than the Redhaven HOA allows and it makes me smile.

Knowing him, he probably left it like that on purpose to spite the Mrs. Appleberrys around town. I even catch a glimpse of clover and late season blooms that must've been nice for the bees and other bugs back in the summer.

As we get out of his patrol car and I grab my things, his parents glance up with grateful smiles.

It's odd to see them aged ten years when it feels like it's just overnight.

Until this moment, I imagined them with a few less wrinkles.

Margaret Faircross' hair not quite so silvery and Jensen Faircross' back straighter and less stooped than it is now. He's still a big man despite advancing age taking the edge off his muscle mass.

Grant raises a hand to his parents.

"Sorry I'm late," he says. "Had a dispatch call. Intruder at Ophelia's house."

Mrs. Faircross' gaze flicks to me, eyes rounding with concern. "Oh, Ophelia—are you all right?"

Next thing I know, she's coming at me full steam.

I don't even get a chance to grab my bag from the car before Mrs. Faircross has me wrapped up in the warmest hug.

It almost hurts to hug her back because it feels like coming home.

To remember that as much as I blame Redhaven and its weirdness and dark secrets for so many awful things, I have people here who are family. It doesn't matter if they're not blood at all.

And Jensen, he makes me feel like the safest woman in the world with just a glance.

"Don't tell me they hurt you?" Jensen pats my shoulder.

I smile at him and shake my head.

I'm half expecting to walk inside to steaming bowls of chili and cornbread, his usual hearty go-to back when he'd feed three kids who dragged themselves in from tromping around the woods all day.

All the best things in life happened with spicy soup and warm bread and friendly conversation around the table.

I think it hit so deep because I never knew my own father. To this day, I don't have any good guesses who he could be.

Mom was always so tight-lipped about it, yet she must have loved him enough to have two children with him.

I only ever knew that our dad wasn't the same as Ethan's, a kind, sickly man who passed away from leukemia before Ros and I were born.

But Jensen Faircross always treated me like I was his own daughter, bridging the awkward father gap until I never even felt the absence.

Next thing I know, he's hugging me as his wife steps aside. I'm caught up in a tangle of Faircrosses while Grant scoops up a laughing Nell.

I let the elder Faircrosses fuss over me a bit, hugging them back and saying a few words about my mother, before I pull back with a smile, gripping Margaret's arms.

"I promise I'm okay," I say. "It wasn't a big deal. Just some confused old guy who rattled me a bit. I'm going to stay with Grant for a bit until he sorts out who it was and if they need help—or an assault charge, I guess. Don't worry."

Margaret pats my cheek, clucking her tongue with soft sympathy. "Such a shame to have you coming home like this! I've missed you dearly, Ophelia. You're practically all your mother ever talks about over tea, you know. She's so proud of you."

I know.

And I can't help the lump rising in my throat.

"Maybe I'll get lucky and she can wake up and tell me herself," I whisper.

Margaret's eyes mist over for a sweet, sentimental second.

Jensen nods warmly again, silent yet completely understanding. It's easy to see where some of Grant's overprotective grizzly vibe comes from.

Then Margaret lets me go, dusting her hands together.

"Well then," she says. "I'll leave you to get settled in." She turns a sharp eye on Grant. "I hope your guest room is livable, young man. You live too much like a bachelor."

Grant clears his throat gruffly as he lifts Nell up on his shoulders. "Bachelor or not, I keep my house clean. I'm not going to have her staying in a damned pigsty, Ma. Jesus."

"You watch that mouth," she retorts. "And don't forget Miss Ophelia is your *guest*. Not your housekeeper. Don't expect her to go picking up after you, either."

"I can clean up for my damned self!" he splutters, cheeks going red above his beard as he scowls at his mother.

"It's cool. I'm really just staying over to help with Nell," I interrupt, if only to give Grant a little mercy. "I heard you guys have been wearing yourself thin. If you both want to run off for a romantic getaway down the coast or something..." I smile teasingly. "Now's a good time."

"Oh, no, we're too old for romance." Margaret laughs. "You two, on the other hand..."

Oh, God.

Oh my God, oh my God.

I forgot this woman is a shameless matchmaker.

The fact that Grant is thirty-nine and still single can't help much.

Also, I'm about to spontaneously combust on the spot.

Honestly, I think I want to be an ash pile just so I don't have to stand here, trying not to die of sheer mortification.

When I was a kid, I always thought Margaret knew about my crush on Grant. She'd invite me over for odd things, especially after I turned eighteen. Always trying to get me and Grant hanging out alone, secretly hoping her son would make a move, I guess.

He never did.

I was just *Butterfly* back then.

Now, I know better.

I've accepted I'll always just be *Butterfly* to him, that last annoying piece of Ethan he still can't let go of.

Even living under the same roof, I'd bet my bottom dollar Grant won't make a move at all.

Even so, I'm tongue-tied.

Frozen while Grant stands there blankly, stone-faced and silent, focusing on prying Nell's fingers out of his hair like he didn't hear a thing.

It's his father who rescues me. Jensen smiles indulgently and shakes his head, slipping an arm around his wife's waist.

"Don't put the kids on the spot, love," he says. "Come to think of it, we could use a little getaway. Maybe drive out to the coast, that little B&B you love so much—the one with the beach that always has a ton of shells?"

"Yes," Grant growls. "Go. Get out. Y'all are on my last nerve."

Margaret thins her lips. "Son, if you think you're too big for a spanking, you'll find out very fast that your mother can still take you over her knee."

"I think I'd kill to see that!" I mutter dryly, smiling myself back into composure—right before a fresh shiver hits me. "Oof, that wind... I'd better get inside before I catch cold. I've been in Florida too long. Didn't come ready for October in North Carolina."

"Grant," Margaret says sharply.

"What, Ma?" Grant groans, rolling his eyes, which makes Nell giggle as she bends over him to meet his gaze.

"Either give Ophelia one of your nice coats or you take her shopping for one immediately," she orders. "Don't let her buy a cheap one, either. I won't have her out here freezing in this house."

"Thanks, but I can shop for my own—"

Margaret charges on like she doesn't even hear me. "Promise me, Grant."

The big lunk looks at the ground and sweeps his foot over it.

"Yeah, yeah, I promise. Now, will you quit harassing us and go plan your trip?"

Mrs. Faircross laughs.

"I'm your mother. It's my *job* to harass you."

I stifle a laugh behind my hand, whispering, "Some things never change."

Grant shoots me a dirty look.

"Somehow, he never did learn enough manners. Lord knows I tried." Margaret leans into her husband, offering me a sweet smile. "We'll leave you be to settle in. But don't be a stranger, darling. I've missed your face around here."

It takes a few more parting hugs and admonishments at Grant before the Faircrosses actually leave.

Even though his shoulders are full with Nell, he insists on taking my bag and carrying it in, dragging my suitcase in one hand with Nell's tiny bright-pink backpack dangling from his broad shoulder.

As we mount the steps to the front porch, I glance back at the last hint of taillights on the Faircrosses' car.

"They haven't slowed down a bit, have they?"

"They're guaranteed to be goddamned terrors until they're ninety, I'm sure," he grumps, unlocking the door to let me in.

I just hold my smile.

Even when he's snarling, it's not hard to tell he complains with so much love.

Inside, Grant swings Nell down and tosses her backpack on the sofa.

"Go wash up, Nelly," he says. "You can have a couple

cookies and a juice for a snack, then I want you buckling down and hitting the books."

"With Adventure Time?" She pouts up at him. "It always makes homework go faster..."

"Not till I'm done so I can turn it off if it gets too weird. You're not old enough for some of the shit on that show." He ruffles her hair. "Now scoot, kiddo."

Nell just beams, flashing me a double-handed wave and she whispers, "Welcome home, Miss Philia!"

Oh, boy.

I want to sputter out that this isn't *home*, but that little wild child's already taking off up the stairs.

I'm just imagining that redness above Grant's beard as he shakes his head, I'm sure.

He turns to lead me upstairs at a slower adult pace.

"C'mon. I'll show you to the guest room up here."

I don't really know what to say as I follow him up, admiring this cozy little cottage house with its soft slate-blue walls and earthy wood tones everywhere.

Until now, it hasn't really sunken in that we'll be *living* together.

Not just seeing him out on patrols or bumping into him at the grocery store.

No, waking up to him every morning.

Seeing him sleep-rumpled and drowsy or relaxing at the end of a hard day.

Falling asleep at night knowing he's just down the hall, that long, powerful body stretched out in his bed, a great beast at rest.

Wondering, when I shouldn't, if he ever finds time to relieve his stress with other women. I've kept my ears perked up for any rumors, but so far, I've heard nothing.

And if he doesn't date, if he doesn't even sneak in a casual one-night stand every so often, what does he do to release that snapping tension that makes Grant so... well, Grant?

Does he just use whatever's in his head on those long, lonely nights? Does he ever get so riled that big hand wanders lower, and what does he think about when he—

"Butterfly, you coming?" He's looking at me intently when my head snaps up.

That shouldn't make my heart thud so hard.

I'm standing frozen at the base of the stairs, caught in thoughts I definitely shouldn't be having.

I mean, it's not like Grant didn't sleep over all the time back when he and Ethan were teenagers. But it made my heart beat like a rock ballad then, too, didn't it?

Yes, even though my thoughts were a little more innocent.

I was only a kid when I'd wake up after midnight and creep down through the house, too curious what stupid things Ethan and his bestie got up to after dark.

I'd wind up sitting on the stairs and clutching the railings, watching them, eavesdropping on their conversations about girls and games and how they were so close to grinding their way to their first million dollars.

Sometimes, the boys would come home after sneaking beer or Jacobin moonshine at parties with the older kids and pass out early. They never saw me when I'd perch in my spot, looking down below at Grant's huge body sprawled out in his sleeping bag on the floor of our living room.

He was big even then.

The sleeping bag was actually two bags unzipped and layered around him like a Grant sandwich because he couldn't fit inside a normal one. Even then, he slept with one thick arm and leg flung out on the floor, his handsome face scowling in his sleep.

I still see that gorgeous, angry boy in the broad lines of Grant's back as he moves up the stairs ahead of me.

It's funny.

No matter how surly he seems, I've never seen him use that strength to hurt anyone.

Upstairs, he guides me down a narrow, blue-carpeted hallway, tapping doors as he goes.

"Things have moved around a little since the last time you were here. Nell's room," he says, then the next one, "My room. Bathroom across the hall." He stops at the last door at the very end of the hall kitty-corner to his room and pushes the door open. "Your room. Laundry's still in the basement if you need it."

"Great, thanks."

He swings my suitcase through the door and drops it just inside off to one side before stepping out of the way to let me in. I brush past him, trying not to be too aware of how that leaves me tingling.

I step into a sunny, neat room with a queen bed covered in homey quilts in various shades of green hexagons, from forest to soft pastel sea green. White lace curtains, a dresser, and a trunk in matching grey ash wood, cozy throw rugs scattered around.

The place is simple, neutral, clean, and cozy.

That's Grant, all right.

Makes sense when this used to be *his* room when he was a kid.

It hits me that I'll be sleeping in the same room he's laid in every night before his parents moved out and he took over the master bedroom.

But I really shouldn't think about that.

Behind me, he clears his throat.

"Listen, this house is old and I'm working on fixing up the insulation. Still gets drafty at night even when the furnace kicks on. There's an electric blanket in the trunk, if you need it. If you're still too cold with that, then I'll buy you a new one."

I turn back to face him.

There he is, standing awkwardly in the doorway, scrubbing the back of his neck with one hand and looking anywhere but at me.

The big moose cares so much.

I can't help a small smile.

"I'm sure I'll be fine with the electric blanket. Jeez, I feel like me being cold all the time is turning into a running gag," I say. "Thanks, though. You don't have to go to the trouble."

His expression darkens into a smoky glare.

"It's no trouble. *You* ain't trouble, Philia."

I blink quickly and duck my head.

Wow.

Now *I'm* the one being awkward and turning away as I blush.

"I, um... thanks."

Way to go, Ophelia.

There's a long silence before he grunts and tosses his head. "Right. I'm gonna start dinner. Come on down once you're settled in and we'll have a chat about Ros."

Blech.

How could I forget?

Hearing my sister's name rips me back to grim reality, away from this beautifully angsty fairy tale where we both try to hide confusing feelings rearing their heads.

I nod slowly.

"Yeah," I say faintly. "Okay. Thanks again."

Grant doesn't say anything.

He just looks at me for a long, hard moment with a gaze I can't decipher.

Then he's gone, leaving me standing in that quiet sunlit

room, wondering why everything keeps throbbing with uncertainty.

* * *

IT DOESN'T TAKE me long to unpack for what feels like the twentieth time.

It also feels a little pointless when everything is so transitory right now.

Or maybe I just have a feeling Grant will be shipping me right back home tomorrow after one of the out-of-towners comes rushing in to apologize because their grandpa broke out of his cabin and wound up lost, running around town spooking people.

Grant will feel silly for overreacting. I'll feel sillier for going along with it, but we'll forget within a week, after my bruises heal.

By the time I'm back downstairs, I find Nell hunched over the coffee table. She's kneeling on the floor and scribbling diligently at a workbook from school while some colorful cartoon bubbles across the TV with overly bright colors and loud noises and a lot of weird, um, stretching.

I stop and lean over to watch her for a moment.

"Whatcha working on?" I ask.

"Book report," she chirps without stopping her aggressive scribbling. "It's about how *The Velveteen Rabbit* is really a book of philosophy. Like how Skin Horse says you can find your real self if you suffer enough for love."

Yikes.

That's pretty freaking deep for an almost ten-year-old.

I arch both brows. "Now where did you learn about philosophy? Last I checked, that's usually a subject for college."

"Miss Lilah!" she answers brightly, her eyes going starry.

"She's the best teacher ever. She says when life gets tough, that's when you find out what you're really made of. A lot of ancient people thought so too and wrote long books about it. Don't much like Aristotle, though. Aristotle *sucks.*"

I burst out laughing at her enthusiasm.

Honestly, it was all Greek to me—pun intended—in the Great Thinkers extracurricular I took, too.

"You have an interesting teacher," I tease wryly, tweaking one of her curls. Then I glance up as I catch a muscular shoulder passing by through the kitchen door.

"Be right back. I'll let you focus."

I follow that glimpse a minute later and the sudden heavenly smell of cooking meat into the kitchen.

Sure enough, Grant changed out of his uniform, slipping into a pair of battered jeans and a plain grey Redhaven PD t-shirt that strains across his chest.

I think I'm in awe.

Seeing him like this, casual and barefoot and so *huge,* breaks something inside me.

This powerful ache of homesickness that doesn't make sense when I'm already here with good people.

But it's not a place I'm missing.

It's a time when things were simpler.

Before we were missing so many pieces of ourselves.

"Need a hand?" I ask.

Grant glances up from flipping homemade hamburgers on the stove.

"Sure," he says. "Fries are just about ready to come out of the oven, if you wanna season 'em."

"On it." I scrounge up a pair of oven mitts as he steps aside so I can retrieve a tray crowded with thick wedge steak fries coated with some aromatic oil. "Spice rack?"

"Cabinet overhead."

"Ah."

I stretch up on my toes to reach in and dig out the salt and pepper, plus the paprika. I know how Grant eats and I know he likes his spicy.

"Only salt on a third of the pan," he grunts. "No pepper or anything. Nell's particular."

I giggle.

"Only because you let her be." I keep myself from pointing out that it's adorable how much he indulges the little girl.

The dirty look he throws me as he pushes the sizzling burger patties around says he knows exactly what I'm thinking.

I watch him sidelong while I season the fries, trying to work up how to ask, before I decide to be direct.

"So," I say. "You want to tell me what's up with Ros? How long has she been this weird?"

He pauses, gathering his words.

"If you'd asked me a few days ago, I'd have said not long at all. Then again, that's mostly 'cause I hardly ever saw her the last year or two with the murder drama and all. Guess that in itself was a little weird, considering she was always around town before. She'd always wave or stop by for a quick conversation."

I frown and pick up one of the steak fries for a taste test.

"Where has she been going? Why can't I get her to come home?"

"No damned clue," he growls. "But I'm thinking it's got an awful lot to do with Aleksander Arrendell."

I'd bitten down on the piping hot fry—and now I choke on it, coughing and coming close to spitting it out.

"Aleksander *who?*" I force swallow and pound a fist against my chest.

"You heard me." Grant watches me in stark silence, then

turns the burner off, sets the spatula down, and rips a paper towel off the dispenser roll before offering it to me.

I eye him intently as he sighs.

"Look, I don't think you're gonna like what I'm about to tell you, Butterfly."

"If it's what I think you're saying, I know I won't like it." I wipe my mouth roughly with the paper towel. "Thanks. But what the hell do the Arrendells have to do with Ros?"

Grant grits his teeth, looking away from me and back again.

Oh, Jesus.

It must be bad if he's steeling himself like this. I brace myself, but I'm so not ready for the moment he says it.

"Ophelia, they're engaged."

"They're—they're—*what?*" I think I'm about to commit a homicide, Aleksander Arrendell primary victim. Rage boils up inside me. I stare at him in disbelief, waiting for him to tell me he's joking or just misspoke. "My baby sister is... is engaged to *that* creep? What the hell? Since when? How do you *know?*"

"I saw them together the day you came back," he bites off. "Up at the big house when I was responding to that suicide call. They were hanging all over each other. She showed me the ring and told me to stop worrying, said they were engaged. She begged me not to tell you."

"Holy shit. Well, I can guess why," I grit through my teeth, clenching my fists. "She knew what I'd say. Jesus, how could she? How—knowing what we know now, about Ulysses, when we've always known. We *knew* they had to be involved that night, and Ethan..."

I can't carry on. The burning thud of my heart makes me incoherent.

"I know," Grant answers bitterly. His voice is heavy and rough, but he's still here with me, sharing the same shock, even if he's not hissing and spitting like a wet cat. "It doesn't feel right. Ros barely reacted to seeing that poor maid hanging there in the big house. I've seen 'em around a few times since and she always seems like she's... fuck, I don't know." He trails off, clearing his throat.

"Like she's what, Grant?"

"Not herself," he replies carefully.

I frown.

"Oh, c'mon. Now is not the time to mince words."

He rolls his thick shoulders. "She's usually intoxicated. Drunk, I'd say, but maybe hopped up on something else."

Sickness punches right through me.

"You think she's on drugs?" I whisper.

It'd make sense, though.

Here I thought she was just being careless, evasive, hiding from what's happening to our mother and pretending it's not real so she doesn't have to suffocate in the fear, the pain, the impending grief.

Only, I remember that man I overheard on the phone.

The weird lightness of her voice.

Now, I get it.

She's been avoiding me because she knows I'll know what's up the second I lay eyes on her.

I hate that it makes a terrible kind of sense.

And I don't realize my legs are going out from under me until I hear the scrape of a chair and feel my vision blanking out.

Grant runs over and spins the chair out just in time to catch me as I drop, still clutching a half-chewed steak fry in numb fingers.

My butt lands hard on the wooden seat.

"Sorry. I think I just hit my limit for too much crap," I say hoarsely, staring at my knees. "I just... everything with Mom, and now Ros, marrying *that* man. He probably knows what happened to Ethan, he—he—"

"Breathe," he commands.

I try, fighting for precious air that feels like napalm scorching my lungs.

"Butterfly. Look at me and breathe," he says again.

Grant sinks to one knee in front of me, those dark eyes locking on mine, demanding that I focus on him as he gently clasps my face.

His hands smolder against my skin as I work out several hard breaths, each one coming a little easier than the last.

His eyes search mine, strong and dark and strangely reassuring.

"That's the other reason I didn't tell you," he says after a minute. "You've got enough shit on your plate. I did want to talk to you about Ethan, though."

I just stare.

I can't seem to look away. Those searching luminous hazel eyes become my focal point until I stop trying to hyperventilate.

"Ethan? What about?"

"I'm reopening his case," Grant growls. "I think there's grounds after what happened with the Arrendells and Celeste Graves. Ethan's case has been a missing person's cold case for years, long past any formal resolution. With Raleigh forensics working on those remains, we might get some answers, one way or another. Hell, if we're lucky, we might be able to retrace his steps, and hope his bones aren't among the remains at all."

My body stops working.

Heart. Breath. Blood. Pulse.

All of me freezes as I meet his eyes, stare at him, stare *into* Grant, into that quiet solemnness and raging gruffness that hides a heart so true.

He never stopped.

He really never stopped looking for my brother all this time.

He still thinks there's a chance he's alive, even if deep down, that seems completely ludicrous. The hope was starved out of me without anyone finding a single clue.

"You... you asshole," I strangle out. My mouth moves automatically. I don't know what I'm saying, why I'm saying it, or why my eyes are welling up and I just can't take anymore. "You overly loyal giant donkey. You... you..."

There's a moment.

A crack in reality when those hard eyes soften.

All those years I spent when we were young, wishing he'd show some emotion.

Something plain and simple and honest.

Something easy, without having to turn myself into a human Grant decoder to understand his growls and loud silences.

Now, he finally gives me what I'm aching for with real concern flashing across his face, the way he leans into me, staring down like he's afraid he's broken me somehow.

"Ophelia, fuck," he says softly. "I won't see you hurt."

No, but he will see me speechless tonight.

If I ever speak again, I'll tell him how wonderfully dumb he's being.

But right now, he's just a giant blur past the tears.

Scalding, stupid, overwhelmed tears I don't want to cry, but I just can't take another bee sting to the heart.

I can't take more confusion, more things to fear.

Holy hell, I don't want to think about it anymore.

Because if I'm thinking, that means I won't do what I'm doing right now.

I won't be laying my fingers on Grant's face, my fingers

weaving through the thick, grey-shot bristle of his bearish brown beard.

Pulling him closer, even as his eyes widen.

I definitely won't be kissing him.

Kissing. Him.

I don't know what comes over me.

It's too instant, too impulsive, too reckless.

Too impossible to be denied.

And now that I've started I can't stop, and I can taste years of pent-up emotion in the salt between our lips as I crush my mouth to his and beg.

Don't hurt me right now, Grant. I can't stand another ounce of pain and disappointment.

Just give.

Give me the fire in that growl, the nip of your teeth, the sweet, sweet rush that makes me tingle.

I'm actually shaking for my longest obsession.

No surprise, the man is a human earthquake when his lips attack mine.

Or maybe it's just the vibration, the shock and awe steaming out of him, tangled up in this sudden hunger I can feel.

Grant goes still for just a second.

The shock radiates through both of us in hot waves so intense they leave me dizzy.

I take a deep breath and wait for it, fully expecting the stab of hurt where he sternly pushes me away and reminds me I'll always be the kid sister.

Nothing but Butterfly.

Not anyone he could ever see as romantic or sexy or remotely desirable.

...only he *doesn't.*

Instead, he wraps his huge arm tight around my waist, possessively jerking me forward, almost off the chair.

My stomach leaps and twists.

Instead of tearing his mouth off mine, he goes all in.

Grant Faircross ravages me with the sudden intensity of a kiss that crashes over me like lightning splitting the night.

Heat blooms under my skin like coffee grounds searing under a hot pour.

His mouth is so firm, so delicious, his teeth taunting and his beard scraping.

The rush of his breaths makes me unhinged as he fits our lips together until they're locked and sliding.

I'm completely captive and I love it.

I don't want to be free.

Not when his tongue teases like he's desperate for another sip of me.

Not when he's taking me over, dissolving my heartache in a universe where there's nothing but this punishing, powerful kiss.

Not when his hand splays against the small of my back, so large and thick I shiver with the sheer masculine force of it.

Holy wow.

I may have been the one who started it, but baby, he finishes.

I'm barely exaggerating when I say I *almost* finish halfway through it, moaning into his mouth.

My cheeks flush so hot I'm boneless.

He steals my control and breaks me down until I'm a gasping, melting mess, tugging at his beard to pull him in closer, deeper, opening my mouth in invitation.

Own me.

A terrible plea, but I'm so past caring.

When one of your deepest, darkest desires is suddenly coming true, it's hard to process anything.

I've secretly dreamed about this ever since I was a little girl.

I just never knew it could burn this good.

I didn't think it was possible to dissolve into Grant like he's this bottomless well of heat and I'm sinking deeper, even as his tongue steals inside me and stirs me up in ways that make me forget how to breathe.

I'm hyperaware of my own body and nothing else. I feel how my toes curl like they never have, kissing anyone else.

I sense every steaming inch of *his* body.

How close he is, the way his chest heaves with every rasping breath, his scent, the rock-hard body as I release his beard and stroke his arms, his chest.

Every savage inch of him underneath that thin grey t-shirt. I—

"*Uh-ohhhh!*" a little voice croons from behind us. "Uncle Grant's gonna be in so much *trou-ou-ou-ouble.*"

Oh, no.

Oh, shit.

We both snap back so sharply I hurt my neck.

We stare at each other for two stunned seconds—*what were we just doing?*—before he stands abruptly.

And I do too, turning to face little Nell, who suddenly has the power of judge, jury, and executioner.

I. Um. I have no earthly idea how to explain what she just saw us doing.

Grant glowers at her with a thunderous scowl.

"You didn't see that, kiddo."

"But..." Nell blinks up at him with a stunned innocence that can only be part devil. "What about the lady, Uncle Grant? The one you were kissing? It's her, isn't it?"

A strangled sound tears from Grant's throat.

"Forget the lady. Do not talk about the lady. You've already embarrassed me a thousand times over about the lady."

The lady? I can't help a little smile, even if I want to curl up and die from embarrassment right now.

"What about the lady?" I ask, clearing my throat.

"Are you her? The special lady Uncle Grant talks about," Nell says solemnly. "The lady's why he's never had a girl-friend. He said he wanted to be with a real special lady but she went away, so now he's all by himself." She turns her wide, mischievous eyes on Grant. "Isn't she gonna be mad that you're kissing Miss Philia?"

"Nell, enough," Grant clips.

Oh.

Oh my God.

I guess that answers the big unknown about his dating life.

Of course there's a 'special lady.'

Someone else he's in love with.

I really do need a nice, deep hole to crawl into right about now. I wonder how the weather is at the center of the Earth?

I'm so *not* the lady and my head is about to spin right off.

I guess kissing me back was just a thoughtless thing, a physical reaction, an impulse.

God, I really did come back here just to get my heart shattered a second time, didn't I?

Why can't I just grow up and get over him?

But Nell's still pouting, waiting for an answer.

"Jeez! I don't get why it's such a big bad secret. And I don't think it's very nice of you, Uncle Grant," she says. "I thought you were gonna find the lady and marry her. You said I'd get to meet her. She's gonna be so sad if she finds out you—"

"*Nell.*" Grant claps one large hand gently over her mouth and holds his mouth to her ear. "Stop it. You've met the damn lady. *Miss Ophelia is the lady.* Now quit embarrassing me. Stop looking at me like you're disappointed. It's not what you think."

...what.

My ears are melting off.

I actually *am* the lady?

Holy hell, I never liked roller coasters.

Every time at an amusement park, I always sat out the rides that flung you up high and dropped you down again like you were addicted to almost dying. It's just not my thing.

So, I'm really not enjoying the emotional rocket ride the last few days—or the last few seconds, really—have tossed me through.

I'm left frozen and numb as Grant gives me an almost apologetic look before turning. He keeps a wary eye on Nell as he slowly pulls his hand away from her mouth.

Nell blinks nonchalantly like a kitten waking up. Almost like she's used to this routine. Then she turns her brilliant little chipmunk smile on me.

"Wowee—the lady! Why didn't you tell me you were the lady Uncle Grant's obsessed with?" She breaks away from Grant, squirming free even as he tries to catch her again with a desperate sound.

Too late.

She's barreling right at me and I'm too stunned to think about moving.

The lady Uncle Grant's obsessed with.

No freaking way.

Nell's just confused... right?

She's only nine.

Actually, *I'm* confused, and blushing so hard I'm woozy.

It only gets worse as Nell throws herself against me, buries her face in my stomach, and wraps her little arms around me in a surprisingly tight, clingy hug.

"Are you gonna be my new mommy?" Her words are muffled against my shirt. "I miss having a mommy."

Ouch.

That roller coaster just had to take one more good, hard turn and chuck me to the moon and back, I suppose.

I work my mouth for a helpless moment, blanking for words that won't come before I rest a hand on top of her head. It's easier to focus on her right now because I think if I look at Grant, I might dissolve into a sticky puddle.

Time to deflect.

"I think I should help you check your homework. Come tell me about *The Velveteen Rabbit* and ethics while we let Uncle Grant finish making dinner, hmm? How's that sound?"

Nell looks up at me, cocking her head, considering it.

Her face slowly lights up in a smile.

"Well... okay!" she says, just like that.

I've never been more grateful for kids and their short attention spans.

The little girl takes my hand and marches us out, nearly dragging me from the kitchen with her pint-sized energy.

I stumble after her, but not without stealing one more wondering look at Grant. If I'm gobsmacked, the look on his face says he's—

I don't even know.

He's wearing that particularly strange, impassable look I've never quite deciphered.

Only, now I wonder if I've just always misunderstood it.

Because I feel like I know that look.

That look screams *want.*

And it belongs to a man who's staring at something he desperately wants and thinks he can never have.

Oh my God.

I'm imagining this, right?

I wonder if the creeper who showed up at Mom's house actually knocked my head into something and this is all a wild hallucination.

Maybe I'll wake up in a hospital bed in a life where

kissing Grant Faircross isn't the craziest thing possible. Because the fact that he might have feelings is.

But when our eyes lock, I feel something tighten deep inside me, swirling emotions drawn up into a sweet knot of curiosity and yearning and—

Hope.

There, I said it.

I've given myself over to the most dangerous emotion possible after I've tried to tell myself for ages I couldn't possibly feel anything for him.

Not after he chased me out of Redhaven with a flaming word of guilt.

Turns out, I lied.

Deep in my bones, there's a fresh hope beating faster than my own rabbiting heart, silently announcing how I've ached for him, and begging him to ache for me, too.

* * *

LOOK, I've been in awkward situations before.

Flubbing my words on an oral exam and saying something very, *very* salacious when I meant something very clinical back when I was grinding away for my nursing license.

Like doing catheter duty and not realizing an elderly man with severe hypospadias had his, um, opening more than an inch below the tip of his junk. He howled with laughter while I searched frantically, and then spent the next hour apologizing until I was blue in the face.

Or the time I didn't realize the friendly older doctor I thought of as a father figure and mentor only asked me to accompany him to a medical awards ceremony because he wanted to get handsy in the back of his car. Yes, I actually had to knee him in the balls and run with my heels dangling from my hand and my pride just as bruised as his balls.

Somehow, it's nowhere near as awkward as the post-kiss-that-never-should've-happened dinner with Grant.

We both avoid looking at each other the whole time like a single glance will turn us into a puff of ash.

The only one who seems remotely comfortable right now is Nell.

In fact, the little monster has clammed up happily.

On the surface, she's being perfectly obedient by not egging on the mess she helped create. But it's not hard to tell she likes watching us squirm.

The little girl stuffs her face gleefully, avoiding all attempts by Grant to awkwardly ask about her school day and my efforts to even *more* awkwardly ask about the "Miss Lilah" she worships so much at school by somehow always having her mouth full.

I get one comment in about how it's not ladylike to talk while chewing—right before Nell stuffs another steak fry into her mouth.

Leaving me looking anywhere but at Grant.

I'm so messed up inside.

The way Nell made it sound, Grant's been waiting for me all these years. But he's the one who told me to leave...

I don't understand.

I have so many questions, but I can't ask them right now. Not when the air feels like a wall between us, and not with little ears listening.

So I finish choking down my food and when we're all done eating, Nell stands and announces, "I need to wash up for bed."

"I'll come up, too. I'll read you a story, if you want," I say quickly.

Grant stands abruptly, his head bowed as he gathers up the dishes.

"You girls run on. I'll clean up in here," he says flatly.

Nell just smiles, sly and too knowing.

That girl is an evil scientist stuffed into a kid's body, I swear. She's just too much for her own good and mine.

I'm still glad she happily waves to me and leads the way upstairs, then proceeds to spend twenty minutes showing me her toothbrush, her strawberry-shaped toothbrush cap, her special bubblegum-flavored toothpaste, and the *right* way to wash my hands with her soap that turns into rainbow foam while you scrub your fingers together.

How charming.

I also snicker because I can already tell she's going to drive some boy wonderfully crazy when she grows up.

I help brush out her wildly curly hair, then we head for her room, which is wall to wall with bookshelves and brightly colored things. The giant floppy blue stuffed unicorn I've seen before is on the lace-frilled bed.

She bounces up to settle against the pillows and holds up the stuffie.

"Here, meet Mr. Pickle," she announces cheerfully. "Mr. Pickle, say hi to Miss Philia."

She picks up one dirty hoof and waves it at me, switching to a different voice, high and screechy. "*Hi, Miss Philia!*"

"Hi, Mr. Pickle," I say carefully. "You're pretty old for a unicorn, aren't you?"

"*I'm just as old as Nelly!*" She continues in her Pickle voice. "*I've been around since she was a baby! Nell's Mommy and Daddy sent me to stay with her forever because they can't!*"

Oh, crap.

My heart wrenches for that little girl.

...was Mr. Pickle the only toy salvaged from the burning house?

God, no wonder it's so stained and worn. I can't blame her for wanting to believe her toy will stay with her forever when her parents left so suddenly.

How do you think Grant feels?

How do you think he feels that you left him?

I shove the thought away and offer Nell a smile. "Did you want me to read you and Mr. Pickle a bedtime story?"

"Yes!" Still clinging to the unicorn, she turns and rummages around in the small shelf built into the headboard. She picks a thin square picture book with a battered cover illustrated with monsters with large yellow eyes.

Where the Wild Things Are.

She thrusts it at me gleefully.

My breath goes tight and shallow as I reach for it.

Oh, wow. It can't be, can it?

Carefully, I open the book across my lap, flip to the last page, the inside cover.

Yep, it's still there in the lower right corner.

O. E. G.

Each letter written in a different hand. The first is so messy it had to be traced a couple times until it actually made a proper O.

O. E. G.

Ophelia. Ethan. Grant.

My lips tremble, but I smile, tracing the letters with my fingertips.

"I remember this book," I whisper. "Did you know I knew your Uncle Grant when he was just a boy, Nell?"

"You did?" She watched me with rapt attention.

"He was my brother's best friend. We were always together, all three of us. The Three Musketeers." It hurts to breathe, but the pain isn't all bitter. "When he'd sleep over with my brother at my mom's house, your uncle would bring this book quite a lot. Sometimes he'd read to us until we fell asleep... and if we didn't fall asleep the first time, he'd read it again."

Nell looks at me with something like awe.

"Dang. You really *are* the lady," she whispers. I blush hotly until she asks, "Where's your brother now? How come Uncle Grant doesn't hang out with him anymore?"

Holy shit, the mouth of babes.

My throat closes up.

"Ethan, he had to go away," I manage slowly. "Kind of like the way your parents had to leave, too."

Nell's eyes glisten, but she beams me the sweetest, bravest smile and then scoots across the bed until she can steal my arm to hug it, leaning herself against my shoulder.

"It's okay if he's gone," she says. "I get it. Uncle Grant tells me all the time it's cool to be sad. I'm only sad because I still love them, and that's not a bad thing."

She's. Killing. Me.

"Your Uncle Grant is very wise—just don't tell him I said that," I joke, kissing the top of her head. "Also, you're very right. It's not bad to be sad. I still love my brother a lot."

"Do you still love Uncle Grant, too?"

I stiffen. My next breath goes down wrong until I have to clear my throat to talk.

"I. Um. Let's start the story so you're not up past your bedtime."

"...if I don't fall asleep, will you read it to me again?" she asks hopefully.

I smile.

"Yeah, sweetie," I say. "I absolutely will."

I end up reading the book almost three times before Nell finally dozes off.

I have to pry her off my arm and it takes a little work to do it without waking her, but eventually she sinks down with a sleepy sigh that tugs at my heartstrings.

Sweet girl.

Even if she can be a little hellraiser.

Soon, I turn off the lights, check her night-light, and leave her there cuddled up with Mr. Pickle. I almost want to bring the book with me now and ask Grant if he remembers writing our initials.

Instead, I leave it on the nightstand and tiptoe downstairs, my heart fast and my blood thick and my thoughts whirling.

I'm hoping I can talk to Grant.

Ask him to explain, to sort everything out, because once again his gentle actions don't match the cruel words that exiled me from Redhaven.

When I step down into the living room, he's unconscious.

Sprawled out on the sofa with his legs stretched out in front of him, his body slouched to one side and his head pillowed on the overstuffed arm.

Sound asleep, and yeah, he still does it.

He scowls in his sleep like he's annoyed with his dreams, grouching at them the entire time they play in his head.

The more things change, they really do stay the same.

Including what I do now.

When we were kids and he'd spread out with his arms and legs all akimbo, I'd creep off the stairs and rearrange his covers so he was tucked in warmly.

He never knew.

Now, I move through the living room and pull the knit throw off the back of the sofa to drape over him. It barely covers his enormous bulk from ribs to thigh.

With a soft laugh, I slip upstairs, rummage around in the trunk at the foot of the bed, and find a couple nice big fleece blankets.

Back downstairs, I arrange the fleeces over Grant quietly, practically making a nest around him.

He doesn't even bat an eyelash, sleeping deep and hard.

He looks so cozy and warm. So peaceful.

And I get cold so easily.

Oh, you know I shouldn't.

But I *want to.*

And maybe tonight giving in to this fierce, beating wanting won't make things worse than they already are.

Biting my lip, chest aching, I settle into the blankets with him, pulling myself against his side.

Against his heat.

Against his silent strength that was always an unbreakable rock when I was growing up, never mind the sharp words that became too much to bear.

There are no angry words now.

Only a warm, firm body enfolding me like a shield.

And him.

Us.

I settle my head against his shoulder, draw the blankets around us, and slide into the most restful sleep I've had in years.

Easy when I finally feel safe.

Because as long as I'm with Grant, nothing bad will happen.

Nothing else can hurt us besides my own desperate mistakes.

IX: ONE AND DONE (GRANT)

*T*his is new.

Waking up with warm flesh curled against me, tucked so close in this lush weight at my side.

What the hell?

I know it's her before I even open my eyes.

I know Ophelia's scent.

I know her feel.

I know how she takes up space with just her presence. This aura surrounds her until even when we're not touching, it's like I *feel* her with every tortured inch of my body.

Worse, I now know how she tastes when I damn well shouldn't.

The only question left is why she felt the need to crawl into bed with a desperate, chaotic fuck who can't keep his lips to himself.

I blink my eyes open slowly, lifting my head and trying not to jostle her as I glance down at her.

I don't remember falling asleep, but I must have dozed like the dead while I was waiting for her to finish putting Nell to bed.

The fact that I'm buried under multiple blankets with no recollection of piling them on?

That brings back memories from half a lifetime ago.

She always thought I was asleep during those calm nights ages ago when she'd creep up on me and fix the covers over me after I'd kicked them around in a mess.

Every time, I felt her cover me.

I knew.

I just kept stock-still so she wouldn't run or die of embarrassment.

Same way I hold still now, letting myself take her in.

She forms this compact bundle like a house cat, small and soft against my side.

Considering how we come at each other with our teeth bared so often, it warms something inside me to know she trusted me enough to settle in this close.

Especially after how awkward last night got—how reckless I made it.

Still can't believe she just kissed me out of the blue like that.

Still can't believe I kissed *her.*

I'm dumbfounded that I gave it back, stoking the messy brushfire she started into a proper fucking inferno.

Not that I'm complaining.

I just feel oblivious when she's been trying to tell me something since we were kids, waving flags in front of my face, but I'm too damned dumb to read the signals. Or maybe I didn't want to.

Of course, Nelly-girl had to go and open her little mouth about *the lady.*

Fuck.

I don't know if I want to hug the kid or ground her until she's twenty.

I let my gaze drift over the morning light turning Ophelia's hair into white gold, pouring an amber glaze over her skin.

For a Florida girl, she's just a hint brown, her summer tan fading fast.

She's still wearing her t-shirt and jeans, but the oversized shirt has fallen off one shoulder in her sleep, baring smooth, curving flesh.

A pale-blue bra strap begs me to tear it away with my teeth, all so I can kiss the crest of her collarbone.

Her body heat soaks into me everywhere we press together.

I feel like a wild animal sunning itself on a hot day, content and relaxed aside from the need building in my blood.

I don't understand.

Ophelia should've hated me all these years after how we left off.

No, I don't just mean the shit I said to her then, pushing her away.

It wasn't just Ethan's disappearance that forged a rift between us. It was more, somewhere around the time when she stopped being *the kid* and started turning into *a girl*.

Maybe when I started seeing her, little hints of a ripening woman.

Suddenly, I was speaking Martian and she was speaking Venusian.

We couldn't agree on anything.

I start to pry myself free as my stomach growls, thinking about coffee and a cold shower to blunt the hard-on from hell I can't do shit about.

It'd be nice to surprise her with some breakfast—but the moment I move, she stirs.

Her eyes blink open and she yawns.

For a moment, that glimmering green gaze is lost, drowsy, unfocused—before clarity sharpens her vision.

She goes tense, tilting her head back with her cheek rubbing sweetly against my arm, peering up at me through long, pretty lashes I can't keep my eyes off of.

"Oh," she says uncertainly. Sleep gives her voice a husky burr. "Hi."

"Mornin'," I answer, arching a brow.

She smiles back sheepishly.

"Um, I meant to wake up before you."

"And sneak off leaving me none the wiser, huh?"

"Yeah. Kinda the plan," she admits, shifting to sit up with the blankets wrapped around us both, tumbling down to her waist. With another loud yawn, she rubs at her eye and glances at the clock over the mantel. "Ick. Way too early."

"Not used to waking up before noon?"

She wrinkles her nose. "No, if I'm being honest. I usually pulled overnight shifts where I'd sleep in past noon."

"They must be missing you. Your work, I mean."

"Not really," she answers wryly. "They fired me right before I got the bad news about Mom. Budget cuts, you know. Half the staff got dropped like hot potatoes, but I guess the timing couldn't be better."

I don't know why that gives me an odd sense of hope.

This idea that she could be back for good, knowing there's no job waiting for her back in Florida.

Though maybe she has other things that hold her there.

Other *people*.

That's an idea I don't like.

Thinking there's some lucky little fuckstick waiting with blue balls back in Miami, texting her every day how much he misses her, calling her *lover*, anxiously waiting for her to come home.

Fuck, I can't.

Though she wouldn't have kissed me if she had someone else—would she?

She damn sure wouldn't have shared another man's bed for a glorified sleepover my cock wishes had turned into more.

I stare at her for a solid minute, searching for a way to ask tactfully.

I'm coming up at a loss.

How the fuck do I even bring up relationships?

The longer I look at her, the deeper she blushes, this pretty pink flush flowering across her cheeks like a drop of red dye spreading through water.

"You can stop staring like that any time, y'know." She ducks her head shyly, breaking eye contact as she tucks a few locks of honey-blonde hair behind her ear.

"Like what?" I growl.

"Like you're trying to figure out what rock I crawled out from under."

I snort. "That ain't why I'm staring, Philia."

"Yeah? Then why?" She peeks at me sidelong.

"One, because you're goddamned gorgeous in the morning light and I've been trying not to look since you came home," I point out. Fuck it. When in doubt, be honest. Her eyes widen as I continue. "Two, I'm trying to figure out how to ask why you kissed me like you were dying last night."

She winces—and turns it into a scowl. "Do you have to make it sound so awful?"

Awful?

Hell no.

"I'm not trying to—goddammit, I am not doing this with you again, I—" My jaw clamps shut.

Every time.

Every fucking time, my words come out mangled and she

ends up mad.

Fine, if I can't talk right, I'll show her.

I ignore the way her pretty face sets in lines of confusion and snapping anger.

Catching her around the waist, I slip under the tangle of blankets to find her, curling my hands against the soft breadth of her.

I feel it when she sucks in a breath, her skin going taut underneath her shirt and my palms.

Before that breath comes out in yet another argument, I pull her close and capture her mouth in a searing kiss.

Fuck.

I feel like I've been waiting to devour this mouth my entire life.

Because even if there's only been one other kiss, it's like I already know her lips inside and out from the countless times I've dreamed about taking her in my arms and tasting every inch of her.

There's a moment of stiffness before she goes soft against me, pliant and willing, her lips opening against mine with a low moan that cuts me open.

Their softness drives me out of my goddamned mind.

This woman drives me insane.

She always fucking has.

How can I keep pretending that I haven't always wanted her to be *mine?*

With a rough growl, I seize her, crushing our lips together, catching the curious flick of her tongue with mine.

We twine tongues until we're shamelessly tangled, all roughness and stroking and teasing as I slick my tongue along hers, chasing that moan.

Give it the fuck up, Butterfly.

I don't deny it's pure lunacy.

She makes me so greedy it's like I'm trying to mark her,

brand her, leave a lingering imprint so she feels me no matter where she is.

Then maybe she'll never run from Redhaven again.

She'll never run away from *me.*

Goddamn, she's the sweetest fire known to man.

The way she clutches at me with her little nails scratching against my chest goes right to my heart and then to my cock.

With a rough groan, I drag her against me, pulling her in tight until we're pressed so close. The soft swell of her breasts crush against my chest, her nipples perked and insistent.

The explosive pressure makes it hard to think with every pulse roaring.

There isn't a coherent thought except how badly I want to be inside her.

When Ophelia feels better than my wildest dreams come to life, it's hard as hell to make myself let her go.

But when she breaks away with a gasp, her mouth swollen to a luscious pink from my teeth, I stop.

I force myself still as she looks at me, dazed, her hands braced against my chest as she puts some sorely needed distance between us.

Damn, what have I done?

"Grant?" she breathes. That sleepy burr to her voice feels silkier than ever, and it's doing some black magic shit to me. "What are we doing?"

"No fucking clue," I grind out. "But I feel like we should've done it years ago."

Ophelia's lower lip creeps between her teeth.

"Nell was serious? You really thought about me all this time?"

Guilty.

I feel like I've been sitting on this secret so long it's almost a sacrilege to root it out and expose it to the light. Or maybe

I've always been so certain it was a lost cause, so I packed my feelings away somewhere I could protect them.

It's hard as hell to admit it.

"Yeah," I force out raggedly.

There's a violent thumping in my chest, a war drum I think she hears.

Her eyes widen and she draws in a sharp breath. "I... I honestly thought you hated me, especially when I left."

"Like hell." I shake my head, catching one of her hands and curling it in my own. Sometimes it's hard to remember how small she is when she's so resilient. My fingers dwarf hers, big twigs against little sticks, rousing that urge to shelter and protect and keep her. "I said some dumb shit I shouldn't have when you told me you were leaving, Butterfly. I've regretted it ever since."

Dark uncertainty flickers in those spring-green eyes as her fingers curl tighter in mine.

"You... you told me not to come back."

"I know. I was a monster asshole about it. Too afraid to face the hurt that was tearing us both up head-on."

I exhale deeply, pulling her in, coaxing her to fit the crook of my arm—all the while hoping she'll let me hold her while I get this out.

I need to drain the poison.

After a worn moment, she nestles herself into my side again, resting her head on my shoulder.

A few wispy blonde hairs tickle my neck and catch in my beard.

"I wasn't thinking straight that day," I admit. "Maybe it was all the time since Ethan disappeared, where we sat there wondering without any answers... but when you said you were leaving, all that grief came vomiting up like it was as fresh as the day he disappeared. All I could think was you were gonna disappear and never come back, too. That I was gonna be alone, stranded with my grief over my best friend and this hole in my family. This gaping fucking pit without you."

These words are brutal.

They come out like hard, jagged shards that cut my mouth.

Especially when I'm forcing every syllable past the hard knot of pride in my throat.

Only, when I think about the damage I did, how much I hurt her, how much those words have been hanging between us all these years like a sword over our necks, I've gotta end this.

Right here and now.

Gotta set things straight.

"Guess I started thinking, maybe it was best if you left after all. This town is a black curse for some folks, and maybe if you were gone, its darkness wouldn't take you, too."

The way she listens so intently, I can tell she's taking it all in.

Turning it over, letting it sink in.

She's always been better at this feelings shit than me.

Absorbing what other people say, thinking it through, using her heart to guide her to the right answer.

I bet it made her one hell of a nurse, too. The kind of bedside saint every patient needs in their darkest hour.

I give her time to think, to decide how to answer me.

I'm definitely not expecting her to say, "I'm sorry."

It's just a whisper, intense and heartfelt.

"I'm sorry I ran away and left you so soon. We were so *close*, Grant, and... and it felt like something broke. Like losing Ethan cut the thread that tied everything together, sending everyone spinning."

"Because we let it," I snarl. "Because even though he was the red thread of fate or whatever that held us together, we could've found a new way to stick. Only, we were young and hurt and scared and stupid. So yeah, you fucking ran. So did I in my own way. I'm sure Ros did too." I press my lips to her hair tentatively. "Hell, some days it feels like I've been running from you half my life."

"I still don't understand. When did you realize..." She can't finish.

She doesn't need to.

"Can't say."

"Grant?" she urges.

My nostrils flare.

She smells too good, all alluring woman mingled with that calming beeswax scent.

I close my eyes, inhaling her as I murmur into that golden crown of hair.

"Just feels like one day you were this bratty thing following us around. Then I blinked and you were still a huge brat, but a girl, too. Then a woman, as time went by. Once I saw you that way, there was no blinding myself again. Couldn't stop if I tried." I smile faintly. "Even though I knew Ethan would kill me."

Ophelia laughs faintly, her body moving gently against mine.

"Did he know?"

"Fuck no. That happened later. The age difference alone would've been lethal. If he was still around, I'd rather stab an eye out with a stick than tell Ethan I was in love with his little sister."

"I wonder if he thought about the future anyway.. I think he knew I was crushing on you and I never told him—and he never let me live it down. Every time your back was turned, he was always picking on me, making kissy faces." She scrunches her nose. "The jerk," she mutters affectionately.

Goddamn, that cuts to the bone.

Mainly because I feel it, too.

That warmth, that easy affection. It's like it keeps part of him around, my best friend egging us both on, no matter how MIA he is.

I can see his easygoing smile even now.

That's just how Ethan was.

Everyone's friend, never met a stranger he didn't like, this charmer with the cocky grin and messy shag of sandy hair.

If he were here, he'd tell us to stop being screwballs and get out of our own way.

Then he'd thump me for the things I'm suddenly wanting to do, with the way my heart catches fire at the words *I was crushing on you.*

I linger on that warm expression of fond memories on Ophelia's face, then catch a lock of honey-gold hair and coil it around my fingers.

"All this time, we both thought it was hate when it was the exact opposite."

"All this time. Crazy," she agrees shyly, a slow smile spreading across her lips.

Only trouble is, it's happening so fast it makes my head spin.

Where the hell do we go from here with two lives apart and endless drama pulling us in different directions?

"So, you still crushing on me now?" I ask.

Do you still love me?

"Don't get ahead of yourself." Ophelia laughs and prods her finger lightly against my chest. "It's been ten years, Grant. I'm still a pain-in-the-ass realist. I barely *know* you anymore." That laughter fades, though, and she cocks her head at me with thoughtful eyes lingering before she adds, "But I think I'd like to." Then she grins, impish as ever as she pokes my chest again. "Your turn, bucko. Are you still in love with *me?*"

I could answer.

For Ophelia Sanderson, I could cut myself open and pour out my soul.

Somehow, I don't think I'm gonna give that beautiful brat the satisfaction, though. Not when we're dancing around our words, saying too much and trying to read between the lines.

I just grin slowly, lace our fingers together, and lift them to kiss her knuckles.

Then I gather her against me in the glowing morning silence, settling down again to hold her while the light rises through the windows, gold and bright and true.

I HAVEN'T HAD a morning this peaceful in a good, long while.

We stay tangled up on the sofa together, now and then stealing a few light, wordless kisses that leave me as hard as a rock.

Honestly, it's a relief when Nell comes thumping downstairs and catches us with an *ooh* and a loud giggle.

That's our cue to start the day.

Soon, we've got all hands in the kitchen throwing together breakfast. We work seamlessly without minding little Nell's clumsy 'help.'

I gotta say, I'm grateful for an extra pair of hands to catch the girl with sharp objects she's not supposed to touch, or her ham-fisted attempts to fiddle with the burners to make our food cook faster. We're real lucky she doesn't burn down the house.

Meanwhile, we're treated to Nell's cartoonish smoochy faces and schoolyard songs about sitting in a tree doing the unspeakable.

Ophelia takes it all in with good humor, thankfully. She also chases Nell into her seat with a frontal assault of tickles.

It's a sweet normalcy I hadn't realized I've been missing until it's right there in my face.

What would it look like if this was my life, my family, every day?

I'm sure I ain't the only person wondering. Ophelia looks at me like she's seeing me for the first time with new eyes, and I think she's pretty damn fond of what she sees.

My heart drums every time I catch her eye over breakfast.

That warmth lingers as we split apart to tidy up, wash the dishes, and get Nell ready for school.

Not long after, I drop them both at the school, Nell kissing my cheek and rushing off to scream after her friends. Ophelia offers a bright smile and tells me she can walk from here since she's planning to stop by the family shop to try to corner Ros before she sets off on another visit to the medical center.

"I'll pick Nell up this afternoon, if you want," she says, leaning her arms on the driver's side window and peering in at me with a smile. "My car's supposed to be out of the shop, so you don't need to worry."

"Not sure how I ever managed before."

And just to see if she'll do it—if things really have changed between us—I tilt my head up for a kiss.

Ophelia glances to both sides, her face flaming such a pretty sky-pink.

Then she leans in and gives it up, pressing her mouth to mine like pure nectar.

It's swift and sweet, this lingering heat that curls through my veins as our lips brush chastely.

I have to hold my greedy tongue back before she pulls away with a flick of her finger against my nose.

"Next time, try asking instead of playing charades," she teases with a smile. "See you tonight."

"Tonight," I agree, pondering how to ignore this brutal hard-on that's fixing to make me black out.

It's hard as hell to pull away from the curb, leaving her behind.

Yeah, I'm reeling with how quickly things keep changing all around me. Despite the nonstop string of bad luck that hits this town too often, for once it feels like things might be changing for the better.

The woman I've always been obsessed with under my roof.

Talking like an old friend.

Sharing meals and bedtime stories with Nell.

Kissing me until I'm redder than a freshly painted barn.

Especially when she smiles at me like I never took an axe to her heart.

Yeah, fuck.

Today's gonna be a real good day, no matter what the universe has planned.

* * *

CORRECTION.

Today is *not* a good fucking day.

I smell trouble brewing the second I walk into the station.

The whole crew's already gathered, huddled around my desk like they own it as usual, but there's something different in the air.

This whole vibe is wrong, tension and quiet so thick it's immediately near suffocating.

When I open the door, they all break away from their semicircle, looking up at me like they're about to announce a death.

Frowning, I shrug off my jacket and toss it over the nearest chair.

"Report. What's got everyone looking so miserable this morning?"

"The Jacobins again," Micah answers grimly. "They've been quiet for too long. Not surprising after their boy went down being an accomplice to a serial killer. But it looks like they're starting to make their move again."

"What?" I frown.

"The unmarked trucks are back, for one," Micah tells me. "No, I can't ever get close enough to see what's going into them without tipping the whole clan off and getting my ass nailed full of buckshot, but there's a lot of coming and going in the middle of the night up there. Has to be the distilleries again, assuming it isn't something worse."

Aw, shit.

I feel like Chief Bowden should be here for this conversation.

Where the fuck *is* the chief, anyway?

Ever since the Arrendell bust, Bowden barely shows up for work, taking his lazy absenteeism to new heights. A hibernating bear would make a better police chief at this point.

Essentially, him being MIA leaves everything in my hands —including making big decisions above my pay grade about our resident bootleg booze makers.

"So, they're moonshining again," I mutter, tugging at my beard. "Goddammit. We've looked the other way on this for ages, but after the way they closed ranks to try to cover up for murder... Yeah, I think we've given them enough leeway. No telling what else they're hiding."

My mind snaps back to what almost happened to Delilah Graves.

The way both Ephraim and Culver Jacobin would watch her around town like they were marking her, two creepy scarecrows eyeballing her on behalf of their master.

I don't like the parallels.

Don't fucking like them at all.

Not when I've seen the same strange man watching *me*, and knowing he also matches the description of the guy who tried to grab Ophelia.

"Uh-oh," Henri says. "Capitan's got that thinkin' look on his face."

"Just drawing a few comparisons. The incident at the Sanderson house—there was a man who fits the description of someone I've seen around town. He's not a local, not that I know of. Which means he's either a tourist, someone from the big house, or—"

"One of the Jacobins," Lucas interrupts, his voice dark.

The hard set of his jaw tells me his mind's falling into the same ugly place as mine.

"Yeah. Only, the Jacobins don't normally wander around in slacks and tailcoats," I say.

"So, staff up at the Arrendell mansion?" Henri asks. "Where we just had a suicide?"

"Yep." I sigh. "Funny how any time there's a death around that damn family, weird shit starts popping off."

"I sure as hell don't think it's funny," Lucas growls. "Considering they almost killed my wife."

"*He*," I correct wearily, even if I don't want to. "As far as we know, none of the other Arrendells had anything to do with the Ulysses situation. Same goes for the Jacobins and their bad seed."

"Fuck, man, and I'm a six-foot green goddamn chicken," Lucas mutters, but he lets it go.

"That doesn't mean we shouldn't keep an eye on them," I say. "Ophelia said that man kept telling her *she's next*. That if she goes near them—one good guess who he means—she'll die."

The entire room goes dead quiet.

Every last one of my officers looks at me with the same grave understanding.

It's Micah who finally breaks the silence, his pale eyes flinty.

"Sounds like we might be looking at a suicide that wasn't a suicide at all," he says. "Do we need to reopen the Cora Lafayette case?"

"Quietly," I snarl. "Let's keep our eyes open, but sweep things under the radar for now. Put your ears out. Listen around town. Ask questions whenever the opportunity comes. Take note of any strange comings and goings up at the mansion, off record, and you guys let me know ASAP if anything stinks."

The men nod with a sense of heavy duty sinking in.

"The flood of movie stars and CEOs has slowed down since the last round of trouble, at least," Lucas points out. "Xavier prefers to do his business elsewhere, and I hear Aleksander's got himself a hometown girl."

"Yeah. About that." I grind my teeth. "If y'all see them around—just fucking watch them, okay? I'm real worried Rosalind Sanderson's in over her head. Might be in trouble."

"Rosalind? Abusive relationship?" Micah asks.

"Probable substance abuse," I reply. "Look, I don't wanna have to arrest her and give her a drug test, but if she looks like she's in trouble, don't hesitate to intervene. I'd rather have to apologize than end up being too late."

Lucas salutes crisply.

"You got it, Chief." Then he frowns. "By the way, how's Ophelia settling back in?"

"She's staying with me for now," I say, ignoring the slow grins turning my way. "Whatever. Mind your own damn business and get to work. Dismissed."

X: ONE STOLEN KISS (OPHELIA)

I don't know if I can handle a fight right now.

Which is why I'm standing outside of Nobody's Bees-Ness with my hands stuffed in my pockets, huffing cold air and very seriously pondering turning around and just walking off until I find somewhere to buy a decent coat.

A little comfort shopping.

A little escape.

A little doing anything I can not to create a rift in a family that's lost so much. I'm so afraid we're going to face that kind of loss again far too soon.

God.

The thought of fighting with Ros while our mom is dying absolutely guts me. I never once thought we'd be facing this apart.

But I don't think confronting my sister over avoiding me is going to go very well, either.

Who knows, maybe I'm being pessimistic.

There's still a chance it'll be fine.

And if it isn't?

Well, then I'll just save that comfort shopping trip for later and take out my feelings with a little impulse spending.

Okay.

I suck in a deep breath for courage and push the door to the shop open.

The familiar jingle of the bell rips me back in time.

Ever since I was a little girl, this shop was a magical place.

The shelves are dark mahogany wood and mirror glass, with more mirrors paneled along the walls. Everywhere you turn, it's glinting reflections and the soft amber light from paper lanterns dangling throughout the store.

True to the name, this place is like stepping into a beehive.

It even smells like warm honey in here, eternally shrouded in the thick scent of fresh beeswax.

Faint ambient music pipes through the store, floating over shelves lined with my mother's handmade honey and beeswax products.

The little signs are still lovingly written in her handwriting like she only put them up yesterday.

It's all here: lip gloss, soaps, shampoos, lotions, ointments, candles, little honey candies, fresh dripping honeycombs, bottled honey, and royal jelly supplements. Several more shelves hold tiers of gift baskets bulging with sweet delights.

There's a beekeeper on the edge of town who sells his products almost exclusively to this shop, giving Mom the freedom to experiment with new ideas. Whether it's cooking up new scented blends of beeswax fragrance melt cubes or creating milk and honey blends for soothing lip scrubs, she's always got something new in the works.

The close, dimly lit space always seems like it demands whispers.

Almost like it's some kind of secret library of warm, cozy

things meant to be taken in with reverence for all the delicate objects crafted with such care.

That feeling of familiar wonder goes cold as I draw up short just inside the door, letting it swing shut behind me.

The noise is jarring.

So is seeing someone besides Mom standing behind the counter and realizing that strange woman behind the glossy glass display case is my sister.

She doesn't look like the Rosalind I remember at all.

My baby sister was always a shy, bookish thing, sweet and romantic with a bit of a dorky introverted side.

When we'd take day trips to the beach, she was always the girl who wouldn't even take off her t-shirt to go swimming, wearing it over her bathing suit instead.

That's always been Ros. Once Mom and I realized she was comfortable that way, we just let her be herself.

Now, I do a double take.

What the...?

She's wearing a see-through light coral cardigan over— not much of anything.

There's a single button fastened between her breasts while the rest hangs open over her bare stomach. Underneath, she has a magenta push-up bra in lace with wired cups that lift her breasts into the kind of straining, full mounds that make me think that underwire's got to be cutting so *deep.* I cringe in sympathy.

Her jeans are pure street princess, low and tight and ripped, showing the little creases of flesh along the bottom curve of her stomach that dip down toward her crotch. There's even a hint of the tiny ladybug tattoo stamped just over the curve of her hip bone.

Ladybug.

Our mother was always about bees and Ros loved ladybugs.

Me, I have a small blue butterfly tattoo on my ankle, just as small as that little red dot on Ros' hip. The ink is just as weathered since we'd gotten them together that day, holding hands and trying not to flinch as the needles marked our flesh, giggling in that goofy way only sisters can when something crazy goes down.

And she normally wears her blonde hair in a sensible bun while she's working, but now it's blown out, falling down her shoulders and chest, framing a face I struggle to recognize.

She's made up with sultry fuck-me red lipstick, glossy vixen red nails, and a solid smoky eyeshadow, though I don't think all of the darkness around her eyes is makeup.

Some of it seems almost sunken. Bruised.

These hollows match the dips in her too-thin cheeks.

Yikes.

Now, I see why Grant thought something was up.

It's not the new look. Not at all.

If Ros just decided on a whim that she wanted a punky makeover to come out of her shell as a flirty, sexy girl, that wouldn't be a red flag of the apocalypse.

No, it's the way her pupils jitter as she looks up from wiping down the counter and her gaze lands on me.

It's the haunted nervousness in her eyes.

The way her fingers look almost like claws as they grasp the paper towel.

Plus, the syrupy falseness in her smile as she brightens, watching me with a mix of delight and wariness.

"Ophelia!" she cries like she's just completely forgotten I was in town.

Only it comes out strange, thick and slurred, like her tongue is swollen and a little numb.

I'm definitely a little numb as she comes flitting around the counter, moving with this wild energy that can't be Ros, and pulls me into her arms.

She buries her face against my shoulder, hugging me so tight it hurts.

"It's awesome to see you," she says. "We missed you so much..."

"So much that you haven't come home for an hour since I've been in town?" I ask, unable to help the sharpness in my tone.

Ros pulls back with a pout. "Not fair. I've been busy as hell keeping the lights on here."

"So busy you can't even come home to *sleep?*"

With an offended gasp, Ros fully lets go, stepping back defensively.

"Hi, Ophelia. Welcome home, Ophelia. It's good to see you too, Ophelia. I missed you, Ophie." She clucks her tongue. "God. And here I thought maybe we could start there instead of you bitching me out." She scowls. "You've been gone for ten years. You don't get to show up and start acting like the big sister out of nowhere."

Brutal.

A beeswax candle to the eye would've hurt less.

Guilt knifes through me, but it's not enough to dampen my rising temper.

"Look, Ros... I'm not trying to be the big sister and chew you out. I'm not here to assert authority or whatever you're thinking. I'm just trying to figure out what's going on with you. Our mom is *sick.* This might be the last time we get to spend with her, and—when was the last time you even went to see her?

She looks away, her eyes going dark with irritation.

"Ros, don't lie to me. The staff said I was the only visitor all week."

Whirling around, Ros glares, her green eyes glassy and glazed with hurt.

"Don't you lecture me! You think I *want* to see her like that?

You think I'm not hurting? Jesus, Ophelia. I can't look at her like that when that's... that's not Mom in that bed." She pauses, chewing her lip before she continues. "That's a memory. A memory I don't want after she's gone. You think she'd want us to remember her like that? No. No, I'm doing the next best thing. I'm protecting her legacy. I'm taking care of the shop because she wouldn't want it closing down just because she's too sick to work. What do you know about any of that?"

My lips thin. I stare at her, trying to soften the blow.

"I know about Aleksander," I say point-blank. "Is he one of your distractions, too? Does shacking up with one of the nastiest playboys in town make it easier—all so you don't have to think about Mom?"

Ros' eyes bug out and she sucks in a harsh breath.

"How'd you—" She groans. "Grant. Oh my God, that snake."

"He only told me because he's worried. Just like I am," I retort. "Honestly, I don't blame him one bit. Ros, what kind of lifestyle does Aleksander Arrendell want you to share? Look at you..."

"At *what?*" She props her hands on her hips, throwing a snapping look at me. "What're you saying? That I look like a whore? Just because I'm enjoying myself for once and finding something to be happy about?"

"You look sick," I point out softly. "You don't look well. That's what I was going to say."

I try stepping closer.

Seriously, I can't stand this, fighting with my sister when all I want to do is hug her and help her. I need to know what's really behind that foggy look in her eyes. Then maybe I can pull her back from the brink before it's too late.

Good thing there are no customers, or else we'd be the talk of the town for the next two weeks.

The Sanderson sisters bickering in broad daylight while their mother lies dying in her hospital bed.

Ha.

But before I can reach her, the door behind the counter to the back stock room pops open.

Oh, good, here comes the man of the hour, oozing out like a stack of slime.

Aleksander Arrendell.

Tall, lithe, his longish hair spilling down and framing a face so angelic it could only be part demon.

The man does not look human.

More like Lucifer's nephew embodied in the flesh. A fallen angel who decided to make tortured Redhaven his personal playground.

He's wearing a pair of designer jeans and an oversized linen blouse that probably costs more than my nursing degree. The blouse is half-buttoned and the wide lapels pulled back like he's trying to flaunt the lipstick imprinted on his collar.

On his throat.

On his lips, still a little smeared around his wide, carnivorous mouth.

He's showing off today—way too deliberately—almost like he's marking his territory. He wants to be sure I know damn well what he and Ros were up to before I showed up.

"Did I hear my name? My ears were burning," he growls in that mockingly cultured accent, swaggering around the counter to join us.

The possessive arm he slips around Ros' waist makes me gag.

And he pulls her in close, stamping a possessive kiss on her shoulder.

"I hope you ladies aren't bickering over little old me.

There's nothing more important than family, you know, and I'd hate to come between loving sisters."

Prick.

His words are devoid of guilt. The words sound false, smarmy, sardonic.

The man drips grease from his pores.

I so don't get what Ros sees in him.

Unless she's just bewitched by the wealth and glamour, the usual Arrendell black magic.

I also wonder what the hell he sees in Ros. She's from another world where money doesn't grow on trees. No wealth, no connections, no way to help him be richer and more powerful.

And although she's perfectly pretty, sure, this man has been with *supermodels.*

I looked him up to confirm the whole sordid history and found a trail of exes who look like mythic goddesses. Never any local girls until now.

It just doesn't add up.

A terrible uncertainty churns in my belly, so many ominous unknowns with no easy answers and too many threats.

Too many ways to lose my sister if he sucks her into his family's black void and sweeps her away from me forever.

I bare my teeth in a smile that feels more like a cat puffing up its tail.

"Aleksander."

"Ophelia," he greets me with a warmth that makes my skin crawl, velvety and inviting. Borderline flirty. *And right in front of my sister, oh God.* "Come now, I know we were never chums growing up, but surely you can spare a little hug for your future brother-in-law?"

No effing way.

And who the hell talks like an English aristocrat in

twenty-first century North Carolina?

"Don't mind her, Sandy," Ros squeaks in this cutesy baby voice I've never heard her use in my life.

Sandy?

Holy crap.

All I can do is stare like a deer in the headlights while she gives Aleksander a sultry pout, reaching up to brush her thumb over his lower lip.

"Ophie's just being weird and stuffy. I told you she wouldn't approve—not unless she really knows you. She's overprotective like that. Big sisters, go figure..."

"And didn't I say I'll do whatever it takes to win her over?" He lifts her hand and kisses it.

Yep.

I'm about to be sick.

Though Aleksander sure as hell isn't winning any brownie points with me right now as he presses his mouth to Ros' thumb, then parts his lips to catch it between his teeth, flicking his tongue over the tip while she giggles.

It's like I'm not even here.

Except I am and they just don't care.

I can't decide what's worse.

But when Aleksander stops doing—ugh, *that*—to my sister's thumb, he turns another oily smirk on me.

"I do mean that sincerely, Ophelia. I know my family reputation makes this seem like an odd situation—"

"Like that's the only reason," I spit.

"—but I do want us all to be one big happy family," he continues, undeterred. "Frankly, I'm dead set on marrying your sister and making her mine. I only hope you'll come to accept that. Not tonight, certainly, but in time."

Not in a million years.

It's funny how he says it, too.

Making her his.

But he never said one word about actually loving her.

This time, when I bare my teeth at him, it's deliberate. "You'll have to excuse me if I don't consider you family just yet."

I've also heard enough.

So I turn my back on them—on Ros' hurt, angry glare and the strangely knowing chuckle boiling from Aleksander's mannequin-like throat.

As I turn to walk away from this circus, completely done with this crap, Aleksander's voice drifts after me.

"See? It's like we're already family. Bickering just like siblings, Ophelia dearest!" he calls. "You just need to come to grips with that fact."

Flipping creep.

I don't need to come to grips with anything besides my mounting temper.

I stalk out of our shop and welcome the biting fall air that stings my cheeks until they burn.

I'm not in any mood for shopping anymore, or even to see Mom.

Honestly, I wouldn't enjoy shopping when I'm this angry, and I don't want to bring this bitter energy into the hospital. I might not buy into the New Agey energy healing stuff, but I can't help thinking all this negative energy won't do our mother any good.

So I just stand there restlessly for an agitated moment, ignoring the people strolling past with curious glances and rude whispers that always carry more than they think.

Sigh.

I'm so sick of being talked about like the town pity case.

I should just go home. Back to Grant's place, I mean.

Except the house will be as empty as Mom's with Nell in school and I'll be stranded with my nerves, rattling around alone.

I shouldn't be doing this when I start moving.

Yet somehow, my feet take me to the left, down the street, a few blocks away to the Redhaven police station.

It's an old-timey brick building, smaller than most shops, and when I push the door open it's easy to fit basically everything in one big room. There's a broad wooden reception desk with an old computer sitting dormant, and beyond that the small cluster of desks where our small police force sets up to work when they're not on patrol.

It's still a little jarring for me to see Lucas Graves in a uniform, though it doesn't surprise me when he was so dead set on finding justice for his sister, Celeste. He and Mallory Cross are the only ones in the office.

Mallory glances up with the same warm, genuine smile she always wears while her phone pipes something at her in —Korean? Whatever it was, it sounds flirty and dirty.

I can't help a flash of disappointment that Grant's not here, though.

I stand around awkwardly for a few seconds, lips parted, trying to pull an excuse for why I even came here—but there's no need.

Lucas looks up from a few open folders in front of him. He's settled at one of the smaller desks, his chair tilted back on two legs, feet crossed and propped up on the desk.

He gives me a shrewd, thoughtful look, then leans back and reaches over to rap on the closed office door with CHIEF BOWDEN stenciled on the frosted glass inset.

"Grant," he calls. "Company."

He gives me a knowing smirk that makes me want to march over and make up for every grade school spitball in my hair with a good, hard tweak to his nose.

"Glad to see you home, Miss Ophelia," he says, his smile softening, a touch of sympathy in his catlike green eyes. "You doing all right?"

Just like that, I almost burst out crying.

It's just this familiar face from my childhood, offering me kind recognition and a genuine welcome home. I can't make a sound, my lips trembling.

No, I *won't* cry when he just asked me a simple question.

But I'm relieved when the door to Bowden's office swings open and Grant's big, bearish frame slips out with more grace than any man that huge should have.

He takes one look at me, crosses the room in three long strides, and presses a heavy, hot hand to the small of my back.

"C'mon," he says. "Come sit down with me."

Swallowing and wiping at an escaping tear, I let him usher me toward Bowden's office. As I pass Lucas, I offer him a watery smile.

He just snaps off a two-finger salute, his eyes glittering with quiet understanding.

I think he gets it, even though he never left this place.

By trying so hard to forget Redhaven, I forgot how many good people I left behind here, too.

I'm pushing the tears back by the time Grant leads me to one of the upholstered club chairs in Bowden's cramped office and closes the door behind us.

Instead of reclaiming the chair behind the desk, he settles on the second club chair next to me.

The tiny space feels so cramped that his knees bump into my thigh.

I need that.

I need his presence.

I need him to fill the space around me, so nothing besides Grant can get in.

Maybe then I can push all the bad things out.

"Butterfly, what's wrong?" he asks. Direct as always, but I'm honestly not used to him just coming out and asking me about feelings. "Did that stalker freak show up again? Did he hurt you?"

"What? No, I—" Instinctively, I brush my fingers against the bruises on my arms. They're already turning that gross yellow-purple as they're healing. "No, it's silly. It doesn't matter." I look around, biting my lip. "So you took over Bowden's office?"

"For now. The guys were giving me a headache about—" He breaks off, and I swear there's a redness under his beard as he looks away. "Never mind."

"What? No never mind!" I reach over and poke his arm. "About what?"

"About you," he grumps, ducking his head and swiping his dark-brown hair back from his face.

My heart skips.

"Oh? What about me?" I ask innocently.

Grant glowers. "Woman, don't think playing Miss Innocent is going to help you deflect today."

I wince. "I'm that obvious, huh?"

"As much as I'd like to think you stopped by just to make me smile, I have a feeling that's not all there is to it."

Whatever I'd started to say just stops cold in my throat.

I've had a lifetime of sullen, withdrawn, walled-off-with-his-feelings Grant.

A whole freaking decade of avoiding what his silences mean, and everything changing the minute I break through them and it sinks in.

That's why I have no armor when it comes to him being nakedly honest.

There's no stopping how my face flares, burning like a fever.

"...you're not smiling," I stammer.

Grant stares intently for several long seconds.

Then he reaches for me with this slow, careful movement

169

that makes me think of a giant shrugging whole mountains off his shoulders as he clasps my hands in his.

He envelops me in his warmth, his coarseness, his strength.

Like he's showing me how he could eclipse me so easily, but he'd be protecting me with his shadow.

Then he smiles.

Slow, warm, just a flash of white teeth through his beard and a softening of his stormy hazel eyes until they look like my fondest memories.

Happier times set in dark bronze like bugs in amber.

Loyal friends and family—plus one beast of a man who never lost his faith.

God.

That quiet explosion of feeling blows my heart to pieces.

My breaths turn shallow and I'm pinned in place by this big manly smile that leaves me in stitches. It's like witnessing a unicorn, rare and amazing.

I think I can still count on one hand how many times I've ever seen a real smile out of this man.

And it hurts so good that he's smiling this way just for me.

"There. I'm smiling and you're happy," he rumbles matter-of-factly as his face relaxes, squeezing my hands. "Now tell me what's wrong, Philia. I know you're hurting."

"Dude. You're not supposed to read me that easy." I swallow past the thickness in my throat.

"It's easy because I spent every damn waking moment fixated on you," Grant snarls. "I'd be ashamed of myself if I didn't know you by now."

Oh, crap.

If he keeps going, he's going to break me for sure.

It's like being caught in the eye of a storm, this one spot of calm while the fury of my life rages around me. I curl my fingers in his, biting my lip.

"You really wanna know? Ros and I had a big fight," I whisper, everything tumbling out in this rush of upset. "I went to see her at the shop like I told you. I just wanted to know why she's been avoiding me and Mom, but I almost didn't recognize her. You were right. There's something wrong—it totally creeped me out. She's too jittery, her eyes are weird, and she's starting to look hollowed out. But Aleksander was there, too. And she wouldn't listen to a word I said. Not as long as she was hanging all over him like he hung the stars." I shake my head angrily. "I don't get it. I don't get how he has this hold on her, but there's something about it that *scares* me, Grant."

"Hush," Grant soothes.

He releases one hand so he can curl his fingers against the back of my neck, coaxing me in.

Next thing I know, I've buried my face in his shoulder, wrapping my free arm around his neck.

I'm not crying. Not yet.

But my entire body shakes with the force of holding it in.

Grant, he just—

He lets me be.

He weathers my confusion, my sadness, while I turn into a complete wreck against him, sheltering me, his hand kneading softly against the nape of my neck until the pressure relaxes me and I melt against him.

I shouldn't feel this content when I was a total mess ten minutes ago, but that's the thing about Grant.

Sometimes his silence is infuriating.

But sometimes, it's medicine, knowing he's as unshakeable as a mountain.

He finally breaks the stillness with a thoughtful growl, though, the vibration thrumming against me.

"I didn't want to presume," he says. "Not with Ros. But if we both think there's cause for concern—"

"What can we do?" I whisper. "She's a grown woman. We can't override her own decisions and we can't make her stop seeing him."

"We're still her family."

We. He says it so casually it warms my heart.

I smile.

"If she can see it's coming from a place of love, maybe she'll stop being defensive and listen. If not for her own sake or for yours, then for your ma's. Can't imagine Angela would want this at all," he says.

"No. Then again, Mom would want her to be happy, even if 'happy' doesn't look like what we'd expect..." I idly stroke my fingers along Grant's throat. "I'm trying not to judge. I just... I don't think she's actually happy right now. Not if she was in her right mind. How could she be when she knows— she knows—" I stop, the words dying on my tongue.

"It's more distant for her, not like how it was for us. Don't forget that. She was so young when Ethan disappeared."

Ever the voice of reason.

I want to hate it, but I can't.

Suddenly, Grant shifts his hold, gathering me into his lap and pulling me across the small, awkward space between us until I'm settled on his thighs. I curl up there, tucking myself snugly against his body while he rests his chin on top of my head.

"The three of us were fucking inseparable. Ros probably felt like an outsider when she's so much younger and Ethan's memory isn't as strong. Not to mention how much we all tried to shelter her from the worst of it, from our suspicions."

"Yeah, but after all the rumors, and what happened with the Arrendells and Celeste Graves..."

"I know. That might be what's behind it. Ros has a rebellious streak under that shy girl surface. Maybe dating Aleksander was a way to defy the rumors or face them in her own way after she got sick of all the whispers and nosy-ass glances. Then she got pulled in deeper than she could handle."

"I could see that," I say wryly, curling my hand in his uniform shirt. "This feels weird, you know."

"What? My shirt?"

I smile faintly, tapping one of his glossy buttons. "Sitting in your lap like a little girl asking Santa Cop for presents."

Grant's snort sounds suspiciously like a repressed laugh.

"Don't even start that Daddy mess. You used to—"

"What? Call you 'Dad' every time we got in a fight because you'd start snarling at me to stop following you and Ethan everywhere and getting in the way?"

"It wasn't *getting in the way*," he growls. "It was getting hurt. We were doing all kinds of dangerous shit. Dicking around the hills too close to Jacobin property, setting off contraband fireworks, drinking our weight in beer like every dumbass kid. Too dangerous for a little girl still in high school."

"Just dangerous enough to be interesting to an adventurous, enterprising little girl," I correct and push myself up to look at him, touching my finger to his nose. "Don't you know the more you warned me away, the more I wanted to go?"

Another snort.

Disgruntled, surly.

See? Big old man-bear.

"You and your hero worship, wanting to be everywhere Ethan was," he rumbles.

"Not just Ethan." I lean in and press my nose to his, replacing my finger. "I wanted to be everywhere *you* were, idiot."

"Whatever. I think you just liked poking the bear."

I grin. "Why not when he made such funny noises?"

Grant obliges me with a funny noise right now, an overly dramatic growl, and I laugh.

Guess it's easier to laugh like this, cradled up in him with his scent surrounding me and his arms wrapped up so tight, his thick beard scratching my cheek.

"Will you stop being annoyed with me if I kiss you?" I offer.

"Who says I was annoyed at all?" he counters, tilting his head and brushing his lips across mine in a tease that makes my blood sing. "Think I'll take that kiss. Call it Butterfly insurance against future irritation."

"Mm, yes, you're so certain I'm going to annoy you again?"

"*Yes*," he deadpans, and I scowl, trying to force down a laugh as I shove against his chest.

"No kiss for you!"

"Too damn late." And with one firm arm around my waist, he swings me back in, refusing to let me escape.

Not that I want to.

No way.

Not when, the second he pulls me against his chest, his lips descend, slanting hard against my mouth and erasing all sense, all reason, all worry from my mind.

Holy hell.

I've never been kissed like this.

Every man who tried fell a mile short and a day late.

Every man who wasn't Grant kissed like I was an object for his own selfish purpose.

Like they were checking off this laundry list inside their minds, all the things a man had to do in a specific order to be this cool sex god, until it felt mechanical and bloodless.

But Grant kisses like he's so consumed by me he can't do anything else.

He kisses like he wants my soul, the best and worst of me.

His lips tease mine, fitting together perfectly, delving like he already knows me inside and out.

And he does, doesn't he?

He's had an iron grip on my heart for so long. Every kiss is just the key that opens my body.

He leaves me trembling, pressing so hard into him, letting him take me over, tease me, shiver me down.

I gasp as his teeth flirt with my lower lip, shifting from gentle grazing to stinging pressure.

As every stroke of his tongue leaves behind raw sensations like hot embers flying across my lips.

God, he tastes *wild*, so much vivid passion erupting behind his stoic face.

Even his beard drags against my cheeks, and as his tongue twines with mine, something flows inside me like liquid honey.

My blood thickens with desire.

These slick, hot, panting sounds slide between our lips, turning this into something achingly forbidden.

Kiss by steaming kiss, he shatters the walls of friendship, leaving two lovers tangled up in each other, in something burning.

Something that doesn't know what it is.

Something that shreds me like paper.

Something with its own inertia we don't have a prayer of stopping.

Oh my God.

Oh. My. Grant.

I'm so tingly and wet it hurts, melting for him helplessly, and it's so amazing to feel his heart banging against his chest.

His pulse ticks against his throat as I run my hands over the hot, taut lines of his neck.

He inhales roughly, a human volcano building with pure sweet madness.

Is it bad that I like making him crazy?

Knowing I can torture him—that he's not indifferent—that I'm all he's ever wanted...

It's enough to get a girl drunk with reckless thoughts.

When his huge, rough hands slip under my shirt, pushing it up to drag coarse skin over the small of my back, to clutch me against him, I'm willing to do anything.

Anything right here, right now, right in this cramped office.

Until there's a sudden rapping at the door.

We both gasp, breaking apart like we've touched a live current.

Just in time as Mallory pokes her head in. "Captain Fair-cross? We've got a—*oh*. Oh, my."

Ohhh, crap.

I fall out of Grant's lap, torn between a humiliated giggle and the need to hide like a roach from sheer mortification.

Breathing hard, I brush my hand across my damp lips.

Grant looks worse, I think, wearing half my lipstick smeared around his mouth.

"Hi, Mallory," I say shyly.

She just blinks at me before shaking her head with an indulgent smile.

"Welcome home, Ophelia." Her gaze shifts to Grant. "We've got a pink problem again, Captain."

Grant groans and presses his fingers into his eyes.

I can't decide if I'm sad or relieved to see his usual control take over.

He's already shuttering, back to being the gruff police captain, but I want to think there's still a certain softness to him that wasn't there before.

Or maybe he just looks really hot in shades of red.

"Again? Aw, hell. Didn't we have another pink run just last week?"

"Pink problem?" I ask. It sounds vaguely familiar, but I don't remember why until—oh, right. "You mean the Jacobins are still letting their pigs escape?"

"It's a Redhaven tradition at this point. Like the running of the bulls, only it's a pig stampede down Main Street at least once a month," Grant snarls. "Fuck, I *just* got my car cleaned out after last time, too. If they don't fix their fucking fences, I'm going to write them up and drop five pounds of pig shit back where it belongs. Right on their porches with their hogs. Fines might get the gears in their heads turning."

Mallory laughs wildly and taps her mouth. "Oh, but you might need a tissue before you make that ultimatum, Captain Faircross! The rest of the team's already en route."

Then she closes the door and we're alone again while Grant frowns, puzzled.

"Tissue?"

"Um... Grant." I'm almost dying, biting back my laughter when he looks so adorably confused. With a loving sigh, I fish my compact out of the pocket of my jeans and flip it open to show him his reflection in the little round mirror. "See? It's a good color on you."

"Goddamn!" Grant gives me a disgusted look like he blames me, leaning over Chief Bowden's desk to snatch up a few tissues from the dispenser. Leaning in, he squints at his reflection in my mirror and starts wiping at his mouth furiously. "Shit. If I go out there like this, people are really gonna wonder what I did to get those pigs into the car."

"*Grant!*" I snicker. "You're awful."

"You only think so 'cause you've convinced yourself I've got no sense of humor. And maybe you like kissing awful men."

Now I'm the one turning red.

"It just takes knowing you to get what you're saying between the lines." As he pulls back and tosses the balled-up tissue in the trash, I snap the compact closed with a smirk. "So, I have to let you go for pig duty, huh?"

"Unfortunately." He stands and his bulk takes up so much space in the tiny office, delightfully overwhelming. It's a miracle he doesn't have to stoop to fit the low ceiling. Hazel eyes soften as he looks down at me. "But there's always tonight."

"I guess there is." I shouldn't be so giddy knowing I get to go home to him when the whole reason is some weirdo stalker hurling death threats. But I smile anyway, tilting my head up and pursing my lips. "Kiss me goodbye."

"I just got your lipstick off me and you're still this bossy?"

"I've hardly got any left at this point. You're safe."

Grant chuckles, then bends and brushes his mouth across mine.

The hurricane is gone.

This is a soft, sweet breeze full of promises. But there's nothing chaste about the way my body lights up at the lightest touch.

I catch myself leaning into him as he straightens, drawn like he's a human magnet and I'm all iron. Before I pull back, I clear my throat, smoothing my clothing.

He catches a lock of my hair and tweaks it. "Go shopping and get yourself a better coat. I'm taking you and Nell out tonight."

"Where?"

"Nothing special. Just dinner and an age-appropriate movie."

But it is special when it's you and me—when it's us, I think.

Of course, I keep that to myself, only smiling brighter.

"You just want to take my mind off everything."

"Maybe I do," he says, absolutely serious.

It's so Grant.

So many little things, the way he tells me I'm important with such subtle gestures. Maybe dinner and a movie isn't much to most girls, but it's Grant Faircross wanting to spend time with me, wanting to help me forget the myriad ways life keeps going wrong.

It's Grant showing me he *cares.*

For now, that's enough to leave me quiet with a thousand feelings flopping around as he bends to kiss my cheek one more time, then tucks my hair back with one last long look before turning to go.

My knees still feel hilariously weak from that first kiss.

Oh, this is bad.

I'm in big trouble and I don't think I care.

I wish I could hold on to that feeling.

But by the time I pick up my newly repaired rental car from Mort's, I'm already dreading the short drive across town.

That cold feeling becomes a lump of frozen lead as I step into the medical center.

The nurses at the front desk just wave me through.

No need to check the hometown girl, I guess. It's one of the rare times when I wish everyone in this small town didn't know my business, just so they'd stall me for a minute or two, making me sign the visitor register or something.

Anything to delay the inevitable—seeing Mom in that bed again.

I'm already an emotional mess by the time I get to her room.

Yes, I want to be with her, to comfort her, to hope that my presence will help her fight to a miraculous recovery, knowing her girls are waiting for her—but I also can't stand how frail she looks, like a skeleton that hasn't remembered to stop breathing yet.

I can't stand that she's *still* not waking up.

This doesn't feel like a restful sleep. More like the precursor to the very end.

With a deflated sigh, I sit next to her bed and clasp her thin, bony hand. With my free hand, I stroke back the wisps of blonde hair left so dry by the chemo and other drugs they're pumping into her system to keep her alive.

"I'm not ready," I whisper, pulling her hand against my chest. "I'm not ready to lead this family, Mom. Ros is a mess. I think she's making a big mistake and I don't know what to do. I don't know how to help her, how to help you..."

My voice cracks.

I can't hold in the tears anymore as this chill rakes down my spine. I squeeze my mother's hand, trying to be strong for her, trying not to shake.

Not strong enough to stop the torrent.

I cry.

Quietly. Secretly. Intensely.

Sobbing over her fingers until they're wet, sucking in heaving breaths, barely managing to creak out words that feel like angry porcupines.

"I miss you."

I can't deny it any longer.

As much as I might blame Redhaven for my brother's disappearance, I've missed this place, too.

Miami never totally felt like home. Just a distant place to escape to.

Home is here.

Home is with my family.

With Mom and Ros.

With Grant.

But right now, I feel so alone.

For just a breath, my heart leaps.

There's movement. A subtle twitching against my fingers.

I sit up sharply, staring down at the hand clasped in my own. My mother's fingers curl feebly, just barely there, but unmistakable.

"Mom?" I stare at her hopefully, my heart threatening to burst, scrubbing at the tears on my cheeks. "Mom, are you awake?"

She doesn't move.

No sound at all.

Not even an eyelash flutter.

But her hand grips mine like a ghost.

Just enough.

It's not just me holding her. She's holding me.

As if it's the only way she can tell me, *I'm still here.*

The rough cry that boils up my throat is raw. This time, the tears aren't so quiet and civilized.

The ugly cry that's been building up inside me for a long time rips out as I weep over that hand clasped in mine.

"Please hold on," I croak. "Please hold on for me."

Still no answer.

But I don't let her go, and she doesn't let me go until visiting hours are over.

I'm reluctant to leave when the time comes.

I've been glued to this chair for so long I think my butt is molded to the seat, and it hurts to unlock my limbs and stand. But everything closes early around here and I don't want to be the reason the day shift staff can't get home and turn things over to the meager night crew.

So I force myself away, fondly touching Mom's cheek one last time.

"I'll be back soon," I murmur. "I won't leave you alone."

No response, of course.

181

But I'd like to think she hears me in there, somewhere.

I turn to let myself out with a nod for the receptionist at the front desk. She offers me a smile full of the pity I hate—and when I smile back, it feels like defiance, as if I'm saying *no, not yet. She isn't done.*

It's not time to give in.

Angela Sanderson raised two stubborn daughters because she's a freaking rock.

She had to be, to get by on her own.

No husband, no man, not even a boyfriend.

I've never met the father I share with Ros. No one knows who my mom dated, saw, slept with after her first husband—Ethan's father—died.

I shouldn't know that, honestly.

But, well, I guess some mysteries were never meant to be solved.

A little ironic when this is a town where everyone knows everyone else's business—and what they *don't* know, they talk about.

Sometimes in earshot of little ones who don't need to hear those rumors at all.

Mom would never tell us the truth, even when we begged for answers.

All Ros and I know is that we have the same father. Two sisters sharing the same unknown DNA.

Even if we don't feel so close anymore.

My nose wrinkles and that bitterness works its way up my throat.

I hate that Aleksander Arrendell is taking her away from me.

A few months ago, the very idea would've been unthinkable.

As I walk out to my car, I turn that over.

Am I overreacting?

Do I just hate this thing with Ros and Aleksander because I'm one of those family members who feels like my sister belongs to *me?* Does Aleksander disgust me because of who he is or because I'd feel the same about any interloper taking my sister away?

Part of me could see it.

It's hard not to loathe any man inserting himself in her life when it's just been us and Mom for so long, relying on each other, close-knit and inseparable.

Only, Aleksander Arrendell isn't 'any man.'

He's velvet trouble and hidden heartbreak and high-strung demands. And if Ros doesn't watch her butt, she's going to wind up—

Oh.

A long, swift-moving shadow stops my thoughts.

There's someone near my car.

I stop halfway across the lot, keys clutched in my hand as my heart stalls.

There's a big old Ford SUV parked next to my rental Corolla, blocking my view, but I can just make out a tall, lean shadow through the Ford's tinted windows, someone milling around in the space between the cars.

"Hey!" I dart forward, pelting across the parking lot. "What are you doing? Get away from my car!"

I go swinging around the bumper of the Ford, ready to tackle whoever's messing around with my vehicle until—

You guessed it.

There's no one there.

My heart jams in my throat as I stop cold, straining to breathe, just staring at the yellow line between the parking spots.

Nothing.

What the hell? Did I imagine it?

Is this what too much stress does?

I shove myself between the cars, staring past the narrow band of grass beyond the edge of the parking lot to the trees bordering it before I pull myself away and walk to the sidewalk, looking left and right as I go.

Still no one around aside from a few kids just getting off the bus halfway down the block.

A few other people look bored, mulching leaves in their yards with mowers or covering their gardens with tarps for the coming winter. A middle-aged woman I don't recognize pushes a stroller, but I don't see that tall, quick shape anywhere.

Not him.

Not the panicked oddball who grabbed me and told me I'd die.

Ugh.

However much I downplayed it for Grant and wanted to believe he's a harmless dementia case, maybe it did get to me.

I'm actually seeing things.

I must be.

Shaking my head at myself, I sigh and head back to my car. But just to be safe, I give it a quick once-over, popping down and peering under the wheels even if I don't know what I'm looking for, exactly.

Evidence of tampering, I guess.

Anything that might be stuck to the car.

I've read enough thrillers to freak out about stalkers and GPS trackers. Unless they're making them smaller than bugs now, I don't see anything like that.

I don't feel it either when I run my hands around the wheel wells for good measure.

There's a dramatic moment when I unlock the driver's side door and imagine the car blowing up the instant I pull the latch, just like in the movies.

I almost laugh. Now I'm being ridiculous.

A stalker, that's my worst case. Not winding up on a mafia hit list.

Of course, nothing happens.

Not until the *Door Open* alarm starts pinging as I stand there with my breath thick, just waiting for something to go *boom*.

Yep.

Still being ridiculous.

There are better things to focus on.

Like the fact that right now, I have a quasi-date.

Grant is waiting for me tonight and I'm ready to let him take my mind off all the worries streaking through my brain.

XI: ONE BAD SEED (GRANT)

I'm just leaving A Touch of Grey, our main local furniture store, after a late call came in from Talia Grey. Easy business after wrangling pigs for over an hour.

The poor girl was flustered, panicked about somebody lifting money from their cash register. Turns out, it was her own grandfather.

Gerald Grey is still one hell of a master artisan with everything wood, only he's going a touch senile in his seventies.

When the old man told his granddaughter he'd make the bank run to drop off the cash, he wound up losing it under an old box of chair legs stuffed in his truck. Damn good thing I thought to look when I saw how upset he was, swearing up and down that nobody ever stole from the store in its fifty plus years—and of course, there was no way they'd start on his watch.

I walk out with two happy, relieved faces behind me, trying not to dwell on the ravages of time.

Sometimes, it comes in like a berserker, daggers drawn and ready to shred the heart.

Other times, it's just a slow, insufferable march to heartbreak.

We all have an invisible hourglass counting down our minutes like grains of sand.

That makes me all the more eager to get the hell home.

Knowing I'll see Nell and Ophelia again is the only thing that keeps me from slipping into a fully shit-mad melancholy mood—until I walk past December Fifth just off Main Street.

There's a familiar, ugly damn mug staring at me through the green-tinted window.

The place is one of our most popular local bars, styled like an old-timey speakeasy and named for the day Prohibition ended.

It's the first time I've seen Aleksander Arrendell there, tucked into the small wooden booth and gesturing to me through the window.

What now? What could human slime possibly want?

I've got half a mind to storm past and keep going, pretending I never saw him.

Too bad I've made eye contact.

Worse, he's not alone.

I find that out the second I step into the dimly lit bar with its tall black leather booths and shelves of glossy bottles soaring to the ceiling.

"Captain!" he calls to me, snapping off a half-mocking salute which jostles the sleeping lump of Ros on his shoulder.

What does this asshole need?

Nothing good.

I can already guess that much as I stalk forward, trying my damnedest not to show my teeth like the angry wolf he turns me into.

"Something I can help you with?" I growl.

"Relax. I wouldn't dream of putting any trouble on your very broad shoulders while you're presumably off duty," he says smoothly. "I just wanted to thank you for coming by the house and dealing with our nasty situation. Mummy was *so* upset, finding that poor gal swinging there."

My eyes narrow.

The polite response would be a curt *you're welcome* and a cold, quick escape.

Only, he's already dragged me in here and I ain't feeling the least bit polite.

"Something you're holding back, Aleksander? You got something we missed on our sweep?"

"Please, call me Sandy," he slurs, his eyes glazed with too much of that godawful cocktail in front of him that smells like smoked rocket fuel.

I will not.

He shakes his head slowly, huffing out an exaggerated sigh. "Gods, do I wish I did, Captain. I always adored poor Cora. If I only knew how she was suffering—if any of us did, really—we'd have gotten her the help she needed and spared no expense."

My eyebrows go up and freeze in place.

Right. And I'm the fucking tooth fairy.

I just wish I could decide if he's so drunk or high he's speaking with a guilty conscience right about now.

If only one of these miserable, cold-blooded fucks would slip up.

"That it then, Sandy?" I snarl the nickname. "Look, if this is you hinting you're feeling a need to talk to somebody to set your mind straight, there are plenty of folks around who are better qualified than me. I can't take away any crosses for you or your folks to bear. That's above my pay grade."

He looks down sheepishly, staring into his drink.

Next to him, Ros whimpers in her sleep, smacking her lips.

"Certainly not, Captain. Nothing of the sort. Truth be

told, I was being a tad selfish when I saw you passing by and waved you in." He meets my eyes again. Finally, a little truth. "I just wondered if you might consider putting in a good word for little ol' me? For Ophelia Sanderson's sake? She wasn't so open when I tried."

What the shit?

He can't be serious.

I cock my head and stare as Ros stirs against him again.

There's a tall empty glass with a fruity smell like raspberries next to her. I wonder how many she's had to put her down in a bar that's already getting noisy with the evening crowd trickling in.

"What about Ophelia? And what's that got to do with me?"

A flash of teeth, too sharp and bone white.

He sweeps his shaggy hair out of his eyes, holding up a burgundy tablecloth—or is it a handkerchief—that looks oddly textured as he wipes his mouth.

"Ros here tells me you've always been rather close to her Ophie—and you know as well as I do how this little town loves to talk. In fact, I've heard you and Ophelia are quite inseparable." His smile widens, indifferent to the swords flashing in my eyes.

I start to open my mouth, searching for the most tactful way to tell him to fuck off in public, but he raises his hands.

"It's not my business, Captain Grant. Suffice it to say it's wonderful to see you enjoying yourself with a lady friend again. I never imagined you'd—"

"Get to the point, Arrendell," I bite off.

He holds his tablecloth up and sniffs.

"I simply hoped you might join us for a drink or two? We'll sit, we'll catch up, and if I can turn that scowly frown into a smile, perhaps you'll see there's nothing for dear Ophelia to worry her pretty little head over. Ros and I were *made* for each other." He pauses, this sneering smile spreading across his lips. "Did you know this dear creature convinced me to do laundry? I never touched a washing machine in my life before she began trusting me with her unmentionables."

Fucking. Gross.

It's a real effort to keep the revulsion off my face.

Especially as he makes a big show of capturing her hand and pressing it to his lips. Weirdly without releasing that little scrap of cloth in his hands, which keeps finding its way back to his cheek.

Who knew an Arrendell needed a security blanket?

"That's between you and the Sandersons," I say flatly. "If you remember anything else about Cora Lafayette, you know where to find me."

"About that drink—"

"No." I'm so done. And I'm already turning when I stop and throw a look back over my shoulder that I wish was scathing enough to banish him to hell.

"Ah. You disappoint me, Captain." He holds up that bundle of—whatever the hell it is—clutched in his hand and breaths it in like potpourri.

Syrupy joy clouds his eyes.

My gaze flicks to Ros who's basically out cold in his arms. She's barely moved the whole time.

Holy shit.

Is he so out of it he's abusing some nasty substance in public? I swear, if he's here huffing some chemical shit, powdered opioids, cocaine, right in front of me—

My hand moves faster than my brain.

Lunging, I rip the thing away from him, spread it out, scanning the wine-purple surface for any sign of drugs. If I see one damn speck of narcotics, I'll arrest him on the spot.

Then it hits me what I'm looking at.

I stumble back like I've been punched, clumsily thudding into a table behind me.

I drop the thing like it's suddenly on fire.

Aleksander doubles over, laughing like a deranged hyena, banging his fist lightly against his head.

I'm not goddamned amused.

Frankly, I'm not sure how I'll ever live down shaking out a pair of panties in a busy bar. Especially if they really belong to Ros Sanderson.

"Are you out of your damn mind?" I barely resist the urge to yank him out of that booth and fling him around until he stops fucking *laughing*.

I get my way a second later when his fit stops and the broken smile fades, leaving a watery-eyed glare fixed on me.

"Hardly, Captain Faircross. There's another word you're looking for. *Obsessed.* Truly, completely, inseparably. Don't tell me that's a crime?"

He kisses Ros' forehead and clutches her head. Even with all the commotion and at least a dozen people staring at us now, she's still grogged out.

Fuck me.

I back away slowly.

A second later, I'm almost tearing the door off its hinges. I've never been more grateful for a face full of cold air.

I need to get out of here before I do something monumentally stupid.

Unfortunately, Aleksander Arrendell hasn't committed a crime by being a depraved, psychotic, creepy fuck.

But I *will* if I spend another second in his presence.

When I get to my vehicle, wishing I could give my brain a bleach bath, there's a text from Ophelia apologizing. She's running late to get Nell from school.

Don't worry about it. On my way now, I send back.

Then I settle in, gripping the wheel until my knuckles turn white, trying to breathe.

How do I do this?

How do I have a normal evening with my girl when her sister's shacked up with Lucifer?

And I'll be damned if I let his nauseating insanity throw another wrench in her life—or in mine.

Before I leave, I put my hand over the badge on my chest, swearing a silent oath to Philia, to Ethan, maybe to God himself.

To everything I am.

I *will* get that demon fuck away from the Sanderson girls, come hell or high water.

I just need to breathe, bide my time, and wait for the scum to give me a chance.

XII: ONE LONG NIGHT (OPHELIA)

*B*y the time I make it back to Grant's house, he's already home.

Both his truck and patrol car are parked neatly in the driveway.

Nell's out front, bundled up to her neck against the cold as she kicks her legs on the tree swing. Another nice reminder I forgot to go shopping for a coat yet again.

I'm a little glad Grant stepped in to pick her up.

It almost completely fell out of my head after thinking I saw someone lurking around my car.

Whoops. I hope they won't be mad.

When I park and step out with a hundred apologies ready for the little girl, though, Nell goes rocketing off the swing and launches herself at me.

"Miss Philia!"

Laughing, I catch her as she glues herself on in a tight hug, burying her face against me.

"Hey, hon." I ruffle her hair and crouch down. "You have a good day at school? Sorry I missed you."

"Yeah! I always do," she announces triumphantly. "I'm the smartest in my class."

"And not shy on confidence, either." Grinning, I tug at one of her springy curls. "Where's your uncle Grant?"

"Upstairs, showering." She scrunches her nose up dramatically. "He smelled like *pig poo*. So he was really in a hurry." Eyes wide, she leans in, whispering to me in the loudest whisper I've ever heard. "And I think he didn't want *you* to smell him."

"Well, good." I laugh again. "I wouldn't want him to smell me if I was doused in pig stink."

She brightens. "'Cause you like him a lot?"

I sputter, then sigh. "Because I like him a *whole* lot. I have for a long time. Maybe since I was as small as you."

Nell's eyes go round. "Are you gonna make more kissy-faces at the movies then?"

"Not in front of you, kiddo." Not to mention everyone else who shows up for a family-friendly film. I stand, idly draping my arm around her shoulders. "C'mon inside with me. It's getting dark. Did you finish your homework?"

"Not yet," she pouts, but follows me in without protest.

"Why don't you settle in and wrap up while I go get changed and say hi to your uncle?" I kick the door shut behind me, already heading for the stairs, but that little imp's voice follows me.

"You gonna make yourself pretty for Uncle Grant?"

I look back with my eyes narrowed to find her bouncing onto the couch, watching me over the back of it with a wide, knowing grin.

"And if I am?"

"You worry too much," she announces decisively. "He'll think you're pretty no matter what! Even *if* you smell like pig crap."

"I—you—" I clam up.

I must have it *bad.*

If a nine-year-old girl can get me this flustered over a crush and make me blush this hard, I'm so screwed.

"You're red, Miss Philia. Is that part of your look too?"

I mock-scowl.

"Do your homework, babe, or I'll feed you to the gremlins."

"Psssh, gremlins aren't real." Totally unfazed, she flips herself around to start digging in her backpack.

Little monster.

Still struggling with my red-hot face, I head upstairs and crest the top of the landing just as the bathroom door opens.

There goes the slightest hope of killing my blush.

Grant steps out, gloriously naked except for the towel wrapped around his waist.

His muscle-bound dad bod is so thick the flimsy towel barely holds the tattooed god underneath, hanging open in a slit over one brawny tanned thigh.

Somebody save me.

He's added some serious ink over the years and it only makes him hotter.

I haven't seen Grant this shirtless since he was a teenager —the old family trips to the lake, the beach, his parents and my mom teaming up to drag us all along. Back then, he was strong and golden and toned, but still a boy.

A little lanky. A lot less built. Not filled out by raw power and life and testosterone like he is now.

The beast before me now is all man.

And even if I tell myself to stop, stop—

Lord help me.

His go-to police uniforms and flannels tend to slim him down a notch, masking just how broad he really is.

Now I'm face-to-face with this wall of a man, solid and

strong where most guys would probably wear that bulk awkwardly.

Not him.

He's the perfect balance of rakishly fit and furiously large, a walking sculpture, crafted by hard work and a harder life until everything fits together *just right.*

Grant Faircross is a natural wonder.

Designed to rip your breath away, not just with his sheer size, but with naked, simple beauty.

I don't even know if beautiful is the right word.

But he's too handsome for life, his skin tanned and weathered into a dusky brown. A few scars form paler marks, giving his body character like a mountain and its fault lines.

Thick hair the same deep brown as his beard and hair furs his chest, marching down in a thin line, dusted here and there with the same sprinkled silver appearing everywhere else.

His shoulders are so wide he has to angle to fit through the door.

His pecs are like stone slabs, the barrel of his rib cage layered in dense ripples that cascade down to narrowed abs so lethal you could sharpen a knife on their edges.

With his hair wet and slicked back, his beard and his chest dotted with water, his skin still gleaming with steam...

God.

He's so purely primal it hurts.

The unexpected sight of him awakens something scary.

Something that takes me over until it's like I'm submerged in molten lava rising to secret places that have been dormant for way too long.

We both freeze, just looking at each other.

Grant caught mid-stride with his powerful calves flexed.

I can't talk, my mouth bone-dry and my palms sweaty.

Oh God, I can't help that I'm breathing faster.

I shouldn't be this turned on just *looking* at him.

I almost hate how much he affects me.

And I wonder just how obvious I am, when the glint in his eye sharpens.

Just a heated flicker, turning hazel to melted honey. He spears me with a long look until it feels like he's undressing me with his eyes.

I can feel my nipples peaking, teasing against my bra, my shirt.

My breasts suddenly feel too heavy, too sensitive, too empty, aching for large, rough hands.

I scrub my hands against my thighs, licking my lips and struggling for words.

Finally, he breaks the silence with a slow, heated smile.

"Shower's all yours," he says, moving toward his bedroom.

Aaand I'm speechless.

I almost let him go without another word, my tongue too knotted to move.

"Th-thanks," I manage. "Oh, and I'm sorry you had to get Nell. Mom kept me around longer than I expected."

Even if my mind's so far from anything else I can't even remember *why*.

"Good thing you did," he drawls, pausing with one big hand on the doorknob, but all he's doing is giving me a distracting view of the way his waist dips toward his Apollo's belt. "I almost forgot you were picking her up and might've went out there anyway. Would've panicked for a minute trying to figure out where she was."

I nod.

Concern darkens Grant's eyes as he tilts his head, studying me. "Did something happen? It's not like you to forget."

Um, yeah.

That's when I remember the shadow, the figure by my car.

The stalker I probably hallucinated.

I don't want to worry him.

So I just pin on a smile and shake my head, letting that sobering thought drag me back to reality so I can stop drooling like I'm just discovering hot men for the first time.

"I just have a lot on my mind," I say. "Worrying about Mom and Ros, you know. But I'll get Nell next time for sure. Have to earn my keep around here somehow."

"Like hell," he growls sincerely. "I'm glad you're around."

Right.

From the way my heart's thumping like it's about to split at its seams?

This new, honest, uncensored Grant might kill me.

Especially with that slow smile, almost like he *knows*.

"What about you?" I ask.

Somehow, there's this extra weight in his eyes that wasn't there earlier when I saw him at the station.

"Can't complain. Survived another bout of code pink and got into the shower before the smell set in."

"Lucky man," I say, snickering. "Are you sure you're still up for a movie tonight after all that?"

"Gotta take the edge off wrangling pigs some way, don't I?" He smiles. "Yeah, Butterfly. Wouldn't miss it for the whole damn world."

And off he goes.

Before he disappears into his room, a shaft of evening light spills into the hall, kissing every line of his body with lickable gold before it's gone as the door shuts.

Leaving me marooned, dizzy, and nearly panting and hot around the collar, plus a few other rebellious places.

Oof.

I've never had a conversation that felt like foreplay before.

"Gonna faint?" chirps behind me.

I yelp, whirling with my heart skipping a beat.

Nell grins up at me, her eyes far too knowing for such a little girl.

"You look kinda winded, Miss Philia. You got asthma? My friend Sadie does. She's got a nee-hale-er."

"Inhaler," I correct absently, then shake my head. "And no, I don't. Grant just startled me, that's all. I'm fine. You didn't finish your homework, did you?"

She bats her eyelashes. "I'll finish it after the movie. It's history tonight, easy as pie. I wanna pick something fun to wear."

"Uh-huh." I eye her skeptically, holding out my pinky. "No trying to stay up late to watch cartoons. Homework, then bed. Promise me?"

Nell hooks her pinky in mine.

"Pinky promise one hundred percent."

Laughing, I tug my hand free and tickle her lightly. "Go on and get dressed."

She runs off with a messy giggle and disappears into her room. I look after her, feeling a smile spread across my lips.

I don't know how I fell into this situation.

But it's nice.

Feeling a little calmer, I shower off quickly, deliberately cranking it to cold before I wimp out and switch it to hot water.

When I'm done, I wrap myself in a towel and bolt for the guest room, skittering past Grant's door.

If he ever sees me naked, I can't be looking like a wet cat with my hair jabbed out everywhere.

If, huh?

Getting awful hopeful there, girl?

Shut up, brain.

Flushed, I shut myself in the guest room and lean back against the door, pressing a hand over my fluttering heart.

Holy hell, just what *am* I hoping for tonight?

I shake myself from my thoughts and rummage through my things until I find a pair of low-rise jeans that aren't too low for a family film. They're comfortably snug but not skintight and a few little rips over the thighs could be innocent or double as a subtle tease.

My white silk camisole hangs loosely, paper-thin when it catches the light. I pair it with an open-knit cardigan that ties across my breasts, a sunny yellow shade. Like that'll convince the thin thing to actually keep me warm tonight.

Everyone and their grandma keeps distracting me from getting that coat.

I pull on a pair of cute brown leather ankle boots and step out to meet them.

He's waiting at the bottom of the stairs with Nell, who's dressed up in pink, complete with a pair of strap-on butterfly wings. She has Mr. Pickle tucked under her arm, while Grant—

Oh my God.

I don't think I've seen him clean up so nice since he went stag to his senior prom with Ethan.

I don't know where he even finds clothes that fit him, but his button-down shirt fits like it was tailored just right, skintight with the buttons straining over his chest.

The pale blue brings out the swarthiness of his skin and the rich darkness of his hair.

His dark blue boot-cut jeans look sharp, well worn and casual, clinging to his hips and strong thighs. The black leather of his belt completes the look with the same coarse pattern as the leather of his boots.

He looks like a rough and tumble rancher ready to ride out with six-shooters at dawn, a gunslinger's dream.

Especially when he has *Ethan's hat* again, clasped against his chest as he tips me a polite bow.

Oh, my.

...it wouldn't be a night out with Grant without a little hint of heartbreak, would it?

"Ophelia," he says.

It does weird things to me—him saying my name with that hat clasped in hand and that look on his face that says he's only seeing me.

I try not to go to pieces as I pause on the stairs, drinking him in before I force myself to look away and refocus on Nell as I descend.

"So this is your prettiest outfit, huh?"

She smiles so wide I see the gaps in her teeth. "My absolute princess-est outfit ever."

I give Grant a skeptically amused look.

He only shakes his head.

"Don't try to argue. She'll strip and streak down Second Avenue if you make her change."

"...let's avoid that. I—"

I stop cold as Grant holds out his arm.

Oh, crap, it's happening.

This really is a bona fide date, isn't it?

Maybe it's a family date, sure, but *it's a date.*

Swallowing my nerves, I slip my hand into Grant's arm— and suddenly find my other hand occupied with a tiny set of fingers.

The trust in the gesture melts me like butter.

Together, we start toward the door until Grant stops at the coatrack, frowning.

"You still didn't buy a jacket, did you?"

"Um, I forgot?" I press my lips together, trying not to smile.

Grant gives me the fiercest look.

While Nell watches us with a giggle, her uncle yanks his fur-lined leather jacket down from the coatrack and pulls it open for me with a commanding glare.

Wear it, he tells me without words.

I blink at him.

Welp. I'm never going to stop blushing at this rate.

After a moment, I let go of Nell's hand and slip my arms into the jacket sleeves, letting Grant wrap it around me.

Wrap *him* around me, his leather and scent enveloping me as I tilt into his arms.

That heavy coat is so large it dwarfs me and I don't mind one bit.

Then he pulls back.

"What about you?" I finger the collar, turning to face him shyly.

"I've got my police jacket," he says gruffly, tugging it down from the hook and sliding into it with a flex of his chest so strong it looks like he could snap the buttons right off. He gives me another fierce, guarded look that sets off butterflies. "Let's go."

No argument here.

Nell and I exchange an almost conspiratorial look.

She slips her little hand into mine, and I slide mine into Grant's arm again. We step out into the night like this is the new normal.

Our normal, period.

Like somehow, it's just this easy, falling into this patch-work family.

I try not to think too hard about what that might mean.

The ride to the restaurant—a local steakhouse—is quiet and comfortable.

Nell carries on a conversation with Mr. Pickle in the back. Apparently, she doesn't want us knowing his business, frequently bending and whispering in the unicorn's ear.

I alternate between watching her in the rearview mirror and watching Grant next to me.

Every now and then, I catch him watching me, too.

Dinner is lively, mostly gentle teasing and trying to keep Nell from splattering herself with steak sauce.

I almost don't taste my food, not when I'm so alive in this happy moment, this feeling of togetherness like we all belong at this table.

Once we're done stuffing ourselves, we get out just in time to head to the movies.

It's a short drive, and soon we're surrounded by the buttery scent of movie theatre popcorn and pretzels.

In the concession line, Grant pulls Nell up on his shoulders so he doesn't lose her in the ballooning late night crowd. Another thing that never changes in Redhaven.

The theatre always turns into a madhouse in the fall, the cooler weather driving people in.

It's the usual townsfolk doubled by tourists coming for a quiet date night in our rustic little theatre that still looks like it belongs to the Vaudeville era.

How many hours of my life did I spend in this place growing up?

Usually tagging along with Ethan and Grant—and just as often sandwiched between them so I could have my two favorite men to myself.

As we file off to the room marked on our tickets, we exchange a fond look.

I think he's remembering older, easier days, too.

It's like stepping back in time, but this time without the charged, uncertain potential of our younger selves.

Now, we're all grown up and so many things are set in stone.

But it doesn't bother me tonight.

Not with him.

It's also no surprise when Nell parks herself between us.

We trade indulgent looks over her head.

So much for make-out sessions.

Not long after the previews, Grant presses one big hand over Nell's eyes and leans across her to brush his lips on mine over her head, lingering in a way that heightens all the sweetness inside.

"Later," he promises against my lips, mostly mouthing the words.

A vow that reaches down inside me, stoking a wildfire.

And I shiver from the hot flash before settling down with Nell happily snuggled between us and already sleepy. Her small head falls against my shoulder and her feet spill over the side onto Grant.

I never thought I'd have this much fun watching a kids' movie.

It's another movie with the squeaky yellow things in overalls. There's got to be like thirty of them by now, yet Nell wakes up and laughs with delight like she's seeing their antics for the first time.

But I'm honestly more entertained by Grant's scowling.

He watches the film like it's personally offending him with how illogically silly it is, only for his glower to soften whenever Nell kicks her feet and giggles.

I don't know how I hold it in.

It's the sweetest first date ever, this little girl tugging at my heartstrings and that big lunk making me so warm every time he snorts and shakes his head like it weighs a ton.

Halfway through the film, his arm stretches across the back of Nell's seat so his forearm rests lightly on my shoulders. Grant walks his fingers up and down my arm, something I can feel even through the thick jacket.

I love this vibe.

This quiet, simple thing might be the cure I need.

Erasing all the pain, all the hurt, all the bad memories of this town for just one night, making this place feel like home again.

My face hurts from smiling by the time the movie ends.

It's like the first half of the day never happened.

I never thought I could go so easily from feeling so upset, so hurt, to so enchanted.

Like all my problems fade away into a dream and soon I'm back where I belong.

Nell looks hilariously drowsy by the time the lights come up. Toward the end of the movie her shrieking laughter died down to a quiet smile.

Now Grant lifts her up to ride piggyback, one arm hooked under her knee.

His other hand tangles in mine.

Quietly, easily, such a small thing and yet it fills me with brightness.

I'm pretty sure Nell's totally out by the time we buckle her into the back seat.

I'm expecting to head back to Grant's house, put Nell to bed, and if I'm lucky get a long kiss at the door to the guest room.

I'm not expecting it when Grant turns off a more familiar street, instead, and drives us to his parents' house.

The porch light is already on.

His folks are waiting—wait, was this planned?

They come out and gather Nell, but not without hugs for me.

They're huggers by nature, always have been, and that feeling of *home* intensifies.

As Mrs. Faircross lifts Nell up, though, Nell reaches for me, her fingers fumbling sleepily.

"I'm... m'gonna break my promise..." she mumbles with her eyes closed. "About my homework."

Grant gives me a puzzled look. I smile sheepishly.

"She didn't want to finish her homework before the movie," I explain. "So she pinky promised me she'd do it after if I let her go pick out an outfit."

"Ah." He nods at her pink dress, then leans in and kisses the little girl's forehead.

Yep. He's trying to turn my ovaries into live grenades tonight.

"You can do it in the morning, Nelly-girl," he tells her. "It's my fault you broke your promise to Philia. You didn't do any wrong." A little smile sneaks past his beard. "Love you, rug rat."

"Uncle Grant." Nell sighs, lifting her head to press a kiss into his beard. "Love you, papa bear."

"Papa bear?" I look at him, barely holding in a laugh.

He shakes his head rapidly.

Margaret Faircross smiles fondly and nudges Grant's arm. "I've got her, Son. Go enjoy the rest of your night out. Both of you."

Wow. I still don't know what's going on.

But Grant set this up, didn't he?

Having Nell stay the night over at his parents' place... that has to mean he really wants me all to himself.

Alone.

Eep.

I give him a wide-eyed questioning look as we climb back into his truck.

My heart's stuck in my throat as he starts the engine and glances over with a faint smile.

"Somewhere I want to take you," he tells me, backing the truck out to the street.

Tentatively, I scoot across the wide front seat and lean against his arm.

Soon, he's driving one-handed with his other arm wrapped around me, gathering me close against his side, making me feel him in every breath.

I'm certain I could stay like this forever.

I'm not even thinking about where he's driving us. Not when I'm content to snuggle into his arm and just stay there, breathing him in.

Most girls don't grow up and actually get the guy who haunted their daydreams.

Especially not after he busts their heart like an ornament and only shows up again so many years later.

Tonight is special.

For once in my life, I feel lucky.

Like the karma wheel might finally be paying me back for all the bad luck.

When Grant pulls the truck to a halt and kills the engine, I open my eyes and lift my head, blinking curiously.

My breath catches the instant I make out the wrought-iron fence, the arched iron gate.

Oh, crud.

Are we really here?

The shapes of headstones leave no doubt, glinting like grey bones in the headlights until he turns them off.

"Grant?"

"Do you know," he says, his arm still heavy around me, his gaze trained thoughtfully through the windshield, "we've never come here together?"

"O-oh. You're right," I whisper.

For a breathless second, I stare at the gate, my heart

beating slow and heavy before I reach for Grant's hand and hold it tight.

"Okay," I breathe. "Let's go see him together."

It's so strange, walking through the tall grass together, breathing in the scent of old flowers left behind on the graves of people who will never get to smell them.

It always hurts, every time I come here—even if I haven't dropped by in nearly a decade.

The last time I was here, the grave marker was still fresh, and so meaningless when there was nothing buried there.

Just Ethan's name on the headstone with no date of death. Because we don't know if he's alive or dead, but we decided to honor him anyway.

Like that'll satisfy his ghost, or at least that haunted feeling hanging over us.

Like everyone just wanted to bury their old pains when we couldn't find a body.

Shockingly, it doesn't hurt so much tonight.

With Grant's hand in mine and his silent presence at my side, his warmth, his steadiness, it feels like something else.

Maybe like a duty that needs to be done.

Like something I need to really, truly come home.

Most people find graveyards pretty spooky at night. But the Redhaven Cemetery is a quiet place full of old bones, old roots, old history.

Serenity lives here.

Old spirits sleep like they should without any disturbance.

The only sounds are a few owls calling through the night. The faint scratchy whisper of naked tree branches rubbing together. Our feet on the grass, moving together at a steady pace.

The moon looms over us, huge and autumn-orange, and

the stars are so bright in the clear sky I can see the Milky Way sprawling across the nightscape.

It's a refreshing sight.

In Miami, the only stars I could ever see were the shooting meteors of taillights moving by the thousands on broad highways.

Maybe there's something to love about this place, after all.

I look at Grant.

He hasn't said a word, but there's a certain gravity in the air. I wonder if he's talking to Ethan in the back of his mind.

I know I am.

My big brother, forever alive in my heart, wherever he is.

And our feet lead us automatically to the quiet corner plot beneath an old satsuma tree with low-hanging branches.

Ethan's plot is right next to his father's. The headstone looks newer, but it's more worn than I remember. Moss has started growing into the inscription.

ETHAN SANDERSON
Baby, come home.

GOD.

I remember my mother crying while she worked out what to write. And then bawling her eyes out even more when she finally found the right words.

Not that anything will ever sound *right* when you had to bury a son with no body and no answers.

A son who may be alive out there somewhere, no matter how slim the odds.

We stop together, though, standing peacefully side by side.

His hand tightens in mine and I smile, my mouth aching with a sweet pain.

"Hi, Ethan," I whisper. "Long time no see."

"Hey, dumbass," Grant growls. "It's been a few. Where you been hiding?"

I can't help a choked laugh and I turn my face into his arm.

"I can see it now," I murmur. It hurts my throat, yet I'm still smiling so much and I can't explain why. "He'd put you in a headlock for that and ask who's the dumbass now."

"Like he could reach." Grant snorts affectionately. The growl in his voice seems more tender. "So he'd just end up hugging me like the big lanky softie he was."

"Right. Until he tackled you at the knees and put you on the floor," I tease.

"Good luck knocking me down with a thousand hours of training and years on the force. I wouldn't move an inch for that guy."

Liar.

The softness in his dark-mocha eyes tells me he'd jump off a cliff taller than a skyscraper just to have one more conversation with his best friend.

Oh, I'm so gutted, but I'm smiling.

Pulling my hand loose from Grant, I raise both hands with my fingers curled. "I remember how he got you. Every time."

His eyes widen and he takes a wary step back. "Butterfly, don't you dare. I'm a grown-ass man and this is hardly the time or place—don't tickle—fuck!"

What can I say?

Since Ethan isn't here, someone has to do it.

So I lunge at him and Grant hops back with the most ridiculous, funny sound I've ever heard.

I never knew a man his size could *squeak* in baritone.

We both freeze, him staring warily, me looking on in surprise, my fingers still curled and reaching for him like claws.

"I wasn't actually gonna," I whisper sheepishly.

Grant startles me again with that rich, hearty bass laugh that trembles my heart.

I can't help myself.

I'm laughing too, and we're falling into each other. I lean on him hard.

Yes, there's a saying about whistling past graveyards, but... let's hope laughing our heads off in one isn't too blasphemous.

I needed this.

Call it catharsis.

And I'm so much more relaxed as I slump against him, resting my cheek on his chest and curling my hands against his arm.

"I think he'd like this," I say. "Us, here with him, I mean. Laughing like we're still teenage screwballs. Ethan wouldn't want us wallowing in misery."

"We have been, though," Grant answers. "Or maybe it's just me."

"No, no... I'm just as guilty. Even in Florida when I thought about this place, about my brother... *you* were always in the back of my mind." I push my arms around his neck. "I always felt alone in Miami. Part of me was scared to come back here, I think. To all these memories. Even though the only people who could possibly ever know how I feel are here."

"The people who miss Ethan the most," he finishes.

My heart dives. It's like he's read my mind.

"Yeah. That." Shaking my head, I burrow my face into Grant's massive chest. "But I'm also talking about the people who look at me like I was somehow involved in that whole mess. It's almost worse, now that the truth is out about what really happened to Celeste Graves. Just feels like they pity me."

"And you," Grant says, slipping his fingers under my chin and tilting my head up, "are too damn proud for pity, Miss Sanderson."

I giggle.

"I thought you'd say too bratty." I smile up at him. "I'd ask for a kiss, but..." I tilt my head at the gravestone and nod.

"Woman, if I could kiss you in front of your brother, you'd have known how I felt a lot sooner," Grant growls, glancing at the headstone thoughtfully. "Feels damn weird saying that when we both know he's not really in there."

"But it feels like he's here anyway, doesn't it?"

"Yeah," Grant answers after a pause. "It does."

We stand there for a few minutes, hand in hand, his warmth and his big jacket and his bigger presence wrapped around me like a blanket.

For the first time in ages, I don't feel so alone.

It really is like Ethan's right here, right now, standing with us.

Hopefully, giving us his blessing.

I feel like that blessing stays with us as we slip away, still hand in hand.

It's a serene walk back to the truck with Grant's fingers in mine, chasing away the October chill.

In the car, I'm happy to bundle myself up in his jacket like a blanket and snuggle against his side, drowsing while he drives.

Nothing breaks the quiet growl of the engine and the soothing whir of tires on the road until we're almost home.

Then Grant's voice rises up like low thunder between us.

"Sorry it wasn't anything spectacular tonight," he says. "First date in a cemetery—if you want to call it that."

"It was exactly what I needed. No fooling. Plus, we had dinner and a movie. Extra points for that."

He snorts with amusement.

I rub my cheek against his shoulder before I make myself pull away as he turns into the driveway and parks. We slip out together, and as we walk to the door, I steal his hand, tangling our fingers together.

The possessive squeeze he gives me sends a fresh wave of butterflies spinning through me.

"I needed to feel like I was part of something," I say softly. "To feel like I was home. Everything's been so off-kilter for so long, Grant." We climb the porch together and stop, locking eyes in the shadows and the pale-gold glow of the porch light. "I've never felt like I fit in anywhere. Now, I wonder if it's because I was so busy running away from the only place I ever did."

He gives me one of those long, stern Grant looks I used to find so unreadable.

Only, now I realize he's just taking me in.

Staring because he wants to.

Because he wants to *see* me.

Because he wants to warm me to my core with nothing more than a glance that says, *woman, you are beautiful.*

Mission accomplished.

I'm burning just as much from his gaze as the heat of his palm settled against my cheek.

"And where do you fit here?" he whispers.

"...not sure yet." I sway toward him, smiling like I'm about to come apart. "But I'd like to find out."

The kiss comes like a summer rain.

Slow and quiet, then suddenly it's a rush of pure adrenaline drenching me as his lips take mine, possess me, drown me in a world that's nothing but Grant.

Here, there are no worries.

I can't be sad or stressed or afraid. Not when his arms wind around me this tight and his beard tickles my throat.

The raw, rough taste of him melts against my lips like the warmest salted caramel.

I'm so hard-wired with need that I moan almost instantly, some hot tight core inside me knotting up even as the rest of me goes loose and melty with desire.

His shoulders feel so strong under my palms, manly muscle stretched over iron bones.

I can feel his heartbeat against that powerful barrel chest, a wild thudding that echoes my own—and for a moment that tender, slow kiss turns thieving and renders me breathless, so powerful my knees go out and my whole being ignites.

Holy hell.

When we break apart, I'm panting.

Clutching my trembling fingers in his jacket and looking up at him in a daze.

He's so *handsome*, and the evening light flutters in his dark eyes like moths searching for a gold-lit heaven.

"Inside?" I whisper hopefully.

Please say yes.

This ache for him that's built inside me my entire life might tear me apart.

Grant's only answer is a loud, needy growl before he pulls away and practically breaks his house key, jamming it into the lock like a man possessed.

I bite back a giggle, covering my mouth with my hand.

I feel like a giddy little girl again, knowing he wants me *that* much.

And that feeling only intensifies when he gives me a familiar dirty, disgusted look. But it's also so much more now.

There's no mistaking what's underneath, coursing like blood.

That smolder.

The same heat that burns incessantly in my core and trembles through me as he shoves the door open and pulls me inside the dark house.

God, I want him right here, right now, but I don't want the anticipation to end.

As I slip past him, I deliberately pull away just out of his reach, backing toward the steps and loving how intensely he looks at me.

The man stalks after me like a hunter and fills me with a thrill.

This big, powerful beast—and I've practically got him on a leash, drawing him after me with every step.

"You wanna play games, Butterfly?" he rumbles, his voice scorched.

"Maybe I just want to be civilized," I tease, reaching back to find the stair rail and guiding myself up the first few steps. "At least use the bed. Don't make me beg you to take me over the back of the sofa like a heathen."

His expression darkens deliciously as his eyes rake me from head to toe.

"Ophelia, fuck," he snarls. "There ain't a goddamned thing civilized about what I'm about to do to you."

Holy hell.

There's a frozen moment where I realize what he's about to do as his body tenses and lowers slightly.

And I let out a laughing squeal and turn, bolting up the stairs with a wild man hot on my heels.

I don't make it far.

He has too long of a stride—and let's be real—I *want* to be caught tonight.

I want to be *his* more than I want my next breath.

And it fills me with electric excitement and heady joy

when he catches me on the stairs and sweeps me into his arms, holding me tight against his chest.

The reality of Grant wanting me and making no secret of it is better than any childish daydream. I can't help grinning as I twine my arms around his neck, looking up at him.

"Oh, no," I lilt tauntingly. "The big bad wolf's caught Little Red. Whatever are you going to do with me?"

"Drop you on your knees and put your brat mouth to work," he growls, even as his grip on me tightens and he carries me toward his bedroom with determined steps. "Or I could just throw you down here, make you sit on my face, and eat you alive."

Dead.

I'm sure I'm not alive anymore as I look at him and whisper, "I don't think I'd mind being eaten."

"Woman, you're gonna regret saying that when I take you literally," Grant says, then elbows the door open and carries me into his room.

I barely get a flash of the moonlight-drenched space, the dark masculine colors, the Spartan neatness, the heavy solid furniture before he's tumbling me onto the bed.

I sprawl out on my back against the comforter, and my entire world becomes Grant.

Him kneeling over me and his bulk takes up my entire field of vision.

His hands fall, flanking both sides of my body until his arms cage me.

His eyes glowing like bonfires in the darkness, that handsome face hovering over mine, gleaming with a hunger I've never seen.

My heart throbs violently.

I reach up to stroke his jaw, his beard—and his animalistic stare softens as he leans into my touch, rubbing himself against my skin like the wild thing he is, stealing my breath away.

Feral.

Powerful.

Stubborn.

Harsh.

And allowing me to touch him like I'm the only force in the world that can ever tame him.

Oh, I want this man to make me his so much.

"Grant," I whisper, trailing my fingers down his throat. "Grant, kiss me."

"I never wanted to stop," he exhales roughly, sinking down to reclaim my mouth.

There's a tremor now, almost like he's holding back a raging river with the flimsiest dam.

The way he kisses me with such gentleness, but with such tension lashing through his body.

A body that presses down slowly as he lowers over me.

And God, I almost forget the feeling of his lips against mine when I discover how delicious it feels to be under a man this huge.

There may have been a couple men in my life while I was away from Redhaven, sure—but no one had Grant's sheer size or overwhelming presence.

No one else could ever take his place.

Not in my mind.

Not in my heart.

Definitely not in the desperate craving of my flesh.

I crush myself against him, arching my back, leaning up into the heat of his wild, surging kiss.

His mouth nearly bruises mine, all harsh beard and seething lips.

His teeth torment in taunting nips that make me clench

in places I'm pretty sure no man has ever touched—and I desperately want him to.

Moaning, I run my fingers feverishly through his beard, letting my mouth go slack in total surrender, giving myself over to his tongue, every lick and tease that lays claim in the most obscene ways.

But not nearly as obscene as his hands skimming over my body, dragging at my clothes, gripping my flesh like he's trying to *shape me* in the image of his darkest desires.

Everywhere, his touch leaves a burning handprint.

It's like I'm already naked.

And when he angles his hips, when his broad body shoves my legs apart so I have to strain to fit him and I'm spread so open that I feel it as his hips ram mine and that hard straining spear of his cock presses against me...

I nearly fall apart forever.

"Grant," I pant, rolling my hips, shuddering and almost *flinching* when my panties press into delicate flesh as he rubs against me.

Until now, I never knew the phrase 'dripping wet' could be a real thing.

"*Grant.*"

An agonized groan spills out of him as he tears his mouth from mine and drops his brow to my shoulder.

I twine my arms around his neck.

That's when I realize it's not just me.

He's shaking, too.

His entire body feels so tense he's nearly trembling, his hands gripping me so hard.

"You're about to fuckin' break me, Ophelia. You know that?" he rasps against my shoulder, his voice thick and feral and electrifying.

"Grant," I whisper again, running my legs along his.

His eyes pinch shut and he exhales a breath like pure dragon smoke.

"Don't say my name like that again. You'll murder me."

Somehow, that delights me.

I've always had a bratty streak with this man.

After the briefest hesitation, I turn my head, brushing my lips against his ear.

"*Grant*," I purr.

It's like flipping a switch.

His entire beastly body goes rock-hard.

His cock pulses against me so violently I feel it jerking, straining against his jeans like it has a mind of its own.

Growling, he braces his hands against the bed and pushes back, gazing down with heat and shadows in his eyes like a leaping campfire.

Right before he very deliberately begins stripping my clothes off.

I've never had anything like this.

You can barely call it foreplay.

But it's the silent intensity in Grant's unblinking, burning stare that makes me a mess.

The slow, calculated movements as he teases the little ribbon tying my cardigan shut.

The manic way he touches me with every movement, his knuckles grazing my breasts as he tugs the cardigan open.

It's so sexy, yet never quite satisfies, leaving me aching for more, my nipples throbbing and peaking, dying for his hands and mouth.

It's beyond hypnotic.

"Damn, woman. Goddamn, you are fucked."

No kidding.

I just wish he'd make it happen faster.

He has me in thrall, helpless to even move, trapped in his carnivorous eyes as he lifts me up with one broad hand.

He handles me effortlessly, peeling the cardigan away and pulling my thin camisole over my head.

I can't even whimper as he lays me back down and slowly runs his fingers through my hair, fanning it out in a halo.

This vibe, it's almost frightening.

It's so *raw*, so real, so alive with feeling I have to curl my toes so I don't black out.

Big bad wolf, indeed.

I never imagined I'd be the delicacy he wants to swallow whole, but here I am, willing prey and all.

There's definitely a slow, wolfish smile on his lips as he presses his fingers to the apex of my ribs, slowly dragging them up, engraving the roughness of his skin in my flesh.

As his middle finger hooks under the clasp in the center of my bra, I inhale sharply.

The lace cups drag against my sensitive nipples, pulling a whimper from the back of my throat.

"Gra—"

"Hush," he demands.

There's pure command in the soft, gritty sound that liquefies my bones.

And then makes my heart skip, my stomach flip, as a deliberate flick of his thumb releases the clasp, leaving me naked and already wrecked.

I almost want to hide from his eyes.

Almost.

Except I've wanted this man to want me since before I was old enough to have the dirty thoughts rampaging through my head.

It's almost unbearable to have him look at me like he's always wanted me just as much.

It hurts when I think of the last ten years, the two of us apart and still burning for each other.

Always in denial when I could have had *this* if I hadn't

run, if he hadn't put a shark-infested moat between his heart and the entire world.

But I'm too caught up in the moment to dwell on the past.

I start to lay a hand across my chest—then Grant catches my wrist.

I flush as he pushes my arm down on the bed, pinning me lightly by the wrist. He holds me captive as he pushes one bra cup aside and then molds his hand over the curve of my breast, fully enveloping it in the heat of his large, masculine hand.

I'm so sensitive it almost hurts as his fingers sink into my flesh, making me feel my own softness in his strength.

I bite down on a husky noise spilling out of me, swinging my hips, gasping when I clench my thighs and grind him deeper into me.

Oh God, *deeper.*

He's made me such a mess, the lightest touch tearing me apart.

This feeling of yearning *emptiness* inside that just wants him to touch me and fill me and bring our bodies together until we can't tell ourselves apart.

But Grant seems intent on this slow, sweet torture.

Even as I twist under him, he burns me with little heat-shocks as his calloused thumb traces slow circles over the peak of my nipple, toying with it, sending waves of pleasure cascading through me.

I close my eyes in rapture and throw my head back with a needy cry.

I'm so not ready.

Completely unprepared for the moment when his hot mouth descends again, kissing me so lusciously deep.

When his body lowers on mine.

When his hips rock like mad, taunting me with the friction of what I need so bad, stealing my breath away.

He kneads my breast, teases and pinches and thumbs my nipple.

Always with this perfect rhythm until I can't help moving against him.

I barely notice when his hands go lower, flicking my jeans open, dragging the zipper down and flinging them aside.

My belly sucks in, clenching as he skims his fingers over the waistband of my panties.

I whimper against his mouth.

But that only makes him slide deeper, his lips dominating mine, nearly fucking my mouth with slow, lazy strokes.

Heaven help me.

I'm hyper-tuned to the lightest touch, shivering with how *close* he is to the heat pooling between my thighs as his fingers search the scalloped line of lace clinging to my hips.

When his fingers hook in the fabric, I'm breathless.

He stretches it away from my flesh, cutting sizzling movements against my pulsing, wet lips.

I rise up with a cry, sinking my teeth into his bottom lip before he shreds my panties.

He actually tears them in two as he tosses them aside.

Holy shit!

I try to cling desperately, but he breaks the fusion of our lips, catching my eye with a devilish smile—right before his mouth descends on my jaw and I finally start to get what it means to be *devoured*.

His lips and teeth are everywhere.

Sucking, biting, skating down my throat, across my shoulders, my collarbones.

It's an onslaught I'm powerless to defend against as every sting of pleasure just keys me up higher and higher until I'm writhing chaos, kicking my feet against the sheets, curling my toes, clutching at his hair—and fisting a handful as he takes my nipple into his mouth.

"Grant!"

I'm so gone.

The suction, the wetness, the heat—*oh, the heat*—I feel it plunging to my depths like lava.

My vision whites.

My breath stalls.

It can't be.

But it is.

Unbelievably, I'm already coming.

Grant flipping Faircross just owns me that good.

And judging from his rough growls, he enjoys every evil second of taking me apart, leaving me speechless and still begging his name with every breath.

His tongue continues marching across my skin when he's done with my nipples.

Down, down.

The swell of my breast.

The slope of my stomach.

My upper thighs, my inner thighs, his face sliding down my twisting body, and then—

I feel his breath.

There.

The scratch of his beard, high on my inner thighs.

His shoulders, pressing my legs apart, forcing me open, exposing me to the heat of his skin invading my most secret places.

I rake my fingers through his hair, the nerves drawn up tight inside me as I look at him with my eyes narrowed.

"G-Grant..."

So, he was serious about devouring me whole. I'm just not sure I'm ready—will I ever be?

But the way he looks up the length of my body...

I already know there's no mercy in those eyes.

And absolutely no scenario where they won't fulfill every devious promise beaming into my soul.

"You said you wouldn't mind being eaten," he mocks.

My eyes widen.

"Oh, you—*ah!*"

One fast lick.

That's all it takes to steal my breath, my thoughts, as his tongue sears my clit—and then a long, slow lick with just the tip, tracing wet-burning lines on my quivering flesh.

Feeding a slow-moving explosion demanding release.

How?

Just how does he make me feel like this when it hasn't even been five minutes since the last time I erupted?

Everything inside me tightens in a screaming knot.

I squeeze my thighs hard against him, whining in the back of my throat.

Yes, it's only the beginning.

He tastes and teases me in almost sadistic strokes, never letting me doubt as he scours me with broad sweeping licks and then stings me deep with savage thrusts of his tongue.

It's unpredictable, shocking, rocking and tearing me apart.

But when he thrusts his tongue fully inside me, teasing that emptiness inside me while his lips suck and caress—

I lose it.

I've wanted this for too long.

I have no defenses left whatsoever.

No resistance to the brute pleasure he slams through me and the wondrous beat of my heart.

No hesitation as I hear him in every thrust, growling *come for me, Philia. Give it all up.*

It's just a few thrusts of that rough tongue inside me, rhythmic and demanding and swift, before the knot inside me bursts.

My vision goes white-hot.

Full body whiplash.

I wrap my legs around Grant's shoulders, screaming, every inch of me twisting in convulsions.

I come hard enough to break my lungs, wringing myself dry, dancing to his whim as he licks my overstimulated flesh to the brink of insanity.

And I don't come down until he says I do.

Until I'm spent and he's good and ready and softening his strokes.

Even as the orgasm fades, he's still running his tongue over me like he wants every bit of hot, sticky sweetness spilling out of me.

Only now I'm a human live wire.

My skin, one raw nerve.

I'm nearly sobbing as I tug at his hair.

But he won't stop—and I think I could even come again—when Grant lets out a satisfied rumble and finally lifts his head, looking at me with lazy satisfaction on his face.

"Not sorry," he says with a slow, unapologetic grin. I blush deep enough to burn at the sight of his beard dotted with my slickness. "Just couldn't get enough of you saying my name like that while I took your pussy to the moon."

I make a spluttering, embarrassed sound.

"I... I wasn't... I didn't say your name!"

...*did I?*

Um, I might have confessed to murdering Julius Caesar while he had me like that.

So high on pleasure I didn't know my own name.

And it looks like he knows that as he pushes himself up with his grin widening.

"Even better," he rumbles, unbuttoning his shirt and shrugging out of it, then stripping his undershirt over his head.

He bares the broad expanse of his chiseled, tanned, scar-pecked chest. I love the way the dark hair outlines the inner grooves of sharp, mounded abdominal muscles and the stylized tattoos that start on his biceps and curl over his shoulders like the stripes of some large exotic cat.

"You must've been enjoying it, at least, if you didn't even know you were screamin' for me like a banshee."

Oh, I want to kill him.

But I want to kiss him more.

He's so good at pissing me off in the best ways.

When he moves up my body to kiss me again, when I taste myself on his lips as he smothers my mouth and crushes my body with his, I'm so ready.

A full decade worth of killing desire that's been building up inside him comes bursting out in wild urgency, this need to be inside me.

The loud rasp of his zipper.

The crinkle of a condom packet.

Suddenly, that flesh that was only teasing me through layers of fabric before is pressed against me, nothing barring skin from skin but a paper-thin layer of latex that does nothing to buffer his heat.

The anticipation destroys me a hundred more times.

Grant's kiss gentles as I press my thighs against his hips.

He brushes my hair back, cupping my face.

Those honey-brown eyes are so tender, but so possessive I can never imagine belonging to anyone else.

He kisses me again with the weight of the world.

"You sure you want this, Ophelia?" His tone tells me his leash is on the verge of snapping and yet it's so powerful to know he's holding himself back. Making sure it's really okay. "You sure you want me?"

"I've never wanted anything more, Grant. Never," I whisper, brushing my lips against his.

With a raw sound, he fuses our mouths together.

He catches my wrists, pinning them to the bed, leaving me helpless and open for him.

His hips go to work, rocking, teasing, gliding the length of his cock up and down against me until I whimper against his lips.

When he finds the perfect position, all the better to ruin me, it's on.

The pulsing head of his cock storms the emptiness inside me.

Hot pressure.

Animalistic power.

One slow, fateful, all-consuming thrust.

Then he glides into me to the hilt, molding me around his thickness like a force of nature.

So intimate I almost want to hide, yet I can't dream of stopping this.

Of course, he's just as big below the belt as the rest of him.

I swear, I can feel every vein as his cock splits me open.

It's like he's breaking me in half, but the sharpness is glorious and wonderful and addicting.

I just want more—*more!*—wrapping my legs around his hips, digging my heels into the small of his back, lifting myself up into him.

I don't even realize I'm biting his mouth until I taste the sharp metallic hint of bruises.

But he bites me right back, marking me.

His breaths rush so hot, the rough hair of his chest scraping against my breasts in shivers of pleasure.

His body moves so hard against me as every muscle tightens like a spring.

Low, guttural pleasure sounds melt between our warring lips as he sinks deeper, *deeper.*

I feel like he's kissing me from the inside out, marching sensations with every inch of him that fills me.

He drives the breath from my lungs, my chest aching and hurting by the time he gives one last short, sharp, sanity-shattering thrust and buries himself in fully.

Our bodies lock.

If I thought I was sensitive before, it's nothing compared to the wildness that ripples over my skin now.

And I clench my fingers, tossing frantically under him, still begging with my body.

"*Ophelia.*"

He whispers my name into my lips.

Imprinting his desire like a prayer.

And then, oh, *then...*

He moves.

He takes.

He demolishes.

He leads me in his rhythm, in his power, until the world pivots by the slow, deep strength of those plunging strokes, piercing me deep, stroking me from inside only to draw back, leaving me empty.

That spot his cockhead teased before throbs.

I'm falling apart, trembling into ruin as every thrust comes a little faster, a little harder, a little more broken.

Honestly, I think he's testing just how much my body can take when I already know the answer isn't much.

Not when I'm close to dissolving with each second.

Not when he's a human storm made flesh, and pleasure hammers me down every time he draws back and slams deeper, filling me up with such force he arches my body off the bed.

Harder.

God, harder.

The air itself ignites.

Our breaths come in rushing tandem, moving together, faster, *faster*—

It's like we're racing each other.

I'm not sure who gets there first.

I know it doesn't matter.

We finish together and there's this glorious moment when I feel him swelling inside me and his back arching and his body shuddering and his fingers clamping down on my wrists.

A moment when his breaths skip and mine shudder and he's somehow *deeper*, thicker, and I'm so much fuller.

A moment when I flipping break.

When everything inside me focuses and all I can feel is Grant Faircross.

When my pussy locks down on his cock and convulses with the surging ecstasy of his girth, marking me as his forever.

And then it's his name on my lips, slowly being kissed away, swallowed by his ravenous kiss.

With a breathy sigh and a claiming touch, I dissolve in his electric glory.

"Philia, fuck!" His voice is pure thunder as Grant lets go, releasing like the sky splitting open.

Finally, he roars and pulses and gives me everything I've ever wanted with one last greedy thrust.

XIII: ONE AND ONLY (GRANT)

There's a lot of shit Ophelia doesn't know about me.

Like the fact that for a couple of years after she left town, I did a short stint with the National Guard.

Wasn't much, mostly local deployments helping out with disasters. I did it less out of any desire to be a soldier and more just wanting to see the world beyond Redhaven.

I've seen a dozen natural wonders from the back of an armored truck or a helicopter.

Nothing like the Grand Canyon from a thousand feet in the air, or standing under the largest tree in the world, looking up at branches so far away they feel like they're a gateway to the sky on another planet.

I've been all over North America and seen it all, yet every last one of those wonders pales compared to the sight of Ophelia Sanderson in my bed, bathed in morning light.

She's too fucking sweet to be real.

Everything that makes a woman eye candy.

The curve of her neck, where she curls on her side with her body tucked against mine and her head on my shoulder, her hand still splayed on my chest.

The dip of her waist that lets the golden sunlight pour over her like raw honey before it flows up over the rounded swell of her hip.

I also love how she's not stick thin.

Nothing wrong with that, but this boy needs meat.

Thank God my girl has a real-ass belly. Living proof she's content to enjoy life, and all the more to shake when I pull her on top of me and split her open.

Then there's the way the morning catches her hair, turning it into a spun gold halo. Every individual strand looks lit, even in the messy tangle left from sleep.

It gives her the wild-tossed look of a woman who's just been claimed, ridden hard, and left deliciously ruined again and again till she's nothing but a sleepy knot of sated flesh.

You'd better believe there's a possessive pride in me for that, knowing I'm the big asshole who left her that way.

She was so tired by the end of the night that she could only look at me with sweet exhaustion hazing her green eyes. A soft, almost wondering smile lingered on her lips as she kissed me before tucking herself against me with total trust.

She looked at me like she couldn't believe I was real.

Hell, I know the feeling.

Because I still can't believe I had Ophelia Sanderson.

Still can't believe that after all these years, she's home where she belongs, snug in my arms, her body warming my flesh while her scent leaves me drugged and hungry to be inside her again.

"Do you ever stop staring?" she mumbles drowsily without opening her eyes.

I bite back a smile.

"Nah. Didn't realize you were awake." I tighten my arm around her. "Good morning, sunshine."

"Mmmm... have been for a while. But I like mornings where I don't move. Especially when I'm this comfortable.

You don't know what a luxury it is for a nurse to sleep in." Her eyes blink open, glimmering like still pools.

I dip my nose to the nape of her neck and inhale her, savoring the way the slightest movement makes her silky skin slide against mine.

"You never liked waking up early long before you had the RN. Remember Ethan tossing you over his shoulder and damn near dragging you to the school bus in your pj's?"

She laughs. "Um, I remember *you* did that once. I wouldn't speak to you for over a week." She pokes my ribs. "I wasn't wearing any *pants* under my t-shirt, you idiot."

"The bunnies on your panties were cute," I say solemnly.

Now, she's definitely awake, letting out a squealing laugh as she swats at my chest.

"Maybe, but the entire neighborhood didn't need to see them!"

"Relax, woman. Wouldn't dream of doing that shit now," I growl, running my hand down to her ass. "My eyes only. Anybody else who gets a look will spend the next month finding some overpaid fuck to put his nose back on his face."

"You wouldn't!" She gasps.

Would.

I beam back a vicious glare.

"Besides, you got no right to complain. You got me back pretty good. Don't tell me you forgot?"

Those pretty pink lips curl smugly.

"Yep. I bit you on the ass—and you deserved it."

I grin. "You want to do that again? It'll end a whole lot different this time."

"Oh my God, no. I haven't even had coffee. Let me wash my face at least and get some caffeine in my blood before you go wearing me out again." Smiling, she settles with a sigh, folding her arms against my chest and resting her chin, looking at me with lazy, half-lidded eyes. "It's so strange, isn't it? All these old memories... Like, we're still the same people, but something else, too."

"Yeah. A whole lot's happened in ten years. Makes you someone else entirely." I catch a lock of her hair, twining it between my fingers. "We got a lifetime of history, but we've missed a lot of little moments. All the shit in between that's made us who we are now."

"It's crazy," she says quietly. She's like a lazy feline, turning her head to rub her cheek against my wrist. "It'd be nice to fill in that ten-year gap. Find out just what you turned into."

"Me? I'm not so different, really. Just bigger and more tired."

The morning's magic makes her damnably hypnotic.

I bury my fingers in her hair, fisting it as I pull her in for a morning kiss.

Her body pressure makes her breasts crush against me and I groan.

I'm taking my sweet time this morning, savoring her lips in small hot sips before pulling back. "A little more honest, maybe. I'd sure as hell love to know what you've been doing in Miami all this time."

"Wandering around in circles, mostly," she answers.

There's a sharp moment when she just looks at me, something haunting her gaze before she smiles.

There's a hell of a lot there between the lines.

Old pains, regrets, a life she never settled into—and having her here like this, thank fuck she didn't.

Ophelia rests her head on my shoulder again and I hold her close like I've always wanted.

"Truth be told, I think I was looking for home," she says slowly. "But home was always here. Maybe not this godforsaken town, no, but Mom. Ros. *You.*" A deep sigh drops her shoulders. "It shouldn't have taken Mom getting horribly sick again to bring me back. I'm kind of embarrassed..."

"Don't be. Space has its uses. You needed to find out who you were away from the bad vibes here," I point out.

That strange smile returns.

"You make it sound so easy, Grant, when here I've been struggling to figure out how to say that for years. But yeah, I guess I did. Not sure I found anything new... I'm still just Ophelia Sanderson, now with an RN behind my name."

"Do you miss it? Your work, I mean?"

"...a little," she admits after a silent moment. "Maybe not as much as I should."

I skim my fingers up her arms, feeling the goose bumps they give back.

I've never been good at comforting words, but I can be here for her.

I can hold her close, listen to her worries, hang on every word.

"You want to tell me more?"

"I don't know, honestly. I just—" Her fingers settle against my hand, stroking me like some kind of animal, then playing through my chest hair. "I think I did it out of guilt, if I'm honest. I tried orthopedics at first, but it wasn't the right fit because there was something missing. Like the fact that if I was going to leave home behind, then I thought I should do something to help people like Mom. Only, they weren't lucky enough to recover. Hospice care is hard work."

I nod solemnly.

My heart drums with the fact that I'm looking at one of God's own angels, dropped on this miserable spinning rock to bring a little comfort to the sick and dying.

"First you learn to care for these people," she continues,

biting her lip. "Then you learn to let them go when it's time. You have to—that's part of life and death—but it never gets easier. The same rough cycle, over and over again. Not something I ever thought would be my calling. But I *cared* about them, still." There's a telltale quiver in her voice, in her mouth. Her brows pinch together. "I don't know... you'd think after saying goodbye so many times that I'd be okay with Mom, whatever happens. I just wish—oh, God—" Her voice breaks.

"Enough of that."

I push myself up against the headboard so I can gather her more securely into my arms.

She's shaking, and with a muffled, hurt sound, she burrows into me.

I stroke a hand over her hair, down her back, resting my chin on top of her head and holding her as tight as I can.

"Don't give up on Angela yet. She's tough as nails and she's beat this shit before," I say. "She's not down for the count. Just taking a breather."

"How can you say that?" she chokes out. "You... you saw her. You saw how bad off she is. This experimental treatment, it's far-fetched. They told us not to get our hopes up for good reason. She's barely alive, Grant."

"But she's *alive*," I growl, trying like hell to convince both of us because I'm not ready to give up and give in to one more Sanderson family tragedy. "And since we don't know who your Pa is, I gotta say, that Sanderson stubbornness had to come from somewhere."

Ophelia's laugh is brittle, but real.

"Ethan used to tell me I was pretty as a flower and stubborn as a skunk."

"Skunks are stubborn and not just stinky? Good old Ethan. Guess he wasn't wrong."

"Hey!" Ophelia whacks my chest lightly, but she's smiling when she lifts her head to look at me. She sniffs and rubs her nose. "You're really gonna pick on me after last night?"

"If I didn't pick on you, you wouldn't know I care." I trace my thumb under one gleaming eye.

Smiling her gaze falls lower, stopping on my right bicep.

"No way. Is that...?" She reaches out, gently touching the black butterfly on my skin.

"Took you long enough to notice, Butterfly," I deflect.

She smacks me playfully, wiping a tear that speeds down her cheek. "You prick. You secretive, magnificent, soft-hearted *prick*. When did you get it, Grant? And why?"

"When do you think?" My brows dart up until she gives back a look that says she knows the answer. "As for why, you can take a good guess. How shit ended with us before—that last stupid fight—it didn't sit well with me at all and I was too chickenshit to go down to Florida and get in your face. So, I settled for what I could do in the here and now. I'm man enough to admit it. I was a little damn obsessed. I needed you haunting me, Philia, the same way I've held onto Ethan all these years. If only so I wouldn't let myself forget you. Not then. Not ever."

"Holy shit," she whispers, desperately sweeping another tear away. "You're the worst."

I suppose I am.

I certainly don't regret being terrible as she kisses my cheek with so much love in those lips it spears my heart like a marshmallow.

"You gonna be okay?" I stroke her jaw with my thumb.

"Yeah. Yeah, I think I'm just off-kilter from everything. Ros, Mom, that weird guy showing up again..."

I frown. "What do you mean, again? You see him?"

She chews her lip.

"...maybe?" She winces, peeking at me guiltily.

"Fuck, why didn't you tell me?" I demand.

"Sorry! I didn't want you to worry." Sighing, she shakes her head. "I'm not even sure it was him, anyway. Probably just me jumping at shadows. When I left the medical center, I thought I saw someone by my car. But when I ran into the parking lot, there was nobody there."

"Forget stinky. You really are goddamned stubborn," I huff, pulling her closer. It's like I'm fucking hardwired to protect her, to shelter her, to keep her near me, even if it means using my brick of a body as a human shield. "Maybe you imagined it. But maybe you fuckin' didn't, too. Next time you even *think* you see him skulking around, you call me. Understood?"

She goes stiff against me, but soon she melts, her arms twining around my neck.

"Okay, okay. Guess I'll be calling you every time a blowing leaf startles me. That only happens ten times a day lately."

I snort.

"And I'll answer every time. Better to call you crazy than dead." I bend my head, resting my temple to hers, just leaning into her and soaking her in. Part of me still remembers the spindly girl she used to be, but right now my arms are over-flowing with the lushness of pure woman.

"If you insist, Grant," she says matter-of-factly.

"I do. I got a bad feeling. Think that shitstorm that started with the Arrendells and Delilah Graves hasn't fully died down. That man who jumped you, I think those clothes he's wearing were Arrendell livery. Y'know, staff uniforms. They might've sent him down here to watch us. You, me, I'm not sure which."

Ophelia makes a thoughtful sound, sucking her lower lip in a way that makes me want to bite it.

"Why would they be after me?"

Good question.

"It could just be keeping you away from Ros, if our boy's on Aleksander's payroll," I say. "Everyone and their grandma must know you wouldn't be happy about her marrying that mannequin-looking fuck. So maybe Jeeves is tailing you so you won't try to break things up."

"Psssh, like I could stop Ros from doing whatever she wants." She smiles bitterly. "But why would they be following *you?*"

"Because I got a weird fucking feeling about that suicide up at the house," I say grimly. "Maybe I'm just jumping at spooks or being paranoid myself. Who knows. Still, something ain't smelling right."

"You know..."

"Oh no." She's got that look in her eye, thoughtful and goddamned obstinate. I eyeball her something fierce. "What? What are you about to say? It's gonna piss me off, ain't it"

"Yes? What doesn't?" Ophelia grins. "I was just thinking there's an easy way to find out."

"No."

"Grant, it wouldn't be that hard."

"Absolutely not."

My blood heats.

"Come *onnn.*" She sticks her tongue out, wrinkling her nose. "We're all adults here. We might as well take the direct route and just ask him. If he shows up again, I'll get him to explain why he grabbed me and what he's talking about, death threats and all. Sometimes even mentally unwell folks just want to be heard."

I side-eye her hard.

Like hell I'm going to approve something that crazy.

But I can already tell she's made her mind up and nothing I say or do is gonna sway her.

Groaning, I thump my head back against the headboard.

"Whatever. Just don't let him corner you alone, Ophelia—if he actually pops up. I don't trust it. You catch him in public, around other people, fine. But if you're alone, you get the fuck out of there as fast as you can shake your tail."

"Shake my tail, huh?"

Her wicked little smile is my only warning before there's a lush, hot body on mine.

Even if I'm not fully awake, it doesn't take much more than the pressure of Ophelia's weight against me to make sure there's a certain part of me absolutely up and fucking ready by the time she slides her gorgeous thighs across my lap and straddles me.

So much for staying mad.

She's so goddamned breathtaking it floors me, this vision of gold flesh straining against the thin sheet wrapped around her body till she looks like one of those old statues where the folds of carved fabric look translucent, tempting me more than concealing.

Her tits strain against the white fabric, threatening to spill free from the hand barely holding the sheet in place as she settles against me.

And while that sheet may be hiding her from my eyes, there's nothing between us to hide skin from skin as that wet soft place I feasted on last night moves against my cock.

Her little ass drags against my shaft as she gives a playful switch of her hips.

"Thought you wouldn't want me shaking my tail for anyone but you," she teases.

Fuck, I'm about to lose it.

"Philia," I snarl, curling my fingers against the back of her neck to drag her down into me, seizing her mouth while those gold tumbles of hair fall around me.

I can't stop.

Stampeding bison couldn't hold me back.

I grasp at her body like a man deprived, gripping hard.

Anywhere and everywhere I can hold on, feeling her filling my palms while I taste her, twining our tongues together in this hot, slinking lock of wetness and heat that goes right to my gut.

Goddamn.

I can't help how my hips stab up, rubbing my cock against her pussy, already slick as hell for me.

I'm so ready to just grab her hips, lift her up, and impale her so I can seat myself fully inside her and that perfect wildness all over again.

I almost rip the sheet in half.

Bare her body, curving and glowing in the morning light.

I bite her lower lip, loving how she moans, shudders, and melts for me.

Yeah, I'm going to take her so hard she'll—

A noise cuts me off a split second before I plunge in.

I release an explosive curse as I realize it's my phone shrieking from the nightstand, playing the old Kenny G tune I set for my ma. She's got the weirdest love affair with that guy I've ever seen, so it was fitting.

Groaning, I break away, thumping my head on the headboard like the pain could possibly clear the lust from my brain.

"Sorry," I mutter regretfully, reaching up to trace my thumb against the corner of her mouth. "Ma calling. Might be something up with Nell."

Ophelia gives me a shaky smile, gathering the sheet against herself again as she slides off me and tucks herself against my side once more. "It's okay."

It is, I realize.

She means it.

It's not just doublespeak where she's saying it's okay

because it's polite, but she's secretly upset at being shoved aside for a kid.

She's relaxed, content against me, patient, and understanding.

She gets how much Nell means to me.

How important that kid is in my black hole of a life.

Shit, Ophelia gets *me*.

I must be smiling like the biggest fool ever born as I snag my phone a second before it goes to voicemail.

"Hey, Ma. Everything okay?"

"Oh, everything's fine, dearest," my mother answers cheerfully. I hear the noise of her car in the background, that hollowness that comes with being on speaker in an enclosed space. Also, the distant sound of shouting, cheerful kids growing quieter by the moment. "I just wanted to let you know I dropped Nell off at school right on time. I know how you worry."

I can't help chuckling as I wrap an arm around Ophelia, settling comfortably against the pillows with our bodies fitting so perfectly together. "You know me too well. Did she behave herself?"

"Like a little angel. Mostly. She wouldn't go to sleep until I read *Where the Wild Things Are* six times, but once she was out, she was out. Didn't even have her usual two a.m. bathroom run to drink six gallons of water straight from the tap."

Smiling, I shake my head. "Be glad she's past waking you up to make you get it for her. Glad she was good. I'll get her after school this afternoon."

"Are you sure? Darling, you've been so good with her, but you haven't taken a day off for yourself in ages that isn't police business. Even parents take a vacation, Grant. Your father and I can keep her for a few more days before we run off into the wilds for our romantic getaway." She lets out an indulgent laugh. "Believe it or not, Nell thinks

241

she shouldn't go home for a *week*. Apparently, she's very invested in you getting plenty of 'kissy time' with 'the lady.'"

Shit.

"Ma, I—she does *not* need to be talking about that. Now, she's really coming home tonight," I growl.

Ophelia snickers at my side. "Nell started singing about us kissing in a tree again, didn't she?"

"Probably," I grouch from the corner of my mouth, then turn my attention back to my mother. "I appreciate it, Ma. I really do. Still, I think it's better if Nell comes home. Whatever is or isn't going on with me and Ophelia, I don't want Nell feeling like she's got to cut herself out to accommodate us. Don't want her thinking she's in the way. Whatever happens in my life, Nell's a part of it."

There's a sweet, soft sigh at my side.

Ophelia's hand rests on my arm.

I look down to find her watching me with such a gentle smile, her eyes warm with approval. My heart warms, too, beating just a little harder.

My mother clucks her tongue, but there's a fondness to it. "You always do take your responsibilities so seriously, but I understand what you mean."

"Thanks, Ma. Don't know what I'd do without you."

We say our goodbyes and I drop my phone back on the nightstand, pressing my lips to Ophelia's hair.

"If Nell's already off to school, that means I'll be late for work."

"Aww. I want to be selfish and tease you into staying in bed a little longer, but I'll be good. Don't work too hard." Ophelia rubs her cheek against my chest, then shoots me a playful look. "So, whatever's going on with you and Ophelia, you said? What would 'whatever' be?"

"No goddamned clue," I admit, tipping her face up to steal

another kiss. "Don't know what I'm getting myself into or what we're doing. But I'd sure as hell like to find out."

The way she lowers her lashes and blushes is all I need to get my blood racing and ready to make it through another day.

"Yeah," she whispers, pulling me in for one more slow, lingering kiss. "I think I'd like that too."

* * *

I'VE GOT enough energy to tow a Mack truck by the time I shower and leave with a scrambled egg and ham sandwich Ophelia threw together.

The whole thing hangs out of my mouth as I shrug into my jacket.

She just charges me up this much. I grin as I take the half-eaten sandwich out and swallow so I can kiss her at the door before ducking into my cruiser and heading off.

I wolf down the remaining sandwich while I drive, flipping back into cop mode even if I'm not technically on duty yet and my head's overflowing with Ophelia damn Sanderson.

It's a rotten habit—observing everything, scanning my surroundings as I make my way through town.

That's how I spot them.

Aleksander Arrendell.

Rosalind Sanderson.

...and fucking Ephraim Jacobin.

They're standing close to the street corner, thick as thieves next to the local cheese shop, tucked in an out of the way place between that building and the next.

My stomach churns, thinking back to that fucked up encounter at the bar. I couldn't bring myself to mention that shit to Philia.

I also wish he'd given a reason—just one—to arrest his deranged ass on the spot. There are still a few public obscenity laws on the books, sure, but good luck dragging a man as rich as an Arrendell to court over it. His lawyers would rebuff anything short of public masturbation—and even then I think the scum would get a community service slap on the wrist.

I slow down at the crosswalk to let a few moms with strollers pass in front of me, using the extra time to observe the scene.

Aleksander's dressed to the nines as usual in a white linen suit today. Ros has a silvery designer dress on, all slouchy bits of fabric that leave her two seconds away from flashing half the town. Her hair's a mess, her mascara sweat-runny—or is that from crying?

My blood temperature drops a few degrees.

Damn, I don't know, but she doesn't look all that distressed. She's just wearing the same neutral out-of-it look that's becoming too normal for her.

Ephraim Jacobin is the one who really seems out of place here, coming down from the hills to hobnob with an Arrendell.

My hands tighten on the wheel.

Remembering what happened with Delilah Graves, it wouldn't be the first time, and we know what was going on there.

Ephraim leans in close to them both, this human scare-crow in handstitched overalls and a cotton shirt under a huge grey trench coat, his thick grey-black beard pouring down his chest. The rest of his face is hidden as usual by the broad brim of his hat.

I still get a nasty flash of his hard, shielded eyes and his teeth as he glances over his shoulder.

Something changes hands between them.

Both Ephraim and Aleksander tuck something into their pockets.

Nope. Don't like this shit at all.

Shame I got no probable cause to stop them just for having a friendly conversation in broad daylight, but dammit, I want to.

Nothing about this scene sits right with me.

I'd bet both nuts it's something shady.

Of course, I've always had my suspicions about the Jacobins, what with their unmarked trucks full of moonshine and God only knows what else—especially after their favorite son was found with a brick of cocaine before his arrest.

Maybe it's nothing.

But maybe it's a whole lot of something, too. Especially when there's no chance in hell Ros would be slumming around with the hillfolk in her right mind.

More importantly, the last time the Arrendells had big dealings with those moonshine-brewing dickheads up in the hills, women wound up dead.

Are we really gonna sit here and let tragedy strike twice?

Last time, the new girl in town almost became their latest victim.

This time, the new girl in town is *my* girl, and no, maybe she's not in overt danger—not yet—but I don't think it's unconnected.

When something weird's up with Ros, Aleksander, and the Jacobins right around the time someone in Arrendell livery is stalking my girl, it reeks to high hell.

I shake my head instinctively.

I won't let anything happen to Ophelia—or to her little sister, no matter how big of a mistake she's making with Aleksander.

I'll be keeping my eyes glued to that slimy prick, every second I'm not watching out for Ophelia.

One bad apple off the gnarled Arrendell tree already raised too much hell in this town.

Letting another one strike so close to home would be too tragic—and definitely too soul killing to ever live down.

XIV: ONE SPICY DINNER
(OPHELIA)

I wonder if Grant still likes his meals slathered in sriracha.

I stand in the grocery store aisle, studying a few bottles from different brands.

Hot sauce was a staple back when we were kids. First the good old Louisiana pepper sauces, then the more exotic options that started trending and seems designed to make you cry.

Ethan and I couldn't handle the spicy stuff—but Lord knows we pretended to keep up and gave into stupid kid food dares—while Grant could probably eat a mouthful of Carolina Reapers whole without blinking.

I remember the first time Ethan brought his new best friend home for dinner. Grant brought his own freaking hot sauce and offended my mom mightily by dumping it all over her cooking.

Eventually, she realized that's just Grant, and the insult turned into an ongoing joke that never failed to make us laugh.

Oh, if Mom could only see me now, staring at these neon-red bottles of hot sauce and wondering if there's anything I can cook that will be fiery enough for that giant grump.

He found you pretty fiery last night, at least.

Oh, God. That's terrible.

Laughing at my own dumb joke, I cover my mouth with one hand.

Yeah, I'm a flustered wreck right now.

Grinning for no good reason, blushing every other minute, and all I'm trying to do is pick up groceries.

I certainly didn't have 'domestic goddess' on my coming home to Redhaven bingo card, yet here I am.

Is it really just this easy? Is anything?

Grant and I just falling back into each other, only it's ten times better than just being friends.

Because now all my girlish dreams have come true and then some.

I just wish Mom and Ethan were here to see it.

I wish they could give me endless crap about it, teasing me up and down.

I'd kill to hear them tell me my stubbornness paid off, this hopeless girl mooning after an oblivious moose of a man for a flipping decade.

That's pretty sobering.

So is the grim fact that Mom's more likely to see Ethan again than her waking up and seeing me with Grant.

My laughter dies and the butterflies in my stomach go dormant again.

The bottle of eye-burning sriracha in my hand blurs. With a hurt breath full of the broken shards of my heart, I drop it into my cart, turning away.

I want to believe what he said—that my mother's too stubborn to let go when she's beaten this disease before.

But if this round of ultra-experimental chemo and its induced coma doesn't work, I know what's next.

I can't think about it.

Struggling to breathe, I turn away, gripping the handles of my shopping cart—only to draw up short as a voice behind me calls my name.

"Ophelia? Ophelia Sanderson, is that you?"

I take a few seconds to compose myself and pull on a smile for Janelle Bowden.

Such a sweet woman.

It's been ten years since I last saw her, but she's still the same vibrant, warm lady with a trim figure and a no-nonsense bob. Looks like the red in her hair has almost fully gone grey, but I still see a few faint ghosts among the silvery strands.

There's something else different about her, too, I think.

Her smile looks harder to find and there's something haunted around her eyes. Like she's faced unspeakable tragedy over the last decade, the sort that can age a person well beyond their years.

Oh, no. What happened?

I try to remember anything Mom or Ros might've told me, but I'm blanking.

Her husband's still alive, so it can't be him.

There's been no terminal illness, she's been fine as far as I know.

Right now, she's putting on a front of enthusiasm as she abandons her cart to approach me, reaching out for a hug.

"It *is* you! Why, you've grown up into such a beautiful young woman."

Oh, boy.

I don't try to escape.

This is Redhaven, after all.

If you're from here, you're *always* from here, and if you leave for so much as a week, you're going to get hugged to death by the nice people when you come back.

So I just smile and pull Janelle into my embrace.

It's a good distraction, a bit of comfort, this motherly woman holding me close for a few moments to ease my wandering thoughts.

"Good to see you, Janelle." I pull back. "How've you been?"

"Oh, you know," she says with a little cluck of her tongue. "No big changes. I'm as boring and predictable as a summer squash. But *you*." Her soft sound of sympathy is twinged with pain. "Oh, sweetheart, I wish you were coming home under happier circumstances."

"...yeah. Me too." I swallow hard, brushing my hair back from my face, forcing my smile to hold. "But it is what it is. I'd rather be here for her than not."

"You are a sweet girl." Janelle cups my cheek. "Are you settling in all right? How's Ros taking things?"

"I..." For a second, I almost spill everything.

It's on the tip of my tongue, this rough, angsty confession, but I can't.

Janelle is way too lovely to trouble with my drama.

So I just shrug and smile.

"I'm managing, you know? Seeing old friends helps a ton. Grant, he's been wonderful. Ros, she's..." I shake my head. "I think she's just super busy. But I can't blame her, it's a big job running the shop."

"Yes, I'm sure." Something strange pinches Janelle's face with a worried look. "...about that."

My eyebrows go up.

I hesitate.

"Is there something I should know?"

"Maybe, maybe. Honest to God, I'm not sure." Janelle screws her lips up before she glances over her shoulder, patting my arm. "Finish your shopping first, dearie, and then I'll treat you to coffee. What do you say?"

* * *

JANELLE FLIES through catching me up on ten years of town history as we finish our shopping together—little things like who moved away, who came back, the new out-of-towners who bought the Yardsdales' lovely old vacation home, the tourist who drowned in Still Lake about six years back, who adopted a dog, who had a kid, and who had three boyfriends in one year.

All those little tidbits of small-town gossip you end up steeped in day in, day out, condensed into a single hour until I'm dizzy.

I'm still pretty grateful for the distraction when her ominous little comment stoked my worries again.

But I'm patient and I wait until she's good and ready.

I'm also not sure how to ask.

Though once we make our way to the local café and settle at the outdoor tables with our drinks, the air feels lighter.

It's a lovely fall morning, bright and sunny and colorful. Crisp enough to make the chill a pleasant nip instead of a stinging discomfort. The light carries that gold-red tint that only comes with an autumn morning, turning the shadows into champagne bubbles.

Honestly, it feels strange to see Janelle so grey, like the light just doesn't quite touch her anymore.

I curl my hands around the warm ceramic of my cappuccino mug, watching her as she stirs precisely half a packet of sugar into her black coffee.

"Janelle?" I murmur. "Is something wrong? You've seemed a little off all morning. Is something on your mind?"

"Oh—what isn't these days?" She ducks her head, her lips curling in a dry humorless smile. "Everything's been so strange in Redhaven the past year, you know. I suppose I'm just carrying a lot of it with me, dear."

"I don't follow." I shake my head.

"Well, I'm sure you heard about what happened earlier this year, didn't you? With Delilah Clarendon—pardon, *Delilah Graves* now."

"Yep, I heard the news. Mom filled me in on some of it. So did Grant."

"Yes, well..." She sighs. "That whole nasty business, I feel like I could've prevented so much of it if I just hadn't been so naïve and trusting. Poor Delilah trusted me with a safe place to stay and I practically handed her off into danger. I sent her to that house. I told her *he* was safe to trust and I said the Jacobins were harmless. They weren't, none of them. Not when she was being lured in from day one, and they would have disposed of her body in the filthiest way when they were done with her. And my useless potato of a husband, he just—"

She stops, compressing her lips and stirring her coffee fiercely. The spoon clinks harshly against the sides of her mug.

It takes me a second to absorb that from Janelle Bowden, of all people.

She's East Coast prim and proper to a fault, never has a mean word, wouldn't speak ill of anyone. And she and Chief Bowden have been happily married for so long.

I'm totally confused.

"Hey, I don't think you should blame yourself for any of that. Nobody knew Redhaven had a home-grown serial killer," I say softly. "You want to see the best in people. That's natural, and it's hard to believe any normal person would do something like that, killing those poor girls. You had no reason to believe it was happening. But I guess I don't under-stand—what about Chief Bowden?"

Janelle stares down into her mug, her eyes glassy before

she looks away sharply, staring across the street with something distant and strange in her expression.

"It just didn't feel right, that's all," she mutters, more to herself than me. "He acted like he didn't even *want* to investigate the entire affair, always looking the other way, dismissing disturbances, brushing them off as unimportant. It didn't sit right with me. It *doesn't* sit right with me now. Any time I mention the folks up at the big house or the hillfolk, he just glazes over and stomps off to trim his nails."

She stops again.

Her jaw goes tight with a swallow.

"Sorry. I didn't know I'd married such a weak man," she whispers. "All he cares about is not rocking the boat. I realize now it's all he ever cared about. I'm sorry, Ophelia. I'm sorry he never tried harder to find your brother. Especially with what we know now."

Those words hit so hard they practically blow me out of my chair.

I don't know if I fully get what she's implying about her own husband, but...

Has Chief Bowden been complicit in covering up the Arrendells' and Jacobins' crimes? Or is he just plain lazy?

Does he pretend not to notice so he can claim not to know?

That fall chill in the air suddenly feels ten times colder.

Pressing my trembling fingers against my mug isn't enough to warm my cold skin.

"It's not your fault," I hiss faintly, struggling for words. "I'm so sorry, Janelle. I had no idea things were so rough between you two."

"Don't we just look like the perfect couple? If people only knew..." she answers bitterly, then glances back at me with a hard, almost angry smile. "Well. Not that anyone sees us together much anymore. I barely know where he even goes these days. But I'm sorry. I just erupted all over you, didn't I?"

"It's fine," I reassure her. "Way better out than holding it in. I know sometimes it's easier to talk to someone who hasn't been wrapped up in every day of your life for the last ten years."

"Yes, well, the walls do have ears in this town, don't they? I'm grateful you won't be sniggering about me behind my back and gossiping over the neighbor's fence." She frowns. "Though lately it seems your sister's more the talk of the town."

"Ros?" I groan. "It's Aleksander, isn't it?"

She cocks her head.

"I'm afraid so, dear. Everyone's acting like it's our own hometown Cinderella story. I suppose they need to, seeing how we're all still reeling over the Celeste Graves business. People want some happy news, something to redeem our local royalty." But her voice falls flat when she says it, and she takes a slow sip of her coffee. "I wish I could say Aleksander Arrendell was our prince."

"He's a *creep*," I snap without thinking. "Sorry. But I don't get what Ros sees in him. He's just weird, and she acts so different when she's around him. I barely recognize my sister..."

"Young girls do get starstruck sometimes," Janelle whispers. "But I hope you won't think I'm too forward in saying I don't like it, either. The whirlwind of it bothers me, yes. It's not hard to see poor Ros is running away from one bad thing into another. There are far healthier ways to manage your emotions."

"I tried talking to her." I sigh. "We just wound up yelling at each other in Mom's shop before Aleksander barged in. He was all over her, right in front of me."

Janelle wrinkles her nose.

"That boy never did have manners. I think he's the worst one of the bunch, frankly, always too focused on preening over himself." Her upper lip curls. "I hope she doesn't go through with it. There are things she doesn't know."

I frown. "Things like...?"

"Well, nothing certain. You can take this with a grain of salt and it's just an old woman's speculation, but this old woman has seen a lot." Janelle watches me knowingly over the rim of her mug. "Forgive me, but I remember a time when your mother was just as bewitched by the Arrendell glamour. Always up at that house—until one day she wasn't."

My breath catches.

"What? Mom? But... but she practically avoided them when I was growing up. We never—I never knew she had anything to do with the Arrendells."

Janelle looks down.

"Yes, yes, certain people do keep their business as private as possible and that's their right." She rubs the side of her nose with one finger. "Oh, I wish I could tell you more, dearie. But it's been some time, and back then we didn't have smartphones documenting everything. Much easier to be secretive in those days, too. Still, I don't want to worry you with bad rumors and old, half-faded memories."

"No, no, that's... fine. I appreciate you telling me."

It's not fine.

I feel like I'm tied to a windmill.

What the hell did the Arrendells ever have to do with my mother?

And does it connect to Ros and Aleksander, and this bizarro engagement that's looking more and more sus by the day?

I wish Mom was conscious enough to ask.

But it's possible Ros knows something.

And I know one thing for certain.

Whenever I corner my sister again, next time I'm holding my ground.

I'm not letting Ros go without some real answers.

* * *

JANELLE and I finish our coffees over more idle conversation before she gets dragged off by Linda Manson from the Ladies' Aid—which I can't believe is still a thing.

Then again, certain parts of Redhaven feel like they never left the Civil War era.

With Janelle gone, I head back home to Grant's to putter around and unload my groceries.

I know he didn't bring me here to play housekeeper or cook, but I need to keep my hands busy so my mind doesn't implode.

I go to work, tidying the house up from top to bottom before tucking myself into the kitchen to prep dinner.

I've just gotten two meatloaves together—one normal for me and Nell, the other burning hot with chili, garlic, and hot sauce for Grant—and put them in the oven when the front door opens.

Little Nell's happy laughter announces their return.

I wipe my hands on a dish towel and lean around the kitchen door, watching as Grant squeezes through the front door with Nell perched on his shoulders, swinging her arms everywhere.

It's a masterpiece of strategic movement, him walking with his legs half-bent and twisting every which way. I'd say she's getting too big to carry around, but Grant could give *me* a five-hour piggyback ride without breaking a sweat.

It also looks like something he's done enough that it's almost second nature. I can't help smiling as I step closer.

"Welcome home," I say.

Grant lifts his head, looking at me with a slow smile that just makes my insides twist.

Neither of us get to say another word to each other, though.

Because with a joyous shriek of *"Miss Philia!"* Nell launches herself from Grant's shoulders and throws herself at me, her backpack trailing behind her like a parachuter's kit.

"Nell!" I dart forward to put myself between her and the floor—just in time to catch an armful of hyperactive kid. "Oof."

She's an armful.

I don't know how I don't go down ass over elbows, but I catch her and hug her against my chest. She latches on tight, sealing both arms around my neck.

"Hi," she chirps with a knowing giggle that says she knows exactly what she did.

"Hi, yourself." I sigh, unable to help smiling. "Let's not hit the floor face-first today, okay?"

"Oh, I knew you'd catch me," she announces confidently.

"You have more faith in my reflexes than I do, kiddo." I tap her nose. "C'mon. I just put meatloaf in the oven. If you help fix the potatoes, I'll help you with homework later."

"Deal!"

As she slips her trusting little hand into mine and marches me off to the kitchen, swinging our arms wildly between us, it feels like all my troubles disappear.

For now, it's just me, this wonderful little girl, and the amazing man who's stepped in as her father, watching me with something in his eyes that makes heat flash through my cheeks and stir my belly.

We trade soft, lingering smiles before Nell drags along, practically pulling my arm off.

God, this feels so different.

Like something I wouldn't mind coming home to every day.

In another life, of course.

I'm not letting my hopes run away with my heart just yet.

I put Nell to work scrubbing potatoes while I peel and slice them. Before long, I've got a big pan of scalloped potatoes swimming in cheesy sauce in the oven next to the meatloaves.

By the time I take Nell to wash up, I find Grant already changed out of his uniform and sprawled out on the sofa in a pair of casually sinful jeans and a black short-sleeved undershirt that looks painted on with how devilishly tight it is.

My God.

It's almost *worse* now that I have some idea what that body can do to me.

I give Nell a friendly pat on the back and send her upstairs, lingering over the back of the sofa, peering at the open folders in Grant's lap.

"What's that?" I inhale sharply as I see the name at the top of the cluttered page.

Sanderson, Ethan Ronald.

Holy crap.

"Old case files. Ethan's report," he says, flipping the folder shut and tilting his head back. A quick kiss is all it takes to distract me, so easy and familiar it strikes my heart. "How was your day?"

"Um, interesting. I ran into Janelle Bowden at the grocery store and we ended up having coffee. I'll tell you about it once Nell's in bed."

Dark hazel eyes flicker thoughtfully before he nods. "Thanks for being so good with her. That kamikaze jump would've knocked anyone else on their ass."

"Hey, I learned by keeping up with you and Ethan. Be ready for anything." Smirking, I catch a strand of his hair and give it a light tug, coiling the short brown lock around my finger and looking at the silver shot through it. "But I see why you're going grey so early."

"That's genetic and you know it. My old man had a silver head before he was fifty." He snorts. "So, meatloaf for dinner?"

"Meatloaves. Plural. One normal, one spicy enough to burn down the house."

Grant's eyes go round like I haven't seen for years, boyish and starstruck. "You're telling me you made a hot one just for me?"

"...I remembered how you like your food. What?" Laughing, I tug his hair again. "Hot enough to start a nuclear reaction, right?"

"Woman, I haven't had the patience to cook separate meals for me and Nell. Most hot grub I've gotten the last few years is those spicy pickles down at the corner store." He's looking at me like I've just handed him the Holy Grail. "Thank you."

"It's just meatloaf. Thank me when I've made you a five-course gourmet meal or something."

"Don't tease me," he growls.

I brace my hands on the back of the couch and lean over him, stealing a quick upside-down kiss.

I'm high on the fact that I *can*, though just to reach I have to pull my feet off the ground.

He leans into me, catching me off guard with a sudden searing-hot rush of pressure—but I make myself pull back before he knocks me off-kilter and makes me forget dinner totally.

"Be good," I mutter. "At least while Nell's awake."

"And after Nell's asleep?" he growls hopefully.

"Then you can be as bad as you want."

The way his eyes ignite this time when he looks at me are definitely not like a little boy's.

They're all man, wolfish and knowing and rogue.

And the way it tangles me up, it's like there's nothing else that could break the magic.

I want to cling to it.

Even as I realize it's a bit hypocritical and maybe I have no good reason to criticize Ros for finding her own ways to hide from reality and its punches.

I know.

I know I'm burying myself in Grant Faircross and this fast-moving illusion of a life together. Probably to avoid having to face my mother and the death clock ticking down day by day.

Am I really so different from Ros? Knowing she's hiding in the illusion of Aleksander, too.

Ugh, I hate that thought.

But this thing with Grant, it's not dangerous or weird.

It's not hurting me.

It's not *changing* me for the worse.

What's going on with Ros and Aleksander feels like a textbook toxic relationship.

I know it and I think Ros does, too, or she wouldn't try so hard to bury it.

I break Grant's honey-brown gaze just as Nell comes spilling down the stairs, brandishing her still-damp hands proudly. "All clean!"

"Right." I force myself to look away from the handsome beast-man still watching me like I'm everything. "C'mon then. Let's go set the table."

It takes twice as long to put out plates and cutlery with a little girl underfoot, and three times as long with a giant lunk of a man coming to 'help' but pretending he doesn't know where the forks and glasses go, just so Nell can correct him and set everything right.

My smile is glued to me, watching them together.

No, it's not just them together.

It's *us*.

This is what coming home should feel like.

Family.

I can practically hear Grant's stomach rumbling by the time I pull everything out of the oven and fill our plates. Nell insists on saying grace—she really respects her grandparents and their traditions—then wrinkles her nose at the spicy meatloaf.

"It smells... itchy," she complains from her seat on one side of the cozy square table. "It makes my nose scratchy."

A second later, she sneezes into her elbow dramatically.

"Good thing you don't have to eat it," I tease, dropping a thick slab of meatloaf flecked with chili flakes onto Grant's plate. "That's all for the big guy. Let's see if I can make him breathe fire tonight."

I wink at him.

"You can do that without the meatloaf just fine," Grant mutters under his breath.

Nell blinks, her little eyes rounding.

"You can breathe fire, Uncle Grant?"

I snicker and nudge him under the table. "Be nice."

Nell's a little too smart for her own good. Plus, if he makes me blush any harder, she'll figure out he's not talking about spicy food.

But my blush comes back for a different reason as Grant takes a bite, then lets out a low, pleased groan. "Oh, yeah. God *damn*, that's good."

"No bad words at the dinner table, Uncle Grant! Grandma's just chomping at the bit for me to start that swear jar," Nell proclaims proudly.

I smile. "One time when I went to this Podunk town in Montana, there was this little girl at the inn who was all about the swear jars. Buuut I think we can let your uncle live just this once." I tuck into my own safely unspicy meatloaf. "Now eat your dinner, hon."

The meal is a pretty rowdy affair with Nell dominating the conversation.

Grant chuckles more than I've ever seen him laugh in all the years I've known him.

Being a dad suits him, even if Nell isn't actually his daughter.

It's like all the rough edges he had as a younger man get smoothed away around this spunky little girl. He turns soft in ways I never imagined.

And I can't take my eyes off him, especially not when his gaze catches mine across the table.

Nell pulls him back to her with another outlandish observation about her classmates and her very pregnant teacher.

But she grabs *my* attention as she abruptly pins me with those wickedly innocent eyes, a broad smile on her lips. "So Miss Philia, are you gonna stay with us for good? You could be an almost-mom. Kinda like Uncle Grant is my almost-dad?"

I nearly spit out my drink, going up like a five-alarm fire. Maybe I got some of Grant's spicy meatloaf by mistake, but actually...

"Um."

I'm speechless.

"Almost-dad. That's what I told her to call me." Grant smiles across the table.

I fumble, looking between him and Nell.

It hasn't taken long to figure out that she loves putting people on the spot, but this is too much.

Because she's not just being a brat. There's something

serious in her nosy question, considering this is the second time she's asked me.

This isn't just a little girl playing pranks.

It's a lonely little girl who misses having a mom, a complete family.

"Honey..." Clearing my throat, I gather my thoughts and say, "I'm happy to stay as long as Grant needs me."

That wins me a smile from Nell. "Then it's settled. You're here for good. 'Cause he's really dumb without you, Miss Philia."

"Is he now?" I laugh, though I suddenly feel shy enough to shrink into the floor, all elbows and awkwardness. I'm right back to being that knock-kneed girl I used to be, flustered in front of her crush. "I don't think I know how to make Grant less dumb, Nell. He's been like that since before you were born."

"I'm right here, ladies," Grant growls, scowling—and just like that, the awkward tension at the table dissipates.

The rest of dinner passes with more quiet teasing and tales from the schoolyard.

When we're done, Grant promises to wash the dishes while I take Nell up to bed and read to her. She bounds into the bedroom after brushing her teeth like an overexcited puppy. Before I can shoo her into bed, she grabs her favorite book and jabs it at me.

It's so weird to feel like that book is part of coming home, right down to the familiar creases in the cover, worn deeper with time.

The same pages I've touched lovingly time and time again.

I'm happy to sit down at her bedside and read it to her until she falls asleep. One hand stretches across the covers, quietly reaching for me.

I curl my fingers in hers and hold them gently for a while, just feeling their warmth, watching her sleep.

She's not mine, no. A few weeks ago I didn't even know who she was.

But I could easily see myself loving this little girl and getting completely wrapped around her little finger just like her uncle.

The door creaks open softly and Grant peeks in.

"She asleep?" he whispers.

I smile, carefully disentangling my fingers from Nell's.

"Out like a light," I whisper back, standing up.

He's changed in the time it took me to put Nell to sleep, standing in the doorway with a pair of loose blue-and-white striped pajama pants straining to keep their hold on the thick breadth of his body.

The drawstring stretches to its limit and the knots in the cords barely hitch on the holes at the waist.

There's almost no difference in the definition of his naked chest above the pajama pants and the details I can make out below them.

The ink snaking up his arms and lining his shoulders.

The hard muscle of his iliac crest and brawny thighs imprinting the thin fabric—and imprinting me as I draw closer to the doorway and he slips an arm around my waist.

He pulls me in with an effortlessness that makes me feel as light as a feather.

"We should probably follow suit," he says with a hopeful lift of his eyebrows. "If you'd like to join me."

I bite my lip on a smile, walking my fingers up his chest. "Is that your way of asking if last night isn't a one-time thing?"

"Might be." A rumble wells under my fingertips. "I could be more direct and just ask you to fuck."

I gasp.

Just hearing him shift to something so dirty does terrible things to me.

"For the record, you don't have to ask." Stretching up on my toes, I brush my lips to his. "Take me to bed, Gra—*ANT!*"

His name becomes a squeal.

He doesn't even let me get the words out before he's sweeping me up in his arms, carrying me against his broad chest and the wild beat of his powerful heart.

I barely clap my hand over my mouth to silence myself, pulse pounding, before I accidentally wake up Nell. Grant's smirk makes me want to shove him and kiss him all at once as he carries me down the hall.

But as he elbows his bedroom door open and tumbles me down on the bed, hovering over me with his body blocking out the light and the moon's glow gliding along his shoulders, I know which one I'll choose.

My body goes slack as his mouth attacks mine.

This time, I'm so ready with an anticipation that's been building my entire life.

My nails rake his shoulders as I draw him in, mating my lips with his.

XV: ONE OF A KIND (GRANT)

*Y*ou can't imagine what the fuck it does to me when Ophelia kisses me first.

It's a wild thing, a fireball affirmation that she wants me just as bad.

Hell, the fact that she's here in my bed, in my arms, willingly and eager and soaked knocks something loose in my head.

All those years I thought she hated me after I ran my mouth—when really she was just waiting for me to stop being a dumbass and make my feelings clear.

I still remember how she writhed under me last night.

And I'm hard in an instant at the thought, especially when I feel her flesh yielding under me as I sink into her kiss, twining tongues before I take the fuck over.

I'm a demanding fuck in bed.

I need to be.

Need to own her, to possess her, to claim her, to make every inch of her mine.

I'm hardly aware I'm shredding her clothes.

She hisses when it bites into her flesh before being

dragged away.

I'm pure hunger tonight, ravenous as hell to have her skin under my fingers.

And Philia's so soft to the touch.

My fingers sink into lush thighs and curving hips, the hot round swells of her breasts.

I goddamned well devour her with my hands, never breaking away from a kiss that leaves our mouths wet as I savage her with teeth and needy tongue-thrusts, starving to taste her.

In mere seconds she's thrashing under me in total sweet surrender, her mouth slack and needy, her nipples hard against my palms.

I can't fucking wait.

I feel like I've got ten damn years to make up for and I want to brand her into my flesh until my hands remember the feel of her even when we're apart.

So I touch her everywhere, finding the forbidden places that make her moan against my lips, that shake her apart. Everywhere that makes her go so tense she's trembling.

Her tongue lashes mine with silent curses that only encourage me more.

I'm possessed, thumbing her nipples, framing her waist with both hands, sliding over her hips, spreading her wide for me.

"So fucking wet. Good girl," I mutter, lashing a palm against her ass.

The crisp smack of skin only excites her more.

When I slide my fingers over her dripping flesh, she bites me.

Her hips shudder in a sharp jerk, and when I delve two fingers into her hot little pussy, her knees grasp at my waist and dig in.

That's it, darling Butterfly.

Let the fuck go.

Everything about her cuts me open.

From her whimpering cries against my lips to the way she writhes, impaled on me, her fingers dragging through my hair and telling me how bad she *wants* me.

I savor that, plunging my fingers inside her again and again—twisting them, curling them, stroking her and learning how she feels, all softness rippling and slick and soon-to-be devoted to my cock.

I need to feel her again.

I need to feel how good it gets when she's clenching on my cock, binding us together as we tumble into pleasure together.

It nearly kills me to tear myself away and pin her down under me.

To let go of that kiss, slip my dripping-wet fingers from inside her, fumble a condom from the nightstand, and shove my pajama pants down.

I have to fight to get the rubber on when my cock is pulsing like mad, this unruly bulge of straining energy and single-minded heat.

That heat becomes an inferno as I look down at her, gloriously open and naked beneath me, so tiny, so vulnerable, so ready to be *fucked* good and proper.

And she looks up at me with such trust through the haze of lust, flushed with desire, doing nothing to hide that lush body from my ravenous eyes.

Her pale skin glows in the moonlight.

Fuck, I almost say it.

I almost blow everything to little flaming bits by telling her I love her.

I already damn well told her once before, but with everything else going on, I don't think she was ready to hear it.

I definitely don't want to scare her off with those

words now.

Don't want to break this new, fragile thing we're building.

So I keep those words to myself and breathe until the air tastes like raw fire.

Snarling, I kiss that feeling into her lips instead, showing her my need to possess her.

I grip her thighs, hitch her against me, and seize her mouth.

I barely press my cock against her soft entrance before she's pushing herself against me.

So needy, so wanton, aching for my cock and needing to be filled.

A rough growl boils out of me.

Her hunger bleeds into me, rips away my control.

With a vicious groan, I slant my mouth harshly against hers, thieving her moans as I crash down to meet her, pinning her body to the bed.

In one hard surge of steaming flesh we merge till I'm buried balls deep inside her and all I can feel is Ophelia.

Her heat.

Her straining pleasure.

How she clutches at me so intently with arms and legs and shivering flesh, holding on so hard it's work to move and draw it out.

But I fucking need to.

The rush has taken over and there's no stopping it, drawing my hips back and losing my breath as the friction of our joined bodies drags over my cock.

It leaves me fucking fiending, insane to be inside her again.

Steeling my muscles, I arch my back and drive in harder.

Fuck fuck *fuck* I can't take it.

She's too good, too hot, too tight.

I can taste my name etched on her lips in every fluttering

moan.

My eyes pinch shut.

I can't even look at how beautiful she is against me or I'll lose it in a few messy seconds. Not when she's already driving me to the edge.

"Give that pussy up," I rasp. "Fucking mine, Ophelia."

She shudders deliciously.

With her body under mine, I fill her again and again, falling into a brutal rhythm like a rutting beast, venting a decade of pent-up need in every thrust.

This feels like a chase.

Like I'm chasing this pleasure, chasing her heart, chasing the love I need no matter what I have to do to earn it.

Panting.

Raw.

Groaning delight.

Merciless claws of pleasure savage me, but not just that.

Her nails find my back and their sweet sting pushes me higher, higher, drawing more primitive, uncontrolled heat from me until I'm slamming her into the bed.

And she's still rising up to meet me with frenzied breaths, her lip pushed between my teeth like a strawberry screaming to be devoured.

I oblige.

My thrusts match hers in every way as she fuses to my cock.

We rut on in sweat-slicked tension, in a quivering peak that towers over us like a wave, crashing and inevitable.

I bury myself in her one last time until something unspeakable hits.

A firebolt.

An invisible hand that reaches up inside me like a puppet and rips my pleasure out until I'm pouring it into her, baring my teeth and snarling like an animal.

Into her tight-locked depths.

Into this body that flows and fluxes and ripples and shudders just for me, and now I can't help but open my eyes to drink her in as we come together.

She's pearl and gold in the moonlight, her skin gleaming and her head thrown back.

Her back arches so beautifully, thrusting her tits toward me like an offering.

Watching as she loses herself in sheer ecstasy is a hundred proof shot to my soul.

It's like falling in love all over again.

It's like finding myself when I didn't know how lost I was.

It's like I've been waiting my entire life for this.

For *her*.

As she soars on my cock and slowly comes back to me with her eyes flitting open, staring up at me in wonder, I can't imagine a world without Ophelia Sanderson again.

SHE'S gonna kill me tonight and I'll die a happy man.

I feel like my heart's giving out as we collapse in a sweaty tangle—and I narrowly avoid crashing down and smothering her.

She's so delicate under me, this tiny thing I could crush like a hummingbird. One thing I love about her is that she's never been the slightest bit afraid of me or intimidated by my size.

Other people act like I'm one second away from hurting someone just because I'm big. They only see how easily I could bowl over a small crowd or turn a man's face into a sack of busted skin and bone.

Always looking at me like they're trying to find the threat.

They move different around me.

Keeping a certain space, like if they get any closer, they're afraid they'll get sucked into my gravity and compacted into tiny bits.

Not Ophelia.

She's never been afraid to get in my face and tell me what an asshole I am with the absolute faith of knowing that no matter how I react, she can handle it.

She can handle *me.*

Hell, I think she's handling this *sex* better than I am right now.

Because while I'm still shaking, shattered by just how goddamned good I feel right now, she's a content little bundle.

She barely waits for me to sprawl out on my side before she tucks herself into my arms and takes her place against my chest like she belongs there.

I'd sure as hell like to say she does.

Do I even know what the hell we're doing?

No.

All our lives, we've been part of each other's landscape, sharp rocks and all.

She was always my best friend's little sister, but we were friends.

We didn't talk about it.

We didn't admit it.

We didn't dare.

She was just part of this unspoken thing that made us, and now I see that *us* didn't break when Ethan disappeared, even if it took one hell of a beating.

I just never knew she had feelings for me, though I guess I was pretty damn good at hiding how I felt, too.

Still, just 'cause she's living with me temporarily and we fell into bed together doesn't mean we're something more. Something *solid.*

As I press my lips into her hair, gathering her close and breathing in the sweat misted on her skin, I wonder.

How the fuck do I ask?

How do I even know what I want from her?

All I can think about is the present, this magic moment, how perfect she feels when she's curled up and trusting me with her life.

"Mmm." She sighs, rubbing her cheek to my chest. "That was a much better way to end the day than it started."

I chuckle. "Was this morning so bad?"

"Not *that*." She swats my chest lightly. "I liked waking up with you. Remember I was out grocery shopping and ran into Janelle Bowden?"

I open one eye. "Yeah? She adores you. What happened?"

"She's..." Ophelia frowns, tilting her head to peer up at me through her sex-mussed hair. "She's still carrying a lot of guilt over what happened to Lucas' wife, I guess. And she doesn't trust the chief anymore, as crazy as that sounds. Almost like she thinks he was complicit, instead of just being his lazy self and close enough to retirement to stop giving a crap. But she also said some weird stuff about Ros being engaged—and about our mom, too."

I stiffen.

Anything I was about to say in defense of the chief and my own worries flies out of my brain. I stare at her.

"Your ma? The hell you mean?"

"I don't know," Ophelia whispers, laying her head on my shoulder with a fretful knit between her brows. "But she hinted Mom used to be pretty close to the Arrendells, way back before I was born. She didn't have anything else to say, but that makes me wonder even more what Aleksander wants with Ros."

"Me too," I say too quickly.

I gather Ophelia close, wishing I could protect her from more worries and dark thoughts.

Maybe it's nothing.

Though Janelle Bowden wouldn't go stomping around spreading rumors lightly.

That gives me a sneaking suspicion it isn't, and it hangs like an axe over my head as I hold Ophelia till sleep finds us.

* * *

I NEVER SLEEP LONG that night.

Eventually, my girl drifts off in a relaxed bundle against me, her soft breaths tickling my chest and shoulder.

But me?

My brain's spinning too many circles to let me rest.

Mostly, I'm knee-deep in my memories.

Being older than Ophelia, I was around Angela Sanderson since I was in grade school, back when Ethan was her only kid.

That was how we met.

Some of the kids at recess were picking on him because he was moping around and didn't want to talk to anybody, always curled up with his Tolkien books. I thought he was gonna get completely pounded, but he was a scrapper. Ethan threw himself into the fray like he didn't care if he got murdered by a bunch of pipsqueaks.

I didn't like it.

So I turned that fight into two on ten and somehow we came out of it alive—beat to hell and back but *alive*—and friends before we even knew each other's last names.

That was how I found out his dad died of leukemia and it was just Ethan and his ma.

That he wasn't moping 'cause he was a 'big nerd' like the kids called him, but 'cause he missed his old man like any normal boy would. Even when we were munchkins, I remember being so mad anyone could pick on him for that that I could spit nails.

The rest of it, that's where I blank out.

I can't remember seeing Angela Sanderson with the Arrendells one time.

Could just be holes in my memory. Muddled stuff from childhood that doesn't like to stick, the same way your old life falls away like a dream as you grow up.

I dunno.

Something about this ain't adding up, though.

Feels like it's right in front of my face.

I just can't fucking see it.

There's some bigger picture coming together here and I'm too close to make out what it is. I can't shake the weirdness.

It's almost like you're being watched.

Like the shadow of the Arrendells looming over Redhaven is this invisible force, always staring down from every corner, leering and watching your every movement—

Crack.

I go stiff as something *snaps* outside.

Wrapping my arms tighter around Ophelia, I gather her close.

Maybe that feeling ain't just my imagination after all.

Because that sure as hell sounded like somebody stepping on leaves in my yard.

Moving stealthily, I lift myself up to peer through the window over the headboard without jostling her.

There's a solid view of the front from there.

While common sense tells me it's just a critter or the wind skittering yard debris across the driveway, my instincts smell a rat.

Or rather, a tall, ominous skinny figure standing on the

walk right outside my fucking house, staring up at the window like he knows I'm looking back.

Same dude.

Thin. Grey hair. Tailcoat.

The asshole stalker.

Pure primal instinct takes over—can't let him escape again.

I jolt out of bed with Ophelia's startled cry trailing me, pelting across the floor and leaping downstairs two at a time.

Pure frustration drives me like I'm a human engine and someone just poured white-hot fuel through me.

That man, whoever he is, can't be up to any good.

He's a threat.

The fact that he scared the bejeezus out of the woman I love is enough reason to pound him senseless.

Like hell I'll let him get away.

I streak through the house, momentum throwing me to the front door and out to the porch.

The moment I tear the door open, the man starts, stumbling back.

He's fucking real.

Not just my imagination.

Definitely not an illusion as I catch a glimpse of a haggard, wrinkled face, fearful black eyes, and a mouth pulled down in a sagging curve.

We lock eyes for a split second.

I smell pure dread in his face.

Then he turns and bolts into the night.

He's spry for an old stalkery fuck, and he's got a head start —not that it stops me from rocketing after him.

I barely feel the cold air or the rough wooden porch boards on my bare feet—then the asphalt, the ground, cracked twigs stabbing my calloused feet as I chase him through the trees.

How is he so quick?

His long legs fly in a blur, tailcoat streaming behind him, breathing loudly through clenched teeth.

Asshole, no, you don't!

I pour everything into the frantic chase, closing the distance one ground-eating stride at a time, fists clenched as I pump my arms, faster, *faster* until—

He vanishes into the tree line at the edge of my property.

Fuck.

Snarling, I plunge in after him, the shadows under the branches swallowing me whole.

Boughs and shrubs scratch at my arms, my shoulders, my chest.

I shove the foliage aside, scanning left and right, searching through the dense tree trunks, but there's nothing.

Nothing but the earthy smell of autumn and the screech of a startled owl.

Dammit all.

I can't see more than a foot or two in front of my face.

Even with the trees mostly stripped of their leaves, the branches are a thick net. The black starless sky doesn't help tonight, either.

Sighing, I stumble to a halt, inhaling and exhaling roughly, my breaths puffing in white clouds of rage.

Shit.

I've lost him.

And what the fuck just happened?

What *was* that?

What does he want with me and Ophelia?

* * *

"I DON'T KNOW," Ophelia answers, after I voice the same question out loud.

I've got a funny feeling I'm about to get my head ripped clean off and honestly, rightfully so.

"But look at you, Grant—you didn't even put shoes on. You're a mess..."

Her eyes shine with sympathy.

Wincing, I make myself hold still while she dabs an alcohol wipe over a long scrape down my forearm, thin and shallow enough that the blood's mostly dried.

I didn't even feel it when it happened.

The moment I came stomping out of the woods and found her standing on the porch in nothing but one of my shirts with her phone clutched in her hand, 9-1-1 already partially typed in, she insisted on parking me on the sofa and checking me over.

Wouldn't that have been a riot?

Calling 9-1-1 from the police captain's house.

The boys would never let me live it down for the next decade.

While she cleans my arm, I pluck a dead leaf out of my hair.

"Sorry," I grind out. "Never meant to startle you like that —or worry you. When I saw him, I had to—"

"Had to what? You scared the *shit* out of me, Grant!" Ophelia smacks my arm, right above the scratch. That honestly stings more than the little abrasions all over my chest and shoulders, though there's a deeper one on the sole of my foot from a sharp stick that's starting to throb. "Just tearing out of here like crazy, you didn't even *say* anything. I just woke up to you running and no idea what the hell was going on. What about Nell? If you'd been a minute later, I'd have called the cops first and asked questions later."

Goddamn, this woman.

Nell's no relation to her, yet her first thought isn't for herself. It's for my little girl.

She's brave as hell.

By some miracle, Nelly-girl snoozed through the ruckus. I'd like to keep it that way, so that's why we talk in low, rough voices.

I also get it.

Even now, she's hiding behind anger, but her cheeks are flushed and her lips pressed together into a nervous line. Her lashes quiver as she glares down at her hands, her fingers clumsy as she fumbles with the cap on the alcohol bottle.

I reach out to cover her hand, stopping her, and tip her face up to kiss those trembling lips.

My heart wants to stop, knowing that tremor is for *me*.

That she cares so goddamned much.

I remember what I was thinking about before I heard that snap.

I don't know what we are to each other, but I sure as hell want to have that conversation.

I can't imagine letting Ophelia slip out of my life.

Not unless she really wants to go.

Not unless she plans to run off again and leave the dust of my heart and the ashes of this freaky town in her wake for good.

Tracing the line of her lips, I draw back, stroking her cheek.

"I'm fine now," I murmur. "More worried about you, Philia. This man's clearly stalking you. You feeling okay?"

"No," she answers, though with less force than before. "I'm *angry,* Grant. What does he want with me? Why is he doing this?"

"Wish I knew," I reply before firming my voice into a promise. "Tomorrow, I'm going up to the big house—and I'll be damned if I leave before I get some answers."

* * *

FRANKLY, I don't know if I'm going to get shit.

Certainly not without a fight.

I stand in the grand hall of the Arrendell mansion with Montero Arrendell just over my shoulder.

He's hovering, sticking just close enough that it's obvious he's trying to make me uncomfortable.

If I actually gave a shit, he might be intimidating.

Right now, I'm too far past that.

I'm laser focused on the full staff complement lined up in front of me. Men and women in maid uniforms or tailcoats and livery.

Seeing these girls with their hair skimmed back and their demure black dresses just makes me uncomfortable, remembering the dead woman dressed in the exact outfit not long ago. Same woman we found swinging from the chandelier of this very room.

My frown becomes a scowl.

No one looks like they're over the age of forty-five here except for one wrinkled little man in breeches. Montero identified him as the stableman—how weird is having a stableman in the twenty-first century?—but when you have the money...

I sweep them all with hard looks, thumbs hooked in the belt loops of my uniform pants, then turn my head over my shoulder to Montero.

"And this is everyone?" I ask skeptically. "No one's called in today?"

"Not one," he announces in his deep, rolling voice. His charming confidence doesn't work on me any more than this invasion of my personal space. I just eye him. "They're all live-in staff, Captain Faircross. If someone else was missing, I'd escort you to their quarters personally myself."

"Uh-huh."

I turn my gaze back to the staff.

Every last one of them stares at the ground, averting their eyes. Nobody meets my gaze except for a few halfhearted glances and quick smiles.

Wonder what the hell they'd tell me if Montero wasn't in the room.

The men's outfits are dead ringers for our stalker.

My memory wasn't failing me when I made that connection.

Exact same cut, same colors, same fit as the man who's been trailing Ophelia like a demented ghost.

Yeah, something ain't right here.

Montero claps his hands together.

"All right, everyone, please return to work. You'll be compensated with an hour of overtime for the inconvenience." He says it pleasantly, but there's an undertone there —*you've inconvenienced my staff and inconvenienced me by having to compensate them for it, you stupid cop*. And that nastiness lingers as he steps forward to look at me. "Captain, could you kindly be a tad more clear what this is about?"

It's a question, but he frames it like an order.

I sigh, taking my time before answering.

"You had any thefts here lately, Mr. Arrendell? Even petty stuff? People raiding the linen closet or anything? Stealing uniforms?"

His aristocratic black brows draw together. "Well, I don't exactly monitor inventory in the linen supply closet myself."

"Somebody should," I growl. "You're swearing no one on staff meets this guy's description, but maybe someone stole some of their duds."

"For *what*, Captain Faircross? What possible motive?" An edge of cultured exasperation enters Montero's voice. "What is this man accused of, that you come storming up to my doorstep—as if we're somehow to blame?"

I don't get a chance to answer.

He wouldn't like what I'd have to say, anyway, 'cause right now I'm not telling him *shit.* Nothing he can use to deflect if he is somehow involved.

And I'll be damned if he isn't.

I've seen Lucas' folder.

All those newspaper clippings showing Montero back in the seventies, eighties, and nineties, gliding through high society and hundreds of women like a Grim fucking Reaper, always trailing death in his wake.

No evidence, of course.

But nobody stacks up that many coincidences.

Wherever this man goes, tragedy follows.

And it feels like I'm watching a new tragedy unfolding in slow motion as the staff scatter like startled mice into the walls.

Two familiar faces come strutting in through the main entryway.

Ros and Aleksander, clearly dragging themselves in from a night of hard partying.

Her rumpled bright-red dress gives me a heart-shot of sick rage and cold fear.

For a second, I'm seeing another beautiful young woman in red.

Emma Santos, dead on the floor of that little house where Delilah Graves was living.

Then Delilah herself, sobbing in the back of an ambulance in another red dress while Lucas held her so hard, all while she stammered out the shocking details of what happened for her police report.

Ros is right here, I remind myself.

She's not in danger—yet.

She's alive and well and God willing, I'll keep it that way.

I just need to drive her away from that drug-addled, panty-sniffing fuck.

She doesn't even notice me, completely absorbed in Aleksander, stumbling against him with clumsy movements and his arm holding her up.

Damn, are they always like this?

I can't remember the last time I saw her sober. Had to be months ago.

Worse, she's mooning at him like he's a rock star, so awestruck she's barely breathing.

Aleksander, he's not looking back at her.

The prick stares at me, his green eyes glacial and unblinking like an alien winter.

His smile slow, cruel, and knowing.

Now that I think about it, I think it wasn't drugs or booze in the bar that made him act that way. He wanted to show me a little glimpse of his real self. Selfish and reckless and arrogant as hell.

A young man who's so used to getting his way he flaunts it in my face, sneering and asking, *What're you going to do about it, Captain?*

That hollow smile says he's making me a promise.

I just don't know what it means or how I've pissed him off today.

As they stagger past, my blood runs cold.

Aleksander makes a big show of gathering Ros possessively close and kissing her right there in the middle of the grand hall.

Not just for me, I realize.

Because while Montero watches them, his eyes distant and thoughtful, his face changes.

His smile is all teeth and edges, his face a mask.

There's no shaking the terrible feeling I'm witnessing something vile.

Like I'm looking at the face of the Devil himself, just daring me to stop him before it's too late.

XVI: ONLY ONE REGRET
(OPHELIA)

*C*oming home to Redhaven felt like traveling back in time to a frozen past that hasn't changed much in the decade I've been gone.

But nothing highlights the differences more than the fact that I'm standing behind the counter at Nobody's Bees-Ness, minding the shop, totally isolated with the scent of beeswax, honey, and loneliness.

I didn't know Ros hasn't opened the shop in days until one of the locals called the home line saying she'd been by to pick up her order for a baby shower and found the shop closed every time.

Ugh.

I've tended the family business before, but it was *different* then.

Minding the register while Mom took a lunch break or ran cash over to the bank.

Keeping an eye on the register while she was in her cluttered workshop in the back, her delicate fingers working over a special personalized custom order.

Making Ros sit in the break room and do her homework while Mom was out talking to suppliers, and my brat of a sister doing everything she could to test my patience.

God.

Even when this shop was empty, I never felt alone here.

I always knew Mom or Ros would be back soon.

We were *together*, even when we were apart.

Now, that feeling is gone.

It's the same homey scent, the same oasis of cute wax goods, but the vibe has shifted.

There's just me, basking in the silence of the golden lights and willing myself to believe it'll all be okay in the end. Somehow.

The hole in my chest feels big enough to fall into.

Sighing, I slip away from the empty storefront into the back.

It's both a storeroom and a workshop, the shelves lined with rows of bottled honey, jars with bits of honeycomb, plus larger wedges and sheets delicately wrapped up and kept in temperature-controlled coolers.

A long, weathered oak table runs the entire length of the back wall, still covered with my mother's tools. It's like she was only here yesterday, lovingly hunched over her creations.

There's a massive industrial stove kitty-corner to it.

My mother's worktable is half sculptor's workbench and the rest mad scientist's lab. The shelf perched over the table is filled with dried herbs in mason jars, along with more drying flowers hanging in bunches from strings overhead.

Their faded scent adds to that honey-beeswax aroma like a wish I can't quite capture.

This was Mom's home as much as our little place in town.

She did everything here.

New ways of distilling beeswax and essential oils, always playing with crafting little beeswax sculptures carved with needle-fine details. Crafting small hand-rolled sticks of lip balm littered with vibrantly colored petals that turn them into masterpieces.

There's still a half-finished project sitting there—a beeswax candle rolled from an entire sheet of solid honeycomb, carefully formed to keep the hexagon sheets from warping.

She was delicately building tiny people inside each open block of the honeycomb, using bits of flower petals and glue with tiny tweezers to craft a scene.

Everything from a little flower person mowing the lawn to another watering their garden, another knitting. As the candle burned down, it would slowly expose the little scenes before burning these precious things away forever.

Just like Mom's time on Earth, melting away as quickly as wax.

She's burning away right now.

An incomplete masterpiece just like this.

A life left unfinished.

Not again.

I'm *not* going to cry over my mother's worktable.

Absolutely not.

I've done enough crying in the last few weeks for several lifetimes.

Sucking in several deep breaths, I focus on tidying up, always keeping an ear out for the jingling bell over the shop door.

No one's dusted back here since Mom went into the hospital. So I wipe down the shelves and organize, telling myself I'm getting it ready so it'll be in perfect condition when she gets better and comes home.

There's not much else to do.

Though we have a good glut of tourists at the moment, they tend to get their shopping done in the early days of their long visits so they can spend the rest of their time exploring the outdoors or trying out local restaurants.

It'll pick up again around Christmas when people want rustic gift baskets to give away.

The big-city folks love that, proudly announcing that they found some handmade kitsch in a cute little shop in back-woods North Carolina. I just wonder who'll be running the store for the holidays.

If Ros doesn't get better...

Oh, here we go.

The hoarse sob braying out of me hits me like a baseball bat to the face.

I drop my rag and clap both hands over my mouth.

I can't think of still being here at Christmas.

I can't think of what it'll be like with just me alone in that house and Ros swept off to God knows where with Alek-sander Dickhead like nothing else matters.

Mom *gone.*

What do I have to keep me here if she passes?

Grant?

Yes.

But also, no, it's too soon.

He has a life here I can't just intrude on permanently with my heart torn and bleeding.

...and am I honestly thinking of staying in this little red-gabled hellmouth just because my childhood crush suddenly likes me back?

It's not like gravity-defying wonder-sex means there's a future.

Not even real feelings mean that, no matter how compli-cated they might be.

He doesn't owe me anything.

His life is complicated enough, and the thought of dumping my drama, my mess, on Grant and that sweet little girl...

The lump in my throat feels like a cactus.

We haven't talked about it, of course.

It just happened.

We tumbled into this together.

And I'm in such free fall that adding another layer of uncertainty doesn't help anything.

But I still think of Redhaven as home.

Some childish part of me thinks that if I just hope hard enough, everything will turn out fine.

Mom will pull off a miraculous recovery.

Ros will come to her senses, or somehow, I'll find out that Aleksander's a pretty decent, misunderstood guy underneath his creeper façade.

Grant and I, we'll—I don't even know.

Settle down and live happily ever after?

Maybe little Nell wouldn't mind that when she's already got me wrapped around her little finger.

Then I won't have to sell the family house because Mom will be there, growing old, clucking her tongue at me because I haven't brought my man and kid around for dinner in a few weekends and... and...

Sweet Jesus.

I'm deluding myself, aren't I?

Weaving a ridiculous fairy tale so I don't have to face the hard truth that everything I love is falling apart and the only thing stable right now is Grant.

I wonder if he'd mind if I called him.

Just to hear that slow, drawling voice, that gruffness that's so gentle when you learn his language.

The thought makes me feel better, like he's reaching out to comfort me.

I wish I could be home with Grant right now, curled up on the sofa with a bowl of popcorn and a goofy movie and Nell snuggled between us, demanding our attention.

Then the bell over the shop door jingles.

It hits like a gunshot, but it's what I need—a reminder to get out of my own head, keep it together, and take on life one minute at a time.

And right now, I have a customer, so I splash my face with water from the little sink in my mother's work area, take a deep breath, and put on my best smile before I walk to the register.

"Welcome to Nobody's Bees—"

I freeze.

This time it's not a gunshot to my chest.

It's a cannonball.

The door swings shut with a rattling jingle before my vision stabilizes.

My stalker takes several reeling steps into the shop with blood dripping past his stained lips and running down his chin.

I stare at him, my mouth trembling, my body rooted in place.

"Oh my God," I whisper. Concern and fear rip through me. "A-are you...?"

He clutches at his stomach—and I notice his hands are filthy, grimed with mud.

He stops like he's just realizing he isn't alone.

His head lifts sluggishly and muddled eyes look at me from beneath the disarrayed mess of his silver hair, his gaze set deep in rough hollows.

He lets out a guttural sound, gurgling pain.

Then he turns and nearly flings himself out the door, making it bang violently with his weight as he stumbles back onto the sidewalk.

"Hey—wait!" I yell, stretching out a hand.

But he's gone, disappearing into the street.

I only hesitate a second before I find my strength, my head.

Some wild urge hurls me out after him.

Yes, I know it's risky, but I have to know.

What does he want with me?

I burst out into the frosty afternoon, sucking in cold, searing breaths, looking left and right.

No sign of him, but there's something else.

Blood.

Right on the sidewalk.

Small gory droplets leading left in an uneven line.

I follow the faint trail until it vanishes between Mom's shop and the pâtisserie next door.

Then I duck into the alley between the buildings, just in time to see the flash of his tailcoat behind him.

I don't know how he moves so fast in his condition, but he's a whole two blocks down, struggling past the buildings on the opposite street toward the thick clumps of trees leading into the hills.

"Hey!" I call, racing after him.

I go careening off the side of a building as I rush down the pavement, pumping my short legs as fast as they can go, desperate to catch up.

Stalker Guy has a visible limp.

As injured as he is, he shouldn't be able to keep so far ahead of me, but he's as tall and leggy as an ostrich, so his unstable steps cover two of mine. There's a stitch in my side and my ribs hurt by the time I break past the buildings, just as he vanishes into the trees.

Panting, I bend over for a second, hands on my thighs, sucking in a few harsh breaths.

"Not again," I gasp.

Then I decide I've had enough.

I'm not letting go this easy.

Gathering my last strength, I plunge into the woods after him, ignoring the burn knifing through my whole body.

It's like chasing a ghost.

Just glimpses of him up ahead, always too far away.

I'm stumbling through underbrush, tripping over fallen branches, flailing and just barely catching myself before forging on.

This time, it's different.

If I don't catch him, I never will.

It's like I'm electrified, something unnatural pushing me on, forcing me after him, because there's something *here*, some answer, some secret I have to know.

And even if there isn't—

He's hurt. Bleeding from the mouth, limping, obviously dazed and confused.

If I don't do something, he could die out here.

But I'm worried I've lost him.

I can't hear anything but my own crashing footsteps and raging heartbeat.

No more of those glimpses, no snapping twigs up ahead, no sign of him at all, but I keep moving.

And I nearly smack right into him as I break through a gap in the trees into a clearing thick with stacks of orange and brown leaves.

He sways in front of me.

Only for a second while I stop in my tracks, staring.

Then he collapses like a falling tree, wheezing as his lanky frame falls down in a pale tangle of limbs at my feet.

At first I don't see it, not when I'm on my knees, searching for a pulse.

But once I see he's still alive, the churned-up patch of dirt next to him catches my eye.

There, the bones protrude from the ground, sharp off-white fingers of human ribs stabbing up at the sky.

XVII: ONE GOOD TURN (GRANT)

*W*hen you've been a cop as long as I have, you learn to trust one thing.

If something smells bad, it's probably rotten.

Right now, this whole situation stinks to high heaven.

The clearing in the woods on the west side of town, just on the far edge of the tiny central shopping district, is a riot of color.

The violent yellow-orange of October leaves.

The retina-burning contrast of red and blue patrol lights flashing, clashing with the red and orange of the whirling ambulance flashers.

The black-and-white patrol cars.

The vibrant green of the last few pine needles slowly turning dull for winter.

Then there's the blaring red of that man's blood, so coppery crimson it's loud.

It spills down his chin, turning muddy brown as the splatters left behind soak into the disturbed earth.

Also, the sickening paleness of those bleached bones.

The skull is just a dome protruding from the dirt. One

empty socket partly exposed, staring at me like it's waiting for me to give it a name.

Now I get why some folks say the dead can be more demanding than the living.

God-fucking-dammit.

Every time I think I've learned just how fucked up the secrets in this town are, something darker turns up.

Some*one* else.

This deep instinct inside me twitches, aching to know, but also afraid to find out who.

I might not like knowing who those bones belong to.

Still, it's part of the job.

Tearing my gaze away from the unmarked grave, I refocus on the paramedics carrying that man to the back of Redhaven's lone ambulance. They push the stretcher up the small slope of hill to the highway visible in snatches just past the woods.

My crew stalk through the scene like scavengers, staking out the clearing with police tape, cordoning it off in yellow lines that add another garish splash of color to this unholy ground.

One of the EMTs breaks away, giving the man one last troubled look before jogging over with her brown ponytail bouncing.

"Captain Faircross?" she says breathlessly. "Hey, I'll get you a full medical workup for your police report once we've had a good look at him at the medical center, but..."

"But?" I prompt.

"Right now, it's looking like attempted suicide," she says reluctantly. "From taking his vitals, he's going into organ failure. Vomiting blood was a classic sign. Some sort of toxic substance, I bet. It's possible he tried to kill himself with rat poison, antifreeze—there are a ton of household cleaners that could do the trick. Even overdosing on some OTC meds.

Actually, I'd put my odds on that, this dude wandering off under the influence. Anyway, once we run toxicology, I'll have a better idea for you."

"Thank you," I grind out. That's the only thing I can manage when my mind's still stuck on her very first words.

Attempted suicide.

Second suicide in less than a month.

Don't fucking tell me it's not connected to the Arrendells.

No matter what Montero said—no matter what fucking front they put up, parading their staff in front of me—that uniform doesn't lie.

It's the same suit every other butler there wears.

They're connected, somehow.

Cora Lafayette's death and this strange man's attempt.

They can't *not* be.

No way in hell.

The ambulance starts its siren and the EMT gives me an expectant look.

I nod at the vehicle.

"Go on. I'll wait for y'all to call. Gonna work the crime scene over in the meantime."

She stares at those bones significantly, then snaps off a sharp nod before jogging back through the trees. I watch her until she vaults over the highway guardrail up the slope and vanishes into the back of the ambulance. The door barely slams shut before the thing goes rocketing off toward the outskirts of town, screaming like a banshee the whole way.

Leaving just me.

My team.

Those bones.

Plus, the slim figure huddled in the back seat of my patrol car, leaning against the window and watching Micah, Henri, and Lucas move around the crime scene efficiently. My men hold up well, putting down evidence markers and noting points of interest, all the places that could possibly hide other graves.

Right now, nothing's off-limits as far as possibilities go.

If anything, this shit promises to be weirder than anyone would think.

As I step closer to the squad car, Ophelia turns her head toward me, her green eyes haunted in the shadows.

I rip the rear driver's side door open and prop my arm on the roof, leaning in.

"Hey. How're you holding up?"

"Still pretty shaken up, honestly." She smiles weakly. She's wearing my uniform jacket again—I have *got* to talk this woman into buying a proper winter coat—and she pulls it around herself tighter, huddling under it like it's an emergency blanket. "Think you could drop Captain Faircross long enough to be just Grant? I wouldn't mind a hug."

"I can do both, if you don't mind talking a little." I ease into the back seat and stretch one arm along the back.

In seconds, I've got a blonde burr against my side, huddling against me and making herself small.

She *feels* so small it worries me as I pull her closer.

I can feel her trembling under my arm.

Fuck, I hate that her homecoming has been nothing but one ugly shock after the next.

"You're safe," I whisper, resting my chin on top of her head, holding her tight. "For what it's worth, I don't think that guy was trying to hurt you. Medic said it's looking like an attempted suicide."

"Suicide?" Ophelia inhales sharply. "Then why...?"

"He might've had second thoughts. Or he might've been hopped up on something that messed with his brain. Maybe he went looking for help and tripped over you."

"God. And it just happened to be *me?* After he's been

following me around town," she points out skeptically. "What else? What are you not saying, Grant?"

I snort loudly.

"You know, you're the only person who can read me like that, and some days, I swear..." I trail off into a grunt. "I just got a funny feeling, Philia. Those bones, that man, another suicide connected to the fucking Arrendells. The maid who hung herself weeks ago, and now this guy turns up half spun out of his mind, wearing their uniform."

She's silent for a terrible minute, her head resting on my shoulder and her gaze trained outward thoughtfully.

"Aokigahara," she murmurs.

"A-oki-huh? You speaking Japanese now?"

"Yeah. I read about it in the news once after this YouTuber caused a huge scandal by being disrespectful. It's this place in Japan called the Suicide Forest," she says softly. "So many people go there to end it all that the rangers can't keep up with all the bodies, even though they try to keep people out. They even try to talk people out of doing something awful. Some people say it's just a trend, but others think there's something dark out there that convinces people to kill themselves there. Sorry. I know what I sound like. I just can't help thinking..."

She trails off, but her head turns, gazing at the big rise over the town. The one where that big house squats like some terrible demon of bleached bone with its windows gleaming like orange demon eyes.

If anywhere could be haunted enough to drive people to suicide just from stepping foot on its grounds, it's there.

The Arrendell mansion.

"But you don't think it's suicide at all, do you?" she finishes.

"Don't know yet," I say. "I've got some odd hunches.

Something itching at the back of my head, y'know? But I need to think. Sort things out. Wait for toxicology."

And possibly an autopsy, if our mystery man doesn't make it.

"I feel a little weird myself." Ophelia's eyes gravitate to the spot where Micah's crouching next to the unearthed bones, delicately sweeping the dirt away with gloved fingers. "Who do you think that is, Grant?"

I don't answer.

The question hangs deathly heavy between us.

I think we're both wondering the same thing, even if the possibility's mighty slim.

So many people have disappeared in Redhaven over the years.

Residents.

Random hikers.

Punk-ass kids who took their mischief too far and wound up in real trouble.

Sometimes, we find folks in the woods looking kind of like that suicide forest she talked about. People get lost, wander off the paths, disappear into some little niche where nobody can find them.

It's dense as hell out here beyond town. You could walk three feet and not even notice them there, frozen to death or torn up by coyotes or cougars. The odds that it's Ethan are slim.

Even so, I still get that *feeling*.

"Hey," I say. "You wanna run what happened by me again? A little more detail this time."

"I kind of stumbled over that when I was screaming into the phone, huh?" Ophelia smiles painfully. "There's not that much more to say, honestly. I was in the back storage room at the shop, tidying up, when I heard the bell over the door. I went out and he was just standing there, pale and reeling, bleeding from the mouth. He didn't say anything. He just turned and ran, taking off between the buildings. Crazy stamina for a man with internal bleeding, but..." She stops. When she speaks again, her voice is hushed, her eyes lidding over. "I guess I felt like he was leading me somewhere. Into the woods, then here. I bet he's the one who dug up those bones. I don't know, maybe he wanted it this way. Maybe he wanted me to—"

"He wanted you to see them," I finish softly.

"Yeah."

"Only question is why?"

"No clue." Ophelia shakes her head. "But I think you're asking the same questions I am, right now."

Damn right.

Like how long that man's been working up at the manor and who he is. It's definitely easy to find out when the Arrendell house runs parallel to Redhaven like its own little insular world.

Folks can spend years working up there without anyone in town catching hide nor hair of them.

We don't know if he was around ten, fifteen years ago.

Or whether or not he knows shit about people who disappeared back then.

What secrets has he been sitting on?

Did he know about Ulysses and the hillfolk?

About what the rest of that vicious clan get up to?

And who would stage a suicide—hell, maybe *two* suicides —to keep those secrets quiet?

I don't like it.

I like it even less that Ophelia seems to be at the center of it. All because this man's fixated on her for some bizarre reason—and I doubt that's coincidence.

Redhaven is a place where coincidence goes to die.

Just have to hope like hell he wakes up and starts talking soon.

I've got some important fucking *questions*, all right.

Like what I can do to keep Ophelia safe, besides staying by her side as much as possible. I have to make sure the Arrendells don't get a single step closer to her.

After all, it's not that house that brings misfortune.

It's not that house that brings death.

If there's a stain on this town, it's them.

It's in their blood.

And I damn sure won't let it consume the woman I love.

XVIII: ONE PLUS ONE (OPHELIA)

J don't know why Grant keeps acting like I've gotten less stubborn as I've gotten older.

When he tries to tell me to go home and rest, I tell him he knows exactly where he can stuff it. I won't take no for an answer until he lets me tag along to the medical center.

I need to know what's going on with my stalker and I'm hoping—

Actually, I don't know what I'm hoping for.

Maybe that my own nursing expertise might help find answers somehow, even if it's nothing more than a little analysis to help with the case report.

But it depends what he was poisoned with, and maybe a few vitals that might show whether he took it on purpose, by accident, or by force.

It's hard being here again so soon, standing outside the big observation window looking in at a room that's almost identical to Mom's. Right down to the same yellowish curtains on the outside windows.

It's not a big place.

She's down the hall, too, just a few doors away.

It's hard to remember I'm not here for her, though Grant's presence at my side helps.

He's grimly silent, his hazel eyes fixed firmly on the man's lanky, pale figure as the doctors and nurses work, stripping him out of his tailcoat and the shirt and slacks underneath.

He's wasted with more than just age.

Sunken ribs, grey skin, and his breaths come in shallow wheezes.

It's painful to watch as they intubate him, forcing his throat to take the respirator tube. IV needles run glucose and whatever they think he needs to counteract organ failure.

They're going to have to pump his stomach, probably, since he's not conscious to take liquid charcoal or anything else to voluntarily expel the poison—assuming it's not already too deep in his system.

There's a foamy froth around his lips where the tube goes in.

My stomach flips over.

I have to close my eyes and look away.

"I can't believe this was suicide," I whisper. "His body's shutting down in one of the worst ways possible. I just... I can't imagine anyone dying that way voluntarily. If he over-dosed on sleeping pills, maybe. Slipping away unconscious where you can't feel the pain. But bleeding from the inside like that..."

"He's not your mother, Butterfly," Grant says quietly. One large, warm hand settles on my shoulder, a comforting weight that eases the shock of that sudden insight. "It's not the same. You're not watching your mother die. And she didn't choose to suffer, either."

My throat starts closing, my next breath coming ragged, but I manage to choke it back.

"I know." I lean into him, resting against his side and letting his presence take the edge off being here. "I just hope he survives. Not so we can pry out whatever he knows, or why he's been following me. Because nobody deserves to die like that."

"That's my main concern," Grant growls.

"You were right, though." I curl my hand against the rock-hard tautness of Grant's forearm. The thick hair there tickles my palm. "I don't think he was trying to hurt me. Maybe trying to warn me."

"Yeah, but about what?"

Before I try to guess through too many swirling thoughts, one of the nurses breaks away from the huddled heads bowed over the man's twitching body and steps out of the room.

Without a word, she offers something to Grant.

A simple black leather wallet, slim and folded shut.

Grant grunts his thanks and takes the wallet.

The nurse answers with a nod, then ducks back into the room and joins the rest of her team again.

With a questioning look for me, Grant flicks the wallet open.

There's not much inside, what looks like a debit card, a security access card, an ID, some cash, a few receipts. Grant slides the ID out and tilts it so I can see.

"Mason Law." I read the name out loud slowly. Even his photo in the ID looks gaunt and sad. From the birthday, he's sixty-four years old. "Is there a Law family in town?"

"Nah. Nobody with that name's moved in since you've been gone. He's not from here, I'd say, though I'll get started on a real background check ASAP." Muttering to himself, Grant fishes out the receipts. "Nothing really damning here. Looks like grocery shopping, mostly. Stopped by the hardware store yesterday. Bought a hose." He frowns. "What the hell? Was he gonna try carbon monoxide poisoning first? Lock himself in a garage?"

"God, I hope not." I shake my head, glancing at Law. "Honestly, if I had to guess..." I flick my gaze over his half-closed, empty eyes, the way he's starting to convulse so stiffly. "Wait, he's seizing, Grant. That's a classic symptom of ricin poisoning."

"*Ricin?* Like in the TV shows?" Grant does a double take. "Where the fuck would a civilian get ricin in this day and age, let alone use it to try to off himself?"

"It's not that hard to make from certain beans," I point out. "The internet makes it pretty easy to get a crash course in all sorts of crazy stuff. Plus, it's so potent, you only need a little. It only takes a pinch to make the body shut down and crash. But it's just weird, to me."

"Weird how?" Grant asks.

"There are easier ways to do it. Ways that don't hurt so much. Substances that don't have to be made so precisely. So many over the counter meds that'll let you slip off in your sleep while your liver shuts down."

He stares at me.

"If you weren't a nurse, I'd be really damned disturbed that you know that." Grant watches me carefully. Like he's worried for me that I have to know these things. "You deal with a lot of suicides back in Miami?"

"I worked in a hospice center," I point out. There's a pain there that tells me that no matter what happens to Mom, I might not be able to go back to my old career. I don't know how to handle torturing myself like that again, no matter how much it helps comfort someone else.

There's only so much fuel in the soul before your tank runs empty.

"Right," he mutters.

"Sometimes people just want to choose how they go out, instead of waiting for their bodies to finish fading away naturally. Sometimes, other people step in, their loved ones wanting to help. So they sneak in ordinary stuff that wouldn't be questioned."

"Feels cruel." His warm hand presses against the small of my back, bringing me in closer, as if he can protect me from dark memories that have already passed. "To have to choose one end or the other, with no hope of recovery."

"Well, the ones who succeeded... they usually have a DNR. So we let them go when it's too late because it was their choice." The look he gives me cuts me in two.

He's everything holding me together right now. As I watch them working on Mason Law, I see so many other faces from the past.

I see *myself* in those nurses, struggling like hell to pull someone back from the brink.

"Philia?" he urges.

I shake my head. "Don't get me wrong, it wasn't always peaceful. Most of the time, they did it wrong. It almost hurt to save them, to bring them back, because they'd done just enough damage to make the end more painful and more prolonged."

He must see what's really on my mind, the worry and pain etched on my face.

"That won't be your ma. She's not looking to go anywhere," Grant promises fervently, as if he has any control over that. "And you're not there anymore. You *aren't*. I get why you left, Philia. I do. But you don't have to go back to that dark place."

What else is there?

What else can I do, when I've been the Grim Reaper's errand girl for my entire career?

"I don't know, Grant. I don't—"

Anything I wanted to say vanishes as Mason Law's eyes snap open.

He pulls up as sharply as the strings tethered to my heart.

Even with the doctors and nurses grabbing at him, he sits up like a toy skeleton popping out of a trick coffin, a human jump scare with his throat working around the tube. He reaches out in a trembling, accusing spear.

Pointing right at me.

Oh, God.

His eyes lock on and I freeze.

Heart palpitations shudder through me in a wild rushing mess.

He gags, and Grant peels away from me, striding into the room, his massive bulk radiating pure authority.

"Get that damn thing out of his mouth," Grant barks. "Let him talk."

One of the doctors looks up, his face tight. "Captain, he—"

"He might be a goddamned murder victim," Grant clips. "Whatever he's got to say, this might be the only chance to find out who the fuck did this to him. *Let him talk.*"

The doctor gives him an uncertain look, even as the nurses grab Law by the shoulders and wrestle him down.

He's still staring at me, fighting them with surprising strength.

I duck into the room quickly, stepping closer to the bed.

"Mr. Law?" I say. "Are you all right?"

His eyes roll wildly.

He lets out a choked sound as the doctor eases the tube out of his throat. Law coughs, his entire body convulsing so violently I just want to hold him, my heart wrenching when it looks like he's about to snap in half.

But as he subsides, his head falls to the side toward me.

More foamy red spit bubbles past his lips as he lets out a wheezing breath. "You y-you're not... s-safe," he croaks. "H-have to go. T-take her... take h-her and *go*. D-don't don't... let him h-have her."

"Who?" I demand, pushing closer to the bed, my heart climbing up my throat. "Ros? My sister? Is Aleksander hurting her?"

He turns paler when he hears 'Aleksander,' his skin bleaching white, but when his lips work open and shut, nothing comes out but strange gurgles.

"Did he do this to you?" Grant asks urgently, looming over the bed. "Do you work for the Arrendells, Mr. Law?"

Law's head rolls toward Grant.

Law looks up at him with a weariness in his eyes, something I've seen far too many times—the glazed exhaustion of someone so sick of fighting their own broken body that they're ready to give up.

"V-valet," Law whispers. "F-for for nearly forty years..."

"Mother *fucker*," Grant spits. "They lied to me. They fucking lied. Swore they didn't know him."

"Please, Mr. Law," I plead. "Can you tell me if Aleksander Arrendell is hurting my sister? Please, I need to know."

His head turns weakly toward me again.

But he only lets out a soft, rolling sigh before his eyes slip shut again.

And the monitors hooked up to him go wild as his vitals take a sharp dive.

"He's crashing!" one of the nurses cries, and suddenly we're being shoved out of the way, thrust toward the door by the bodies clustering around Law and trying to secure his hold on life. "Everyone who isn't staff, *out*. Now!"

Grant and I exit dutifully, regrouping in the hall and watching helplessly.

I don't realize Grant's trembling with anger until his hand finds mine, wraps it up tight, seeking as much as giving comfort.

I hold on for dear life.

"I shouldn't have forced it," Grant whispers. "Shouldn't

have tried to make him talk in that state."

"You didn't do this." I shake my head. "He was in bad shape, Grant. He'd have hurt himself more trying to fight them to say what he wanted. You helped him."

"I don't even know the old bastard." It comes out rough. The ridges of Grant's knuckles print hard against my palm. "Hell, half an hour ago, I was ready to throttle him for stalking you. Now, I'd give my left arm to keep him alive."

"It's hope. Because there's already been too much death around here."

He doesn't answer.

But that tight grip on my hand never wavers, keeping us locked together.

We stand together for what feels like hours, watching as the doctors get Law settled, bringing his vitals back to a modest baseline.

It's a good sign.

Anything that could give him those symptoms of organ failure—ricin or otherwise—would be a slow, quiet killer. It's possible he ingested it days ago and only found himself feeling a little off before it started to really hit.

But even when it passes that crucial threshold, it's still not quite the point of no return. Organ failure deaths are slow and agonizing.

For now, there's a chance to save him, if he's holding through this.

There's still a chance to pull him back from the cliff.

Please, God.

Hasn't there been enough suffering in this town?

But I have a funny feeling God isn't listening to me right now.

Because even as Law settles into a fitful sleep, intubated and sedated again, the respirator forcing his chest to rise and fall...

That same cacophony of screaming machines rises.

Not from Law.

But from a room several doors down the hall.

Cold sweat sweeps over me as I jerk toward that direction, drawn like a magnet.

I already know what's happening before a throng of nurses comes rushing down the hall.

My nails dig into Grant's hand as I pray, I pray, I *pray* that they pass my mother's room—

No.

Room 110.

The door jerks open, people go funneling in, voices rising and calling out commands, demands for—the words aren't even clear.

Everything narrows down to a tiny distant pinprick in my vision.

I think Grant's calling my name, but I've dropped his hand and I'm running—*running*—racing through a wavering nightmare of runny colors.

But I can't stop.

Just like I can't stop the churning thud of my heart or the slap of my feet against the cold tiles or the way the icy sterile air pours down my throat and hurts my lungs.

I have to save her.

I *have* to save my mom!

They don't love her enough.

Yes, they're professionals and they'll do their jobs, but they won't *fight* the way someone who loves her will. I have to—

"Ophelia!" Grant calls roughly.

Then there's nothing at all.

I don't know what I'm thinking when I hurl myself into my mother's room.

When I see those doctors and nurses perched over her

bed like vultures, like soul reapers coming to take her away.

She's so pale, alabaster white.

And I let out a soft scream, flinging myself at her bed.

"*Mom!*" I can't even see her anymore, not when it's just bodies and limbs in my way, my eyes overflowing. I'm grabbing at the emergency cart, digging through wrapped syringes of emergency injections. "Her kidneys are failing—you have to—she needs, she *needs*—"

"Ma'am—*ma'am!*" A nurse blocks my path, barricading my mother's bed with her body. "What she needs is for you to get out of this room and let us do our jobs."

"Damn!" Another voice erupts from behind her—followed by a long, sustained beep. That eerie sound I've heard more times than I can count, but this time it's my mother, it's my *mom*— "Flatline, we need the crash cart right—"

I throw myself at the nurse, but she shoves me back, then barks, "Captain Faircross!"

I'm fighting her, trying to claw my way through her, but now I have arms around me.

Huge, hugging arms I can't fight.

Strong oak tree-trunk arms that bind me up and pull me against him, filling me with hate and wonder and another anguished scream.

Grant takes me hostage as he sweeps me away from the room.

He drags me along as gently as he can while I lose my shit, twisting and thrashing and shrieking through the hot, drowning tears skating down my face.

"Mom, no—*Mom!*"

She can't die like this.

She can't be alone.

Not suffering, with Ros nowhere to be found, her body too weak to hold her strong, bright spirit.

"Ophelia, stop," Grant growls, clutching me against him.

He wrestles me into the hall until my mother's creeping death is just a surreal portrait through the window. A still life painted in crisis and pain.

"Ophelia, will you listen? They're going to fucking save her. They *are*."

"Clear!" comes from inside the room, followed by a terrible liquid zapping sound.

I can't bear to watch after the first time my mother's body jerks like a puppet shaken by some angry child.

The fire goes out of me and common sense comes flooding back.

Oh my God, what have I done?

"Ophelia," he whispers again, pinning me to his chest.

That embrace becomes my world, overtaking the horror, the fear, the impending loss.

This man truly is a bear, forever bigger and brighter than the great one in the night sky.

He's certainly holding up my entire world.

This time, I don't fight Grant when he turns me away, running one big hand down my back.

I bury my face in his chest, smothering my sorrow in his bulk.

"Clear!"

Then more of that hellish zapping.

I can't really hear it now, but it's still in my brain, the ugly sound of my mother falling limply against the hospital bed and losing her hold on life.

It's breaking me in slow motion.

Imaginary noises hollowing me out horribly, but I can't hold it in.

Can't escape that hell sound even with Grant's arms wrapped around me like he can block out every evil and protect me with the soft wordless silence he offers.

His drumming heart is so strong under my cheek, though.

And I know—I just know—if he could only take some of his strength and give it to restart my mother's heart, he would without hesitation.

Why does tragedy always feel like forever, though?

In reality, I think it's only a minute.

It can't be much more than that when there's so little time between the heart stopping and brain death due to lack of oxygen. They'd quit working before they'd revive her as a vegetable, I know that with the DNR, and yet it still feels like a thousand years condensed into one brutal moment where they charge and clear, charge and clear, all choreographed in perfect sync to my sobs.

Until that flatline tone stops.

Until it becomes a slow, yet consistent beeping.

I turn my head sharply, terrified to hope.

Afraid to think Mom cheated death once again, only to be wrong.

But that green line on the screen doesn't lie.

The slow zigzags tracking cardiac activity, and suddenly that flurry of motion around her turns quieter, gentler, settling her into place.

Closing up her hospital gown over the subtle burn marks on her skin from the shock paddles, a small sacrifice to keep her alive.

Her eyes are closed, her lips slack.

But her chest rises and falls while that slow beep echoes over the room.

I go down limply against Grant. My knees won't hold me up any longer.

I don't know if I'm sobbing with relief or if I'm still petrified and pre-mourning. I can't decide.

I just know it feels like the medical staff bought me a little more time to say goodbye.

XIX: ONE MORE TIME (GRANT)

J can't remember the last time I've seen Ophelia Sanderson this exhausted and drained to the bone. No, actually, I can.

The last time her mother went through this, and Ophelia was right there with her, every step of the way.

She was much younger then.

And she almost feels like that younger version of herself now when she's unconscious in my arms, so weightless it's like she's barely there.

Like her very essence bled out with her grief.

She refused to leave the medical center, even after the staff settled her mother and drifted away. Hours in a chair at her mother's bedside, holding Angela's fragile hand.

When Ophelia finally passed out, I carried her to my car and took her home.

She doesn't even stir as I settle her in my bed and pull her shoes off before tucking her in, adjusting the pillows under her tangled gold hair.

Flaky lines of tears linger on her cheeks in glistening

tracks I gently brush away, lingering on the hollows under her eyes.

"Wish there was something I could do for your ma, Butterfly," I whisper. "Anything. I'd do any goddamned thing to bring her back for you, safe and sound."

Ophelia's only answer is a sigh, turning subtly toward me in her sleep.

I sigh, too.

I can't work miracles. There's nothing I can truly do for Angela when she's waging a lonely war.

On the other hand, I can do something for Ophelia. For Ros.

That means getting to the bottom of this shit show with Mason Law.

My resolve hardens into granite.

I dig around in my pocket till I find the little notepad I use to write down case notes and scrawl out a quick note just in case Ophelia wakes up and worries where I am. I leave it on the nightstand.

GONE UP to the big house to follow up on a few leads. Be back soon.

Don't you worry about dinner tonight. I'm cooking. My folks got Nell and I'll grab her when the timing's right, too.

Just rest, Butterfly.

-G

I ALMOST SIGNED IT *LOVE*, but fuck.

I don't think that's a discussion either of us can handle right now.

It's hard to talk about feelings when you're stretched over a hungry abyss, and even if we weren't, it's no easy conversation.

Hell, we're both still acting like this is a silly damn child-hood crush reborn in our adult lives.

With the way she's feeling, I don't want to dump the L-word on her when that's just more emotional pressure.

Still, it's hard to pull away from her.

I linger just a little while longer, brushing her hair back from her temples before I drag myself away and head out to scare up some answers.

I'm prepared to storm a bullshit factory and take no prisoners when I drive up to the Arrendell mansion and go stomping out of my vehicle.

I refuse to hand my keys over to the valet waiting to take them, curling my lip.

"Sir," the valet says, his nose pointed up above the exact same uniform as Mason Law, "I'm afraid you can't just leave your car—"

"I'm afraid I damn well can," I snap off, brushing past him and pocketing my keys.

The man's eyes bulge.

What's he gonna do, call the police?

"I won't be ten minutes," I say. "You've got room to fit an eighteen-wheeler past my car. Deal with it."

Offended, sputtering pleas trail me as I mount the steps without looking back.

Here we are, poised at the gates of hell.

The huge, gleaming double doors open before I can reach for the knob or knock. Another uniformed man looks down his nose at me.

"Whom should I say is calling?" he asks.

Like these fucking people don't see me at least once a month with all the odd shit that goes down around here. Not to mention the occasional summons from the exalted First and Second Selectman to stand in for Chief Bowden in budget discussions, wherever he's fucked off to.

I fold my arms.

"And whom are you calling for?" the man asks again.

"His or Her Highness, who else? Can't say I give a shit which, though both would be better," I growl. "And you know damn well it's Captain Faircross, *Peter*."

"Ah, yes. You'll have to excuse me if the uniforms start to blend together sometimes," he lies. I only remember his name because I heard Lucia yelling at him during another visit. "Please come wait in the receiving room."

I follow him inside, keeping a standoffish distance between us as we cross the red carpeting through halls with towering walls and glowing golden sconces.

After thinking for a few moments, I step closer, leaning over his shoulder and lowering my voice.

"Mason Law," I say. "You worked with him, yeah? Just like you worked with Cora Lafayette?"

Peter's shoulders go stiff.

"It's a rather large estate with dozens of staff, Captain," he says coldly. "We all have our assigned areas. It's quite possible for us to go our entire term of employment here without meeting everyone."

"Uh-huh."

Like I believe that crap for one second.

I expect him to show me to the same posh velvet-adorned receiving room where I'm left to twiddle my thumbs every time I have to come up here. Whenever it's not about taking me right to the site of a dead body.

Instead, he takes me a little deeper into the manor.

He raps lightly on a heavy mahogany door, listens, and then—when there's not a single sound—pushes the door open on an opulently decorated office.

"Mr. Arrendell isn't in residence today," Peter says icily, which makes me wonder just where Montero is. "However, the Lady of the house will be in to see you as soon as she's available. Please have a seat and wait."

The *try not to dirty up the place* is clear in his acrid tone, and in the snobby look he rakes over me, from my uniform down to my boots.

Whatever.

They're still a bit muddy from tromping around in a clearing splattered with blood and bleach-white bones when I haven't had time to clean them.

But there's something else there, too.

A sort of nervous fear.

As he walks away stiffly, he glances back, his eyes rolling like a spooked horse.

There's something in that look that almost seems to say, *Save me.*

You know the saying, if walls could talk?

What would these servants say if they felt free to run their mouths without catching a pink slip or worse?

I step into the office—so much red fucking upholstery everywhere, what is with these people and their red, it looks like a seventies porno shoot—and hunker down in a chair that really ain't made for someone my size.

The polished wooden legs creak a little in warning.

I'm itching to do a little digging, but if Lucia walks in and catches me rooting around in her files, I'm not gonna leave with my head intact.

No surprise, the office has the same glamorous gothic vibe as the rest of the place.

I still can't help looking around, taking in what I can.

An oil painting of a younger Lucia and Montero with their four sons as kids, including the supposedly disgraced and exiled Vaughn. Even in that painting, he's standing a little apart from the others, like there's something walling him off from the rest of them. Kid's got an overly serious face, and the painter captured something troubled in his eyes for sure.

The others are different.

Feels like looking at human masks painted over the oily, hissing faces of snakes.

Everything else is priceless vases, odd little old statues from Egypt or Greece, awards for charitable contributions and philanthropic acts.

A framed doctorate on the wall.

Never knew Lucia Arrendell had a PhD in psychology, but it makes me a little more wary of what I'm dealing with and that fluttering façade she likes to put on.

I'm just glancing at her desk and realizing the brochure sticking out of her bristling planner is for a wedding florist when I get a face full of liar. The door opens behind me and the Lady of the manor comes gliding inside like her feet never touch the ground.

She's stuck in a bygone era, her shimmery pearl-colored dress swaying around her calves. Its fringe lashes with dancing steps that belong to a younger woman.

She's lean as a rake and her mouth is a violent red, painted and stark and smiling below eyes that don't reflect any warmth at all.

Like I said.

Human mask. Serpent underneath.

The conspiracy nuts would go wild with this family, certain they've found their lizard people.

She offers both hands like a little coquette, fluttering her lashes.

"Captain Faircross! I'm so sorry to keep you waiting. I trust you haven't been languishing too long?"

Damn.

Just because my ma raised a gentleman, I stand and take

off my hat—Ethan's hat—and hold it to my chest as I take one of her hands.

I'm not playing courtier, though, and instead of kissing ass, I just give it a firm shake.

"Wasn't here long, no," I say. "Hope not to stick around, either."

"So this is a business call then." She rounds her broad wooden desk and settles behind it in her high-backed chair, tossing back her icy, white-streaked blonde bob.

"It's always business, ma'am. No reason to be up here otherwise." No point in holding back today. I settle back in my chair, slouching down and folding my hands over my stomach, studying her. Think I'll take a roundabout approach first. I nod toward the planner. "You putting together a wedding?"

"Why, yes. *Trying* to, but the bride is being rather difficult." She gives an exaggerated roll of her eyes, sighing deeply. "Of course, she wants to wait until her mother's out of the hospital, the poor thing. Now, I don't want to be uncharitable, but..."

She stops cold.

I can't hide the anger in my face.

I can't help bristling and struggle to hold it in, scratching the back of my neck like it's just a late season mosquito that's got me annoyed.

A whole damn legion of them has nothing on the bloodsucker right in front of me.

Fuck, I don't like this woman talking about it like Angela Sanderson's death is a foregone conclusion.

"I'm sorry, Captain. Family business. Don't you know our Rosalind's a stubborn girl? I suppose that's why Aleksander was so smitten..." She smiles demurely, flicking her hand through the air. "Wait for this, wait for that. She's driving my boy quite mad—and wanting to save herself for marriage, can you believe that? Honestly, I thought *I* was old-fashioned."

What the—

It takes a second for that to click, and when it does, I go a little green.

I really don't need to know that about Ros, even if it's a small pleasant surprise when I figured Aleksander already had his dirty paws all over her.

I also don't want to know why Lucia knows that.

What kind of son talks about his sex life with his mother?

"So Aleksander's in a hurry to tie the knot, huh?" I ask coldly.

"Oh, you know how boys are when they get to a certain age." She gives me a sly look, like she's counting me in with that. "Eventually they get tired of catting around, and then it's all about wanting to build a family and having a little woman to come home to. Honestly, I'm glad he's gotten his wild oats out of his system. I was starting to worry about him, jetting around the world with all these vapid models. Such a bad influence."

"Uh-huh." I nod slowly. "Is this wedding drama the reason you lied to me about Mason Law?"

There's a telltale moment.

A certain stiffness.

A cruel blackness that falls over her aristocratic face, turning it into a caricature of frozen fury. It's so fast that if you blinked, you'd miss it.

I even wonder if I imagine it when she just blinks at me after that half-second pause, the perfect picture of cultured confusion.

"I'm sorry, who?" she asks, but there's a little too much of a delay.

"I ain't here for it, Lucia," I say tiredly. "Cut the bullshit. You put on that big show—you and Montero both, trotting out the staff for us, pretending like you never heard of this man. Turns out, he's one of your goddamned valets. Now he's in the hospital, fighting for his life after ingesting an unknown poison. So, yeah, I think you might wanna stop playing cute with me right the fuck now, because if you think I won't put a Selectman in cuffs for obstructing an investigation, you got me *real* fuckin' wrong, lady."

Lucia pinches her lips, folding her hands primly atop her planner.

"That's hardly necessary—and neither is your language," she clips, suddenly all business. "You'll have to pardon me for trying to protect the man's dignity. I had no idea what condition he was in."

"You wanna explain what you mean about protecting his dignity?"

"Mason Law was fired," Lucia informs me crisply. "Some time ago. He continued living in his servants' quarters up until recently. We gave him a good deal of time to remove his possessions and find a new residence and employment elsewhere, considering he had nowhere else to go. However, we told the whole truth and nothing but when we said he didn't work for us, Captain Faircross. It's sad, really. He was a loyal, hardworking employee for many years. I chose not to humiliate him by spreading his disgrace around so callously."

"Yeah, that's your reason." I arch a brow. "Why'd you fire him then?"

"Oh, he simply wasn't able to keep up with the rigors of the job in his advancing age," she replies, almost before I finish asking the question. A little too eager. "Frankly, I believe he may have been suffering from a touch of dementia, possibly substance abuse. He started behaving erratically, sometimes turning hostile with the other staff. He was only a few years away from retiring with a pension. It was a shame to let him go, really." She clucks her tongue. Dutiful sympathy. "I never thought being fired would push him over the edge, though, the poor man. Suicide? God. If only he'd taken our advice and gotten professional help."

There's that psych degree at work, making her a magnificent storyteller.

I just stare at her for several long seconds before I say, "I never said it was a suicide."

She freezes, but her eyes betray nothing.

"Well, yes, but what else could it be?" she asks, almost impatiently. "You tell me he's been poisoned—there's no one who would hurt a dear old man. And with how he was behaving, it seems entirely in character."

"Sure it does." I lean forward, propping my elbows on my knees, watching her intently. "So that's your story? You fired him and it drove him to suicide by poison, and now you've got no earthly idea why he's been running around town acting all weird and scaring people?"

"Scaring people?"

I nod. "Just a few encounters. Always startling and unpleasant."

"How terrible. My, I'd have to say it's the dementia," she says glibly. "I do hope now that he's in the right custody, he can get the help he needs."

Dementia.

Right.

Guess that's her story and she's sticking to it.

I also don't think I'm gonna get anything else out of her tonight, though.

Not without telling her things that might get her and Montero and possibly that sleazy fucking son of theirs sniffing around.

Trouble is, they hold too much weight around here.

If they tried to get in at the medical center no one would

stop them, not even after overhearing what me and Ophelia said to him about the Arrendells.

So when Lucia asks, "Is there anything else I can help you with, Captain Faircross?" in an expectant tone, I shrug.

"Not right now." I heft myself up from the chair. "I'll be in touch, though."

"Come now, Captain," she says, and dimples at me with girlish innocence, so out of place in her razor of a face. "I hope that won't be necessary, will it?"

I storm off without answering.

* * *

YEAH, I really don't know how I'm gonna tell Ophelia I haven't gotten much of anything.

Though it's kind of implied.

TV likes to show you these genius cops who crack hard cases from sunrise to sundown, wrapping things up quick and easy. That's not how it is.

Real police work is slow and plodding, chasing every tiny detail, one long waiting game that might not have a payoff at the end.

Sometimes you gotta be the ticker in Poe's *The Tell-Tale Heart*, beating away under the floorboards until just by knowing you're there, waiting, your suspect cracks and does the hard sleuthing work for you.

Still, I wish I had something to tell her when I get home and drag through the door.

Something besides waiting around while forensics tests those bones, seeing if we can get a match on DNA or dental records to ID the victim.

Especially when I find Ophelia curled up on the couch and crying her eyes out.

Every thought of Mason Law, Cora Lafayette, and the scummy Arrendell clan goes flying out of my head.

I barely remember to close the door as I cross the floor quickly, dropping to my knees in front of the sofa and reaching for her hands.

"Philia?" I breathe. "Butterfly, what's wrong?"

"No—no, I—"

She shakes her head quickly.

Fuck, it nearly wrenches my heart to bits when she pulls her hands away, rejecting my touch.

It almost breaks me, but I let her.

I ain't gonna force her through that much hurt.

Sometimes all a man can do is know when to give his woman space.

Craning my head, I try to catch her wide, wet eyes again.

"Ophelia, talk to me. What happened? Did they call about Angela?"

"No, but they *could!*" she bursts out. "That's... that's the problem, you see."

She's got this pleading look.

Like she expects me to have an answer when I don't even know the question.

"Babe, hey. Hey, whatever's upsetting you, we can talk through it, okay?" I reach out tentatively, holding her chin up with my fingers. "Can you slow down and start over? Rewind a little and clue me in. I'm right the fuck here. I'm always listening."

Sniffling, Ophelia doesn't say anything for a few seconds, looking away from me and rubbing her red, raw nose.

When she finally speaks, it's through trembling lips. "I just—I can't do this, Grant."

I know what she means before she explains it.

I know the feeling when a sledgehammer crashes into your heart, but I still have to ask.

"This?" I bite off.

"*Us!*" she flares miserably. There's a lashing anger in her voice, but it seems like it's more for herself than for me. "I'm... I'm just all over the place. Everything hurts. I'm up and down all the time, falling for you and learning to love Nell while my mom's dying and we don't know what's up with the Law guy and... and I don't even know what's going on with Ros. But I'm scared for her. I'm so scared, and I just can't take all these feelings ripping me around. Grant, I..."

She can't finish.

Not when she meets my eyes.

I hate that she can see I've been flayed the fuck open.

This girl, she's breaking my goddamned heart.

Same way she did the night she decided to leave, only I was the fool who broke us then.

And me, being the complete buffalo-brained idiot I still am, I'm dead inside.

I don't care about my own feelings.

Snarling, I push myself up on the sofa next to her and gather her into my arms.

"Just let me, okay? As your friend. Nothing else. Stop crying and c'mere, Ophelia. Let me hold you."

She resists for a trembling moment, then glues herself to me the same way she always does, this tiny bundle hiding against me.

"I'm sorry," she rattles out. "I'm sorry, I'm *sorry...*"

"Don't be." I stroke my hands over her back slowly. It's killing me—*fuck is it killing me*—knowing I could lose her just as soon as I found her again. She's hurting, though, and I ain't gonna make that worse. "You're going through pure hell, Philia. That's what's going on. You gotta do what helps you first and last. It's okay."

"It's not okay. D-don't you lie to me, Grant Faircross."

"I ain't lying. Promise. Cross my heart and hope to die, split a camel if I lie."

That gets a weak smile from the bundle of woman in my arms.

"I never did figure out how you and Ethan came up with that camel splitting thing..."

I snort.

"Honestly don't remember. I think we were trying to make it about how a camel will spit in your eye, but we were kids and it got all mixed up and corrupted." I chuckle, even though it feels like chewing broken glass, and hold her closer. "Look, I don't care if you're breaking up with me. I'm still your friend. I've always been your friend."

And I've always been obsessed.

A dead man walking, wishing like hell I could be so much more.

"...the best friend I've ever had," she whispers. Her hand creeps out from her knotted-up tangle and curls in my shirt. "It's... it's not forever, Grant. Let me get through this. Let me think. That's all I'm asking. I need to get to the other side of this—of everything—and then I can breathe. Then, maybe I can think about us."

My eyes burn like hot coals as I smile.

There's a little hope still burning, but it's honestly the last thing on my mind.

All I know is the woman I love is hurting like hell and I can ease her pain.

I can help her deal with it by accepting what she needs right now and being there for her.

"We'll talk when you're ready," I promise, smoothing her hair back to try to get a glimpse of her face. "For now, we're gonna do what we can with what we've got. That means figuring out what's really going on with Ros and helping her out whatever way we can. Okay? 'Cause something sure as hell ain't right. I went up to talk to Lucia today. She was all about Aleksander pushing for a quick wedding. Does that sound like Ros to you?"

"No way." Ophelia shakes her head raggedly. "Not at all, she always wanted to take her time. She was such a shy girl, barely ever dated. I used to tease her about finding a man before fifty at the pace I thought she'd go. But that was the Ros I knew. Old Ros..."

"Yeah. Old Ros is still there, Philia. Lucia said she's holding up the show because she wants your ma there. *That's* Old Ros. That's the Ros who still cares about her family, no matter what else she's going through. For Aleksander, this must be about something else. He's getting something out of it." I reach over, wiping a tear off her cheek with my thumb. "So you sit tight. We're gonna figure out what that something is and then we're not gonna stop talking sense until Ros fucking listens, okay?"

The worry in her eyes just piles up a little higher, a few more sharp stones on an avalanche of hurt, but slowly, she nods.

"Okay. I guess that makes sense," she says. "Anyway, if you'll give me a little bit, I'll grab my stuff and get out of your hair. We can talk tomorrow and—"

"And not a goddamned thing," I growl, holding her hand too tight. This possessive streak whips through me. "Maybe Mason Law's in the hospital, but I've still got a bad feeling. You're safer here with us. The guest room's still yours."

Her face crumples. "But after I—"

"Woman, you're fine. Wouldn't dream of sending you back home, letting you out of my sight."

Her face smooths. She knows I won't budge on this lone condition, keeping her close.

Leaning in, I press a kiss to her forehead.

I have to remind myself that right now, if I can't be her

lover, I'll damn sure be family. I'll look after her the way Ethan would've wanted, just like an older brother would.

"Okay," she whispers back with a shy smile.

"Go on up and get some rest. I'll fetch Nell from my folks and then get everybody fed."

XX: ONE OF A KIND (OPHELIA)

I am the absolute worst human being.

I wake up feeling like I just got beaten to death by a bag of bricks.

Crying up a storm in one day will do that, though I barely remember falling asleep.

I just know I grabbed a few of my things that crept into Grant's bedroom during our brief fling, relocated them to the guest room, then curled up and passed out. It was all I could manage after letting go of the one thing that brings comfort when everything sucks.

Never mind the special anguish of hurting this wonderful man in the process.

He hid his wounds pretty well, but I could tell my words cut him to the bone.

I'm just surprised he didn't pull a Grant on me. It feels worse that he didn't.

If he'd gone cold and stonewalled me the way he used to when we were kids, whenever anything happened that might force him to have an *emotion*, that I could've handled.

But the fact that he was so kind?

So gentle.

So understanding.

Like all he cared about was making me happy.

For a confused second, I almost took my need for space back right then and there...

Only, I can't.

I'm too much of a messed-up wreck right now to have my heart in the right place for anyone.

I'm not stable enough for a relationship or even a job.

I'm living my life balanced on a freaking tightrope between order and chaos, love and loss, life and death.

I shouldn't even keep staying here, probably, but I don't think I could stand to crawl back home to the old house, either. I can't go there and rattle around alone with the ghost of my dead brother and the shades of two women who aren't dead yet, but who've already left me behind.

I think I'm the luckiest heartbreaking bitch alive because Grant let me stay after I pushed his soul through a cheese grater.

And I wake up to another wrenching reminder of what I'm walking away from, snuggled against my side and sleeping blissfully.

Nell.

She's an adorable pile in a cute pinafore dress with her curls pinned up in a prim, ladylike cascade. Somehow, she managed to wedge herself into the curve of my body without falling off the edge of the bed.

She sleeps like a kitten, and that ratty old stuffed unicorn is right there with her, clutched in her arms and pressed up between us.

Grant must've told her I had a rough day.

I don't know why she's so attached to me, close as a kitten, but the feeling's mutual.

Painfully so.

Maybe that's what's got me extra screwed up right now.

The fact that this return to Redhaven feels like skipping right past all the normal stages of a relationship and going straight to a settled life with a husband, a daughter, a family, a *home.*

I'd be lying if I said a deep, restless part of me hadn't craved that like a slice of caramel-drenched cheesecake.

I love this little girl.

About as much as I love her uncle-slash-cousin-slash-dad.

About as much as I love my own family, and that's when it punches me right in the feelies.

How much I miss Ros.

I've been so caught up trying to sleuth out the mystery of her weird behavior that I haven't seen her as my sister ever since I came home. More like another problem to be solved.

But I miss my *sister*, the little girl who'd follow me around just like Nell follows me now.

A bittersweet smile pulls at my lips.

I can't count the number of times I'd wake up in the middle of the night to a shaking figure tucked against my back, hissing at me not to look because that brat would never admit she was afraid of the dark.

Of course, she couldn't make it through the night without her big sister.

I still remember the first time she wanted to talk to me about a boy, too. The first time she got rejected. Her first date, an awkward night out with a boy in her class band that went exactly nowhere.

Braiding flower crowns in the garden behind our house and plotting our dream weddings.

Chasing each other through the woods with glowsticks in the fall, weaving through endless trees like fireflies.

How we always knew she'd be taking over the shop one

day because she idolized Mom like a goddess and adored sticking her hands in fresh-warmed beeswax more than anything. She'd spend hours playing around with it, completely fascinated by everything our mother made.

No, I don't just want to save my sister.

I want to be her best friend again.

I want to *stay here* and remember what it's like having roots that run so deep with people I care about, and who still care about me for reasons that are increasingly hard to fathom.

I'm careful not to disturb Nell as I reach over and pull my phone from the nightstand. Scrolling through my texts, I stare at the history of unanswered messages I've sent Ros and sigh.

No matter how much it sucks, I have to try again.

I slowly type out a message.

Mom flatlined today. They brought her back, but I want to go see her in the morning. The treatment took a harsh turn and I talked to the doctors. I hope you'll come with me?

My thumb hovers over the small paper airplane icon, then stops so I can add something else.

I miss you. I hope you're okay.

Then I hit Send and curl myself around Nell with my phone clutched against my chest. All that's left to do is hold that sweet little girl tight and pray I'll feel my phone buzzing against my fingers soon.

But there's nothing.

Nothing but Nell's quiet, sleepy breaths and the soft little mewling sounds she makes as she starts to wake up.

Her eyes drift open and she blinks at me drowsily before smiling.

"Miss Philia?" She snuggles closer to me, still half-asleep.

"Hey, munchkin." I smooth back the loose spray of curls lining her brow. "Decided to take a nap before dinner?"

"Mm-hmm." Closing her eyes, she noses into my shoulder with a slow yawn. "You looked sad. Mr. Pickle said I should keep you company."

"Did I? Well, that was very nice of Mr. Pickle. Your unicorn's a sensitive guy." I certainly *feel* sad, weighting my smile as I try to force it for her sake. "I'm okay, kiddo. But you can hang around any time."

She hesitates, then peeks one eye open. "...what about when I'm sad?"

"Of course when you're sad, too!" I wrap my arms around her. "Are you sad right now, Nell? It's okay if you are."

Her mouth quivers as she lowers her eyes.

"I... I miss Miss Ros. You look so much like her, just a little older," she whispers. "She doesn't play with me anymore. You're her sister, huh?"

"I am." My heart feels like it's splitting in two. I kiss the top of Nell's head. "I miss her, too, hon. She doesn't play with me much anymore, either. She's been going through a lot. Did you two hang out a lot?"

"Uh-huh." Nell nods, burrowing into me. "She cleaned up Mr. Pickle for me. He used to smell like smoke. Really bad. Like all the bad burning things. Oh, plus she'd let me come play in the store. She showed me how to make honey candy."

All the bad burning things.

It takes a minute for it to sink in.

Then I remember Grant telling me how Nell's parents died, and how Mr. Pickle was practically the only thing that survived the fire...

"Oh. Oh, sweetie." I feel like I'm going to crush her with how tight I'm holding her. She squeaks, but clutches back just as tightly. "Don't you worry. Ros is just going through some things, sweetheart. She's still your friend and still my sister. She's just having a hard time, but I know she'll pull herself together soon. She'll have time for you again."

Nell goes quiet against me before she asks, "...is it because of your mom, Miss Philia?"

Holy hell.

She's too good at strumming all my heartstrings.

My breath catches.

"You... you know about that, huh?"

"I—yeah. Sorry. I heard when you and Uncle Grant were talking."

"It's okay, sweetie." I stroke a hand over her hair. "Yeah, it's true. Our mom's really sick, but I hope she'll get better. I'm going to go see her tomorrow morning."

"Can I come with?"

I don't answer at first, biting my lip.

The medical center seems like such a dreary place for a little girl.

Especially when my mother's in the shape she's in. No innocent kid her age should have to see anyone busted up like that, barely kept alive by machines and drugs that feel like a final Hail Mary.

God, it's hard for *me* to see it.

But there's something sparking in her eyes when I look down at her.

That's when it hits me.

She never got to see her parents before they died, did she?

For little Nell, death had no gentle introductions.

It never kept its distance.

It was just her waking up in the middle of the night with fire everywhere, nothing but Grant yelling her name and digging her out of the burning rubble.

I'm guessing it would've been a closed casket funeral if her parents burned to death so horribly. And I wonder, does Nell want to come with me because she knows what it's like?

To have to say goodbye without anything to say goodbye to?

My heart feels so wrung out.

Maybe I'm reading too much into it, although she's the smartest little girl I've ever met. She's obviously got a crazy high emotional IQ.

But there's something in her eyes when she looks at me.

Something that says she needs to come with me.

She needs to be there.

She needs to comfort me.

"Okay," I say, and I tell myself I'll march her right out if she can't handle it for even half a second. "Okay, kiddo. We'll talk to your uncle. If he says it's fine, you can come. I bet my mom would love to meet you. Now, let's go see what Grant made for dinner."

* * *

TO SAY things are a little tense around the house would be a mammoth understatement.

Yes, it's my fault.

Grant's quiet as always, yet gentle and warm, and if I catch him starting to reach for me now and then before he drops his hands with a firm glance, it only stings for an instant.

Mostly, it's a painful reflection of what I feel.

I want to reach for him so bad, to hold him tight and never let go.

But I can't ask him to carry the disembodied mess I am right now.

A walking piece of crap who told him to his face I can't commit.

Jesus.

I only hope he'll wait for me, knowing full well I don't deserve it.

Also, I know ten years should be long enough for anyone to make up their mind.

I've been love starved and so has he, but my heart doesn't care. It's fallen into a vacuum where time doesn't matter among all the feelings.

I need to get myself together first, to find my footing again, and then I can make it right.

Then I'll hopefully be someone worthy of a hero.

We don't talk much over dinner.

It's paella tonight, and he followed the trend I set, making half of it spicy enough to kill us ten times over and the other half mild.

I'm a little surprised when he gives permission to let Nell tag along after some grave consideration. It's a hard silent moment, dense thoughts clashing behind his eyes, that make me realize that no matter what happened between us, he trusts me with his little girl.

Ouch.

It's beautifully painful.

Things feel a little more normal when I start the usual routine of wrangling Nell into settling down for bed, making sure she brushes her teeth, then sending her off with another story.

It's *The Velveteen Rabbit* tonight.

Once she's out, I kiss her forehead, slip out, and find Grant waiting in the hall.

He leans around the doorframe, peering in at the sleeping little heap of mischief with that slow, fond smile he only ever has for the ones he cherishes.

"She falls asleep faster for you," he says with mock irritation. "Think she wants you to like her so much that she's on her best behavior. Enjoy it while it lasts. When her little mask finally slips, you'll meet the real four-foot monster."

I laugh.

I can't bear to think that I might not be here by the time Nell gets tired of suppressing her inner brat. But Grant seems to realize what he said.

He backs away a few steps, giving me an uncertain look in the dark hall.

My heart sputters.

It's so hard to look at that powerful body gleaming faintly in the moonlight spilling in from a window. He's extra mountainous when he's tense, bare shoulders and the brute strength in his corded arms and massive hands.

Not so long ago I was pressed hot against that body, writhing in his bed, in his arms.

Now, we're only a couple of feet away, but it might as well be a nautical mile. Close enough to catch the faint spicy scent of the oil he grooms his beard with.

But it feels like we're looking at each other over a gulf.

The longing in those mocha eyes might kill me before anything else.

Grant looks away first, ducking his head and rubbing a hand over the back of his neck.

"'Night, Ophelia," he mutters gruffly.

"Yeah," I answer, my voice hurt and hollow. "Good night, Grant."

We stand there for another awkward second before he turns away with one last lingering look and slips into his room.

I linger alone in the pale moonlight, wondering if tonight was just a bad dream.

Wishful thinking.

God, this sucks.

Nell's mask might be holding up, but mine's falling apart like cheap plaster.

The tears come hot, heavy, and brimming with so much guilt.

For a few chilling seconds, I can't breathe, can't move, can't think.

There's nothing more I'd love than to slip into his bed and feel those massive arms around me, except I can't, and it's my own dumb fault.

Eventually, I trudge down the hall to the guest room and throw back a few sleep aid pills from my purse just to knock myself out.

I will myself into a dreamless sleep, hoping I'll wake up with my heart intact.

* * *

GRANT IS GONE by the time I wake up early the next morning.

Nell's already up, parked in front of her cartoons with a bowl of cereal and bouncing on the couch as she yells along with the *Ben 10* theme song.

There's a note on the fridge, too. I rip it off and read.

HAD to go in early for an all-hands meeting about the local crime scene. Raleigh PD's coming in to have a look at the bones. Will keep you posted. Nell's already eaten, so raid the fridge for anything you want.

I CAN'T HELP SMILING.

It's his little way of reminding me I'm still welcome to make myself at home. That I wasn't just buying my place in his bed.

I kinda love him even more for that and forget how disgustingly complicated it's gotten.

I'm in no mood to cook, so I end up joining Nell on the sofa with some honey-tasting cereal of my own.

What *is* she watching?

I have no clue, it's just bright flashing colors and crazy smears of green.

Nell's enthusiastic explanations go right over my head. She doesn't need me to understand, just listen, and I'm happy to let her chatter away.

But when I check my phone, my stomach sinks.

Ros left me on read without even bothering to reply. She saw the message last night.

Awesome.

Jesus, Ros. Do you even care that Mom almost died?

If I didn't have a bouncy little girl next to me, I'd punch the fluffy accent pillow.

Nell's quiet, almost like she senses my heartache, but she doesn't seem upset.

I wash the dishes after breakfast and then bundle her up in her jacket. We share a few laughs over the fact that I'm still slumming it in sweaters to keep the chill away.

Someday, I will *get that stupid coat.*

On the drive to the medical center, she reaches across the front console and quietly rests her hand on my wrist— holding Mr. Pickle tight with her other hand.

How pathetic am I for being comforted by a little girl?

In the parking lot, though, I stop, looking at her worriedly.

"Nell, I need you to know my mom's very sick. They're using a lot of experimental stuff to get her better, but it's pretty rough on her body."

"Ohhh, like sci-fi drugs? Will your mom get superpowers?"

"Yeah. She just might." I smile. "I just mean it might be a bit jarring to see her. If you change your mind and want to leave, I won't think you're any less brave. I'm glad you're here."

Nell looks out the window, her gaze heavy with a strange maturity that makes her look like more than just a little girl.

"...can I tell you a secret, Miss Philia?" She peeks up at me, working at her lower lip.

"Sure, shoot."

"I... I saw some dead people." She gulps. "Please don't tell Uncle Grant, he'll get so mad, but when I was at work with him one day Mr. Henri left his screen unlocked when he went for coffee. I got on the computer and got in the police files. I looked up my parents and... and..." She sputters, her eyes glimmering, but she fights so hard not to cry. "I saw them. Everything the firemen took away. I saw Mom and Dad—what was left of them. Don't worry about me. I'm so strong I didn't even cry in front of Uncle Grant or the other cops."

My blood thins.

"Nell... Nell, honey—" I don't even question what I'm doing as I unlatch my seat belt, unbuckle hers, and pull her into my arms with the stuffed unicorn squished between us. "You don't have to be strong like that. Nobody does."

Holy shit.

I need to talk to Grant about this.

I know he's trying his best—so am I—but I wonder if Nell's a little too curious for her age. Maybe she needs a good counselor as much as she needs a family.

She clutches at me, though, her tiny body shaking.

"My point is, I *saw*, Miss Philia. If I saw that, I can see your mom no matter what she looks like," she whispers against my chest. "I want to see Miss Angela because she's still alive. Even if she looks sick or scary... she's here with us. So I just wanna see her in case she—you know."

She won't say it.

Even at her age, she knows not to tempt death out loud.

But I know exactly what she means, what she isn't saying with that precocious little mouth.

In case she isn't alive anymore, soon.

I get it.

She couldn't say goodbye to her folks.

And since she cares about Ros and my mom, about me...

It means something for Nell to be able to say goodbye to our mom before she's gone, instead of waiting for the grim aftermath.

"Okay, Nelly. I gotcha." I whisper into her hair and squeeze her tight. "But you hold on to my hand, okay? If you want to leave, just say it and we'll go."

With a sniffle, she nods, huddling against me before pulling away with the dignity of a tiny duchess and rubbing at her eyes. "O-okay."

I offer her a brave smile of my own, then get out of the car and round the passenger side to let her out.

Her hand feels warm and small in mine as we head inside.

I still feel a little uncertain about this, but Nell seems steady enough.

I'm the one who's unsteady—even more so when, on the way down the hall to my mother's room, we pass Mason Law's room.

I almost stop dead in my tracks.

I'm not expecting a familiar broad shape sitting in the chair at his bedside, hands steepled, brooding stare locked on Law's sleeping face.

Grant.

He must feel my eyes drilling into him somehow because he breaks away from studying the unconscious man and glances up.

We lock eyes and he offers me a guarded smile.

The whisper of a smile I beam back feels just as unsteady

and full of aching confusion. Then his gaze shifts as Nell leans around me and waves.

"Look who's here! Hi, Uncle Grant!" she whispers loudly.

Behave, he mouths, raising a hand to her.

Pinky promise, she mouths back, holding up a hand with her little finger outstretched.

We linger a moment longer before we make the rest of the trek to my mother's room.

I stall for a second before we come to the window that feels like gazing straight into hell. It's little Nell I'm watching, not my mother, as she comes into view.

Thankfully, Nell doesn't look bothered at all, though her eyes are a little wide as we stop in the doorway.

She just looks in at the wizened, shrunken shape my mom makes in the bed before she whispers, "Hi, Miss Angela."

My mother doesn't answer, of course.

But I'd like to think she can hear Nell, anyway.

The heart monitor and the respirator are the only sounds in the room.

They're steady today, almost soothing.

Mom's chest rises and falls smoothly without a big struggle.

I hope I'm not drunk on hope, but she actually looks a little better today.

There's more color in her cheeks, a little more fullness, almost like her body's finally doing something with the IV cocktail inserted in her veins. A late call with the doctor last night told me that's what overloaded her heart.

The drugs are new and volatile, not yet widely used. It was a miracle Mom got the chance to try them as a last-ditch treatment just as they came out of trials at a prestigious institution.

I hate the thought that this unreliable savior might wind up killing her before the cancer does.

But we're too far along to stop and give up now.

More importantly, her latest scans came back with shrinking masses. Smaller, lighter shadows around her pancreas.

Enough reason to keep holding out and crossing my fingers.

Last night, I gave my blessing to continue—a decision Ros should've been part of. As long as she keeps her mind and her organs don't slip into DNR territory.

After all, it's either this, or absolutely nothing.

I pull out two chairs, but when I settle into mine, Nell ignores the seat I got for her and just leans against it instead.

I'm cool with that.

And I settle into a familiar vigil with Nell cuddled close, one arm wrapped around my shoulder.

With the other, I reach for my mother's frail hand.

I can feel it today.

The faint blood pulsing through her, a subtle ticking rhythm between our clasped palms.

A sign that her body's still working, anchoring her to this world.

A promise that there's still some fight left in her, that she's still in there, trying to find her way back to us.

Please.

Please hang in there.

I never thought I would be answered.

Not until there's a sudden shrill spike in the heart monitor's soft beeps.

Not the abrupt squeal of cardiac failure or another panic-worthy event this time, but just this strengthening, quickening, before my mom's lips move.

The oxygen tube in her nose fogs up slightly.

Her head rolls, and I suck in a sharp breath.

Holy crap.

Should I call the nurse? Should I—

Then Mom lets out a low, tired moan.

Her eyes flutter open, dim slits of faded color rolling around aimlessly before they land on me.

She's aware.

She's awake.

The soft gleam of recognition in her eyes nearly sends me spiraling into tears. Behind the mask, the shadow of a smile flits across her lips, her voice coming in a thready whisper.

"O-Ophelia," she whispers. "Hi, baby girl." Then she turns her head. "Nell Faircross? Hi, Nell."

Nell lights up, the prettiest picture of all the bright, hopeful feelings flapping around inside me.

"Hi, Miss Angela!" She holds up her unicorn. "Mr. Pickle came to see you too!"

Mom lets out a shaky laugh, weak but there, even if it trembles her body in ways that look painful.

I'm flipping speechless.

I choke out a tearful laugh, too, pressing a hand over my mouth so it doesn't sound like a scream.

Jesus, please.

Please let this mean she's coming out of it.

Please let this mean she'll be okay.

"Mom?" I venture. "How... how do you feel?"

Her weary eyes slide over and stop on me. Even that small movement looks like it takes a terrible toll on her.

"Tired," she admits. "H-how long have I been...?"

"Out of it? Not too long," I answer, and her smile fades. "You slipped away the day I got back. Around the time they started the next phase of your meds."

"Oh, my," she says. Her hand tightens in mine. "It's bad then?"

My lips press together.

How do I answer that?

Realistically, her odds are somewhere between surviving a shark attack and winning the lottery even with the new drugs, but dammit, I don't care.

She's still in this.

She's still here, alive and conscious and fighting *for me.*

"It's progress, Mom. The doctors are doing everything they can. Your last MRI came back with less than before. They brought back the specialist from Minnesota to help monitor the next phase. It's all so experimental, but very promising."

Yeah, supposedly.

I hate being so vague with her, passing off this keep-calm-and-blindly-keep-hoping speech a nurse would give, but I don't want to scare my mother into losing her fight.

It's like she knows, though.

She just gives me that knowing Mom look.

"Ros...?"

"Not here," I answer reluctantly. "I texted asking her to come, but..."

Ugh.

Where do I even start?

I pin on a strained smile.

"But?" My mother's brows wrinkle.

What else can I give her but the truth?

"I don't know, Mom." I shake my head. "I've seen her like twice since I came home and we just fight a lot. She ignores my texts. Honestly, I don't—I don't know what's going on with her, but I'm worried I'm going to lose you both." I swallow the massive lump lodged in my throat. "It's her new boy, I think. He's just eating up her time, always pulling her away."

"New boy? Who?" Mom stares at me.

This time, I frown.

Surely, she had some hint of what my sister was up to before the coma pulled her under?

"You-know-who," I offer, but she doesn't say anything. I clear my throat. "So, Mom, how long has Ros been dating Aleksander, anyway?"

I'm not expecting what's next.

Honestly, I don't know how my mother could get any paler, but she does.

Her hand seizes mine, her grip so fierce it digs into my palm with bony fingers.

Her eyes widen and she stares in abject disbelief.

Total horror etched in her face.

"Aleksander? Aleksander Arrendell?" she croaks, her voice breaking.

I nod slowly.

"Well, yeah. The one and only."

"No! N-not him. Not *that* boy. He's not the right one, Ophelia. God, he's—you can't—she can't—you can't let them!"

"Mom, calm down," I urge, leaning toward her, hating that she's so upset. But why? "Believe me, if I could convince her to look at other options, I'd—"

I stop as my mother quivers, her eyes darting around the room as her nails sink into my flesh.

"Ophelia, no. No, it's not right! It's *sacrilege.*"

Holy hell, what?

She trails off with a muffled sigh, like just speaking saps her energy.

And those stinging nails in my hand are gone. Her eyes flutter shut as she sinks into the bed, her head lolling to one side.

"Miss Angela?!" Nell whimpers.

"Mom!"

Nell goes tumbling forward as I surge to my feet and

press my fingers to my mother's throat, feeling for —thank God.

There's still a strong, steady pulse.

I almost had a heart attack myself, but she's fine.

Or is she?

Leave it to Aleksander effing Arrendell to nearly kill her a second time.

"Miss... Miss Philia?" Nell whines, clinging to my leg. "Is your mom okay?"

"She's fine, sweetie." I exhale, dragging a hand over my face before looking down at Nell and gripping her shoulder gently. "It's hard on the brain to wake up when you've been resting for so long. She just wore herself out and fell back asleep, that's all. C'mon, let's give her some rest. I'll take you out for lunch so your uncle Grant can have a break from feeding us."

That gets a bright smile, even if I need to talk to Grant, myself.

Because I have no idea what my mother's reaction means.

Not that boy.

It's not right.

Sacrilege.

Heavy words.

It worries me.

Actually, it scares me, and so does the fact that I have no answers, no idea what to do about it.

It's almost a blessing that Mom's out again. The last thing I need is her freaking out again and overstressing when there's been a flicker of improvement.

I can only hope we dig up something ourselves—and soon.

We need to get to the bottom of this insanity before it's too late.

XXI: ONE OF THOSE DAYS
(GRANT)

I don't know what the fuck I'm doing here.

Staring at this almost-dead man like I can magically see through him, divining some answers from his bones.

From somebody's bones, I guess.

Because goddammit, I really don't know what to do about finding a whole human body out there in that clearing in the same place Law was bleeding out.

That's what Raleigh PD forensics dug up in the end.

A complete human skeleton—and they're gonna want me to have a look at the rotted remnants of clothing to see if I recognize anything.

From the looks of it, the perps stripped the victim naked, buried them, then buried their belongings close by. Not much survived over long years of decomposition besides a leather jacket.

Too much like the jacket Ethan wore when he started riding his motorcycle.

The big asshole just had to play the part, all leather and jeans and tough guy swagger as he grew into a young man.

Once, I had to pull him away from a drunken fight with a dude from the Grizzlies MC. It was bad enough that we snuck into the bar without anybody carding us. Worse that this tank of a man was passing through town when Ethan mouthed off and the biker called him out as a 'chickenshit poser.'

He totally was.

But that boy was *my* poser and my best friend.

My thoughts are unsettled as hell as I frown at Mason Law.

What were you trying to tell us, old man?

How many more bodies will Raleigh forensics find as they work that clearing, churning up the earth and the devil's secrets?

One.

Just one awful secret.

You know that's all it is.

You already know who.

My lip curls into a snarl.

I can't take this shit.

All these years, I thought I was ready.

Now that there's a chance we might find out he's really gone—

Fuck.

In the back of my mind, I've been hoping one day he'd show up on my doorstep with a wife and kids or at least some unbelievable story about running off to Argentina—a place Ethan always fantasized about when we were boys because it was so frigging close to Antarctica. He had a hard-on for arctic exploring even though he shook like a leaf all winter.

Go figure.

Ethan, he'd be a little grey, more grizzled than before. Maybe an early midlife pot belly and a set of bristly

349

whiskers, but grinning with that same shit-eating, disarming grin.

Sorry, man. Wish I could've told you.

But I just couldn't take this dull little town anymore.

So you married my sister, huh? Shit, that's great.

When do I get to meet my niece and nephew?

Stupid.

Stupid fucking cheesy-ass fantasy.

I snort at my own idiocy.

Married to Ophelia with a son and daughter of our own and Nell playing big sister?

Ros safe and sound, busy running the family shop without any goddamned drug-snorting, panty-sniffing Arrendell lunatic in the picture?

Angela Sanderson, miraculously recovered and happily retired?

Then Ethan, coming home to surprise everyone.

Deep down, I knew.

I knew it was fucking *hopeless.*

Guess I never learned to separate hope from the desperate inner ravings of a madman who could never stop wishing for one more day with his best friend.

I'm a realist at heart with everything but Ethan.

Trouble is, shattering that little fantasy feels like the apocalypse. The end of everything.

Every hope that I could somehow fix things for the Sandersons, a family I care about as much as my own.

Every hope that somehow, some way, everything could still be all right.

Every hope that Ophelia might be so overwhelmed with joy that all her problems would disappear and she'd marry me tomorrow.

Shit, no.

I need to get the fuck out of here.

Head out to the crime scene and meet up with the Raleigh team. Check in with Ophelia and make sure she's okay after all the scares yesterday.

I hope she's shaken off a little of her angst.

With any luck, she's back at home with Nell by now. She'll probably keep giving me those guilty looks like she did something wrong, and I don't know how the fuck to tell her she didn't.

I don't know how to tell her I'll wait as long as she needs me to.

Goddammit, Grant.

Get out of your own head and go do something useful.

So I do.

After staring at Mason Law for a few more seconds, I heft myself up with a groan and stretch, rubbing at my ass. I'm sore from over an hour in that little plastic chair. The seats in this joint are fit to put someone in the hospital themselves.

I turn away, grinding my fingertips against the back of my aching neck—only to hear a low moan behind me.

I whirl on my heel.

Law's eyes twitch, his lips parting on a disturbed groan.

Cautiously, I step closer.

His vitals aren't changing—not that I really know how to read that shit, I ain't Ophelia—but the beeping hasn't changed, so I guess he's okay, just waking up.

I should get the nurse.

I turn away again.

Only, this time I'm stopped by cold, bony fingers pinching the back of my arm.

I freeze.

Law clings to me with too much strength for a man in his state, the needlepoints of his emaciated fingers digging into my arm.

When I look back, his eyes are marbles crafted in pure fear.

Bloodshot, entirely mad, red-rimmed—he's awake, and staring right through me with an accusatory gaze that says he sees me.

He's aware.

"The... the letters," he wheezes. His voice has the rawness you'd expect from someone whose throat was burned, first by a flesh-wilting poison and then by a breathing tube. "I... I buried them where they b-buried the bones." Law stares at me like he's trying to grind something urgent into me. "T-tried... tried to w-warn her. Tried to stop her, you... you have to *save* her."

"Save her? Save who?" Alertness spikes flashes of cold through me. Fuck. Was that what he was trying to do? Save Ophelia from something? From what? I step closer and lean over him. "What am I saving her from, Mr. Law?"

He just stares at me.

"*Mr. Law,*" I say again. "I'm Captain Grant Faircross with Redhaven PD. I'm on your side. If you want me to help Ophelia, you've got to tell me more."

"The letters," he repeats in a fading whisper. His grip on my arm goes lax.

Goddammit.

His eyes lose focus and his head falls back against the pillow, staring blankly up at the ceiling.

"I... I was there," he breathes, but I don't think he's talking to me anymore. "The night that boy... that night th-they ran him off the road. I was there..."

...that boy?

"*Ethan?*" I gasp, catching his arm. "You talking about Ethan Sanderson? Did someone run him off the road?"

And he's gone.

Eyes rolled back, closing as he goes slack, his hand falling away to dangle from the bed like a broken doll.

Fuck me.

Looks like I've got some serious digging to do. An old case to reopen and answers to find, even if it pounds what's left of my heart into slag.

I turn to head out again and this time no one stops me.

I stop by the nurses' station and let them know he woke up, asking them to let me know if he does it again, and to record anything he says.

A quick glance at Angela's room shows her alone now.

Ophelia and Nell are gone.

Damn.

I'm on the verge of something massive. I can feel it.

I just have to find out what.

Whatever I have to do to keep Ophelia Sanderson safe.

* * *

THE FOREST CLEARING looks like a battered anthill that was kicked around by some bored kids when I get there.

The whole area has that wet earthy smell of fresh-turned mud you always get in October.

My team is mostly on the sidelines, talking with a few of the folks from Raleigh forensics as they bag and tag more soil samples for evidence. They mostly defer to Lucas to determine what we keep and what goes off to the Raleigh lab for more analysis.

"Anything interesting?" I ask, settling on the hood of Lucas' patrol car.

Our combined weight makes it sag on its front tires.

Together, we watch while the Raleigh crew digs up these neat segmented squares, carving out one orderly piece of ground at a time.

"Full human skeleton. Scraps of clothing, but I'm guessing you knew that. The teeth in the skull are intact, I guess." He glances at me, his cat-green eyes flashing. "Sounds like they might try dental records to get an ID."

I just grunt.

I don't need to say it.

He's a Redhaven native and only one degree removed from Ethan's mystery with his own missing sister for so long.

He gets it.

"Nothing else?" I ask.

"Not yet, but they're still working it, Cap," he answers—just as a call goes up from across the field.

"We got something!" a voice calls.

I glance at Lucas before pushing off the car and speeding across the clearing.

A woman in a white jumpsuit and mask crouches over a hole in the ground, gingerly sweeping dirt off—wood?

Yep, polished wood.

Her gloved hands gently lift up a gleaming box of rose-tinted redwood, roughly the size of a shoebox.

Doesn't look that old—and doesn't look like it's been in the ground all that long, either.

There's not enough dirt accumulation to be as old as those bones.

Plus, the moisture along with the freezing, melting, and heating cycles would've warped the wood bad, never mind insects and worms eating away at it, too.

This thing was buried not too long ago.

The woman gives me a questioning look through her goggles.

I nod.

"Open it."

She returns my nod and pries the latch. The little bronze hook opens smoothly, no rusty squealing, confirming its age.

Inside, I see stacks of folded paper, yellowed with age, thin enough so the handwriting on the other side looks like ghostly scribbles bleeding through.

I stare at the box with Mason Law's voice on replay in my mind—until something brushes my elbow and I just about bust right out of my skin.

When I look up, Lucas stands by my side, holding a pair of nitrile gloves.

I take them with a grateful nod and snap them on, then take the box from the woman and retreat back to the patrol car.

The urge to read the letters wars with professional obligations to treat this like crime evidence—because it is.

No prints, no smudging, so I carefully set an evidence bag on the hood of the car and place the box on top before I settle down and pick up the first sheaf of folded pages, peeling them open.

They're definitely older.

Handwritten.

All blue, sloping ink, a light and loopy feminine style with a slightly older feel I can't explain. The top page is dated over twenty years ago—October, just like now.

Dearest,

It's freezing today. Cold enough to feel the loneliness, your absence, though I know why I can't see you.

Not right now. Maybe not ever.

I told you I won't deceive myself about what we're doing.

I'm lonely, yes... but I'm also convenient for you.

You know how much that makes me smile.

Being yours. Something to distract you from your responsibili-

ties. From how cruel life must be in that cold, loveless house, where you said all the money in the world can't buy you any joy.

Oh, I can tell when your smiles are false. When you turn on the charm for everyone else, playing the part of the dearly respected man for the public.

I'm not fooling myself.

I'm just the only one who understands how lonely, how sad you truly are. It's enough for me to believe you love me right now.

Enough for you to believe you love our beautiful little girl and the child growing in me right now.

Will you come tonight? I don't dare send the ultrasound, just in case she stumbles on it. This letter is damning enough, but there's a little bit of a thrill in the risk, isn't there?

It's a girl, beloved.

Another girl.

Perhaps I'll name her for one of Shakespeare's ladies, too.

HOPING TO SEE YOU TONIGHT,

-Your angel

WHAT THE FUCK am I reading?

I numbly scan the pages of the first letter again.

Something in the back of my mind screams like a startled coyote.

Call it an instinct that's trying to make me look at what's right in front of my dumb fool face. Only, everything else shuts the fuck down and refuses to acknowledge the terrible truth.

You already know what this means.

It's veiled, yes, but it's not hard to decode.

This is a letter from Angela Sanderson to Montero fucking Arrendell.

After the birth of her first daughter, while she was pregnant with her second, and—

Oh fuck.

Oh fuck, oh shit, oh *damn*.

I shove my knuckles against my mouth, barely stopping my fingers from clutching violently at the pages and crumpling them into dust.

Angela Sanderson had an affair with Montero.

A long-running arrangement, from the sounds of it.

Ophelia. Rosalind.

Montero's daughters.

They're both Arrendells.

Which means Ros is about to marry her own *half brother*.

And I get the sickest feeling Aleksander knew it all along.

"Hey, Cap, what's wrong? What the hell did it say?" I hear Lucas asking, but I can't answer.

I dig my feet into the mud, fighting to stand up as my mind strains, wondering what the hell to do with this waking nightmare.

357

XXII: ONE LITTLE SECRET
(OPHELIA)

I'm asleep on the sofa when the door bangs open with a crash loud enough to stop my heart.

I bolt up with a startled scream, my eyes snapping open.

The look on Grant's face when my vision clears doesn't stop the panic slashing through me.

What happened?

What is it now?

I stare at him, standing in the doorway with his face ash grey, his brown eyes stark, his chest heaving like every breath is cement.

"Ophelia," he snarls roughly. "We have to find Ros. Right fucking now."

"Why? What's going on?" I clutch my throat, trying to tame my rabbiting pulse. I'm already scrambling for my phone with my other hand. "What's wrong? Is she hurt?"

"No, not exactly, I don't—oh, fuck." He swipes a hand down his face and steps into the house, moving with a weariness that seems to have aged him a thousand years.

My heart slows to the dull *thump* of the door slamming shut in his wake.

Grant sinks down on the sofa next to me and fully buries his face in his hands.

Holy hell, what happened?

"Grant?"

"I don't know how to fucking say this, Philia. I don't. But I can't keep this from you," he rumbles.

I shake my head painfully.

"Keep what?" I'm frozen, phone pinched in my hand, thumb hovering over Ros' contact. Cold dread squeezes me like a snake. "Grant, you're scaring me..."

He slowly lifts his head, looking at me with haggard eyes.

"We found letters," he says slowly, wetting his lips. "They were buried at the scene where Mason Law showed you the body. He hid them there." Grant's eyes are almost pleading. "They're from Angela, Philia. Addressed to Montero Arrendell."

"...what?"

I am so, so confused the world goes fuzzy.

My phone drops into my lap as I brace myself against the back of the sofa. What else isn't he telling me?

Grant looks at me miserably and shakes his head. He's wearing the same face I imagine he uses as an officer when he has to show up to someone's doorstep with the very worst news.

"I don't understand. What... what are you saying?"

Deep down, I'm scared that I know.

At least, I have an inkling.

I can guess what he's implying, but my mind won't wrap around the words. The very idea feels like a foreign language, something I can't understand taunting me.

Ice knifes through my heart as it all comes flooding back.

The questions about the past Mom always dodged.

How secretive she was about our little family.

About our dad.

What Janelle Bowden said about my mother and the flipping Arrendells.

"He's your father," Grant clips, reaching for my shoulder, the only point of warmth grounding me to a reality that's just flipped upside down. "You always wondered. Montero Arrendell is your old man—and Ros'. That means—"

"No! Oh my God..." If it wasn't for his steady hand, I'd throw up right here. I clap both hands over my mouth, staring at my knees, wretched bile climbing up my throat. "Aleksander, he's—"

My throat clamps shut.

I can't even say it, to speak aloud the full insanity lodged in my throat.

"If it's any comfort, Lucia said they haven't—y'know. Not yet." Grant clears his throat.

"Holy shit. Holy balls. Are you sure? Grant, you're *sure* she's been holding out?"

That's definitely the Ros I know, a sweet, old-fashioned, shameless romantic at heart.

But with the way she is now and that leering creep all over her, I figured there was no way he hadn't lured her into his bed.

"Yeah," Grant agrees grimly. "We have to find her before that twisted prick does something she can't take back. Before he makes this worse than it already is. You understand?"

Sickeningly, I do.

And I don't blame him one bit for dancing around saying it.

My sister and Aleksander Arrendell. *Engaged* when they're half siblings.

I rake my nails over my thighs, grounding myself with the stinging sensation.

"God." It's the only thing I can say coherently, but after a moment something clicks. I lift my head, staring at him. "You think he knew? He knew and... but *why?*"

"Considering his own fucking brother said he liked murdering women because being rich was boring before he died, tricking his half sister into sleeping with him is probably a parlor game. That whole family is completely fucked in the head—" Grant stops and stares at me. "The ones who know what they are, I mean." His voice drips with disgust as he sighs. "Are you okay?"

"No. *No*, I'm not, but—oh God, it's too much." But I can have a breakdown later.

Montero, Montero, why would my mother ever...?

Why is *he* my father?

Why can't my dad be any other man on Earth?

But if I think about it, I can see it.

Terrible little hints of him in my face, in Ros', in our striking green eyes.

When I swallow, it's like sandpaper, and I shake myself loose from my circling thoughts.

Ros has to come first while there's still time to help her.

I shoot to my feet, legs wobbling.

"We have to find her. I'll call, you go get Nell. I left her doing her homework in her bedroom," I tell him.

Grant nods sharply, standing as well.

There's a fraught moment when he starts to reach for me, and I'd have fallen into his arms in a second, desperately needing comfort, damn the complications.

But then he stops, hesitates, pulls back.

There's one last forlorn look between us before he pivots and thunders upstairs, his voice echoing back as he calls, "Nelly-girl?"

Meanwhile, I stab at my phone, lift it to my ear, and listen to the ringtone shrilling horribly. It's too much like horror-movie violins ramping up my nerves with every scraping sound.

Three rings.

Four.

Five.

Then a lonely click—

"Ros?"

—before her voicemail message chirps at me cheerfully. *"This is Ros! You know what to do, I'll call you back when I can."*

Crap.

Crap crap crap.

"Ros, it's me. Call me back as soon as you get this. Please. Make sure you're alone when you do."

I hang up, staring at my phone.

Endless horrible images rush my brain, starting with the slimy way Aleksander touched her, looked at her, kissed her right there in front of me, his eyes swirling with so much hunger—

No, we're not going there. But if I think about my sister alone with him for even another second, I really will puke.

I fire off a text instead.

SOS call back NOW it's life or death please please please Ros this is beyond serious

As soon as I hit Send, I try calling her again.

While the phone rings dumbly in my ear, Grant comes tearing down the stairs again and thrusts a crumpled piece of paper written in screaming red colored pencil at me.

"We've got another problem," he grinds out.

The sound of Ros' voicemail trills at me in the distance as I read Nell's loopy handwriting.

And my heart has a new reason to plummet.

Gone To Find Miss Ros: Dont Try To Find Me

"Oh, no," I breathe, dropping my phone.

When I look up, there's a direct mirror of my confusion, my pain, my disbelief in his face.

Grant's eyes darken like never before, swirling with worry and a cold determination I wish I had.

* * *

WE RUN THROUGH THE HOUSE.

We search high and low.

We pray silently—even if I can only hear it in his footsteps and loud, lonely calls for her—because this shit *cannot* be happening right now.

Oh, but it is.

No sign of Mr. Pickle.

Nell's backpack isn't in her room or anywhere in the house.

She's not answering the little kiddie phone Grant uses to keep up with her, and the tracker signal on it doesn't show. It's like the battery's dead.

My house is locked up tight, the little play area where Nell ran away before untouched. Empty.

She's truly gone.

I want to blame myself, falling asleep and losing track of her, but there's no time for that right now.

Grant's truck roars wildly as we pile in and floor it, heading for the Arrendell house.

The engine churns, fighting the steep incline of the hill.

I try Nell's phone over and over and over again, but she's not picking up.

"Grant," I whisper, and he clenches his jaw, staring ahead at the house with a hard gaze.

"We'll find out where they are, and then we'll find Nell.

We'll put a stop to this bullshit." There's a dark certainty in his voice, something I shouldn't find so reassuring.

But I do.

Grant Faircross doesn't let any horror slow him down.

He doesn't think. He doesn't grieve. He doesn't curse his atrocious luck.

He just springs into action, becoming courage incarnate, and right now I wish that were me.

Listen to him. It's going to happen, I try to tell myself. *No matter what he has to do, he's going to bring her home.*

And you're going to get Ros away from that smiling freak before it's too late.

Soon, we're roaring through the gates.

The tires screech as Grant swerves into the roundabout at the foot of the stairs of that big white mansion. The engine barely has a chance to die before Grant leaps out of the truck, slamming the door hard enough to shake it.

I launch out after him without thinking, racing up the steps right behind him, but as we get to the door, I balk.

We're about to go into the lion's den, and if *he's* there...

I'm part of this.

My God.

Part of this tainted legacy that's poisoned Redhaven. But I shouldn't think about anything but Nell's safety right now.

Later, I'll start to process my feelings, everything that comes with finding out you're part monster.

For now, Grant is my shield, the wall between me and the valet who opens the door, lifting his chin haughtily.

"Sir, you cannot simply show up without a prior—"

"Unless you want to spend the night in county lockup, stand aside," Grant snaps, flashing his badge. "Official police business. Missing child. Get the fucking Lord and Lady of the manor right now. Do not waste my time."

There's a stunned, offended sniff. Then the valet jerks his head and pulls himself back inside. "Follow me, *please*."

We exchange tense looks and I follow him into Hades.

I feel so small here, even in Grant's shadow.

This massive house always looms over the town like a giant fist of judgment.

Today, it feels like its shadow is meant for me personally.

I just stay close to him as the valet leads us through red-draped halls that make me think too much of blood.

Blood bond.

Blood relatives.

Blood—

I have to stop.

Imagine how much better this gets if I panic myself into passing out here.

The butler brings us to the big central hall with its massive chandelier and curving staircases.

Intimidating, but Grant stands tall and strong like nothing unnerves him.

His fists are clenched, his shoulders squared like he's gearing up for a real brawl.

The valet leaves us alone.

I curl my hand against Grant's arm. The muscle feels like stone under my palm.

I don't dare say anything when it feels like the high ceilings would pick my voice up and carry it through the entire house.

My heart beats like a frightened, caged bird in the silence.

Still not as hard as it jolts when the double doors at the far end of the hall snap open.

Lucia and Montero Arrendell glide in like they're making a grand red carpet entrance they've rehearsed a thousand times.

She's as elegant as ever in a sleek grey sheath dress, her

slim fingers brushing her blonde bob back from her sharp jawline, but I barely notice.

I'm staring at my father.

God help me.

He's a dark cameo of old-school style and dashing, devil-may-care looks behind a smooth smirk.

Their eyes flick over us like we're for sale and they're just considering the price, but it's when they look at me that I die inside.

They know.

There's something strange in those haunted green eyes that match my own as Montero Arrendell—as my *father*—looks at me.

As his gaze lingers, weirdly distant, that remote smile fading and leaving something thoughtful and strange.

I might never notice, if not for the other pair of eyes burning like a laser.

But Lucia's stare is all cold hatred.

To her, I'm a living reminder of how often her husband must've strayed, and now I've invaded her house.

My stomach sinks.

I shrink away behind Grant.

Especially when Montero won't stop *looking* at me.

Like he's trying to understand this fantastic new creature in front of him, oblivious to Lucia tossing her hair and eyeballing Grant like a judge ready to hand down a sentence.

"How many times must you barge into my home in one week, Captain Faircross?" she bites off.

"Don't," Grant growls. "Lady, I don't have time for your offended bullshit. My little cousin's missing. Pretty sure she ran off with Ros, and Ros is always with Aleksander. She's not answering her phone. So I'd damn well appreciate it if you could tell me where your two lovebirds went."

Lucia smirks. "I'm afraid they're a little out of your reach.

Come now, what are you worried about? If the little girl's with them, they'll take good care of her, certainly."

The emptiness in her voice makes my heart fall out.

For the first time, I'm afraid for Nell and Ros both.

Grant's knuckles strain in hard ridges as he stomps forward, baring his teeth.

I pull back on his arm, shaking my head with a whisper. "Grant. Don't."

Meanwhile, Montero keeps staring at me like a statue, his gaze blank and impenetrable.

How could he?

How could *they*?

What the hell was my mother thinking?

And with Ros, if they knew—if they just stood back and watched and let it happen, let Aleksander play this sick game...

Grant goes stock-still.

"Don't make me arrest you both," he snarls. "And fuck the consequences to my career. Tell me where they are."

"On the coast by now," Lucia answers haughtily, her lips curving smugly. "They've eloped. My dear son wouldn't wait for a fairy-tale wedding. Since Rosalind's practically *family*" —she pauses and sends me a cutting look—"and since I couldn't be supportive enough of their little relationship, they've taken matters into their own hands, I'm afraid. There's a priest waiting to marry them on Aleksander's private yacht at Wrightsville Beach."

Crap.

Aleksander must have pressured her.

Somehow, he must've known the clock was ticking, so he wants to bring this horrible game to its conclusion before it's too late.

Marry her so she'll stop resisting and he can have his way, and then he'll get what he wants.

An abomination.

"Why didn't you stop them?" I whisper before I can stop myself. I'm talking to Lucia, but I'm locked on Montero, eye to eye, searching for—

I don't even know.

Something.

Some vague recognition of a man I could call my father, some hint of humanity or just regret.

I don't find either as I clear my throat and force myself to speak.

"Why did you let them?"

Montero finally looks away.

He's hiding his face from me now, looking to the side. Maybe there's the faintest human conscience in there somewhere, or he's just annoyed at getting caught.

But it's Lucia who answers confidently.

"Frankly, I'm glad they decided to do it this way. Big weddings are such work, and who am I to get in the way of my son's happiness?" she purrs.

"Get fucked," Grant says bluntly. "Call him right now. Keep calling him until he answers. That yacht better not leave the fucking docks. And you call the wedding off ASAP. That's not a request."

He turns sharply then, stalking away.

"Grant?!" I pelt after him.

"Let's go," he snarls. "It's a three-hour drive to Wrightsville Beach."

* * *

I'M COMPLETELY EXHAUSTED, running on total willpower.

Little Nell's still not picking up.

The last few hours have been a whirlwind from hell.

Constantly calling Nell and Ros while Grant coordinates with both Redhaven and Wrightsville PD officers. He's also sent Lucas and Micah and Henri up to the big house to make sure the Arrendells follow his orders. They report back in when Aleksander still won't answer his phone.

My fingers work the screen furiously between calls, messaging my sister again and again, begging for an answer.

He's our brother! You can't marry him.

Mom had an affair with Montero Arrendell and he's our father.

Wherever you are, run! The police are coming. Whatever you do, don't let him pressure you into anything.

This is so not how I wanted this travesty to go.

But I don't have the luxury of time anymore.

There's no breaking the news to her gently.

Not when this could break *her* if he pushes her into going through with the unthinkable.

When that gets no response, I try Nell again, just as Grant swerves the truck onto the off-ramp for Wrightsville Beach. I'm just about to hang up and try again.

But the call picks up.

I jerk forward hard enough to snap the seat belt against my throat, gasping as someone sniffles out a whisper.

"M-Miss... Miss Philia?"

"Nell! Honey, where are you? Are you okay?"

"You got her?" Grant's head whips toward me.

I shove a hand against his cheek, urging him to keep his eyes on the road. "Nell, sweetie, talk to me."

"I... I can't," she whispers, her voice tiny. "They'll hear me. And he'll get m-mad..."

"Who, Nell? Who's scaring you? Where are you?"

"It's... it's a big boat," she manages. "I hid in the trunk. I didn't think Miss Ros would m-mind, but then the scary man was there and he said mean things to her. He made her get in the car, and I followed them on the boat. But I'm scared. I think he's gonna hurt her!"

"Stay where you are, sweetie," I say, clutching my phone tight, making my voice level. "Stay hidden. We're on the way. We're almost there, and we'll make everything okay, I promise."

"Hurry," she pleads. "H-he... he's—"

My heart becomes ice as she breaks off.

Followed by the sound of my sister's voice in a chilling scream.

Then Nell screams too, belting out, "Miss Ros!"

I reach out helplessly like I can grasp them both, letting out a hurt cry of my own, my heart splitting apart.

"Rosalind! Grant, we have to hurry."

XXIII: THE ONE THAT GOT AWAY (GRANT)

*F*or a law abiding officer of peace, I'm sure as hell breaking at least a dozen laws right now.

Speed limit? I don't know what the fuck it is in this mad flight to save my little girl and Philia's sister.

I'm pretty sure I've cut a few people off without a turn signal, whipped around a couple semis, and left one red-faced old man shaking his fist and calling in my plate.

Ask me if I care.

Nothing else matters besides Ophelia's pale, tear-streaked face.

Plus, those heart-wrenching screams I heard shrieking through her phone.

Ros.

Nelly-girl.

Both trapped with that blackhearted would-be-sister-fucking psychopath.

We go tearing through the town of Wrightsville Beach toward the docks without slowing down, weaving in and out of traffic. Horns bleat and tires squeal as pissed off bystanders rage around us.

A few sirens echo in the distance through the noise.

Good. That means the Wrightsville Beach PD actually paid attention.

Wish I'd brought my patrol car instead, but not having it doesn't stop me from flying through the streets.

I can't stop now.

I won't.

Three women depend on me too much.

That's all that keeps my brain running at the moment.

I'm still reeling from too many big shitty revelations hitting at once.

The sick and twisted machinations Aleksander Arrendell has been playing at, this long game built up bit by bit, carves a piece out of me I'm not sure I'll ever get back.

Seriously. What the hell?

From day one, I wondered what he saw in her. I never believed the fairy-tale lovey-dovey bullshit coming from this vampire playboy for a minute.

A man like Aleksander Arrendell with fantastically high standards and warped tastes doesn't just up and decide to shack up with the small-town girl on a whim.

Now it makes sense, and it fucking hurts that it does.

Seducing his own half sister into a marriage just so he can get his rocks off?

Getting her hooked on drugs?

Setting a trap to break her for his own sick pleasure?

That's what he's after.

Unfathomable cruelty.

And considering his serial killer brother, I've got an ugly feeling a man like him won't just stop at psychologically breaking a woman, either.

That makes me stomp the gas.

That drives me on, knowing it's life and death and I can't have their blood on my hands.

I'll never forgive myself if I don't make it in time to—

There!

I can see the water glinting through the buildings.

"Hold on tight," I growl, throwing out a hand to steady Ophelia as I wrench the wheel.

The truck rockets around the sharpest turn yet, practically rearing up on two wheels.

I'm glad as hell I remember that tactical driving I did for Uncle Sam in my old Guard days.

She doesn't make a sound when she's so frozen silent, but she clutches my arm, staring ahead and straining toward the windshield like she can somehow lean into the momentum and guide us to them faster.

I stomp the gas again and the truck lurches forward, bouncing around the turn and onto the narrow road leading down to the docks.

Boats of all sizes line up along the quay like overgrown toys, everything from little speedboats to cargo barges to one big, sleek ship towering over the rest.

The yacht.

Then I see the tiny fingers wrestling against the railing.

Two men, one woman.

Goddammit, don't tell me I'm too late.

"Ros!" Ophelia sees it too and screams, reaching out toward the windshield, right before one of the men—not Aleksander, but an older man in black—goes overboard.

I whip the truck into the lot and go tumbling out just as Aleksander drags Ros, kicking and struggling and shrieking, into the yacht's wheelhouse.

Fuck.

The older man hits the water with a splash.

Then the yacht churns to life, the water around it surging white.

The sirens grow louder, police cars careening into the lot, too little, too late.

Because the ship lurches away at a dangerous speed a second later, even as a thin, high scream rises from the rear of it that hollows out my soul.

"Uncle Grant!" Nell screams, clinging to the railing at the rear, Mr. Pickle clutched in her arms.

Ophelia's out of the car after me.

We bolt for the docks and I hold out my arms.

"Nell, jump! Jump in the water! I'll come for you!"

She shakes her head frantically. "I can't swim! I'm scared!"

"Jump, Nell!" Ophelia cries, flinging herself down and leaning over, grasping at the flailing older man who's swimming clumsily toward the cement edge—the priest who was supposed to marry them, I think, judging by his black garb and collar.

Nell shrinks back and then just *shrinks* some more, growing smaller as the yacht surges away.

"Uncle Grant..." she whimpers, the wind taking her voice away.

It's a minor miracle the yacht doesn't plow into anything on its way through the crowded water. Of course, that means it's fucking escaping, going God only knows where.

I'm about to say screw it and dive in after her even though I don't have a prayer of catching up, let alone scaling the damned thing with no equipment, but suddenly we're surrounded by cars.

Officers come pouring out. Several stop to help Ophelia haul the priest up.

Too many people crowding around in the commotion, in my way, demolishing my heart.

I whirl around, glaring at one of the uniformed men approaching me.

"Call the fucking Coast Guard," I snap. "That's my niece

up there. This is a kidnapping and they've got to intercept that—"

"We've already called," he answers before barking something into his radio. "They're at least forty minutes out."

Shit.

Forty minutes too long.

Drenched with sweat, Ophelia pulls away from the tangle of people helping the gasping, red-faced priest and launches to her feet.

"That's too late!" she yells. "He knows we're onto them. Grant, he's going to hurt her. There's no way they'll get to her in time—"

"Ophelia." I catch her arm, despair rolling through me. "If the Coast Guard hauls ass, they'll—"

"Fuck the Coast Guard!" she cries, ripping away from me.

For a second, I watch as she races across the marina.

There's no shortage of rubberneckers at this point. People who were fishing, people working on their boats, even people who'd pulled over on the side of the road to stare at the spectacle and the growing riot of police cars.

One rubbernecker stands at the helm of his speedboat.

His mouth hangs open, slack-jawed while he stares through the swarming cop cars at the rapidly retreating yacht.

Only now his gaze flicks to Ophelia as she storms onto his boat.

What's she doing?

"Ophelia, no!"

I snap out of my trance and dash after her just as she stops in front of him and thrusts out her hand.

"Keys," she demands.

"Uh. What?" The man blinks at her.

"I need your *keys!*" Ophelia flings her hand out at the water. "My sister is on that boat with a man who's going to hurt her, maybe even kill her. So is a little girl I love very much. By the time the Coast Guard gets here, they could be dead. Can I please borrow your boat so I can save them, or am I going to have to throw you out of it with my bare hands?"

Goddamn.

Only Ophelia Sanderson would still say 'please' while threatening a man.

She's sobbing by the time she's done, but resolute.

This tiny powerhouse, jacking a boat from a man twice her size for the people she loves. She stares up at him with tears streaking down her face.

With a soft, sympathetic sigh, the man fumbles his keys from his pocket and hands them over without protest, giving her an almost awed look.

"Do what you gotta do, ma'am," he says. "Just try to return her without a scratch."

Ophelia grabs the keys and turns to face me, her chin thrust out stubbornly.

"Well?" she demands. "Are you coming or not?"

XXIV: THE LAST ONE LEFT (OPHELIA)

*C*onfession time.

I've never driven a speedboat before in my life.

If you think that's going to stop me? Ha.

Not after I saw him.

He was *hurting* her.

Ros wasn't there willingly, not after seeing my texts. No matter how messed up she is—no matter what he's done to her—I know she wouldn't.

She's a hostage now.

And there's nothing I'll let come between me and saving my sister.

Not now. Not ever. And with Nell trapped on that boat with them?

I swear, I'll ram this speedboat right through the hull if it means saving them.

The yacht's a big boat, no question.

Its high-powered engine roars as it churns out to sea—charging forward like there's no one at the helm. But the boat I've 'borrowed' was made for speed.

I lean into the yoke hard, gripping the wheel tight enough

to make my fingers go numb, as if I can urge the boat forward with my entire body.

"We're closing the gap," Grant says tightly at my back. He's been with me every step of the way, not even hesitating a second to vault into the boat after me and kick on the engine. "Get ready."

The boat skims the waves, ice-cold spray snapping at our faces and the wind cutting with knifelike precision.

"Get ready for what? I didn't exactly come out here with a plan!" I pant, sucking freezing breaths through my teeth. *Closer. Closer.* My heart's about to burst as the yacht looms larger. It's so close now I can hear the waves slapping against its sides and the angry droning of its engine.

"I've got one, Butterfly," Grant promises, reaching for the wheel. "There's an emergency ladder they didn't pull up before taking off. Just noticed it hanging off the side. You're lighter, so you'll make the jump better. You let me steer."

I stare at him, wondering when my life turned into an action movie.

"If I didn't think you could make it, I damn sure wouldn't ask. You get on board and slow it down, I'll be right behind you. Just move fast and don't let him see you. If he's armed, you hide."

This is the Grant I've never seen.

Battle-hard. Steely. Certain.

The police officer in action, the protector, the warrior.

Honestly, the love of my life.

That's never been clearer than right now, cutting through the drama and stupidity.

The man who will stand strong with me through anything and come out the other side bleeding and battered but victorious.

I start to answer—until a scream splits the sky, so loud it rings my eardrums.

I whip my head up and realize we're almost neck and neck with the yacht, almost on a collision course.

Crap.

"Ophelia, now!" he growls.

Wrenching the wheel, I bring us parallel in a panic, but I can't take my eyes off the deck overhead.

Nell's nowhere in sight now.

But Aleksander and Ros are at the front of the ship, wrestling too close to the railing.

Ros yells desperately as she claws at his face—only for him to force her away with a leering, inhuman grin, holding her by the wrists.

Oh, that asshole.

The fact that he's clearly enjoying this makes me see red.

"Ros!" I cry, only for Grant's bulk to shove me aside, his hands brushing mine off the wheel.

"Let me. I'll get you closer. Woman, don't lose your nerve now," he demands.

Another twenty seconds pass in breathless, brutal silence before he barks one word.

"Go."

No time to hesitate.

No energy for the fear clawing up my throat, trying to smother me.

If I want to save my sister and that sweet little girl, I have to act now.

I have to be half as brave as Grant Faircross.

It's his selfless courage—knowing he's with me and that he's had me through this whole awful homecoming—that buoys me.

The speedboat swerves in close to the yacht, slashing forward and then dropping back as Grant adjusts speed.

He angles our boat, tries to keep an even pace until we

come up to the rungs of the unretracted ladder on the outer hull.

I take a breath, hold it, and wait.

Closer, closer, inch by inch.

All I need is the magic word.

"Now!" Grant shouts.

I don't think.

I just gather my body and throw my strength into my legs.

A real-life leap of faith.

For the longest second, the world is empty air under me.

The terror when I realize if I miss, I'll be smashed between the hulls of both boats like a bug before I hit the water.

Then my grasping hand hits the ladder's rung.

This loud *slap* stings my palm and reverberates through my arm, whipping me back from that frozen moment into fast-rushing reality.

Hold on.

Hold on tight.

I grit my teeth and ignore the instinctive panic, latching on hard with my other hand. The stakes are so much higher than doing pull ups back in high school gym class.

My body slams into the yacht's hull with a hollow *boom.*

I'm going to have the worst whiplash tomorrow morning, if I make it home alive.

Sucking in hot, rushed breaths, I scramble my feet until I find a lower rung. The water keeps lapping at my soaked heels as I fight for footing.

For a nanosecond, I glance back at Grant.

Flashing hazel eyes lock on mine, burning with certainty and encouragement and a love that almost makes me implode.

Go, go, his eyes say. *I fucking know you can do it. Life has been dragging you around, leaving you helpless.*

You're not helpless now, Butterfly.

You can do this.

You can help me save them.

I'm with you.

Always.

I nod fiercely.

Just in time for the boat angling away under his touch as I turn and scale the ladder as fast as I can, pulling myself up in quick, short bursts.

When I hit the top, I tumble over the railing and hit the deck.

For now, I'm hidden from easy view by the raised cube of the wheelhouse.

Thank God for small favors.

Every second Aleksander doesn't see me is one more bite of hope.

I can still hear Ros, though.

She sounds miserable.

I can't make out what she's saying, but as long as she's talking, as long as she's making noise, she's alive, she's on this boat, and I can still bring her home.

Crouching low, I creep along the deck, flattening myself against the wall of the wheelhouse and reeling with every step on the rocking waves.

We're going too fast, I think.

No one's paying much attention to piloting the ship. Another problem.

At first, I'm thinking don't wait for Grant.

Just get to navigation.

Stop the boat.

Then get between Aleksander and Ros—until another scream floats over the deck.

"Leave her alone you—you weirdo! Leave Miss Ros alone!" Nell screams.

Just past the wheelhouse, I catch a flash of blue with rainbow—Mr. Pickle—right before a pint-sized blur flings itself at Aleksander and my sister.

Baby, no!

With one brutish hand still locked on Ros' wrist, Aleksander whirls around just in time to catch Nell cannonballing against his forearm.

He blocks her and shoves her back.

She goes tumbling to the deck with a heartbreaking cry.

"Well, well," Aleksander leers, glaring down at Nell with a smile full of murder. "What do we have here? You're a little young to drown, brat, but if you want to play rough..."

"No! Don't you dare!" Ros cries, jerking violently on her wrist. "Don't touch her!"

Aleksander whirls on her with that same awful grin.

"Oh? What will you do for me if I don't, *dearest sissy?*"

Gag.

I'm going to be sick.

He effing knows.

We knew it before, but to have this horrid confirmation...

He knew who and what she was the whole time.

And it's no wonder she's fighting him with everything she has, rejecting this man like a poison when before she was glued to him.

Ros goes still, staring at him with a pale, horrified look.

All the blood drains from her already pale face.

"You're disgusting," she whispers. "All this time, stringing me along, I... I *kissed* you."

My gag reflex almost overwhelms me this time.

Especially when Aleksander leans closer, smirking, bringing his mouth near Ros' while my sister turns away cringing.

"And you loved every filthy, fucked up minute of it. How wet did you get, Ros? Why won't you just admit you find this exhilarating?"

Holy shit, enough.

I can't take it anymore.

I'm about to do something monumentally stupid.

Anything to make it stop.

There's no warning, though.

One second, Ros is frozen in place, her familiar green eyes wide with terror.

The next, a resounding *slap* echoes over the boat.

Her hand smashes across Aleksander's cheek so hard his head twists.

There's my moment.

Aleksander reels, probably seeing double, his face blooming red, ugly-handsome features transformed into a mask of violent rage.

His grip tightens on Ros' wrist and his hand flies up to strike her.

Before he can regain his balance, I charge forward.

I may be short.

But I make a way better cannonball than little Nell.

I slam into them with all the force I can muster, flinging myself between them and shoving Ros back from Aleksander, forcing him to let her go from pure shock.

Thank God.

We all go tumbling down.

Aleksander in one direction, me and Ros in the other.

As my sister and I hit the deck, clutching at each other, tangled up in the silk folds of her white dress, my heart scrambles.

Nell's scream cuts through the chaos.

Ros gives me a panicked look before we're moving again.

Only to freeze almost instantly.

Aleksander rises up on one knee like a snake that just won't die, his hand snaring Nell's hair, dragging her against his body.

Something metal materializes in his other hand—a compact black pistol from inside his designer white tux.

Shit, shit, no.

He can't.

He won't.

I start inching forward again, then go completely still as Aleksander smirks, aiming the gun dead at us over Nell's shoulder.

"Ah-ah-ah. Not very smart, little sister. One little flick of the hand and it'll be her just as easily as you."

"You animal," I hiss. "She's just a little girl. Leave her alone!"

"She was old enough to follow us into trouble, wasn't she? Such a clever little thing..." He makes the most disgusting kissy face toward a trembling Nell and my heart wrenches. "Too smart for a little *brat*. If she wants to fight like an adult, she can die like one, too."

"No!" I thrust a hand out. "No, look, you can do anything you want with me. I swear, we won't say a word, we just— please don't hurt her."

I'm at a loss. Reduced to begging this demon for a miracle because I don't think he's capable of mercy.

He looks at me flatly.

I think I see what makes his gleaming green eyes so different from mine and Ros' now.

Unlike ours, his are totally empty.

Soulless.

His smile, a horrible clown mask splitting his face until it looks like plaster cruelty.

"Liar," he spits. "I know when I'm outgunned. Well. Not literally." He taps Nell's shoulder with the pistol and she cringes. My gut bottoms out every time his finger shifts. "The moment I put the gun down, you'll charge me. Two against one is hardly fair, is it?"

Shit.

I don't know what to do.

I have to talk my way out of this. I *have* to buy time. If I just have a few more minutes—

Except I don't need them.

Because the next time I breathe, the odds are three against one.

My heart leaps as Grant comes vaulting over the railing behind Aleksander, a wild man with his face bristling with protective rage.

I'm not breathing as over two hundred pounds of pure grizzly force barrels down on Aleksander Arrendell like a tank.

XXV: ONE WAY TO SKIN A CAT
(GRANT)

*N*ever.

Never in my life have I felt anything like the murderous rage scalding my veins the instant I hear my little girl's scream.

I don't even remember how I got on the fucking yacht.

I know I meant to jump for the lifeboats bolted halfway down the hull—a target I can actually reach without someone holding the wheel steady for me—but I don't remember actually doing it.

One second, Nell's voice sliced through my heart.

Then the gun.

Ask me if I care.

Now, all I can see is Aleksander Arrendell's back—and then nothing but a smear of color as I slam into him like a freight train.

"Nell!" Ophelia cries.

It happens faster than I can blink.

Nell rushing into Ophelia's arms.

Ophelia grabbing her, pulling her and Ros toward the

wheelhouse and safety—right before Aleksander's bony damn elbow snaps back at my face.

My nose cracks.

My vision explodes in a surge of white.

Pain bursts over me like a roaring waterfall.

Of course, that doesn't stop me from reaching, from grabbing him, from catching his shitty fucking tux.

He's all dressed up with nowhere to go except *down.*

And he howls, cursing like a wounded beast.

I pry my eyes open, vision hazed with pain, and fling myself at him again.

Again.

I'm a human wrecking ball.

The only thing that matters is demolishing this asshole.

I throw him to the ground and grab for his wrist, his gun.

I can't risk it.

Let him hurt me all he wants, but if that gun goes off and strikes one of my girls—

"You ridiculous brute," he grinds out, writhing under me like an eel. His knees jab my gut, throwing me off-balance, pushing me back, but I *won't* stop. "You're ruining the entire thing!"

"Get fucked," I snarl.

I have to take a risk, it's the only way.

I let go of his wrist—and then plow my fist into his face like an angry god.

Blood explodes everywhere.

Aleksander lets out a cry that's pure shock before the pain hits his brain. Then all he can do is make this gurgling sound.

His hand tightens convulsively on the gun.

Wrenching his arm, I slam it down on the deck, but the shot goes off.

It's deafening and just ahead of another noise.

Crashing glass.

Shit.

Then the yacht stops so abruptly we're flung apart.

He goes skidding toward the railing, the gun spinning after him.

I hit the floor, landing hard on my shoulder, then roll and take a leap, snatching at the gun, scrambling for it with both hands.

I catch it just as the engine dies with a shuddering groan.

I'm falling to my knees, flicking the safety on the pistol, while Aleksander flails up against the deck railing.

I'm winded as I glower at him.

"Fucking stand up. Hands behind your back!"

"Oh, fuck you, pig," he says, lying there awkwardly, his face streaked in blood and contorted with hate. "You—"

The yacht's engine growls to life again.

The boat goes jolting forward.

I let out a startled groan, rocking unsteadily while Aleksander screams.

The sudden momentum shoves him through the bars of the deck railing.

Overboard.

Dammit.

I can't decide if I'm relieved or pissed at the tiniest chance he could escape. We have to get him the hell out of the water before he has any bright ideas.

I drop the gun and bolt to my feet, rushing to the railing, looking for him.

Just in time to see his garish white tuxedo and that stark blond hair disappear into the churning waves.

Followed by an ugly bloom of crimson.

The yacht shudders and stops again.

A minute later, a lifeless shape, mangled almost beyond recognition appears.

He's nothing but shattered limbs floating face down, bobbing up to the surface.

"Oh my God, the engine. I-I didn't mean to do that!" Ophelia calls from the wheelhouse, her voice hollow.

I look up and nod.

Nobody's gonna mourn one less psycho, murdering asshole sucking up oxygen, especially me.

I wouldn't have pulled the trigger on him myself unless I had no choice, no. But there are times when I'm damned glad fate doesn't make me choose real justice over my oath to law and order.

Soon, Ophelia's feet patter on the deck, rushing up to me.

"Jesus. Are you okay? Did you—" She freezes, standing at my side, staring over the railing with her mouth a solid ring. Her face goes ashen, one trembling hand pressed to her mouth. "Holy shit. I... I definitely didn't mean to do *that*."

It's the look on her face that clears the adrenaline fog holding me in place.

Without thinking—hell, I can't remember why I ever made myself wait, why she needed distance when life is so fucking short—I pull her into my arms, pressing her so close.

She comes willingly, trembling, burying herself against me while I curl a hand against the back of her head.

Beyond her body, I can just make out Ros with little Nell in her arms.

They both come creeping out warily from inside, edging past the glass of the shattered front window. They're both crying and shaking and wiping their eyes. More importantly, they're whole.

They're safe.

As I hold Ophelia Sanderson tight, I remember how to breathe again.

As I shelter her in my arms, I thank God this situation

didn't end a thousand other fucked up ways it easily could have.

And now I can safely tell her, "It's over. It's all right. You're all in one piece and we're going home."

* * *

THAT WHOLE PROMISE of home would come a lot faster if I knew there weren't a million questions to answer and multiple high-ranking men growling in my face soon enough.

They're sympathetic enough, sure, but they want answers, slaves to law and procedure.

I get it. If I were in their shoes, I'd be the same way, especially when an outsider cop rolls into their town with a stolen yacht and a dead high-profile killer to deal with.

It takes almost an hour for the Coast Guard to zero in on our coordinates and find us—and retrieve what's left of Aleksander Arrendell.

I end up in a pile of girls while we wait, sitting on the deck with little Nell in my lap. Ros is also tucked against my shoulder, leaving Ophelia curled up in an exhausted bundle in the crook of my arm.

Nope, I still can't feel bad for that dead fuck.

Not when he's done this much damage.

The only thing that soothes my tired rage is knowing how much they need me.

How I still have a chance to make everything right.

If they didn't need me so much, I might be shaking from the cold too, but I can't.

For them, I'll be as steady as an oak tree, spreading my branches to cover them.

I don't breathe easy until we're back on the shore and surrounded by EMTs.

They flag us down, guiding us over to the benches along the dock while they fuss over our bruises and injuries.

Ros is going to need more than a few bandages for her scrapes.

She and Ophelia take the bench next to us, Nell still glued to my arm. I stroke her hair like a puppy, willing the last few hours away like a bad dream.

Goddamn, if only it were that easy.

"What's your favorite food, hon?" A kind EMT chatters away, prompting Nell out of her shock with small talk and checking her reflexes.

"Broccoli cheddar soup," I answer when she hesitates too long. "The girl eats it by the pint and she's gonna get the biggest, cheesiest batch of it in her life tomorrow."

That wins me a smile and a laugh. Plus, a few words from Nell about how she's a Bolognese sauce connoisseur too. For the first time since we got off that yacht, I relax.

When the other EMT asks if she has any other conditions, Ros looks down weakly.

"I..." She bites her lipstick-smeared lip. "...cocaine, honestly. And he had these other pills that always left me feeling warm and loopy. Opium, maybe? I think, um... I think I'm still high right now. I-I don't know how it happened. I was with him and he made it seem so innocent. Like harmless fun. I just..." Her face falls, fresh tears welling in her eyes. "Oh, God, Ophelia. I'm so sorry, I don't even know how I got to this point—"

"Shhhh," Ophelia whispers, gathering her sobbing sister close. "It doesn't matter how you got there. What matters is that you're here now, and we're going to take care of everything. We're going to get you better."

For a second, Ros looks at me like she's about to completely break.

I nod fiercely.

I'll take care of them all, if I need to.

Ethan's last unspoken wish and my fate, accepted without complaint.

"How can you even say that?" Ros whimpers against her sister. "Everything's falling apart. And a lot of it's my fault."

"It's not, and some things that fall apart can be put back together," Ophelia says bravely with the same soft, serene strength that's made her who she is. The same power that's always defined her. "Because I love you, baby sister. That's all that matters. There's always a way to work things out with the people you love."

She's talking to Ros when she says it, but over Ros' head, her eyes find mine.

And she smiles, something so luminous in her eyes igniting that it takes my breath away.

I can't help but smile back.

I grin like I'm losing my mind, cuddling Nell against me while the EMT looks her over and pressing my lips to my cousin's hair.

No matter how Ophelia feels about me, I won't ever stop loving her.

That strong, fierce woman who fought for her family, for mine.

That storm of my life, the one I could never forget in a decade-long drought.

The fire of my soul, destroyer of grief, pulsing light of a thousand butterflies that never go dormant with winter.

She is everything.

It's more than half an hour before the EMTs are satisfied and declare me, Ophelia, and Nell safe to go home. Ros is whisked off to the local hospital where they can start treatment for substance abuse.

It's another forty-five minutes before the cops are done taking our initial statements.

I'm gonna have one hell of a fat police report to write when I get back to Redhaven, but I'll worry about that later.

By the time we can breathe again, Nell's passed out, clinging to me like a kitten. She's barely said a word, and it's been driving me nuts that I can't pull away from all this to focus on her.

I just hold her tight.

So she knows her Uncle Grant is never going anywhere, and he's never going to let anything ever hurt her again.

Once was bad enough.

We saved her, yeah, but not without a scratch and a whole mess of fear. Happy endings don't hit like they do in action movies or thriller novels.

Not when real life is so goddamned messy.

I'll only be undoing the damage for the rest of my life.

The sun starts setting over the water, staining it pink and gold. I take a quiet moment to watch it, to breathe, while I hold a sleeping Nell in my arms.

I'm not expecting the soft voice at my shoulder.

"How is she?"

I lift my head.

Ophelia stands there, watching me with a tired, wistful smile. Her hair tumbles down around her, turned into a fiery gold halo around her face by the fading sunset.

"Not great," I say, keeping my voice low, rubbing a soothing hand over Nell's back. "She's been through so much already. I think sleep is the only way she can cope, but I'm definitely gonna have to get her in to a child psychologist soon. I don't know. I've gotta know how to help her without accidentally stomping around and doing more damage."

"You're already helping, Grant. Just being here for her right now is the best thing you can do, but I know you'll do anything she needs. Whatever it takes." Ophelia settles in next to me, sinking down on the bench. "Is there anything I can do?"

"You've done a hell of a lot already, Butterfly. You helped save my little girl." I can't help leaning toward her. "Fuck, you saved *me*. Thank you."

"...it still doesn't feel like enough." She lifts her head, looking up at me with those green eyes.

I don't care what she is.

I'll never think of them as Arrendell eyes when they're too warm, too pure, too full of that gorgeous heart they lack. Her hand rests on my arm, light as snow, yet so much warmer.

"Just wish I could do more for you," she whispers. "I wish I could do everything."

My heart stills in my chest.

I don't want to hope. Not after this shit show with so many raw feelings torn open.

I clear my throat. "What are you saying? Be clear, woman, my head's too spun to read between the lines."

She looks down.

For a second, I'm worried I've scared her off, but then she jerks her face up and looks at me.

"I'm saying I almost lost you," she whispers, tears glimmering in those beautiful eyes. "He could've shot you. That could've been *you* going over the railing. Grant, I—"

"*Ophelia*." I spare a hand from Nell to cup Ophelia's cheek. "You never lost me. Not once. Not even for one second." And I hope she knows what I mean. "No matter what happens, you never will. You've always had the best of me—hell, you teased it out of me in the first place—and it's not going anywhere."

"Yeah?" Her soft breath blends into a slow, hopeful smile.

"Yeah."

"So... maybe we can try again?"

"No damn maybes about it," I growl. She's always needed me to be honest, and I've never been good at it until she came back into my life. Now it's easier than ever to say, "I need you with me, Ophelia. Not just as a roommate, helping me with Nell. I need you to be *mine*. If you need more time, I get it. I'll—"

"No! I don't." She shakes her head quickly, blonde hair whipping around her face. "I'm stronger with you than I am without you, Grant. I've figured that out. So maybe life is messy right now. Maybe I just found out my father is a huge creep and two of my brothers are crazy killers and now *dead*. Maybe my mom's in the hospital fighting for her life and my sister's an addict who almost married our half brother. But... but I can *find* the strength to fight through all of that, to be there for my family—my real family—and to stand strong. And I don't have to search hard as long as I have you... As long as you'll let me hold you up, too, I mean. As long as you'll accept my apology for being stupid and not coming to my senses sooner."

I shouldn't be able to smile again.

Not after the black day we've had.

"You're a little short to hold me up," I say, grinning like a madman.

I cup my palm against Ophelia's cold skin.

Her eyes narrow, but her smile only brightens as she rubs her cheek to my palm. "Don't be an ass. You know what I mean."

"Maybe I want to hear you say it."

Her eyes glimmer, widening, her smile fading.

Her cheeks flush hot and those soft pink lips finally give me what I need.

"I love you, Grant. I never stopped loving you. Not once in all these years."

I'm burning inside like the setting sun as I lean in and claim that lovely mouth.

"Then it's a damn good thing I love you, too," I say, growling with delight. "I've always been obsessed, Philia, and I always will be. As long as I'm breathing, you're mine. Plain and simple."

XXVI: THE ONE FOR ME
(OPHELIA)

I can't believe I'm in this grocery store, buying sriracha sauce again.

We must go through two bottles a week lately.

Between Grant's addiction to spice and Ros complaining about how bland the food is at the medical center and begging her big sister to bring her something better to eat even if technically it's against the rules of her program, we're in a condiment crisis.

Well, since she's doing her best, I'm not going to deny her a little fire-breath.

Not when I'm so glad to have her back—and lucky that Redhaven has a rehab ward so I can still visit every day. Even if 'ward' is a bit of a stretch when it's technically just one big room at the medical center, and that room is currently occupied by Ros while she gets past the worst of detox.

It's been a heart-wrenching few weeks.

She'll be out and on home watch soon enough, but until then, you can bet her big sister's on contraband food duty.

It feels like my life revolves around caring for other people lately, and that's okay.

Making sure Grant eats enough every day.

Bundling Nell up and taking her to and from school with a handmade lunch on weekdays.

Stopping by to feed Ros something with real flavor, check on her progress, then going to see Mom. So far, she's doing better, even if she hasn't woken up again.

The doctors say she could come around any day. Against all odds, the experimental chemo's working.

Her body is slowly rebuilding itself, instead of dangling over a bottomless pit by a thinning thread held together by endless rounds of therapies.

I'm still taking care of the shop, too. Nobody's Bees-Ness will still be around whenever she wakes up, just waiting for her, whatever she decides to do with the store.

Also, I still need to figure out what to do with my life. What's going to be my life's work as this strange and stormy chapter comes to an end and a new one begins.

But for now, I'm content with where I am, one day at a time.

Taking care of everyone by daylight and warming Grant's bed at night.

Yes, I'm blushing like I've downed a whole spoon of sriracha myself as I toss a few more bottles in my basket for the pantry and move on.

We were barely apart and quasi-broken up, yet here we are devouring each other like we have years of lost time to make up for.

Maybe we do.

All those lonely years when I could've been here with him, instead of running from my past and abandoning my home. Trying to carve out a new life in another state that was always missing its biggest pieces.

Back then, I wasn't ready to face him.

Our feelings were confused whispers then. They easily

would've been crushed and silenced forever under the weight of grieving Ethan, back when it was still so fresh and killing.

How could we have loved through the bruises?

How does anyone with an acid pain wearing away their hearts?

We both needed to heal.

Now, for the first time, I feel like I'm no longer suffocating. Healing might look like scar tissue, but we're stronger than ever.

We needed that time.

That distance.

Time apart to let the pain settle until true love could stand on its own in the fresh light of a brand-new day.

And now that I've found Grant again, I never want another day away from him for the rest of my life.

I'm pretty sure my thoughts are written all over my face and everyone can see them.

Though I'm probably being too self-conscious about it, reading too much into the curious glance of the checkout girl and everyone I pass on the streets as I finish running errands and head back to Grant's house—home.

It really is.

He's made it so clear he wants me to stay.

I go to work happily in the kitchen. A couple hours later, there's a spicy lasagna slow-baking in the oven next to a version I can actually stomach without my gut catching fire.

By the time I blow through the house, tidying up and showering, the lasagna's ready.

I cut off a huge chunk and drop it into a Tupperware container, leaving the rest in the oven to stay warm, then head out into the icy late afternoon wind to make my way over to the medical center, humming contentedly under my breath.

It's so strange to break out of this holding pattern I've been in for so long.

It's bizarre to actually feel alive for the first time in ages.

But it also leaves me bursting and bright, feeling cheerful enough to warm me against the cold, even if I'm cursing myself once again for not picking up a coat as winter muscles in, promising the first snow.

Idiot.

That coat always slips my mind every time I'm out shopping.

I'm grateful for the burst of warm air as I step into the lobby. The nursing staff wave me through, familiar with my daily visits by now, including pointedly pretending not to see the container tucked under my arm and shielded with my body.

We share a subtle smile.

They get it.

Back when I was a nurse, I looked the other way on things like that all the time.

When I get to Ros' room, I'm surprised to find it empty.

Her bed's still disarrayed and her clothes are in the dresser, so she's around somewhere, I guess.

Frowning, I walk over to the nurses' station and offer a smile to the woman behind the computer.

"Hey, Brandy," I say. "Have you seen Rosalind? I'm just dropping in to keep her company before she makes you pull your hair out."

Brandy glances up at me, blinks, and does a double take. A huge smile curls her lips.

"Ophelia! I was just about to call you."

I blink back at her.

Common sense tells me that smile can't be bad news, but my heart turns into an anxious little knot anyway.

"Yeah? What's up?"

"About Ros," Brandy says, almost slyly. "You might want to check your mother's room."

Oh?

It takes a minute for what she means to really click.

But when it hits me—

I'm barely aware of dropping the lasagna container on the desk like a brick.

I turn so fast I almost fall over.

My lungs are about to burst as I sprint down the hall.

Hope floods me, a fragile thing that could break again so easily, but please, oh please—

I nearly slam into the door of Mom's room face-first as I go sliding in.

For a frozen second, I'm staring in disbelief.

I stand there with my chest heaving and my eyes filling up with the most wonderful tears.

There she is.

My mother, sitting up in bed, her cheeks flushed with life, her eyes open.

Smiling.

She's never looked happier as her fingers tangle with Ros'. My sister buries her face in our mom's shoulder and sobs.

The choked sounds rise over everything inside me right now.

"Mom," I whisper, the only sound I can make.

Then it's my turn.

I start bawling like a baby as my mother looks up, meets my eyes, and beams her too-bright smile right at me.

Her free arm stretches toward me.

I practically throw myself into the tangle of my family until we're just a mess of happy hugs, grateful tears, sniffles, and incoherent words.

Holy hell, it's not a dream!

She's still weak and frail and recovering, sure, but she's alive.

She's conscious.

She's here.

And so is Ros.

I never let either of them go.

Thank God I didn't.

"I was so scared," I rasp, burying my face in Mom's shoulder. "I was so *scared* for you, Mama."

"I know you were, baby," she says, kissing my hair. "I know you both were. But I can't go anywhere just yet. I know when my girls need me and I had to stay to take care of you."

That's enough to trigger a new cascade of tears.

We're like that for a while, just the three of us and enough sweet relief bursting out of us to make a statue cry.

By the time the emotional bubble breaks, I'm worn out. Ros looks just as tired as she sits up, wiping at her eyes with a frayed laugh.

"Wow. Never thought we'd be rooming right down the hall from each other," she tells Mom. "At the rate you're going, you'll be out of here before I am."

Mom squeezes Ros' hand.

"Stay as long as you need, baby," she says, glowing with the warmth of motherly love. "As long as you take care of yourself."

"You told her?" I catch my sister's eye.

Ros nods sheepishly. "Well, yeah. She deserved to know."

"That's right," Mom says firmly. "Just because I'm laid up doesn't mean I'm not here to support you girls like always." Then her eyes darken and she glances between me and Ros regretfully. "So, I guess the secret's out."

My heart pinches as Mom's heavy eyes meet mine.

"You'll never know how sorry I am that I never told you

girls everything." She sighs. "I just wanted to close that rotten chapter of my life so much... I never imagined the trouble it would cause later on." Her eyes glitter with approval as she looks at me. "Thank you, Ophelia. Thank you for looking out for your little sister—for protecting her where I failed."

"Mom, no." I grip hard at her thin fingers. "You didn't fail. You got sick. But it all turned out okay in the end."

"There's nothing time won't heal. We'll be fine," Ros adds, clearing her throat. But Mom, I have to ask... What happened? Like, how did you end up with *him?*"

"Oh, that." Mom smiles sadly. "Dredging up these old memories, it feels like someone else's life. It was so long ago. I wish I had a better answer. I was different then, too young and hopeful. Too stupid, maybe—is there really any difference?"

Ros and I shake our heads.

Her smile turns grim.

"You don't have to talk about this if you don't want to right now," I say.

"No, Ophelia. You both deserve the truth after the ordeal you've been through." Mom strokes her thumb over the back of my hand. "If you want someone to blame, you're looking at her. There's no excuse, but I was so lonely after my husband died, loves. Zachary had my heart first. I didn't know how to get over him. I was an open wound, lost and confused, pining away after a ghost all the time. Men like Montero Arrendell can smell vulnerability. I think..." she sighs again, wetting her lips. "I think he enjoyed how fragile my heart was when I was so desperate to be loved again. He enjoyed toying with me."

My breath catches and I squeeze Mom's hand.

"And then when I got pregnant with you, Ophelia... he distanced himself like a boy moving onto his next shiny thing," she continues. "Of course, I didn't let that stop me from sending him secret love letters. There was a woman at the house, a maid, Cora Lafayette." Her eyes soften. "Such a sweet lady, not much older than me. She always looked at me with sympathy, like she understood. She'd help sneak my letters in. They weren't always love letters, exactly, especially as time went on. But since he had a daughter, I thought he should know how you were doing."

God, that makes me feel hollow.

I don't even know how I'll look at any Arrendell ever again without exploding in their face.

Though I won't be surprised if Aleksander's gruesome aftermath sends them out of town for a good long while. Maybe out of country.

Fine by me.

It's too strange, knowing this man I've only seen from a distance my entire life, who was just part of the landscape of Redhaven, is the reason I exist.

A fact so revolting it chokes me up.

He's always known so much about me.

All this time, *he knew.*

He saw me, he knew I was his daughter, peeking in at my life through these hidden windows my mother gave him.

"But what about me?" Ros asks. "If you stopped seeing him after you got pregnant with Ophelia?"

Mom goes quiet, her eyes pointed down.

"We didn't stop entirely," she finally whispers. "There was a lull, perhaps a few years. Then suddenly, somehow, he was desperate for me again. Instead of a quiet, comforting thing in the wake of my grief, it was a passionate affair that made me feel young and beautiful again." With a hurt laugh, Mom tucks her wispy hair behind her ear. "Maybe that's why the two of you are smarter. One the soft, steady girl with such deep emotions she couldn't hold them in forever..." She casts an affectionate look at Ros before she turns to me. "And the other, my little firecracker, so much bravery and passion under her skin."

Ros' eyes well up again, and our mom smooths her hair back and kisses her brow.

And I realize then that maybe some of what happened with Aleksander wasn't just his sick, hypnotic influence or the drugs.

Maybe my shy, prim sister really *did* want to break out of her shell.

It's just gut-wrenching that Aleksander took advantage of that feeling, just as his—*our*—father took advantage of Mom's loneliness.

Some bad habits run in the family, I guess.

So does bad luck.

There's still one lingering question, though, and I frown.

"What made you stop sending the letters? I read them all."

Mom sighs.

"There are so many things that came to a head, I think. The fact that he never even acknowledged receiving the letters, for one, on all the nights we spent together. Little by little, I began to see his other side. His callousness, his cruelty. His truth, shining through the cracks of his wealth and intelligence and perfection. I was getting tired of being someone's dirty little secret, and then—" She bites her lip. "Then we lost Ethan. And I knew—I *knew* there were questions about his sons. Your brothers. And Montero saw my grief. He wouldn't even speak to me about it. Wouldn't even let me ask him *why*. He made me realize I was no use to him if I wasn't gratifying his appetites. One day, I woke up and refused to do that any longer. If he ever wanted to be a father to you girls, I told him he could speak to me then, but otherwise to stay the hell out of my life."

"And he never did, did he?" I ask softly, touching the back

of her hand. "That was it. It was always just us... and he went back to his gold tower."

"Yes," she says. "But I wouldn't dare give up the gifts he gave me for the world. He gave me two angels, and I've never been lonely since the day you girls were born."

"Oh my God, stop," I gasp, wiping my eye with a shaky laugh. "I'm going to start sobbing again."

"Well, in my humble opinion, Montero Arrendell can fuck right off," Ros flares, shaking her head harshly. "Wait, should I call him Dad? Dad. Dad can fuck off."

My laugh comes out stronger this time.

"You do you, Ros. I'm never calling him Dad. No tearful family reunions for us."

"I don't know." Frowning, Ros gives me a puzzled look. "Should we? I mean, do you want to say anything to him? Do we want to tell him we know?"

"What good would it do?" I ask bitterly. "Do you really want him as a father now? I don't. I want absolutely nothing to do with that man."

I mean every cutting word.

Call it impulsive, but now that I know the truth about our family, about who my father is?

I wish I didn't.

I don't want him in my life.

I don't want excuses or apologies or explanations—if a stone-cold prick like him ever had it in him to offer any at all.

More than anything, I just want him gone.

After Aleksander went after Ros and Nelly, after the questions with Ethan, after the appalling damage they've done to this town, I just want to escape the Arrendells' stain.

I want to see all their ugly secrets and crimes come spilling out, and I want them to pay dearly.

I want a life untouched by their pain.

Give me distance.

Such a huge, gaping chasm between us and them that I can live a normal life and blissfully forget that I share their toxic blood.

Ros wrinkles her nose. "He saw me with Aleksander. He *knew,* and he didn't try to stop it at all. He could've told me the truth any time. So, no. I don't even want to remember I'm related to... to those people." She chokes on the last two words.

To Aleksander, she means.

I can't blame her.

Honestly, I've never been happier my sister is so committed to waiting until marriage.

"Then it's settled," I say. "We keep our distance. We don't acknowledge him. He won't acknowledge us, and we live our best lives apart. The prick obviously never cared, anyway."

"But he kept the letters..." Ros points out slowly.

Ugh, yeah.

He did.

Which raises another question that makes me shake my head.

"That's what's so weird to me. Mom, you gave those letters to Cora, right? So how did Mason Law wind up with them?"

"Mason Law?" Mom purses her lips. "I don't rightly know, dear. I didn't know him."

"I do," a voice says in a bearish growl at my back. My heart flutters. "Hi, Angela. It's damn good to see you awake. Am I interrupting?"

I have to force myself to move slowly as I turn to face Grant.

He stands in the doorway in a full crisp uniform, handsome as ever in the trim lines of navy blue-black outlining the hard-cut of his figure underneath.

Mom brightens instantly.

I'd bet I'm wearing the same look, only ten times more intense.

"Grant!" she gushes. "Aren't you a handsome sight? Have you proposed to my daughter yet while I was out?"

"*Mom!*" I cough. "You were out for a few weeks. Not ten years..."

"Not yet," Grant answers bluntly.

Boom.

There go my insides again.

He's just too good at scrambling them without even breaking a sweat.

Because *not yet* means that someday, he just might.

And he gives me a lazy, knowing smile, before sobering as he says, "Must be something in the air today setting things right. I've just been talking with Mr. Law and I've learned some things you ladies ought to know."

XXVII: ONE TRICK PONY (GRANT)

I don't think I've ever seen a sight more beautiful than all three Sanderson women together, happy, and whole.

Ros looks a hell of a lot more like herself after a stint in rehab.

Angela might as well have come back from the grave. There's a second life infusing her with a radiance that seems too big for her rail-thin body.

And Ophelia—fuck.

My woman *shines* when she looks at me, her eyes overflowing with pure love.

Every morning, waking up next to her, I still have to pinch myself to make sure I'm not dreaming.

How the hell did this become my life?

I still don't know.

The way she fits right in like a missing puzzle piece to complete my soul seems too natural.

Without any warning, I've got a whole family.

It's almost too easy looking after Nelly-girl together, making our house, doing damn near everything together.

It shouldn't be this easy after the tragedy and scars and absence.

But I guess that's the thing about old wounds.

Once you stop picking at them, they start healing awfully fast.

And healed is what I am.

I'm a new man, greeting each morning with a smile because I get to love Ophelia Sanderson like she never left.

Can't say I care if it feels too easy sometimes.

Maybe love is worth fighting for, but true love ought to come natural. Being with someone who just fits you so well that not even ten years apart can change how you mesh together.

That's not to say the last few weeks have been a cakewalk.

Ophelia's still been beating herself up over everything.

For not knowing enough, for not protecting her little sister, for not pulling some magic rabbit out of her hat that would bring her mother back to life.

Even if she doesn't say it out loud, a man can tell.

Only this time, instead of pushing me away and crawling up in her head, she let me stay.

Let me hold her on those cold creeping winter nights when her soul got too heavy to bear.

Let me kiss her tears away.

Let me see those little moments of shaky hope as the calls came in from the specialists every day, confirming steady progress by inches for her whole family till she knew they would be out of the woods.

Then that beautiful, grateful personality came out in full joy.

The same joy she's showered me with over and over again.

Sometimes with her words.

And sometimes, it's just the way we get tangled in the

sheets, fusing our bodies together like we were always meant for each other. So wrapped up in ourselves that sometimes we forget to sleep.

There are a few mornings I dragged myself in to work completely worn out and haggard. Sleepless because I couldn't get enough of her.

Got plenty of shit for it, too, when every last one of the guys knows *exactly* why I've got bags under my eyes.

The only one I haven't threatened to punch yet is Lucas—mostly 'cause he went through the same bullshit when he finally captured his hellcat of a wife.

Goddamn, I can't wait to devour Ophelia again tonight.

But now isn't the time.

Now, I've got to reach down in my gut and find the right words for this news.

Grabbing the one free chair in the room, I drag it over to where they're all clustered like birds, nesting around Angela's bed, the girls perched on the edge and all of them clinging to each other.

Well, fuck.

I've never been cut out for this.

A hundred years as a cop wouldn't make this any easier.

Never been much good with words, either, but somehow for Ophelia, I learned to speak my mind without snarling them. To be honest rather than sliding into harshness.

Unfortunately, with the shit that needs saying today, this can't be gentle.

Yet it's Philia's encouraging gaze that makes me dig deep, find my voice, and speak.

For her.

Because she needs this.

They all do when they've been waiting far too long.

"I know what happened to Ethan," I begin slowly. "The whole story of the night he disappeared. I knew he never

411

would've left us willingly. I know those bones belong to him —forensics confirmed it this morning. And now I know without a doubt that he had nothing to do with what happened to Celeste Graves. That he tried to *save* her. That he's innocent. It won't bring him back, no, but it lets us have our memories without any nagging questions. Without more wishing or guessing or doubts."

I'm expecting the tears.

What I'm not expecting is that it makes me panic anyway, freezing up as all three Sanderson women look at each other —then burst into rolling grief, grabbing each other, burying their feelings in a big group hug.

They're not saying anything, no, so I don't know if it's relief or horror or if I did this right, if I fucked this up—

"Come here, boy," Angela almost snaps, but there's warmth in her voice. Deep, heartfelt emotion, and she holds her arm out. "You're part of this family, too. Come let me hug you."

Relief then.

Gratitude tinged with sadness.

Oh, thank God.

I'm slow to move, but then Ophelia peeks past her mother's shoulder and gives me a shy, sweet smile, offering her curled fingers as well.

I can't resist.

So I stand, stepping closer to the bed.

Soon, I've got my arms full of all three women, crying on me and hugging like it's the end of the world. In a way, they're not wrong.

Good thing I'm a human tree, I guess.

I ain't gonna cry myself.

I'm not.

But it still feels like years of heartbreak bleeding out of me.

It's finally over.

And there's nothing better than being part of this tight-knit family knot, wrapped up with these girls and able to grieve for real.

Finally, finally, able to let go.

It takes a good while for them to let go—and when I fall back into my chair, Ophelia disentangles herself from her mother and sister to join me.

I'm a little self-conscious about her sitting in my lap in front of her ma when I've got every mind to ask permission for certain things and Angela's looking at me like she knows, but like hell I'm gonna push Ophelia away.

She settles on my thigh, this small thing nestled against my chest with her arms around my neck, looking up at me with sweet expectation.

"Tell us," she murmurs. "Since we're ripping all the Band-Aids off today, tell us everything."

I take a deep breath and nod.

"I've just been talking to Law. He's lucid again and this time he managed to stay up longer than a few minutes. When I told him our suspicions and said I had forensics working on those bones, I think he knew it was up. He spilled everything." I search their hopeful eyes. "Turns out, when the Arrendells lured Celeste Graves up to the big house for Ulysses' sick games, Ethan went after her. He tried to stop her murder. Only, Aleksander was a part of that, too. He thought enabling his little brother was funny—a fucking riot—" I can't hide the growling disgust in my voice. "Sorry. Anyway, he went after Ethan when he knew he was coming. Made Mason Law drive him, chased Ethan off, wound up driving his motorcycle off the road. He..."

My voice breaks.

It's hard as hell to say this, especially when I can feel

Ophelia trembling. She hides her face against my chest as I fold my arms tighter around her, holding her.

"He died in the crash," I grind out. Both Angela and Ros watch me with wide eyes, frozen and listening. "Aleksander buried him there and made Law dispose of the motorcycle debris and other evidence. Law kept his head down after that, stayed quiet all these years because he was terrified they'd kill him next—until Cora Lafayette found out about Aleksander's relationship with Ros. She went and confided in Law about the letters. They swapped stories about a lot of Arrendell dirt. Then her murder happened—"

"Murder? Cora's *dead?*" Angela's face crumples. She curls her hand against her chest.

"I'm sorry, ma'am. She didn't make it easy for them. If it wasn't for Cora, we'd have never learned all this. Because she didn't kill herself. Mason and Cora were close and one day Aleksander overheard her telling him about the letters. He took matters into his own hands. He hung her."

The women gasp.

My heart wrenches with fury, realizing what a fucked up story this is.

Aleksander Arrendell's savagery only hit its limit because he's dead.

"Mason, he couldn't take it anymore," I continue. "He lashed out, stole the letters, and hid them. He was going to try to warn y'all, using them as evidence, but shit kept going sideways. He wasn't in the best place mentally. First, we thought he was a stalker, and then it turns out Aleksander poisoned him before he left their property. Some sort of slow acting agent that wasn't dosed right. That's why it took so long to catch up with him and take him down. Mason was trying to atone, I think. Trying to soothe a guilty conscience, for not doing anything when Ethan died. In his own way, I guess he succeeded, saving you girls."

"Oh my God. God, I never..." Angela shakes her head, struggling to continue. "I never fathomed the *evil* in that house. I never thought—well, it doesn't matter now." She gathers a weeping Ros close. "All that matters is you girls are safe now."

But Ros is stiff and she lets out a choked, "Oh my *God*. Holy crap." Her throat works. "I... I almost married the man who killed my brother." She goes pale and claps a hand over her mouth. "I'm gonna throw up."

Angela loosens her grip.

"Bathroom, dear," she says gently.

There's a frozen hell moment.

With a nauseated sound, Ros bolts into the suite's bathroom and slams the door.

Ophelia turns her head from watching, and when she speaks, her voice is subdued. "...will she be okay?"

Angela glances at the bathroom, her eyes troubled. "She will. She's stronger than you know, dear. Of course, we'll be there to help her through it."

"We will," Ophelia agrees—then squeezes me tight, burying her face in my shoulder. "Thank you. Thank you for telling us, Grant, without leaving out the ugly parts. Honestly, we needed it. We needed the truth, warts and all."

"Philia, no. If there was any other way, I'd have traded years off my life. I'm sorry this truth has to hurt like hell. It's got me torn up just as bad as you ladies," I say roughly, grabbing her hand.

She squeezes me so tight, I hardly notice the warm, soulful smile her ma beams our way.

"Thank you for never giving up. Without you, we never would've found out what happened to him. And that freak, Aleksander, I don't even want to *think* about what he'd have gotten away with if you hadn't stepped in, if you hadn't—" she chokes off, shaking her head severely.

"Ethan was my brother too, Ophelia. Not by blood, but family all the same. Now we can finally give him the rest he deserves." I'm fucking breaking as I say those words, but it's the sun in this room holding me together.

This small woman with the same calm, easy smile as my best friend.

I think that's the one thing all the Sandersons share, that smile, no matter what else makes up the other half of their DNA.

And even if I won't say it right now, finding out the full grisly picture took something heavy off my heart, banishing a darkness in my soul.

The truth will set you free.

That's not just a Bible verse anymore. It's something everybody in this room has lived and breathed.

Only question now is what the hell we do with that freedom.

I haven't figured it all out, not yet, but I've got a few ideas.

Inhaling slowly, I brush her hair back and kiss the top of her head.

"I had to know. Same as you. Now, we've got our answers, and Aleksander Arrendell will never hurt anybody again," I whisper.

It goes quiet then.

Just the sound of running water in the bathroom, the faint beep of Angela's monitor, and the soft sounds of Ophelia breathing softly as she settles in my arms.

I let her stay with me while she processes the shock.

Over her head, I catch Angela's eye.

Her mother studies me for a long moment, something sad yet warm in her gaze, before her mouth curls and she gives me a subtle nod.

That's when my breath stalls and it hits me.

She sees me.

She knows how much her daughter means to me.

She looks at me like I've always been family, and not in the creepy fucking Arrendell way.

And she's telling me it's all right to make that a reality.

That if I want to catch Ophelia while she's spinning, if I want to keep her and never let her go, I don't need to dilly-dally with the usual slow-burn shit.

I already have the blessing of the woman Ophelia loves most.

I just have to man the fuck up and gather my courage.

I have to find the right words one more time to tear my heart open and ask one simple question.

* * *

It's a quiet farewell when we exit the medical center together, leaving Angela and Ros to talk and comfort each other.

We walk silently, hand in hand, until we part ways at the station.

I still need to file a proper report with Mason Law's confession while the details are fresh in my mind.

"I'll be home soon," I promise, cupping her cheek and kissing her in the street, her cold-reddened nose brushing mine.

Her kiss comes slow and delicately wanting, all gentleness and parted lips that beckon me inside like she needs me to fill her. I oblige, sinking into her with my eyes closed until there's nothing but her darkness, her heat, the curl of her breath against my cheeks.

It's so hard to pull back it hurts, but I do, smiling faintly.

"Be safe."

"It's just a few blocks," she teases, her cheeks flushed with more than just the cold. "But I will."

She turns and walks away, wrapped up in one of my flannels and still shivering.

That silly woman has two sweaters on, still too distracted by life to buy a proper coat.

I stand and watch her till I can't see her anymore, then glance at the door of the police station. An instinct pricks at my skin.

You know what?

The police report can wait.

I won't forget anything when all the sordid details are carved in my brain.

Right now, I've got something more important to take care of.

And the woman I almost let get away waiting for me at home, asking for a fresh start to a life we can finally build, without this horrible black hole of grief in the way.

She's made me more than a one-trick pony, obsessed with procedure and haunted by clawing after answers I finally have.

How could I not want to return the favor?

We've always been in this together.

XXVIII: ONE WAY HOME
(OPHELIA)

*I*t's not like Grant to be this late.

Call me paranoid, but after everything that's happened, I don't think anyone could blame me.

It's almost time for dinner, and Nell's looking a little worried, too, though she won't say it out loud.

She's been quieter than usual since everything that happened on the yacht.

The child counselor she's seeing twice a week says that's normal. She needs time to process the horror in terms she can understand at her age.

What she needs most from us is to be there for her, without any pressure to act a certain way or get better faster. My own experiences certainly taught me pain moves at its own pace.

Love and reassurance are the medicine she needs most, knowing her world won't fall apart tomorrow.

That she's not going to lose anyone else the same awful way she lost her parents. Or how she almost lost us.

I can do that.

Loving Nell is easy.

And being there for her... if I'm honest, I don't ever want to be anywhere else.

I want to be here for Nell, for Grant, for me.

But that requires Grant to *be* here, too.

I squeeze Nell's shoulder as I stand up from the sofa.

"Give me a sec, I'm going to call him. He probably just got buried in work and lost track of time. You know what he's like."

She looks up from doing her homework at the coffee table.

For a moment, there's a flicker of fear in her eyes before she smiles sweetly and bravely. "He's a big dumb dorkface like that. Worky-holic."

"He is. But we'll take care of him, won't we?" I return her sunny smile and squeeze her shoulder again. "I'm not going anywhere, little lady. Just getting my phone off the charger."

Her fear eases, her smile growing brighter, stronger.

She hasn't let me or Grant out of her sight since that nightmare happened.

For a couple days after, we kept her home from school, spending whole days snuggled in bed, Nell tucked between us while we let her watch anything she wanted on TV in Grant's bedroom. We also let her talk to us and ask us questions about what happened, about what scared her most.

I see so much of myself in her at that age. A little bit of Ros, too.

Whip-smart, strong, but she still needs those little moments to be a kid.

I get it.

I see how she struggles, the pain making her grow up faster until she's under pressure to be the big girl, to show she's too smart and mature for this, too brave.

But big feelings aren't that easy.

Neither is trauma.

Mrs. Graves—Delilah—at school has been a big help with that. She says Lucas used to call her a human cactus because she was so prickly and dead set on her independence. She *gets* a little girl like Nell, and Nell idolizes her to kingdom come, so Delilah's been a help to us teaching Nell that she doesn't need to be the strongest kid in the room all the time.

It's okay to cry.

And it's okay to reach for a helping hand when you're scared, instead of doing what Ros did and falling down a deep, dark hole.

Not that I'm blaming my sister.

We all do awful things when we're afraid. Some of us turn to bad habits.

Some of us run.

For me, those days are over.

Not unless it's running right down to the station to drag Grant out by his scruff, but we'll try the easy way first. I give Nell another smile and grab my phone off its charger.

Just as I pull up Grant's contact, though, the latch on the front door turns.

He's pushing his way inside when I look up, bundled up in his wool-lined coat—and he's brought company, too.

His parents come bustling inside behind him while Grant grins.

"Look who's here to fetch their favorite granddaughter for cake and hot chocolate!" Jensen Faircross announces.

"Grandpa! Gammy!" Nell shrieks as she flings herself around the coffee table and into her grandmother's arms.

Margaret Faircross laughs, lifting her up and swirling her around.

"How's my favorite girl?"

"Tired! Too much homework," Nell pouts, latching her arms around her gram's neck with a sly look. "I get to stay with you tonight? Does that mean no more homework?"

"It means you get to finish your homework at our house, sweet girl. *But* you also get to have Gammy's special hot chocolate with cinnamon and those extra-big marshmallows while you do it. Trust me, it'll be over in no time." Mrs. Faircross winks while her hubby chuckles indulgently and pats Nell's head before Margaret sets Nell down. "Grant already said it's okay. Go run, pack your overnight bag, sweetie."

I look at Mrs. Faircross and we share a nod.

"I'm sorry to steal her away on such short notice," she says.

"Oh, no. When there's special hot chocolate involved, no need to even ask," I say.

Nell brightens, then pelts toward the stairs, not even waving to Grant. He looks after her with a snort.

"I see where I rank. Somewhere between pet dog and chopped liver," he grumbles.

My heart swells with warmth and I laugh—really laugh—for the first time in forever.

I've missed this easy, happy feeling, so cozy and so *right.*

"On a school night, though?" I cluck my tongue. "You two always let her stay up past bedtime."

Jensen chuckles, a laugh so much like his son's, dry and deep. But it doesn't fill me with the same tingles.

It just makes me feel comfortable, casually accepted as part of their family.

"I think we can indulge her a little longer. It ain't spoiling the kid to let her have a few happy distractions. She still having trouble sleeping?" he asks.

"A little," I admit. "We end up with a burr in bed with us most nights. I mean, she'll fall asleep just fine, but usually she'll wake up in the middle of the night and come into our room to read."

"She was like that after the fire, too," Jensen says

solemnly. "But she just needed time and care, which you two are giving her plenty of."

The warm approval in Grant's father's voice makes me blush so hard I duck my head.

Sometimes I'm a little awestruck.

I don't know what to say.

They've always treated me like family, but ever since I moved in with Grant, it's been *different*, somehow. Like pulling me into the fold and knowing this time, I'm not going anywhere.

Nell saves me from having to come up with a response by tumbling back down the stairs, her backpack only half-zipped and bursting with her pajamas and a change of clothes. Mr. Pickle dangles from the strap by a jingly pet collar she's insisted on using ever since she almost lost him on the yacht.

"All ready!" she announces.

I sigh indulgently.

"No, you're not. Hold still, munchkin." I slip around behind her and tuck her bag in a little more neatly so I can zip it up. "Now you're ready. Oh—wait, no, you're not." I step back and quickly scoop up her books from the coffee table, closing them with a sheet of her notebook tucked inside to mark her place, then unzip the bag again and start to wedge them in. "Don't think I don't know you stuffed this too full for your books."

"Then why are you trying to put them in?" she asks sulkily. "You can't."

"I can. I have magic space-time bending powers." More like enough persistence to compress the fabric until I can slide the books in and the notebooks behind them. After a solid minute of pushing, I zip the bag back up and pat it lightly. "There you go."

Nell sticks her tongue out at me over her shoulder.

"Miss Delilah won't be happy if you haven't finished your homework." I grin.

That works a charm.

Delilah really is like Wonder Woman to that kid.

"Okay! I'll finish it tonight at Gammy's." Nell lets out a huge, dramatic sigh.

"We should get going." Margaret holds her hand out for Nell's bag. "Standing here in the doorway, letting in the chill. I want to get home before the snow starts, anyway."

Snow? I peer past them at the deep, dark winter sky.

Not a star in sight past the porch overhang.

That darkness isn't night sky.

It's low-hanging, slate-grey clouds, heavy with the promise of snow.

"Go on," I shoo. "Drive safe."

Sure, it's only a couple of blocks, but... did I mention I'm a bit of a safety freak lately?

Soon, it's all goodbye hugs, Grant's parents pulling me into a tangle of Faircrosses while Grant looks on with warm amusement.

I'm left dizzy from the whirlwind of back-pats, well-wishes, and then bundling Nell out the door.

After they're gone, I brush my messy hair away from my face before I round on Grant, playfully putting my hands on my hips.

"Okay," I say. "What's up? What's so important that you maneuvered your parents into taking Nell for the night?"

His slow grin tells me he hasn't even tried to fool me.

He jerks his head at the door.

"Take a walk with me, Butterfly."

"But it's about to snow?" And I'm in a light-pink cashmere sweater and jeans.

Fine for indoors, but outside, not even borrowing his

police windbreaker will keep me safe from those bone-stripping winds.

"I have the perfect solution." He holds up a shopping bag I hadn't noticed before in the happy chaos all around us. It has pink stripes running through it, printed with the logo of a local clothing store.

Blinking, I reach for it hesitantly.

It's hefty when he drops the pink handle into my hand.

Curiously, I shove the tissue inside aside, peering in—and I'm rewarded with a glimpse of buttery soft brown leather. Eyes wide, I pull out a lovely fitted leather jacket with a padded inner lining and wool collar.

"Grant! You didn't..." Laughing, I flush as I hug the new coat to my chest. "It's gorgeous. Thank you."

"Had to do something before you froze to death," he teases. "I ain't having my girl turning into a Philia popsicle. Try it on and let's go give it a test drive."

I don't know how it couldn't be warm enough when it feels like a blanket that could beat back any cold. Plus, the gesture itself, knowing Grant cares so much about my well-being—and my absentmindedness.

With a happy sigh, I wiggle into it and let the snugness settle around me.

It's like being hugged by a cloud, and it actually *fits*, too. Which should tell you right now that Grant truly is the ideal man.

Is there another straight guy on Earth who can buy his girl clothes in the right size on the first try?

"Give me a sec," I say, fumbling for the door and my warm leather boots stowed away just under the coatrack.

It takes a minute to lace my boots, and then we lock up and head outside.

I instantly curl my hands into the crook of Grant's arm, leaning on him gratefully.

He doesn't say anything.

Neither do I, really, but we don't need to.

It's nice to just *be* together in the still, silent night. The whisper of snow charges the air with a peaceful, pure energy.

I don't ask where we're going.

It's enough to be here with him, following his slow, strolling steps, breathing in the heavenly scents of my white knight and my shiny new coat.

This is the way we're meant to be, I think.

We just took a long, hard detour getting here, but doesn't it feel good?

I don't feel the cold at all.

The jacket is too perfect, insulating and comfortable. It lets me enjoy the night and the soft glow of the streetlamps shining gold paths through the darkness.

When you forget the darkness, the heaviness of the Arrendells' shadow over this town, Redhaven really is a beautiful place. Picturesque, cozy, and while I've experienced terrible loss and horrifying secrets here, so many people in this town are *happy*.

I'm glad I'm finally one of them.

As we walk, I'm so focused on how handsome Grant's serene, quiet profile looks against the night sky that I don't realize where we're going until we step off the sidewalk and I feel grass crunching under my feet.

I tear my gaze away from Grant and realize we're at the shore of Still Lake.

It sure lives up to its name right now.

Not even a whisper of waves. Completely glass-smooth, reflecting back the dark clouds until it's nothing but a solid sheet of ink, this great shadow vault spread out before us.

Maybe for some that would be a dark image, but for me it's like looking into a scrying mirror.

One where I get to imagine any future I want.

And the future I imagine now is peaceful, safe, and full of love.

Grant seems to want to linger, so I lean against his side, resting my head on his shoulder and watching the water.

When he finally speaks, the low rumble of his voice is a part of the calm night, blending into the smooth darkness like black silk.

"Have you thought about what you're doing?" he asks. "Staying in Redhaven." He clears his throat, a hint of almost boyish uncertainty creeping into that deep growl. "You are staying... aren't you?"

"Yeah. I am." There's no doubt when I say it.

Under my cheek, his shoulder relaxes and I smile to myself, hugging his arm closer against me.

That lunk.

Not wanting to admit out loud that he was worried I was leaving again.

"So what are your plans?" he asks.

"A work in progress. I don't really want to go back to being a nurse," I say. There's no doubt there, either. I've known that for a while now. "Cases like Mom's, they're rare, you know? Working in hospice, you're mostly holding hands until death shows up. I've seen enough of that for one life."

I rub my cheek on his shoulder, so grateful he wasn't one more tragedy.

Neither was Mom or Ros.

"Go ahead and laugh, but I'm thinking about taking over Mom's shop," I admit. "I know she'll want to go back to work once she's out of the hospital, but I know what recovery after a second round of cancer is like. She won't be able to manage alone. And Ros, she needs to find her own way instead of feeling obligated to take on the shop, especially if she was feeling so trapped that she fell into Aleksander Arrendell." A chill breeze blows against me until I shiver, chasing me into

Grant for warmth. "I think I need to do this. That shop is family. It's *home*. And I think Mom would be happier knowing there's someone to pass it on to who really wants it. So, yeah... I want to stay and make a few more memories there. Good ones."

Grant lets out an understanding rumble.

"Only in the shop?" His head turns and he looks down at me with those hazel-honey eyes that warm me from head to toe.

"No," I answer quietly, and stretch up to brush my lips to his, his beard prickling my cheeks. "Do I look like I just mean the shop?"

I feel him smile more than I see it, his lips moving against mine, a lazy sweet thing. A reminder that now we have all the time in the world for every kiss, every touch, every lingering glance, every secret.

Because I'm not leaving this time.

I'm not going anywhere again.

His kiss leaves my chilled lips warmed—way more than my lips, honestly.

But as he leans back, he curls his hand over mine, laying it against his arm and reminding me just how frozen my fingers are, too.

"You forgot your gloves," he says.

I beam back a cheeky smile.

"I could think of a few ways you could warm my hands up."

"I could," he says—and is there something strange in his voice as he pulls back from me? Then he lets me go, his arm slipping from my grasp. "Or you could try putting them in your pockets."

Huh?

I blink, puzzled, a sting of hurt going through me.

It's not like Grant to reject me like this, pulling away so I can't even touch him, but there's something odd in his eyes.

Something intense, deep and searching and not cold at all, making a lie of his actions.

I don't understand.

But I need a second to compose myself so I don't react with instant hurt. Shrugging, I turn away from him to look out at the water, stuffing my hands into the pockets of my lovely new coat.

Then I go completely stiff.

Motionless except for the frantic beat of my heart.

The right pocket.

My fingers brush something—a boxy shape, velvety, a seam under my fingertips, and—I'm not stupid, I *instantly* know what it is—but I don't dare believe it.

Not until I yank the box out with a gasp, holding it up in my palm.

Soft blue velvet, dark as the night sky.

And when I open it, my blood rushing and crying out with joy, I see the unthinkable.

A ring!

It glitters like the first delicate snow drifting out of the sky, diamond-clear, a gorgeously cut stone set in the center and framed by two smaller clear-polished peridots the same shade as my eyes, all on a delicately wrought band of twined silver ropes.

Oh, God.

Oh my God, I'm going to cry.

I'm going to scream.

I'm going to barf.

I'm going to—I'm definitely *laughing*, a little manically, clutching at the box with one hand and pressing the other over my mouth, staring down at the ring and then up at Grant as I try not to hyperventilate.

His smug smile calms me, the gentle way his eyes glitter with teasing warmth.

"Grant?" I whisper in the faintest voice.

"Never met a woman who can find more ways to be so contrary," he says. "Gets herself a brand-new coat and she doesn't even do the obvious thing and stuff her hands in her pockets on a cold night." His grin widens as he snorts. He steps closer, his warmth reaching out to me in a cloud. "But I guess that gave me a chance to find a prettier place to propose than the front porch."

Propose?

Even if I knew it was coming, my brain can't handle it.

I let out a choked sound that's half giggle, half sob as he plucks the box from my hand and sinks down on one knee in front of me. His taut thighs strain against his jeans as the grass crunches under him.

It used to be an art form, knowing how to read Grant Faircross... but right now, the look in his eyes needs no translation.

Not when his heart shines so clear in those hazel depths, in that devil's smile on full, firm lips.

Not when, looking up at me, Grant offers me the ring and so much more as he clears his throat.

"Ophelia Sanderson, I've been chasing you even when you weren't here to chase. I always loved you. Always damn well knew I'd be here one day, if only you'd let me. And now that I have you, I don't ever want to see the back of you again. Stay this time, Ophelia. Stay and be my wife."

Trembling, I reach for the box again, delicately touching the sharp-cut edges of the stones, my eyes blurring.

"That's not even a question," I can't help teasing.

He snorts.

"Give me a yes or no, you brat," he says.

I'm already laughing with sheer joy.

"*Yes*," I cry, flinging myself against him. "Now put your ring on me and kiss me, you big lunk."

There's nothing but laughter between us then, and cold, fumbling fingers as he works the ring out of the box and slips it on my finger.

My God, it feels like the rightness I've been searching for all my life.

A promise.

Proof positive that Grant loves me, and I love him, and that's never changing.

For a moment we both just stare at that small band lining my finger, so heavy with meaning.

Then with another messy laugh, I cup his face and bury my fingers in his thick beard until I find the warm skin underneath.

"I used to daydream about this all the time as a little girl. I never thought it would actually happen. I never thought you'd actually *see* me."

"I always did," Grant promises. "I was just waiting for you to come home."

I can't hold back anymore.

I lean in to kiss him—only to stop as something wet and cold touches my lips, my cheeks.

Something besides my own tears.

Pulling back, I lift my head and look up.

A happy sigh slips out of me.

"It's snowing," I whisper.

I'm smiling like I might break as I watch the first snowflakes of winter falling down in pale fluffy magic.

"Yeah," Grant answers, wrapping his arms around me so tight. "Feels like it's all for us, huh?"

I don't answer.

I don't need to.

I just need to live this moment with him, bursting with love.

We watch the snow for some time, but there's a pull between us, and in the silence we sway closer until we're not watching the snow at all.

His eyes lock on mine.

His lips part, but there are no words.

We don't need them.

We only need our mingled breath and parted lips and the mating mouths.

How does it feel so different now?

Kissing him, I mean.

Somehow, it's like this one simple change from girlfriend to fiancée opens up this deep sealed-off part of me. It's like I'm blown open, my shields down, so much feeling pouring in.

The texture of his lips, brushing against mine until my heart trills with every teasing caress.

The warmth, soaking into me and reaching down, claiming me from the inside out.

The flick of his tongue, so rough and yet so delicate, teasing me in that slow, tormenting way that ignites me like mad.

It makes me tingle with an ache between my thighs and a need for something more.

More than the slow, plunging thrust of his tongue.

More than the possessive grasp of his hands on my ass, promising he'll never let me go.

More than the wet, heated sounds rising up between us as our bodies press together until I can feel every inch of him.

When I pull back, the heat in his eyes matches the molten core building inside me.

Without a word, I take his hand and turn to lead him home.

We walk back in sweet, heavy silence.

Gone is the peace of our earlier stroll. No matter how calm we may seem on the surface, there's a giddy storm building in my blood.

The tension between us is a living thing that cuts as deep as the snowy wind tonight.

Every time his glance reaches me, I shiver with more than just the cold.

It takes everything in me not to *run*, when I need him so much, when I love him to death.

Grant barely gets the door open back at the house before we tumble inside and I sweep the door shut with my foot.

Then we're a human collision, slamming into each other hotly, not even bothering to turn on the lights.

We're lips and teeth and hands, grasping wildly, ripping at each other's clothes.

Upstairs—oh my God—we should go upstairs right now.

But Nell's not home and I don't care where I have him.

I just *need* to have him, rising up on my toes to take his mouth with a heat as deep and heady as the fire he gives back.

The man *devours*, claiming me with a crushing kiss.

"How the fuck do you do it, Butterfly?" he whispers.

"What?"

"Taste this much sweeter the second you're wearing my ring," he growls.

Yep, I'm dead.

And I'm sure my epitaph will say, *Here lies the woman a human bear loved too much.*

Before I can even kiss him again, his hands are on my shoulders.

My new jacket hits the floor, my sweater follows, then Grant's coat, his shirt, and it's my turn.

433

He lets out a startled sound as I throw myself forward, shoving him back, sending him thudding down on the sofa.

He blinks at me for a harsh moment, breathing hoarsely, his huge chest heaving.

And I get my chance to answer his question by flowing down to straddle him.

Holy hell.

It shouldn't feel this good—this devilishly satisfying—with how wide I have to stretch my straining thighs to fit around him.

Don't get me wrong, I've always been attracted to his size, how small and delicate and easily overpowered he makes me feel.

But there's something different in the air now.

The promise in that ring, the lashing fire in his eyes, the *feel* of him under me...

It makes Grant's size more than just deliciously over-whelming.

He's more like a mountain built just for me.

Sheltering and protective.

My war shield, given to me for the rest of our lives, and that vow makes me crazy to feel every inch of him.

It makes me greedy to take him, to worship him, to remind him he belongs to me as much as I'm his.

His hands cup my ass with a growl that vibrates my bones, dragging me in and grinding me against his cock. Our jeans scrape together.

"You need it bad," he whispers, cupping my chin. "You too proud to beg for your almost-husband?"

A blush like flames licks my cheeks.

"What can I say?" I press myself against him, my breasts straining in the bra cups against his chest and my nails digging into his neck. "Something about a man promising to devote his entire life to me just turns me on. Please don't make me wait, Grant. *Please.*"

The way his eyes ignite like burning leaves when I say that special word slays me.

Sometimes, I wonder what I did to deserve a man as loyal as Grant Faircross.

I wonder if he's my prize on the karma wheel for all the terrible things I've suffered.

A man who would wait for me for ten years.

A faithful friend.

A lover who gives me his body, his soul, and his entire flaming heart.

But there's no waiting around now for questions that have no answers.

There's only our greedy mouths merging in a wild, biting kiss, tongues dueling as we grasp and pull at each other.

Half fighting.

Half moving in tandem.

We peel off the rest of our clothes until we're gloriously naked, twined together in the dark.

His body moves under mine and his cock slides against my folds.

I can barely breathe through the pleasure arcing through me as I rock against him.

Even with his hands so hot on my skin, so commanding, making me burn everywhere he pleases as he teases at my aching, wet center, he lets me set the pace.

I'm in control, keeping this great beast wrapped around my little finger, letting me do as I please.

Letting me torment us both with the slow-burn rhythm as I move over him, rubbing myself against his burning-hard cock.

Letting me kiss his jaw, his throat, while I arch my back

into the flow of his hands over my hips and the curve of my spine.

Letting me tease myself until I'm delirious on his girthy length.

Letting me stroke my chest against his, my nipples pricking and throbbing as his coarse chest hair rouses me with enough friction to make me feel divine.

Letting me capture his face in my hands and kiss him slowly, tenderly, as that heat reaches a simmering peak.

Letting me brace for his power as he boils over.

The frenzy between us briefly calms into cool sweetness, this intense realization that this isn't just another night.

This isn't temporary.

It's not another moment of undeniable passion erupting until it breaks our world.

This is a sacred vow.

This is everything we'll ever be.

This is us, welded together in a love so desperate it's totally unbreakable.

And I still want more.

I want to be as close to him as humanly possible.

When he catches my hips, supporting me, he knows what I want without me saying one word as I lift myself up on my knees and position myself over him.

His swollen cock kisses my flesh.

God, I can't stand it.

I reach down, touch myself, spread myself open for him.

His huge hand falls on mine and he guides my fingers to my clit.

"Show me how bad you want this cock, woman. Your pussy gets my dick wet before I'm inside you."

Oh, shit.

I'm so not ready as he leads my hand, tracing circles around that soft nub that's already pure lightning.

And when his fingers push inside me while he urges me to keep going, I'm absolutely gone.

Grant's fingers delve deep and his eyes never leave mine, every gaze and every thrust searing, melting me from the inside out.

A loud moan rips out of me.

"Bring that little pussy the fuck off, Philia. Come for me now."

I do.

I lose control like a woman possessed.

And I guess I am.

I've completely given myself over to this man who owns me, my core burning and my vision going white.

I see snow.

I see stars.

I see those blazing mocha eyes as I come on his hand, ripped apart by sheer ecstasy.

"More," he rasps against my lips.

"Grant..."

"Fucking *more*," he snarls again, his fingers still going and oh God, how does he always know exactly where to touch me?

His knuckle strokes my inner wall and it's like flipping a switch.

My orgasm intensifies until I'm deliciously frayed, every part of me curled, gasping and gushing and going down so hard.

My free hand grips his shoulders so hard it must hurt him.

I don't think he cares.

There's a mission in his eyes.

He's going to ruin me tonight—and I'm happy to let him just as long as he keeps me hanging in heaven.

But we're both so greedy.

A low growl vibrates the room. He barely stops to let me catch my breath.

Then he rears back, just enough to reposition, to let me watch him stroking his massive cock with my slickness.

Holy flaming shit.

"Good girl, Ophelia," he rumbles, bringing his swollen cock to my entrance. "Now, you get to feel me like never before. Get up and ride me."

I don't know what he means as I slide over him again.

Not until a gasping, needy cry explodes out of me as I sink down, engulfing his cock.

"Grant!" His name comes out hoarse, just as broken as the rest of me.

He rises up to meet me, spearing deep.

My legs go weak in under ten seconds and I take him in *hard*, willing him to fuck me as wildly as he wants.

A jolt rushes through me in bright-hot bursts as he fits me perfectly, fills me, makes me feel a wholeness I've never known.

Like I'm not alone.

Like I've run away for so long, hid from what I truly wanted, avoided my home, my family, this love and pleasure that was always waiting but I've been afraid to claim.

That's over.

Every rising, rough thrust of his cock says we're in a new chapter now, and oh, is it glorious.

Grant is mine now and I'm irrevocably his.

I'm not alone any longer in this bed or in this life.

"Look at me before you come again," he says, his thrusts coming faster, harder.

His eyes hold mine.

So do his hands, lacing through my fingers, steadying me with perfect strength.

This rhythm is deep and raw and delirious.

We flow together, one blazing body, where each of us begins and ends hidden in our pleasure.

He's never out of tune with me, never lets me go, always clutching so, so tight.

It's crazy intimate, and as Grant whispers *"Ophelia"* one more time, I'm totally undone.

Melting against him, kissing him like he's my next breath, falling into the animalistic flow and the churning feelings stirring up my everything.

I came to Redhaven under a cloud of darkness.

But now, there's no question what I see as my eyes flutter, as my breath hitches, as we almost break something as he throws himself into it.

As I hear him snarling, "Fucking come with me!"

Light.

Blinding and beautiful, inside and out, overwhelming.

Insane warmth.

Two deprived souls tangled up until our flesh matches our joined hearts.

And with pure wild ecstasy devouring me, I feel *him.*

The way he rocks his punishing hips into mine and buries himself to the hilt.

His face screws up as he unloads and sets me off again and then it's all fire. Waves of burning—

No, not waves.

Mountains.

Towering landscapes of absolute flame.

If it's a sin to come this many times for any man, I accept my punishment.

As Grant pulses inside me and I throb myself numb, we meet somewhere in the brilliant middle.

We make *forever.*

When I come down from the roaring high, I taste salt on my lips.

My own tears, I think, overwhelmed from the depth of what we just experienced.

And I smile into this timeless moment, opening my eyes and finding his sated and so full of love.

He's still watching me like I'm the only girl ever made for him.

Raptly, in the truest sense.

My heart convulses.

No one but Grant has ever looked at me like that—and no other man ever will.

Not since he's claimed me as his.

With his ring, with his love, with his touch, we're one and the same.

Two perfect hearts rescued from the dark.

* * *

Months Later

OKAY, I'll let you in on a little secret.

I always wanted a spring wedding. In my little daydreams about a fairy-tale life with Grant as a little girl, it was always green and warm.

There'd be flowers everywhere.

A sunny day full of butterflies and the smell of blooming plants.

An open-air ceremony under the crisp blue sky with God himself watching and nodding along in approval.

Instead of doves released into the air, we'd have more butterflies, set loose everywhere. Even my dress would be butterfly-themed.

I had it all planned out just like every girl who dreams of her future husband, wondering who she'll get to be with him.

I just never thought my husband-to-be would spoil me enough by making it flipping happen.

A silly comment started it one night after we collapsed in each other's arms, sated and sweaty and deliciously sore.

We hadn't set the date yet, still caught up in the afterglow of getting engaged. Our families were so ecstatic we almost didn't survive all the hugging and back-thumping and laughing shouts.

I used to write about marrying you, I teased him, swirling my fingers through his chest hair. *All the details worked out. I wanted a butterfly dress.*

Yeah? He'd caught my hand, held it tight, kissed my knuckles. *Tell me. Tell me what kind of wedding you dreamed up.*

So I told him.

I just never thought he paid that much attention beyond the idle conversation.

I also never thought Grant freaking Faircross would be the kind of man to take over planning a wedding. I admit I was nervous, when he insisted—but Ros promised to keep him in line and make sure he didn't make a complete man-bungle of it.

It still made me a little skittish, being kept in the dark about my own wedding.

But today, as I look at myself in the mirror, I know.

I know I should've trusted my sister and my fiancé.

There's zero doubt left that I can *always* trust the people I love.

I gave Ros a sketch from memories half a lifetime ago. Then I let her drag me to a dress shop in Raleigh to get my measurements taken, and back again for a basic fitting for a simple sheath dress.

At first, I thought the sheath was the base of the dress. But it turns out it was just a body mold to give the dressmaker what she really needed to work with while still keeping the actual design a secret.

The odd secrecy, everyone working overtime to make something to surprise me, adds a little thrill to everything.

But it's nothing versus the sweet rush that rolls through me as I stare at my reflection while Ros zips me into the dress.

I don't look good.

I look enchanting.

Heck, I feel *enchanted.*

The dress is sleeveless and strapless with a bodice scalloped in the shape of a fluted butterfly's wing on a diagonal down to a high, empress-cut waist.

Delicate lines like the stripes of fragile wings shimmer in a soft hematite glitter against the white bodice. The rest of the dress is layered damask sheeting down to the floor in misty ripples.

Sometimes white. Sometimes a sheer, soft grey depending on how the layers merge. They always catch the light with a shine like the dust falling from a butterfly's wings.

The scalloped hem moves against the floor like waves as I turn—no, more like a butterfly's wings.

I smile until my face hurts.

Behind me, the dipping backline trails out into a train of the same damask.

When I step forward, it's magic.

The lightest brush of air lifts it up.

I try not to squeal.

They've given me wings.

They made *me* the butterfly.

My throat chokes up as I turn to hug my sister tight.

"It's beautiful," I whisper. "Thank you. Thank you so much for doing this, Ros. Thank you for *being* here."

"I mean, I had to, didn't I? Ethan's not around to stuff you into a princess costume made from paper bags." We laugh because it's no exaggeration.

My dumb brother totally would've given me a grown-up version of my favorite Halloween costume as a wedding present.

God, I miss him today.

Ros' voice thickens as she hugs me back. "Besides, you're always there for me. It was definitely my turn. How could I let my big sister's big day be anything but magical?"

"Oh—*crap*." I let out a shaky laugh. "Don't make me cry and ruin my eyeliner."

"Oh, hush. You both know I'll fix it," a warm voice says at our backs.

We pull apart as Mom steps into the small covered pavilion tent set up for the bridal party in the large clearing on Still Lake's shore.

My mother looks radiant today.

No other word works.

Yes, she's still thin, baring the signs of her recovery in the shadows of her cheeks and the bones poking through the shoulders of her dress... but she's *alive*.

She's up and about, bursting with excitement to be my matron of honor in a lovely silk waterfall dress the color of a blue morpho butterfly's wings. A perfect match for Ros' bridesmaid dress.

"Mom," I whisper.

That choked feeling returns for a different reason now.

Not so long ago, I didn't think she'd live to see me at the altar.

I didn't think *either* of them would, honestly.

Yet here they are, right by my side, smiling with so much warmth and love in their eyes.

"Now, baby," my mother chides playfully, tucking a lock of my hair back into the wild tumble of twists and curls my sister made, strewn with flowers in pink and blue and white. "Today wasn't made for tears. I've waited for you and Grant to find each other your entire lives. Go out there and make me the happiest mother alive."

Ros snorts. "Don't let Mrs. Faircross hear you say that. She's already mad she's not in the ceremony when Mr. Faircross is."

"Well, someone had to give me away," I say. "And Jensen Faircross always treated us like family, so..."

There's a chill moment then.

A silent awareness.

The ugly knowledge of who *should* be here to give me away in another life.

But we're not talking about him on today of all days.

True to form, no one's seen Montero Arrendell since he gave his brief police statement on Aleksander.

No evidence linking him to high crimes, of course.

There never is.

I tell myself I don't care.

It shouldn't matter.

Today, at least, it doesn't.

All the little questions that still eat at me are just annoying mosquito bites instead of coyote teeth stripping my skin off my bones.

He's not our father, anyway. Not in any real sense of the word.

He's just bad history meant to be left behind.

But the moment breaks when Mom smiles, reaching out to clasp hands all around.

"Are we ready?" she asks.

444

As ready as I'll ever be for my own little happily ever after.

"Yes. Kinda." I nod breathlessly as my stomach drops. "Um. I'm not ready... What if he changes his mind, Mom?"

"My love, stop." My mother's cool knuckles graze my cheek. "That man loved you every day of his life without seeing you for ten years. He won't stop now."

I nod again, taking a slow breath.

I know that.

I believe that.

It's just nerves.

"Okay. Ready," I say. "Let's do this."

Soon I'm gathered up in tearful hugs.

We're all sniffling, but we manage not to cry, and suddenly Nell flies into our huddle.

She's completely adorable in her little flower girl dress with butterfly wings scalloping the hem. It hits me that she barely speaks, just throws her little arms around me and clings like a blessing.

And then I'm alone, waiting for my cue.

Outside, I hear the wedding march starting.

Delilah Graves recruited the high school band to play it because Nell asked. Another little personal touch that makes my heart mush.

Sure, they're a little clumsy, a little off-key.

But that honest imperfection feels like a better fit when nothing about our love story was ever easy or orderly.

Jensen Faircross leans into the tent, peeking around the flap with his eyes averted, probably making sure he doesn't catch me in a state of undress.

"Ready to be my daughter for real, Ophelia?"

I flush hotly and nod, stepping forward to take his arm.

Yep, I'm speechless.

Everything I've been missing my whole life is here in Redhaven—family, love, acceptance.

445

I wonder why I ever ran away.

Jensen draws me out into the light, standing at the foot of the long white silk carpet laid over the grass and leading up to the altar. The entire Redhaven police force, minus Chief Bowden, is lined up on Grant's side.

My mother, Ros, Janelle Bowden, Nell, and Delilah wait for me on my side. And right there before the pulpit with the priest looking like a ghost in his shadow, I see him.

Grant.

My big lumbering bear of a man has never looked more handsome in his life.

I don't even want to know what Ros did to find a tux that fit him.

It sits on him perfectly, though, wrapping his grizzly frame in this sleek gloss, but it also can't hide what a wild man he is. His hair's slicked back, his beard neatly trimmed, but he's still my gentle giant.

Maybe he's a grouch.

Maybe he's a little feral, sometimes.

Maybe, just *maybe* on some days he can be a bit of a massive asshole.

But I love him desperately.

He loves me.

And there's nothing else that matters in the world except the love shining in his eyes as they land on me and he freezes.

That barrel chest stops rising and falling, his lips parting soundlessly. Without a word, he gives me his reaction.

You take my breath away.

I smile shyly, glancing at Mr. Faircross.

Together, we step forward.

The moment I take that first stride, though, I gasp.

A cloud of blue light erupts around me as several towns-folk let go of the ties on delicate nets I hadn't noticed before.

Before I can blink, I see swarms of glittering, beautiful blue morpho butterflies.

They float up like scattered leaves, rising to the sky.

My gasp of wonder isn't the only one as the family, friends, and neighbors gathered here today stare up at the sky in amazement.

The butterflies fan out in delicate arcs of jeweled wings, shedding their dust in soft motes that feel like they're showering me with magic today.

My heart spills over.

It really is the wedding of my wildest fantasies.

I can't stop myself from laughing with the sheer elation running through me while Jensen and I step forward again.

It's a slow march.

It's supposed to be.

But I'm not a patient girl. I want to break free and just *run* to Grant.

He's magnetic, this constant pull drawing me to his side, and it takes far too long to make that graceful procession. My train flares behind me, shining in the sunlight with a little more dust that fell from the butterflies' wings.

It's over before I draw my next breath, and here I am.

Face-to-face with destiny—and who knew it was so handsome?

Jensen's arm slips free from mine, turning me free.

The only thing stopping me from reaching for Grant is the bouquet of white lilies clutched in my fingers. For a breathless second, we just stare at each other in awe, before he smiles that slow, boyish smile that feels like it's just for me.

"Is it everything you dreamed of?" he whispers.

"Everything and more," I answer. "You really...? All of this, I mean? Just from what I told you?"

"With a little help from your ma and sister." He grins. "They made sure I didn't fuck it up."

I giggle low in my throat. "And what about you? This wedding feels like it's all for me..."

"Ophelia," he growls fervently, nearly stopping my heart, "*you're* everything I ever dreamed of and now you're standing here. If I've got you, what the hell else do I need?"

Wow.

Looks like he's determined to kill me before we finish our vows.

But then the priest clears his throat, glancing at us with indulgent amusement before the traditional words begin. "Dearly beloved..."

Ah, here we go.

Lots of lofty words that land like heavy snow through the happy haze around my brain.

I feel so very *dearly beloved.*

And for me, Grant is the only beloved I'll ever need.

I don't know how I even hold still while the priest recites the vows, the long litany of passages from the book, everything that makes this ceremony complete.

It's just a formality, I suppose.

Everything became *real* the moment I saw Grant standing there, waiting for me without any hesitation or doubt in his smile.

But finally—finally, we've arrived.

My heart just about bursts as the priest calls for the rings.

Grant takes the simple gold wedding band and slides it on my finger, then leans in close, whispering, "Check the inscription later."

Smiling, I nod, a silent promise as I slip the ring onto his finger.

Those coarse, weathered knuckles fight the confines for a split second before the gold band settles snugly. He flexes his hand like he's testing how it feels, the weight of it, before his hand laces in mine, ring to ring, absorbing our heat together.

And when the priest says, "Do you, Grant, take Ophelia to be your lawfully wedded wife..."

"I do," Grant answers.

His voice is rolling thunder, this gruff whisper I imagine only I can hear, this secret just for us, but the crowd strains forward, listening intently.

I do.

My heart beats in sync to those words as the priest turns to me. "And do you, Ophelia, take Grant to be your lawfully wedded husband?"

I become the butterfly again, fluttery and full of shiny things.

"I do," I whisper.

Then the entire gathering erupts into clapping, shouting cheers.

The priest says something about pronouncing us husband and wife.

I'm completely deaf to it.

Grant and I are the only stillness left in the noise around us, completely locked on each other.

I can't sense anyone else when I'm already home, becoming Ophelia Faircross.

"You may now kiss the bride," the priest announces.

Grant rakes his eyes over me, then sweeps me close, pulling me against the hardness of his body.

"Hello, wife," he rumbles.

I laugh, twining my arms around his neck, showering pollen from my bouquet into his hair as I stretch toward him.

"Hello, husband."

His mouth twitches with repressed laughter.

I can't help fixating on it as he leans in closer. *Closer.*

For a second, I realize there's another burst of blue from

NICOLE SNOW

the corner of my eye—a second cloud of butterflies rising up to herald our union—but I'm not paying attention to that.

All the magic is right in front of me.

As Grant's mouth claims mine.

As I fall into him for the first kiss of the rest of our lives, heady and sweet and electric.

He rocks me gently with slow touches I never want to end.

And even with the entire wedding party watching and people roaring behind us, I can't help how he melts me, how he makes my knees weak with every trace of his tongue from one corner of my mouth to the other, leaving behind trails of fire on my skin.

His kiss takes me deep, owns me, leaves no doubt about my fate with every caress and every rough nip of teeth.

I belong to this man, here and now for all the world to see.

I belong, and I'll never miss my true home again.

* * *

THE RECEPTION IS small and intimate.

Most people who aren't direct family and friends linger for the grand toast and a little food. Plus, a chance to embarrass us with noisy spoons clinking against glasses.

They mostly head out before the dancing starts.

Honestly, it's a bit of a mess—people trying to dance in high heels in soft earth and lush grass, but no one seems to mind, tripping and stumbling and falling into each other with raucous laughs.

When I see Mr. and Mrs. Faircross dancing together, smiling at each other with such heartwarming sweetness like they're remembering their own wedding day ages ago, I think my heart grows one more size.

450

It makes me hopeful that can be me and Grant, one day.

Oh, I'm aching for the wonderful life ahead.

Seeing our children off into their own happy lives, and still as deeply in love as the day we were married.

As Grant and I take the floor for our dance, though, I catch my mother standing on the sidelines, watching us with bittersweet emotions I can't totally describe.

I offer her a smile, leaning into my husband.

She smiles back and mouths, *Love you, baby girl.*

Love you right back, I mouth back.

My eyes sting wonderfully.

"You realize," Grant rumbles, his chin resting lightly on the top of my head, "I have every intention of giving your ma grandchildren to obsess over as soon as possible."

"Oh?" I tease. "You do know that's *my* uterus involved in that decision, right?"

"I know. Just had a feeling your lady bits were thinking the same thing."

"...I was," I admit. "I almost lost her. Of course, I want to give her grandbabies while she's still here to see them grow up."

"We will, sweetheart. As many as you want." His hands tighten on my waist possessively. "We've got time. Your ma's a stubborn woman. The Reaper won't be back anytime soon after she chased him off. She's not going anywhere—except possibly being swept off her feet."

"What?" I lift my head from Grant's chest, peering over my shoulder—just in time to watch Officer Henri Fontenot bow to my mother like an old-fashioned gentleman, offering her his hand while she blushes and titters. "Oh, no! Isn't he the new guy you warned me about? The shameless flirt?"

"Yep. Every woman over fifty in town loves him. Old Mrs. Maytree calls in with a 'stolen cane' three times a week and demands Henri come find it. It's always in her bedroom closet." Grant chuckles. "I promise he's a gentleman. Frenchie won't do anything too dastardly to your ma."

I giggle.

"Oh, I'm more worried about her doing something dastardly to *him*," I groan, but it's full of laughter. This entire day is full of good humor and more joy than I ever thought possible. I smile as I look up at Grant. "You know, I think you've made this the happiest day of my life, Grant Faircross. Good job."

Grant smiles, hazel eyes gleaming like bronze stars as he spins me into a stomach-fluttering turn. "Then that makes this the happiest day of mine, Ophelia Faircross."

I think I die hearing him say my name that way.

Sometimes little girls' dreams do come true.

And maybe I'm about to make another little girl's dream come true when it's time to throw the bouquet.

I swear I don't do it on purpose. I toss the thing wildly, blindly over my shoulder, listening to the laughing, shrieking scramble of women.

When I turn around, I see my sister holding the bouquet with her face beet-red.

For a second, Ros looks stricken, but then she smiles, hugging the lilies close and looking up at me with damp eyes.

God, I hope it's her turn soon.

I hope she finds the love she deserves—a good man who'll care for her, cherish her, treat her with the same tender care Grant shows me.

And it's with real tenderness that Grant keeps me on my feet even when my legs go wobbly with exhaustion as the party starts winding down.

With the energy waning, that's our cue.

Hand in hand, breaking away from the others, all of them pretending to chase us but giving up far too soon as we break for Grant's truck.

It's parked on the road through the trees, festooned with cans and ribbons and a garish *Just Married* painted on the rear window. The back is crammed full of camping supplies for our big road trip slash honeymoon deep in the wilds of Vermont.

Nothing but us, tall trees, a tent, a gorgeous lakeshore, and as little clothing as possible, if I have my way.

"Get moving while there's time," Micah Ainsley says, ripping open the door like our personal valet. "I'll distract any stragglers."

His albino skin glows like ivory under the moonlight.

"Thank you!" I gush. "But you don't need to go through this much trouble for us, Micah, if you don't want to—"

I never finish. He's already rushing through the trees, yelling about being attacked by a giant raccoon.

"Oh my God! He's always such a serious guy too." I snicker.

"He's earning his hazard pay today," Grant agrees.

Breathless, still laughing, we tumble into the truck and pull away.

I'm a floofy mess in the passenger seat, my dress spilling everywhere and licking at Grant like waves. I tuck my hair back and pull the skirt in closer.

"Sorry. This dress slaps when I'm standing, but sitting down, it just wants to eat me alive. We should probably change before we head out..."

"Not a bad idea," he says. "First, we've got one more stop."

My curiosity deepens, but knowing Grant, I might as well wait and see instead of asking questions.

I don't have to wait long.

He steers us quietly through the streets of Redhaven—or as quietly as he can with cans rattling behind us and everyone who sees the truck yelling their congratulations and fist-pumping the air as we pass.

The streets grow more somber as we turn down a familiar lane lined with overhanging birches, all bowed toward a wrought-iron fence I know almost as well as my childhood home.

"Oh. You meant this stop," I whisper, staring at the cemetery gates as Grant pulls the truck into a parking slot.

"Thought he'd want to see you in your dress," Grant rumbles gently. "And I thought you'd want to say goodbye."

Somehow, my eyes find a few last tears.

I understand.

It's finally time for us to truly let Ethan go.

Hand in hand, we walk through the tombstones, the procession as solemn as our wedding march.

When we reach my brother's grave, it's almost jarring to see the freshly turned earth there, the grass only slowly beginning to grow over it in a thinner carpet than the neighboring plots.

We interred him right around New Year's.

No more empty grave.

No more missing date of death.

No more gaping questions.

My wonderful brother finally laid to rest, his name cleared... and I remember my resolution that day.

To live a life he'd be proud of.

As I stand here with Grant, I think I'm on my way.

Ethan would be proud of me today.

Of both of us.

He tried to save the woman he loved. He fought for her. He failed, in the end, but I followed in his footsteps.

Together, we saved my family, Grant's family, *our* family.

We fought like hell and we won.

"Hey, big brother," I whisper, smiling even though I'm breaking. "Guess who just married your favorite asshole?"

"Hey!" Grant flares with a chuckle. "Don't listen to her. Well, listen to her, but not about me being an asshole."

"Oh, please." I snort. "He'd be right here calling you every variant of ass along with me."

"Yeah, guess he would." Grant's eyes soften. He squeezes my hand tight as he looks at the headstone in silence.

"Hey, buddy," he whispers. "Hope you know I'll do my damnedest to make her happy. I'll look after her—even when she's giving me the lifetime of hell I'm missing from you."

Be still, my heart.

But that's asking the impossible.

Because I don't think I could ever feel more complete than I do right now.

Hand in hand with my new husband, feeling Ethan's presence.

He's still here, still watching over us from the Great Beyond, and loving the crazy romance we've found in each other.

That's when I remember to check the ring.

I reluctantly pry my hand free from Grant's and work it off so I can angle it just right to catch the light that lets me see the letters inside.

We'll live on in love. Always.

My heart swells as I slip the ring back on and twine my fingers in Grant's.

Talk about heavy.

But it hits deep, hits true, hits until I'm smiling so hard my face screws up because he's right.

When has he ever been wrong?

For Ethan, for Nell, for ourselves, we'll go on.

We'll live on and make the most of these lives.

We linger for some time with our own quiet thoughts, saying goodbye to Ethan in our own quiet way. I think we're both living the same kaleidoscope of memories and emotions that bat my heart around like a tennis ball.

Eventually, by some unspoken agreement, we turn away. But not without me stopping to pull one of the flowers from my hair. A bright-blue one.

Ethan always loved dark, rich blue, too.

I lay it down gently on the grass and kiss the ground.

Then I rejoin my husband.

My love.

My destiny.

My sweetest obsession.

Together, we leave death behind forever, and step into a heavenly new life.

FLASH FORWARD: PLUS ONE (GRANT)

Fifteen Months Later

I will never understand men who stop finding their wives sexy when they're pregnant.

I sure as hell can't stop ogling *my* wife as I help her fold the laundry.

It's a lot easier to do with two pairs of hands when she can't stand on her swollen feet for long, especially with her even more swollen belly.

Her doc warned her that being so tiny would make carrying an eight to ten pound basketball for so many months trickier than usual, never mind hard on her back.

There's no doubt she's been feeling it ever since she started to show, and I've been doing everything I can to help her even when she bats me away and tells me to let her do *something* before she goes stir crazy from keeping her feet up all the time.

I also spend a hundred percent of that time grinning like the big damn fool I am.

Now that she's close, she's so round she can barely walk without waddling—and she's still absolutely gorgeous.

Her face is flushed and sweaty, her hair a mess around her shoulders.

Her clothing clings to curves that have only grown rounder as her pregnancy advanced. She's barefoot in a mid-thigh pale blue maternity dress that might as well be a mumu, she's not wearing any makeup, and I am fucking smitten.

Can't peel my eyes off her to save my life.

Sometimes, I still can't fathom the fact that this amazing woman actually married me. And now she's pregnant with my child.

Even after being married for over a year, I can't get over how I beat the odds, asking how I got so lucky.

There are times when it *scares* me how much I love her, especially when she's—

"*Hey*. Stop staring." Blushing, Ophelia ducks her head, mock-glaring as she folds one of Nell's little t-shirts.

"Can't help it, Butterfly. It's your fault," I tell her, grinning wide and balling a pair of socks that I hope I actually matched right. Last time, I paired up two athletic socks with an inch difference in the calf height and she just about murdered me in a fit of pregnancy hormones. "My wife's right in front of me and she's the sexiest goddamned thing in the world."

"Liar. Or maybe you need your eyes checked," she retorts with a tired laugh, but it's that girlish, sweet laugh that says I can still get under her skin like when we were kids. "I'm so bloated I look like one of those blueberry kids in Willy Wonka. My hormones are nuts, my face is breaking out everywhere, my feet feel like snowshoes, I—"

Enough.

I stop her with a kiss.

I'm on a mission.

If Philia can't see how beautiful she is, then I'll goddamned well show her.

She's so sensitive, too.

The hormone storm might make her plenty irritable, but they make her body quiver for me at the slightest touch, too, and damn do I love that.

All I have to do is press against her from behind, brush my fingers to her breasts, and she's trembling and gasping with delight. Her chest overflows in my hands when I cup those tits and take such pleasure in their weight, their lushness, the way she presses back against me until her round ass drags against my cock.

I've found the sweetest torture.

"Grant," she moans low in her throat. "*Hurry.*"

Fuck.

Fuck, she can get me going in a heartbeat with that sultry voice, that hint of urgency, that way she raises her ass like she's already positioning herself for me.

I know we ain't got much time anyway.

Not with little Nell running loose in the house, but it's not just the kid—it's that magnetism between us that ignites every time we touch. And it's only gotten *stronger* in the year since we've been married.

The jokes about marriage falling into a dull complacency must've been a lie.

With us, I'm still so ravenous I need my hands tied behind my back some days.

I just have to remind myself to be gentle with my pregnant wife.

To handle her carefully even in my urgency, as I press my hand to the small of her back and bend her forward over the edge of the bed, cushioning her belly against the pile of laundry while she braces her hands against the bed to support herself. When I push her dress up, baring her lush, pale thighs and the clinging lace of her panties, I can't help but groan, dropping a kiss to the small of her back, stroking my hands over the curves of her bottom, gripping and kneading the thick, plush flesh, pulling her panties tight against her crotch until she moans and tosses her head.

"Don't tease," she whimpers, and reaches one hand back, tugging her damp panties aside to expose tempting pink flesh that makes my blood lava. "Grant... Grant, *please...*"

Fuck me.

The fact that I can't tell her no is how she wound up in this condition in the first place.

I nearly rip my jeans clean in half dragging them open, freeing my rock-hard cock. She wiggles her hips against me, enticing me, and I let out a growl, catching her ass and holding her in place, positioning her just right, nudging my cock against her.

Then savoring her stifled cry, muffled against the laundry as I rock my hips forward, sinking in deep in a single hungry stroke.

She's so fucking *hot* inside.

So tight.

So sweet for me.

I'm growling as her hungry heat envelops me—then clenches around me.

She tightens her inner muscles until I suck in a breath, nearly losing the strength in my legs as she squeezes my cock till my eyes roll.

Goddamn.

She knows how to drive me stark-raving crazy, pushing me to be an animal.

Any idea of going slow gets lost as she teases me with her

body, dragging her slick flesh over the length of my cock, demanding more with little whimpers, telling me just how much she wants this.

I can't hold back a second.

Digging my fingers into the yielding flesh of her hips, I slam into her again and again, our mingled breaths setting the frantic pace as we crash together harder and harder still.

Flesh meets flesh in snapping hot pressure.

Each thrust overwhelms me till it's like I'm falling downhill and I can't stop the tumble and I don't fucking want to.

Not when my gorgeous pregnant wife is a little fiend under me, rocking back to meet me, completely lost, her hair tumbling everywhere and her lovely face contorted into this mask of ecstasy.

I'm doing that to her.

No one else.

I'm the man making her crave it so bad she can't even wait to finish the fucking laundry before she's spread open and begging for my come.

It still burns fierce, knowing she's all mine.

And the way she's backing up and moaning like she can't stand *not* to feel me is so blinding hot it makes me feel like the dirtiest prick alive, and I don't care.

We're probably gonna need to wash this entire load of laundry again by the time we're through.

Don't care about that, either.

All I care about is the soft heat of her body gloving my cock, the way she's so tight around me, giving up these little moans muffled against her hand so they don't carry to little ears.

I barely hold my own rough noises in.

I'm a savage. An animal. A monster.

Fucking her so hard the bed jolts and digs the legs into

the floor, catching growls in the back of my throat, my eyes nearly pointed at the back of my head with pleasure.

I can't take my eyes off her.

Even quiet, she's so *into* it, her face so flushed, her eyes glazed with desire, her body telling me I'm doing everything right.

This is how it is with us.

She gets me in all the best and worst ways, right down to the primal level.

Everything about her hooks into me, tugging at my heart, my body as her pussy tightens.

"Yeah, fuck. Philia, give it up," I snarl in her ear, pulling her hair.

The pleasure drags me along in its wake cruelly, biting me until I almost can't stand it.

I crash into her harder, seeking deeper, wanting to imprint myself inside her so she feels me forever. Those biting teeth of heat sink deeper, *deeper* and—

And I snap.

It's all-consuming as it washes over me.

This ruthless sensation, the way she leans into it, the way it trips off something inside her that starts that ripple and crush and flow as the raw power of her pleasure moves through her body in crashing waves.

Her greedy little pussy sucks me off as my balls heave pure fire.

I'm not breathing, every bit of energy hurling itself inside her.

She milks me dry, leaves me weak. Almost shaking.

But then, I'll always let my shields down for her.

She's the only woman made who can lay me low.

The only woman I'd ever trust to lift me high with her love.

* * *

WE'VE BARELY COLLAPSED into each other before Nell's voice comes floating down the hall, along with a crash.

"*Oops*," Nell says a little too loud—then follows with a squeak, hushed, as if she just realized we might have heard.

We exchange indulgent looks before I call, "Anything bleeding or broken, kiddo?"

A long, sheepish silence, and then, "...no. *I'm* okay..."

"Which means," Ophelia says wryly, "something else is not. Should we investigate what our little girl is up to?"

"We need to take out Nell insurance on this house." Snorting, I give Ophelia a hand up and help her back into her dress before hoisting my jeans up and pulling my shirt on.

Hand in hand, we slip out and head down the hall.

I already know where Nell's voice came from, the guest room we're repurposing as a nursery. Ever since we started remodeling it, she hasn't been able to stay out of it, so excited about the idea of a *baby* that she's always trying to help with the redecorating.

Only this time her 'help' involves an entire bucket of bright sunflower yellow paint tipped over, splashing the floorboards in a spreading puddle.

Even the toes of her socks are stained, and there are little yellow prints all over the bare floorboards.

Twining her fingers together, staring down at her feet, Nell mumbles, "...sorry. I was gonna paint flowers on the walls for my baby sister."

Baby sister.

That still makes me smile every time I hear it.

To Nell, Ophelia and I are Auntie and Uncle and Mom and Dad and cousins all in one, so she's decided our daughter will be her baby sister, and that she's going to be the kind of big sister to her that Ophelia is to Ros.

We don't have the heart to correct her.

Because if that's how she wants it, that's exactly how it's gonna be in our patchwork family.

For now, though, I sigh. "What did I tell you about messing with paint unsupervised, Nelly-girl?"

"Um. You said not to?"

"That's right. Besides making a big mess, the fumes could get you sick, and I don't want you painting the house with your lunch." She giggles as I rest a hand on top of her head. "Don't make me ask again. I love you too much for that crap."

She perks a little.

The older the girl gets, the more she hates getting in trouble. Still, I try to handle it in a way that says when I'm upset, it's purely because I'm worried for her safety and well-being.

I fuss out of love. Not because she's bad.

Ophelia's caught on quick to that approach, especially after the Arrendell nightmare on the boat. Together, we've coaxed Nell out of her trauma shell and back to being her usual bright, impish little self.

And said imp looks up at me hopefully, then peeks at Ophelia, looking for support. "So I'm not grounded?"

"Oh, you're definitely grounded," Philia says with a dry smirk. "Buuut you know, since you already started the job, we might as well finish it, right?"

She steps forward, planting her bare feet right in the paint before lifting them high and taking several stomping steps, leaving footprints all over the floor.

I blink. "What are you doing?"

"Decorating!" Ophelia answers cheerfully. "C'mon, help us out. The baby needs all three of our footprints here. Come on, Nell. Take your socks off and make some really good prints."

My fucking jaw drops.

While Nell lets out a joyful squeal, whips her paint-stained socks off, and dives in to start stomping and splashing around in the paint, Ophelia's right there with her, the two of them laughing their fool heads off.

My girls.

My wonderful damned girls.

And even though it's against my better judgment...

I step forward and stick my feet in the cold, gooey paint, too.

Soon, I have to grudgingly admit I'm having *fun.*

The three of us reel around each other, stepping over and around each other's footprints, crossing them till the paint puddle is almost gone and the entire nursery floor becomes a mosaic of footprints that look almost like an intentional pattern, rather than proof that the three of us have temporarily gone insane.

We're all laughing like idiots by the time we stop.

Breathing hard, Ophelia leans a hand against the wall, puffing her cheeks out a little.

"Whew," she says. "No stamina anymore. Now we have just one problem..."

"Yeah? What problem?" I cup her cheek, stroking the soft skin.

"How we're going to get out of here without getting paint all over the carpet in the hall."

Nell lets out a shrieking giggle, then claps her hand over her mouth, peeking up at us over her fingers.

"I mean, we could stay in here until the paint dries on our feet," she offers.

"Maybe," Ophelia says. "But pregnancy bladder's no joke, and I already gotta pee—" She stops. Then her eyes go wide and a strained expression crosses her face. "Oh, no. I—that's not—oh, God. Grant, I think my water just broke."

"*What?*" My voice goes up three octaves and I jolt closer to Ophelia. "Oh shit. Shit, are you sure?"

"...pretty sure," she strains out as a puddle splashes down on the floor. She slaps a hand out and clutches at the edge of the empty crib. "Oh. Oh *ow*, yep, that's a contraction. Grant, the baby's coming!"

Fuck.

Fuck fuck fuck, I don't know what to do, I'm panicked, frozen—no, no, I got this.

We talked about this

Okay, *okay*.

"Nelly-girl, help Ophelia downstairs," I say firmly.

Ophelia frowns. "But the paint—"

"We'll sort it out later." I press a hand to the small of her back. "Downstairs. Lie down on the sofa. I'll get your bag. Do you want me to drive or do you want an ambulance?"

"Drive—oh no." Ophelia nearly doubles over, squeezing her eyes shut, and my heart clenches at the pain on her face. "Ugh. We might need the ambulance... I think this baby's as impatient as her father."

With a woeful, worried look, Nell pats Ophelia's stomach.

"Hold on, little sissy," she says, then reaches for Ophelia's hand and takes it with such tenderness it just about breaks me to see it. "It's okay, Almost-Mom. I've got you. Lean on me."

"That's my sweet girl. Thank you." Ophelia gives a pained smile, but lets Nell tug her along.

For a moment, I pull her close and kiss her sweat-sheened forehead.

"It'll be fine," I murmur. "We planned for this. I'll be right there."

Ophelia clings to me for a moment longer, wordless affirmation, then goes hobbling out of the room, tracking spots of yellow on the carpet. I follow on swift strides, detouring to our bedroom, the closet. Even as I yank the door open, I dig out my phone and pull up 9-1-1.

"Mallory?" I clip. "I need to dispatch the ambulance from the medical center. Ophelia's water broke and the baby's in a hurry."

Mallory makes a fluttering sound. "Oh—oh dear, yes—yes —congratulations, Captain Faircross. I'll get right on it, I—"

"Thank you," I say, and hang up.

I don't mean to be rude, but my wife is having a fucking kid right now.

I grab the go bag we threw together when we first realized she was pregnant, packed full of everything she'll need for her hospital stay, then go rocketing out the bedroom door.

I catch Nell and Ophelia before they're even halfway down the stairs and scoop Ophelia up in my arms.

Yelping, she throws her arms around my neck—then lets out a shaking gasp. "Ohhhhh *God* no one told me it hurt *this* much..."

"It'll be over soon," I soothe, carrying her quickly down the stairs and to the sofa. "Lie back. Pillow under your hips and your legs, right? That's how it goes?"

Wordlessly panting, Ophelia nods—but she won't let go of my hand as I lay her down.

So, one-handed, I maneuver a pillow under her bottom, another to prop up her raised knees, while she starts that paced, puffing breathing she learned in our parenting class.

"You're doing good, babe." I squeeze her hand. "Keep that breathing up. The ambulance is coming any minute now."

Just as I say it, I hear the squealing siren, barreling closer.

Ophelia lifts her head, craning toward the door as she lets out a choked laugh.

"Oh, thank God for small towns. If this didn't hurt so much I could've walked to the delivery room."

We're interrupted by an urgent knocking just as Ophelia lets out a strained, hurt cry.

Her fingers crush on mine.

"Oh *God!*"

I grit my teeth, forcing down my own snarl of pain.

My wife's about to break my fingers.

I'll hold on anyway, even when they're sausages, just as long as she needs me.

When her grip relaxes, I shake my hand out.

Goddamn, that woman's got the grip strength of a boa constrictor when she's in pain. "Give me just a sec to let the EMTs in."

"Hurry," she pants. "This baby's coming—the baby's *coming*, Grant, you knocked her loose, you horny asshole—"

Huddling against the arm of the sofa next to Ophelia's head, Nell blinks. "How did you knock the baby loose, Uncle Grant?"

"Not the time for this conversation!" I fling out as I dash to the door and rip it open to find a man and a woman in uniform with a stretcher waiting on the front porch. "She's right here on the sofa. Contractions are really strong and close together."

They bustle past me with tight nods, wheeling the stretcher in and then shoving the coffee table out of the way so they can jack the stretcher down. As they start to reach for Ophelia to roll her onto it, though, the woman stops, holding Ophelia's shoulders, staring at all three of us.

"Why are your feet—"

"You don't want to know," I mutter.

Any response dies as Ophelia lets out another heavy wail and grasps for me blindly. I catch her hand, holding tight as they roll her onto the stretcher.

"We're going, babe," I soothe. "Remember your breathing. Out, out, in. Out, out, in. Like the coach told you."

"Out, out, in," Ophelia heaves. "Out, out—ohhhhhh *FUCK!*"

Shit. Shit. Shit.

I need to call my parents to take Nell, but I can't leave Ophelia. Trailing after the fast-rolling stretcher, I hesitate, then ask the female EMT, "Our kid. There's no time, can she ride along?"

"Everybody that's coming needs to be in this ambulance in thirty seconds," she says briskly, right before she swings Ophelia out of my grip and works with her partner to lever the stretcher down the steps, whisking my panting, crying wife away.

I make sure the go bag is settled on my shoulder, then scoop Nell up, yellow feet and all. "Come on, Nelly," I say. "Ophelia needs us."

She holds on tight with a firm nod as I dash out the door, lock up, and go bolting into the back of the ambulance just in time for the doors to slam on me. The ambulance starts up with a wail and I balance Nell on one knee, reaching for Ophelia, who's still writhing in pain while the female EMT pushes her dress up for a look.

"How the hell are you dilated this fast?" the woman says, then curses. "Okay—you're gonna have to try to hold it for just a few minutes, but I'm gonna give you an epidural now—"

"Hold it? *I can't!*" Ophelia screams, mangling my hand into gravel. "She's coming now—she's coming *now!*"

I have never been more unprepared for anything in my life.

And I'm not fucking going anywhere while my wife wants me here.

It's fast. It's chaotic. It's intense.

Ophelia yelps even after the epidural, her body convulsing and her hand fused to mine.

I am a stone.

It's me and Nell holding on, anchoring her, trying to

bleed our strength into her. Nell's silent and watching anxiously; I'm fixed on Ophelia's face as she tosses her head back, straining.

I can't tell if she's fighting to get the baby out or fighting to keep the baby in but no matter what I keep smoothing her hair back, kissing her brow and tear-stained cheeks, telling her I love her.

I love you, I love you, I love you a thousand damn times.

And I mean it.

Just like I'm gonna love our baby girl to death.

It feels like an hour.

But it can't be more than a few minutes when we're not even at the hospital yet.

Suddenly, there's one last heaving push, a strange sound, and then the female EMT says, "Welp, here we go..."

A loud silence.

And then a squalling cry.

I jerk my head up, staring as the EMT wraps our dirty, slimy, *absolutely gorgeous* baby up in a soft blanket, the umbilical cord trailing. Ophelia collapses against the stretcher, breaths heaving, but she's already trying to reach for the crying, red-faced, perfect little life we made together.

"My... my baby," she rasps. "Let me hold my baby."

"Here you go, mama."

I watch in wonder as the EMT lays our little girl between Philia's deflated belly and her breast. Ophelia's eyes shine as she rests her hand over our daughter and gathers her close.

"Hi," she whispers, a smile making her face glow. "Hi, little one. You were impatient, weren't you?"

I'm motionless, even when Nell lets out an awed whisper.

"Dang. She's so itsy and cute."

She is.

Itsy. Cute. Perfect.

I've only known her for thirty seconds.

She doesn't even know I exist.

And I already love her enough to die for her.

Something cold and metallic presses against my free hand.

I look up to find the EMT smiling at me. "Want to cut the cord, daddy?"

"But the ambulance is moving, I could... oh." I feel the subtle swerve of a turn, then parking, the ambulance going still. I gulp, staring at that tiny sweet baby. "I won't hurt her?"

"Nope. It'll be fine." It's Ophelia reassuring me now, not the EMT, and she turns that beaming, beautiful smile on me. "It should be you. Welcome your daughter, Grant."

Christ Almighty.

Those words are like a landslide.

Slowly, as delicately as I can, I reach out with the shears the EMT gave me and carefully snip that cord. The baby barely gurgles, settling down against her mother like she knows already where her source of safety and security is.

Light comes rushing in on us as the driver flings the doors open, then blinks.

"Huh? Y'all couldn't wait five more minutes?" He grins. "C'mon, folks. Let's get you inside and get both of you looked at and settled in for post-natal. You've still got some work to do and *somebody* needs to get weighed and named."

It's less rushed now as the EMTs handle the stretcher down with Ophelia and the baby.

Nell and I follow, hand in hand, my other hand always twined with Ophelia's against our daughter's swaddling. I can feel her tiny movements inside.

So fragile, and it fills me with an awe that threatens to break me.

"Hey," I whisper. "You were in a real hurry to meet us, huh?"

Ophelia turns her head toward me, her smile softening.

"I'm sorry. I... I think I hate hospitals and all the death there so much that my body just rejected the idea of giving birth there. At least I didn't make a mess on the sofa?"

"Wouldn't have cared if you had. You're worth it and so is she. God, I—fuck. Didn't think I could love you more, love *her* more, but I do." Overwhelmed, I lift Nell up into my arms, giving her a tight squeeze as we make our way to the waiting double doors of the medical center. "All of you. So much. I don't know what my life would be without you."

"Let's hope you never have to find out. We're here, Grant. We'll always be here for you. And that goes double for little Ellie here."

I burst into an ecstatic grin. "That's what we're naming her? Ellie."

"I like it," Nell chirps. "Nelly and Ellie."

I groan, but Ophelia laughs.

"Nellie and Ellie. Our wonderful girls. It has a ring to it." Then she looks up at me with those green eyes that overflow with such emotion. "Our wonderful life. I love you, Grant."

"Ophelia, hell," I whisper as we step into the cool bright halls, so tangled the EMTs can't separate us. "I'm so glad I never stopped loving you like crazy."

ABOUT NICOLE SNOW

Nicole Snow is a *Wall Street Journal* and *USA Today* bestselling author. She found her love of writing by hashing out love scenes on lunch breaks and plotting her great escape from boardrooms. Her work roared onto the indie romance scene in 2014 with her Grizzlies MC series.

Since then Snow aims for the very best in growly, heart-of-gold alpha heroes, unbelievable suspense, and swoon storms aplenty.

Already hooked on her stuff? Visit nicolesnowbooks.com to sign up for her newsletter and connect on social media.

Got a question or comment on her work? Reach her anytime at nicole@nicolesnowbooks.com

Thanks for reading. And please remember to leave an honest review! Nothing helps an author more.

MORE BOOKS BY NICOLE

Dark Hearts of Redhaven

The Broken Protector

The Sweetest Obsession

Knights of Dallas Books

The Romeo Arrangement

The Best Friend Zone

The Hero I Need

The Worst Best Friend

Accidental Knight (Companion book)*

Bossy Seattle Suits

One Bossy Proposal

One Bossy Dare

One Bossy Date

One Bossy Offer

One Bossy Disaster

Bad Chicago Bosses

Office Grump

Bossy Grump

Perfect Grump

Damaged Grump

Heroes of Heart's Edge Books

No Perfect Hero

No Good Doctor

No Broken Beast

No Damaged Goods

No Fair Lady

No White Knight

No Gentle Giant

Marriage Mistake Standalone Books

Accidental Hero

Accidental Protector

Accidental Romeo

Accidental Knight

Accidental Rebel

Accidental Shield

Stand Alone Novels

The Perfect Wrong

Cinderella Undone

Man Enough

Surprise Daddy

Prince With Benefits

Marry Me Again

Love Scars

Recklessly His

Enguard Protectors Books

Still Not Over You

Still Not Into You
Still Not Yours
Still Not Love

Baby Fever Books

Baby Fever Bride
Baby Fever Promise
Baby Fever Secrets

Only Pretend Books

Fiance on Paper
One Night Bride

Grizzlies MC Books

Outlaw's Kiss
Outlaw's Obsession
Outlaw's Bride
Outlaw's Vow

Deadly Pistols MC Books

Never Love an Outlaw
Never Kiss an Outlaw
Never Have an Outlaw's Baby
Never Wed an Outlaw

Prairie Devils MC Books

Outlaw Kind of Love
Nomad Kind of Love

Savage Kind of Love

Wicked Kind of Love

Bitter Kind of Love

Printed in Great Britain
by Amazon

36405905R00268